THE W [illegible] e exploits of brave heroes, and the rise and fall of powerful enemies. Now for the first time the tales of these mythical events will be brought to life in a new series of books. Divided into a series of trilogies, each will bring you hitherto untold details of the lives and times of the most legendary of all Warhammer heroes and villains. Combined together, they will also begin to reveal some of the hidden connections that underpin all of the history of the Warhammer world.

THE LEGEND OF SIGMAR

Kicking off with *Heldenhammer* and continuing in *Empire*, this explosive trilogy tells of the rise of Sigmar as he unites the tribes of men.

THE RISE OF NAGASH

A gruesome tale of a priest king's quest for unstoppable power over the living and the dead begins with *Nagash the Sorcerer* and follows with *Nagash the Unbroken*.

THE SUNDERING

The immense, heart-rending tale of the war between the elves and their dark kin commences with *Malekith* and continues in *Shadow King*.

Keep up to date with the latest information from the **Time of Legends** at *www.blacklibrary.com*

More Time of Legends from the Black Library

· THE LEGEND OF SIGMAR ·
Book 1 – HELDENHAMMER
Graham McNeill

Book 2 – EMPIRE
Graham McNeill

· THE RISE OF NAGASH ·
Book 1 – NAGASH THE SORCERER
Mike Lee

Book 2 – NAGASH THE UNBROKEN
Mike Lee

· THE SUNDERING ·
Book 1 – MALEKITH
Gav Thorpe

Book 2 – SHADOW KING
Gav Thorpe

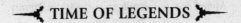

TIME OF LEGENDS

Book two of the Nagash Trilogy

NAGASH THE UNBROKEN

The undead will rise...

Mike Lee

A BLACK LIBRARY PUBLICATION

First published in Great Britain in 2010 by
BL Publishing,
Games Workshop Ltd.,
Willow Road, Nottingham,
NG7 2WS, UK

10 9 8 7 6 5 4 3 2 1

Cover illustration by Jon Sullivan.
Map by Nuala Kinrade.

This is a work of fiction. All the characters and events portrayed in
this book are fictional, and any resemblance to real people or
incidents is purely coincidental.

See the Black Library on the Internet at
www.blacklibrary.com

Find out more about Games Workshop
and the world of Warhammer at
www.games-workshop.com

Printed and bound in the UK.

It is a Time of Legends, a time of gods and daemons, of kings and heroes blessed with the power of the divine.

The arid land of Nehekhara has been blessed by the hands of the gods, giving birth to the first great human civilization by the banks of the winding River Vitae. The Nehekharans dwell in eight proud city-states, each with its own patron deity whose blessings shape the character and fortunes of its people. The greatest of them all, situated at the nexus of this ancient land, is Khemri, the fabled Living City of Settra the Magnificent.

It was Settra, hundreds of years before, who united the cities of Nehekhara into mankind's first empire, and declared that he would rule over it forever. He commanded his priests to unlock the secret of life eternal, and when the great emperor eventually died, his body was entombed within a mighty pyramid until the day when his liche priests would summon his soul back from the afterlife.

After Settra's death, his great empire unravelled, and Khemri's power waned. Now, amid the haunted shadows of Khemri's mortuary temple, a brilliant and mighty priest broods over the cruelties of fate and covets his brother's crown.

His name is Nagash.

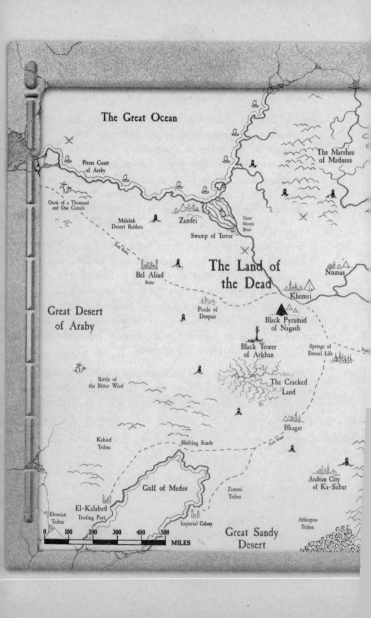

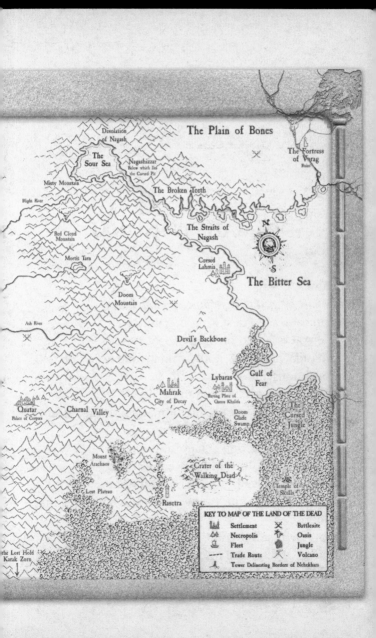

The Plain of Bones

Desolation of Nagash

The Sour Sea

The Fortress of Varag
Ruins

Misty Mountain

Nagashizzar
Below which lies the Cursed Pit

Blight River

The Broken Teeth

Red Cloud Mountain

The Straits of Nagash

Mortis Tarn

Cursed Lahmia

The Bitter Sea

Doom Mountain

Ash River

Devil's Backbone

Lybaras
Resting Place of Queen Khalida

Gulf of Fear

Mahrak
City of Decay

Quatar
Palace of Corpses

Charnal Valley

Doom Glade Swamp

The Cursed Jungle

Mount Arachnos

Crater of the Walking Dead

Lost Plateau

Temple of Skulls

Rasetra

the Lost Hold
Karak Zorn

KEY TO MAP OF THE LAND OF THE DEAD

Settlement		Battlesite	
Necropolis		Oasis	
Fleet		Jungle	
Trade Route		Volcano	
Tower Delineating Borders of Nehekhara			

DRAMATIS PERSONAE

Lahmia
The City of the Dawn, strange and decadent
   Lamashizzar, Priest King of Lahmia
   Neferata, Queen of Lahmia
   Khalida, a young noblewoman and ward of the royal household
   Ubaid, Lamashizzar's grand vizier
   Tephret, most favoured handmaiden of the queen
   Aaliyah, handmaiden of the queen
   Abhorash, the king's champion
   Ankhat, a wealthy and powerful noble
   Ushoran, a wealthy and powerful noble
   Zurhas, a dissolute young noble and cousin to the king
   Adio, a dissolute minor noble
   Khenti, a dissolute minor noble
   W'soran, a scholar, formerly of Mahrak
   Prince Xian Ha Feng, emissary of the Eastern Empire

Rasetra
Former Khemri colony, now an independent city
 Shepret, King of Rasetra

Lybaras
City of Scholars
 Khepra, Priest King of Lybaras
 Anhur, Prince of Lybaras

Quatar
The White Palace; Guardian of the Valley of Kings
 Naeem, Priest King of Quatar

Numas
Breadbasket of the Kingdom
 Amunet, Queen of Numas

Zandri
The City of the Waves
 Teremun, Priest King of Zandri

◄ PROLOGUE ►

New Beginnings

Lahmia, The City of the Dawn, in the 63rd year of Khsar the Faceless (-1739 Imperial Reckoning)

SMALL, SOFT HANDS gripped her and gently shook her. Voices whispered urgently in her ears, calling her back across the gulf of dreams, until the Daughter of the Moon stirred at last from her slumber and opened her heavy-lidded eyes. It was very late. Neru hung low on the horizon, sending shafts of lambent moonlight through the tall windows of the bedchamber. The golden lamps had been turned down, and only the faintest hint of incense still lingered near the room's tiled ceiling.

The sea breeze stirred the gauzy curtains surrounding her bed, carrying ghostly sounds of revelry from the Red Silk Quarter, down by the city docks.

Neferata, Daughter of the Moon and the Queen of Lahmia, rolled onto her back and blinked slowly in the gloom. Tephret, her most favoured handmaiden, was crouched by the head of the queen's sumptuous bed, one slim hand still resting protectively on Neferata's naked shoulder. The queen irritably brushed the touch away, her own fingers slow and clumsy from the effects of too much black lotus and sweet, Eastern wine.

'What is it?' Neferata murmured, her voice thick with sleep.

'The king,' Tephret whispered. The handmaiden's face was hidden in shadow, but the outline of her slender body was tense. 'The king is here, great one.'

Neferata stared at Tephret for a moment, not quite able to make sense of what she'd heard. The queen sat up in bed, the silken sheets flowing over the curves of her body and pooling in her lap. She shook her head gently, struggling to think through the clinging fog of the lotus. 'What time is it?'

'The hour of the dead,' Tephret replied, her voice wavering slightly. Like all of the queen's handmaidens, she was also a priestess of Neru, and sensitive to the omens of the night. 'The grand vizier awaits you in the Hall of Reverent Contemplation.'

The mention of the grand vizier cut through the mists surrounding Neferata's brain at last. She swung her slender legs over the edge of the bed, next to Tephret, and let out a slow, thoughtful breath. 'Bring me the *hixa*,' she said, 'and my saffron robes.'

Tephret bowed, touching her forehead to the top of Neferata's feet, then rose and began hissing orders to the rest of the queen's handmaidens. Half a dozen young women stirred from their sleeping cushions at the far end of the room as Neferata rose carefully to her feet and walked to the open windows facing the sea. The surface of the water was calm as glass, and the great trading ships from the Silk Lands rode easy at their anchors in the crowded harbour. Specks of red and yellow lantern-light bobbed like fireflies down Lahmia's close-set streets as the palanquins of noblemen and wealthy traders made their way home from an evening of debauchery.

The lights of the Red Silk District, as well as the more upper-class District of the Golden Lotus, still burned brightly, while the rest of the great city had sunk reluctantly into slumber. From where Neferata stood, she could just see the sandstone expanse of Asaph's Quay, at the edge of the Temple District and just north of the city harbour. The ceremonial site was bare.

The queen frowned pensively, though she'd expected no less.

'There was no word from the army?' she asked. 'None at all?'

'None,' Tephret confirmed. The handmaiden glided swiftly across the room and knelt beside the queen, offering up a small box made from fine golden filigree. 'The king's servants are in an uproar.'

Neferata nodded absently and plucked the box from Tephret's hands. She carefully opened the lid.

Inside, the *hixa* stirred torpidly. Neferata gripped the large, wingless wasp between thumb and forefinger and pressed its abdomen against the hollow beneath her left ear. It took a few moments of agitation before she felt the *hixa's* sting and the prickling tide of pain that washed across her face and scalp. Blood pounded in a rising crescendo at her temples and behind her eyes, finally receding several seconds later into a dull, throbbing ache that set her teeth on edge but left her alert and clear-headed at last. There was no better cure for the lingering effects of lotus and wine, as the nobles of the city knew all too well.

She placed the *hixa* back in the box with a sigh and handed it back to Tephret, then raised her arms so that her maids could wrap her body in ceremonial robes of welcome. Tephret set the golden box aside and hurried to a cabinet of gilded ebony that contained the queen's royal mask. Made of beaten gold and inlaid with rubies, polished onyx and mother-of-pearl, it had been crafted by the artisan-priests of Asaph as a perfect likeness of the queen's regal face. It was the face she was required to show to the rest of the world. In time, it would serve as her death mask as well.

It would have taken hours for Neferata to fully prepare herself for her husband's return; she impatiently waved aside the proffered golden bracelets and necklaces, and glared at the maids who tried to paint her eyes with crushed beetle shell and kohl. The instant her girdle was pulled tight and the royal mask set carefully upon her face, she snatched up Asaph's snake-headed sceptre from Tephret's hands and hurried from the bedchamber. A servant dashed ahead of Neferata, her bare feet slapping on the polished marble tiles as she held up a bobbing lantern to light their way.

Neferata moved as swiftly as her confining robes would allow, but it still took ten long minutes to traverse the labyrinth of shadowy corridors, luxurious rooms and ornamental gardens that separated her apartments from the rest of the palace. It was a world apart, a palace within a palace that served as both sanctuary and prison for the women of the Lahmian royal bloodline. Not even the king himself could enter, save on certain holy days dedicated to the goddess Asaph and her divine revels.

There were only three small audience chambers where the queen and her daughters were allowed to interact with the outside world. The largest and grandest, the Hall of the Sun in its Divine Glory, was set aside to celebrate weddings and childbirths, and was open at various times to both the royal household and the common folk of the city. The smallest, a dark vault of green marble known as the Hall of Regretful Sorrows, was where long, solemn processions of Lahmian citizens would come to pay their last respects to a dead queen before her journey to the House of Everlasting Life.

In between was the Hall of Reverent Contemplation, a medium-sized chamber built from warm, golden sandstone and inlaid with screens of lustrous, polished wood. More temple than audience chamber, it was here that the king and the noble families of the city – as well as a handful of common folk, chosen by lot – would gather to pay homage to the queen and receive her blessings for the coming year.

By the time Neferata arrived at the hall the great golden lamps had been lit, and incense was curling in dark, blue-grey ribbons from the braziers that flanked the royal dais. A red-faced servant, glistening with sweat, was single-handedly trying to unfold the delicate wooden screen that was meant to shield the royal presence from unworthy eyes. The queen stopped the servant in her tracks with a curt wave of her hand as she stepped from behind the elegantly carved wooden throne and approached the robed figure resting upon his knees at the foot of the dais.

Like the queen, Grand Vizier Ubaid had taken the time to don his ceremonial saffron robes to welcome the king's return. His shaven pate had been freshly oiled and matched the mellow tone of the room's polished wood. Neferata could barely make out the coiling tattoos of Asaph's sacred serpents that wound sinuously about the sides of Ubaid's head and neck. She couldn't help but note that the thin coating of fragrant oil effectively concealed any signs of nervous sweat on Ubaid's high forehead.

The grand vizier bowed low the stone floor as Neferata descended the broad steps of the royal dais. 'A thousand, thousand pardons, great one–' he began.

'What is the meaning of this, Ubaid?' Neferata hissed. Her husky voice sounded harsh and menacing within the golden confines of her mask. 'What is he doing here?'

Ubaid straightened, spreading his hands in a gesture of supplication. 'I swear, I do not know,' he replied. 'He arrived little more than an hour ago with a small retinue and a handful of slaves.'

Like most Lahmian nobles, the grand vizier had a slender neck, high cheekbones and a prominent jaw-line. Years of rich living hadn't softened him, like many of his peers, and despite being of middle age his body was still slender and strong. Many at court suspected him of being a sorcerer, but Neferata knew that he was simply very good at keeping up appearances. He had even taken to wearing golden caps on the ends of his little fingers, each one ending in a long, artificial nail in the fashion of bureaucrats from the Silk Lands across the sea. The affectation did nothing to improve the queen's mood.

'Where is the army?' she demanded. 'The last report said they were still three days' march away.'

Ubaid shrugged helplessly. 'There is no way of knowing, great one. Likely they are still somewhere on the trade road, west of the Golden Plain. Certainly they are nowhere near the city itself. The king appears to have hurried on ahead of the host.'

As well as the majority of his noble allies, Neferata observed, growing more irritated by the moment. Absolutely nothing about Lamashizzar's expedition to Mahrak had gone according to plan, and now he was risking the ire of people whose goodwill he would desperately need in the years to come. 'And where is the king now?' she asked coldly.

The vizier's carefully composed expression cracked somewhat around the edges. 'He's… in the cellars,' he answered in a subdued voice. 'He went there straightaway with his men–'

'The *cellars*?' Neferata snapped. 'Why? To inventory the jars of grain and honey?'

'I…' Ubaid stammered. 'I'm sure I can't say–'

'Asaph's teeth!' the queen swore. 'I was being sarcastic, Ubaid. I know perfectly well what he's doing down there,' she said. 'Take me to him.'

Ubaid's eyes widened. 'I'm not certain that would be proper, great one–'

Neferata straightened her shoulders and glared down at the grand vizier, her golden face implacable and cold. 'Grand vizier, the king has flouted ancient tradition by returning to the city in this… unorthodox… fashion. By custom and by law, he hasn't *officially* returned, which means that I continue to rule this city in Lamashizzar's name. Do you understand?'

The grand vizier bowed his head at once. Over the last year and a half he'd been exceedingly careful to conceal his true feelings about the king's secret dispensation of power. By rights, Ubaid should have been the one to rule Lahmia in Lamashizzar's absence; the queens of Lahmia were not meant to sully themselves with mundane affairs of state. Now, eighteen months later, Ubaid understood what had persuaded the king to make such a scandalous choice.

'Please follow me, great one,' he replied smoothly, and rose to his feet.

THE GREAT PALACE was honeycombed with a network of hidden passageways, built for the use of the household's many servants, and Ubaid led the queen through a veritable labyrinth of narrow, dimly-lit corridors and dusty storage rooms as they made their way to the cellars. Neferata could barely see where she was going within the confines of her mask. The servant's lantern bobbed in the darkness ahead of her like some teasing river spirit, luring her onward to her doom.

Finally she found herself descending a series of long, narrow ramps, and the air turned cold and damp. Gooseflesh raced along the skin of her neck and arms, but she suppressed the urge to shiver. Then a few minutes later she felt the weight of the narrow passageways fall away to her left and right, and she realised that they'd entered a large, low-ceilinged space. Neferata glimpsed stacks of rounded, clay jars sealed with wax, and heard the distant sound of voices somewhere up ahead.

Ubaid led her through one interconnected cellar after another, past jars of spices, salt and honey, bolts of cloth and bricks of beeswax. The sense of space began to shrink again, and the queen reckoned that they were heading into a much older part of the cellars. The voices grew more distinct, until she could clearly make out her husband's hushed, urgent voice.

Suddenly, the grand vizier halted and stepped aside. Neferata rushed ahead and emerged into a small, dripping chamber stacked with wide-bellied wine jars bearing the royal seal. A handful of torches guttered from the walls, casting strange, leaping shadows across the floor.

Lamashizzar, Priest King of Lahmia, City of the Dawn, stood over an opened wine jar and gulped greedily from a golden drinking bowl. His rich, silken robes were grimed with the dust of the road, and his tightly curled black hair was matted and limp with sweat. Half a dozen noblemen stood around the king, all of them travel-stained and reeling from fatigue. Several drank along with the king, while the rest stole apprehensive glances at the slaves working feverishly at the far side of the room. None of them noticed the sudden appearance of the queen.

Neferata studied the men for a long moment and felt her irritation sharpen into icy rage. She took another step into the room and drew a deep breath. 'This is an ill-omened thing,' she declared in a cold, clear voice.

Startled cries rang off the stone walls as the noblemen whirled, their dark faces pale and eyes wide with shock. To Neferata's profound surprise, many of them reached for their swords; they caught themselves at the last possible moment, hands hovering over the hilts of their blades. Yet they did not relax. None of them did. Instead, their eyes darted between Neferata and the king, as though uncertain how to proceed.

Now it was the queen's turn to stare in amazement. Some of the men she knew to be Lamashizzar's closest supporters, while others, though Lahmian, were strangers to her. All of them shared the same tense, hard-edged expression, the same fevered glint in their eyes.

They look like cornered animals, Neferata thought, thankful that the all-enclosing mask hid her startled reaction. Is this what war does to civilized men?

The king himself was no less stunned to see his queen. His handsome face was sallow and drawn; his eyes were sunken and his cheeks hollowed out from poor eating and little sleep, but his gaze was sharper and more penetrating than ever. Lamashizzar lowered the drinking bowl. Red wine trickled thickly down the sides of his sharp chin.

'What in the name of the dawn are you doing here, sister?' he rasped.

'I?' Neferata snapped, her anger managing to overcome her growing unease. 'More to the point, what are *you* doing here?' She advanced on Lamashizzar, her hands clenched into fists. 'There are sacred rites to be observed. The king may not return to the city without first performing the Propitiations of the East. You must thank Asaph for the blessing she gave when you first set out to war!' Neferata's voice grew in volume along with her ire, until her voice rang like a bell within the confines of the mask. 'But the army isn't expected for days yet. Asaph's Quay is bare of offerings from the citizenry. The proper sacrifices have not been made.'

Without warning, the queen lashed out, striking the drinking bowl from the king's hand. 'What happened?' she hissed. 'Did you drink all the wine you plundered from here to Khemri? Couldn't you have waited two more days to slake your thirst? *This is an offence against the gods, brother.*'

For a moment, no one moved. Neferata could feel the tension crackling like caged lightning in the air. The king glanced past Neferata. 'That will be all, Ubaid,' he said to the grand vizier.

Ubaid bowed and hastily withdrew, his robes rustling as he fled from the cellar as quickly as his dignity would allow.

Lamashizzar stared at the queen, his eyes depthless and strange. He raised his hand and laid the tips of his fingers against the mask's curved, golden cheek.

'The gods do not care, sister,' he said softly. 'They no longer hear our prayers. Nagash the Usurper saw to that on the plain outside Mahrak. Did you not read any of my letters?'

'Of course I did,' Neferata replied, suppressing a chill at the mention of Nagash's name. She and Lamashizzar had been born during the height of the Usurper's reign, when the former Grand Hierophant of Khemri's mortuary cult had held all of Nehekhara in his iron grip. It was only when the kings of the east had risen in revolt against Khemri that they had learned true horror of the Usurper's power, and though they eventually triumphed, the cost of victory was almost too terrible to contemplate.

Angrily, she pushed aside the king's hand and stalked past him. At the far end of the chamber, the slaves stopped what they were doing and abased themselves at her approach.

'It doesn't matter if the covenant has been broken or not,' Neferata continued. 'In matters of state – and religion – perception is every bit as important as reality. Lahmia was spared from the worst excesses of Nagash's rule, but the war has disrupted trade with the west for more than ten years now. Fortunes have been lost – to say nothing of the enormous debt we now owe the Emperor of the Silk Lands. If the people had *any* inkling of the deal we struck to obtain their dragon-powder there would be rioting in the streets.'

'That was Lamasheptra's doing, not mine,' Lamashizzar pointed out, bending to retrieve his drinking bowl.

'It doesn't *matter*,' Neferata insisted. 'Father is dead. *You* are the one on the throne, now. The people look to *you* for reassurance. They need to believe that the Usurper's reign of terror is over and that a new era has begun. They need to know that Lahmia will prosper once more.'

The queen's tirade had carried her nearly all the way across the chamber. The slaves were still as statues, their previous labours forgotten as they pressed their foreheads to the earthen floor. They had been in the process of shifting scores of dusty wine jars and dismantling wooden shelves to create a cleared space for–

Neferata came to a sudden halt. Her eyes widened behind the golden mask as she saw the linen-wrapped bundles resting on the earthen floor. 'What–' she stammered, suddenly at a loss for words. 'Brother, what is all this?'

Behind her, Lamashizzar dipped his bowl in the open jar. He stared into its ruby depths, and an ironic smile tugged at the corners of his mouth.

'The dawn of a new era,' he said, raising the bowl to his lips.

They were not jugs of plundered wine or wrapped brinks of lotus leaf. Neferata saw that at once. Each bundle had roughly square sides, some reaching as high as her knees. The linen wrappings were stained brown by countless leagues of travel, and were bound with braided twine. She went to the closest one. Slaves scattered from her path like frightened birds as she knelt beside the parcel and tugged at its bindings with long-nailed fingers. As she did, a stir went through the assembled nobles. Neferata heard angry growls and choked protests, until finally one of the men could contain himself no longer.

'Stop her!' the nobleman snapped. Neferata didn't recognise the voice. 'What is she even doing outside the Women's Palace? She should be in her proper place, not–'

'She is the *queen*,' Lamashizzar said, in a voice as cold and hard as Eastern iron. 'She goes where she wills.'

Neferata listened to the tense exchange with only half an ear. Her dark fingers teased the twine knot apart, and a corner of the linen wrapping fell away to reveal–

'Books?' the queen said. Her eyebrows knitted together in a frown. They were thick tomes of expensive Lybaran paper, bound in a strange kind of pale leather that sent prickles of unease racing down her spine.

'The books of Nagash,' Lamashizzar explained. 'Smuggled from his pyramid outside Khemri. All his secrets: his plans, his studies, his… his experiments. It's all there.'

Neferata felt her heart grow cold. She rose and turned to face the king. 'I don't understand, brother,' she hissed. 'You were supposed to forge an alliance with the Usurper. With the power under your command you could have broken the siege at Mahrak and handed the east to Nagash! He would have agreed to any terms–'

'No,' Lamashizzar said flatly. He took another long draught from the bowl, his face haunted with memory. 'You weren't there, sister. You didn't see the… the *creature* that Nagash had become.'

'We knew he was a sorcerer–' Neferata began.

'He was a *monster*,' Lamashizzar said darkly. 'None of the rumours we'd heard came anywhere close to the truth. Nagash was no longer human, and what he'd done to Neferem–' The king's words dried up in his throat. Finally, he shook his head. 'Believe me, Nagash would have never honoured the terms of an alliance, much less shared the secrets of eternal life.' He gestured at the stacks of linen-wrapped volumes with his drinking bowl, sloshing thick wine onto the floor. 'So. Better this than nothing at all.'

Neferata spread her hands. 'Indeed? Are you a sorcerer now?' she shot back. 'I'm certainly not.'

'You were trained by the priestesses of Neru,' Lamashizzar said. 'You know how to perform incantations, how to create elixirs–'

The queen shook her head. 'That's not the same thing,' she protested.

'It's enough,' Lamashizzar said. He lurched forward, seizing Neferata by the wrist, and pulled her after him as he wound his way drunkenly through the collection of plundered tomes. Beyond the linen-wrapped books lay another shape, stretched out against the dank stone wall. 'We also have *this*,' the king said proudly.

It was a corpse. It had been inexpertly wrapped, and the linen bindings were devoid of the ritual symbols of the mortuary cult, but the shape of the body was unmistakeable.

The king gave his sister a conspiratorial smile. 'Go on,' he said, squeezing her wrist with surprising strength. 'Take a look.' His eyes glittered like glass, sharp and fever-bright.

Lamashizzar's hand squeezed harder. Neferata clenched her jaw and sank slowly to her knees. She heard the slaves shift nervously behind her as she stretched out her free hand and began to gingerly pull away the wrappings that covered the corpse's head.

The face took shape by degrees: first a man's beak-like nose, then a prominent brow and deeply sunken eyes. Next came sharp-edged cheekbones and a long, square jaw that gaped in a grimace of agony, revealing a mouthful of jagged, blackened teeth.

The corpse's skin was pale as a fish's belly and covered in a patchwork of fine scars. The veins at his temples and along his neck were black with old, clotted blood. The very sight of it filled the queen with revulsion. Neferata recoiled from the ghastly visage. 'What in the name of all the gods–'

Lamashizzar pulled her close. 'He is the key,' the king hissed, filling her nostrils with the sour reek of wine. 'This is Arkhan the Black. Do you know the name?'

'Of course,' the queen said with a grimace. 'He was the Usurper's grand vizier.'

'And one of the first immortals,' the king added. 'But he fell from favour during the war and betrayed Nagash on the eve of the great battle at Mahrak. He offered me the power over life and death if I would side with the rebel kings against his former master.' Lamashizzar gave the queen an almost boyish wink. 'After the battle, I hid him in my baggage train during the long march to Khemri. No one suspected a thing. The others thought he'd fled westward with the rest of the Usurper's immortals, so once we'd reached the Living City and the Usurper's troops made their last stand in the city's necropolis, I paid some soldiers to spread the rumour that Arkhan had been seen fighting to the bitter end at the foot of his master's pyramid. No doubt the story's taken on epic proportions since then.'

'And Arkhan actually held to his bargain?' she asked.

The king smiled. 'As much as I expected he would. He led me to the books, deep in the heart of the Black Pyramid.'

'Then you killed him.'

Lamashizzar's smile never faltered. 'Is that what you think?'

Neferata's expression hardened beneath the mask. With a savage jerk, she tore her wrist from the king's grasp. 'You're drunk,' she hissed. 'And I am not in the mood for games, brother.'

That was when the smile faded from the king's face. Slowly, deliberately, he lowered his hand and set the bowl of wine upon the floor. His eyes bored into hers. 'Then perhaps I should make it plain for you,' he said quietly. He spoke again, in that voice as hard and cold as iron. *'Bring them.'*

There was a commotion behind Neferata, and the slaves began to wail in terror. She froze at the sound, and watched as Lamashizzar leaned forward and tore away the linen bindings wrapping Arkhan's torso. The immortal's chest was even more scarred than his face, but what was worse was the blackened, thumb-sized hole in Arkhan's breast, just above his heart.

'He was swift, but the bullet in my dragon stave was swifter still,' Lamashizzar said. His nobles crowded around him, dragging the terrified slaves over to Arkhan's body. 'It's still there, buried in his heart. Here. Let me show you.'

The king crouched over the body and pressed his fingers deep into the wound. There was a thick, liquid sound, and Lamashizzar grunted in satisfaction. When he drew his hand away his fingers were covered in a black fluid as thick as tar. A fat, round metal ball was gripped between his fingertips. He held up the bullet and studied it for a moment.

'You see?' he said. 'Such a wound would have killed one of father's mighty Ushabti, much less a mere mortal like you or I. But to Arkhan it was nothing more than an *interruption*.'

The king bent close to the immortal's face. His voice dropped to a whisper. 'He's still in there,' Lamashizzar said, but whether he said it to Neferata or to the immortal himself, the queen could not be certain. 'Locked in a cell of flesh and bone. So long as his heart cannot beat, Nagash's elixir cannot circulate through his limbs, nor fan the flame of his cursed soul.'

The look on the king's face sent a shudder through Neferata. This was not the libertine who had led his father's army to Mahrak. The things he had seen on the field of battle – and possibly within the pages of the books he'd stolen from the Usurper's crypt – had left an impression in the young king's mind. Blessed Neru, she thought. What if he's gone mad?

Lamashizzar chuckled to himself, entirely oblivious to his sister's mounting unease. 'I have had many discussions with the former vizier on the journey home, and I believe we have reached an understanding. He will serve us, unlocking his former master's secrets and teaching us how to create the elixir for ourselves. If he serves well, then we will share the draught of life with him. If not…' he paused, and his expression grew hard. 'Then we will send him back into his cell, and we shall see how long it takes for an immortal's body to collapse into dust.'

The king tossed the bullet aside, then nodded curtly to his noblemen. Without a word they drew knives from their belts and began slitting the slaves' throats.

Hot blood sprayed through the air. The slaves thrashed and choked, pouring out their lives onto Arkhan's still form. As they died, Lamashizzar picked up the pale leather tome and began turning its pages.

'The world has changed, sister,' Lamashizzar said. 'The old gods have left us, and a new power has risen to take its place – a power that now we alone possess. We shall usher in a new age for Lahmia and the rest of Nehekhara. One that we shall preside over until the end of time.'

At their feet, the blood-soaked body of Arkhan the Black drew in a terrible, shuddering breath. His bruised eyelids fluttered, and Neferata found herself staring into a pair of dark, soulless eyes.

The Wasteland, in the 63rd year of Khsar the Faceless (-1739 Imperial Reckoning)

NIGHT CAME SWIFTLY to the wasteland.

As the last rays of Ptra's hateful, searing light disappeared behind the jagged fangs of the Brittle Peaks, stealing away the heat of the day and filling the narrow gullies with inky shadow, the hunters of the dead spaces began to stir from their lairs. Deadly vipers slithered from beneath rocky overhangs, tasting the air with their darting tongues. Scorpions and huge, hairy spiders crawled from their daytime burrows and began their hunt, seeking sources of heat against the contrasting coolness of the rocky ground.

In one shadow-haunted gully, half a dozen lean, spotted shapes came nosing along the broken ground, tracking the scent of death. The jackals had been following the trail for many nights; it had rambled and looped back upon itself many times, like the path of a beast lost in madness and on the verge of collapse. Now the hunters sensed that the prey had been run to ground at last. Sniffing at the chill air, they edged towards a low overhang carved deep into the gully wall.

Within the darkness of the overhang, a bundle of rags stirred fitfully at the jackals' approach. The scavengers paused, ears forward, watching as a single, bony hand groped its way painfully from beneath the overhang. The skin was blackened and leathery, the nails yellowed and splintered by months of scrabbling over rocks and burrowing in the dry earth. The skin of the knuckles was split, peeled back like shreds of dry parchment to reveal grey flesh inlaid with grit.

The jackals watched as the long fingers arched, digging into the earth for purchase. There was a rustle of fabric and loose dirt. A trio of sleek, black lizards bolted from beneath the overhang, startled as their refuge began to shift beneath them.

Slowly, shakily, the figure dragged itself out into the night air. First an emaciated arm, then a bony shoulder, then a thin torso clad in grimy robes that had once been the colour of blood.

A bald head, blackened and blistered by the sun god's merciless touch, emerged from the shadows: a man's face, once handsome, now ravaged by the elements and the horrors of war. Dark eyes, set deep in bony sockets, regarded the jackals with feverish intensity. The man's face was gaunt to the point of being skeletal, his cheeks and nose frayed by brushes with rock and the mandibles of burrowing insects. A ragged hole, wide as a man's thumb, had been punched into his forehead, close to the left temple. At one time the ghastly wound had grown infected, causing the flesh to swell around the rim of splintered bone and the veins to distend with corruption.

The jackals lowered their heads and began to whine softly as the figure continued to drag itself from its refuge. This was not what they expected. Indeed, their would-be prey exuded a sense of *wrongness* that their animal brains couldn't quite comprehend.

Death hung over the man like a shroud. In addition to the awful wound in his head, his left arm was coiled uselessly against his chest. Another hole had been blown through the upper limb, shattering the bone and constricting the muscles into immobile knots. The scent of old bile rose from a puncture in the man's belly, and another wound in his chest carried the reek of old infection.

Dead, the jackals' minds said. The man ought to be dead long since. And yet still the leathery muscles worked, creaking like old ropes. The eyes still burned with an almost feral rage. Thin, cracked lips drew back from blackened teeth in a snarl of challenge.

Nagash the Usurper, Undying King of fallen Khemri and for a time the master of Nehekhara, pressed his palm against the stones and grit of the gully floor and with a bubbling growl pushed himself to his feet. Once upright, he swayed slightly as he turned his head to the gleaming face of the moon and let out a long, ululating howl of hate.

The jackals flinched at the awful sound. It proved too much for the leader of the pack, who let out a nervous bark and sped from the gully with the pack hard on its heels.

Nagash continued to howl long after they were gone, emptying the last dregs of air from his lungs in a long, wordless curse against the living world. The exertion left him shivering and weak, his skin burning with a fever that had no basis in the sicknesses of living flesh.

Like the jackals, he turned his face skyward, casting about for spoor. The scent of power hung above the emptiness of the wasteland, emanating from the slopes of a dark, brooding mountain that always seemed to lie just beyond the far horizon. It had a flavour unlike anything he'd ever tasted before; not dark magic, which he knew well, nor the fitful heat of a human soul. It was something furious and unfettered, primal and alien at the same time. It shone like a beacon in the emptiness, promising him vengeance against those who had betrayed him and cast him out into the wastes. He thirsted for it, and yet, like a mirage, it seemed to recede into the distance with every step he took. Lately, even the scent of it had grown vague. It was getting harder and harder to sense it past the pain of his ravaged body and the fever buzzing in his skull.

You're growing weaker, a voice said. *Your power is almost spent. Darkness waits, Usurper. Darkness eternal, and the cold winds of the Abyss.*

Nagash whirled, hissing with rage. She stood just a few feet away, her translucent body silhouetted by moonlight. Neferem, last Queen of Khemri, looked much as she did the day she died: a withered, ravaged husk of a woman, transformed into a living mummy by Nagash's sorceries. Only her eyes, large and brilliant as cut emeralds, hinted at the beauty that had been taken from her. Her ghostly figure was clad in ragged samite, and the golden headdress of a queen rested precariously upon her brow.

The Usurper reached out with his hand and clenched it at her like a claw – but his febrile mind failed him. The words of power that once bound the ghosts of Nehekhara to his will had been somehow stolen from him. Rage and frustration boiled inside his brain.

'*Witch!*' he hissed. His voice sounded somewhere between a growl and a groan. '*I am Nagash the*

*Immortal! Death cannot claim me! I have passed beyond
its grasp!'*

So have we all, Neferem replied soundlessly. Her
eyes glittered with hate. *You saw to that at Mahrak. The
paths to the Lands of the Dead are no more, swept away
when you used me to undo the sacred covenant with the
gods. Now none of us shall ever know peace.* Her shrivelled face contorted into the ghastly semblance of a
smile.

Especially you.

Snarling with fury, Nagash whirled about, tasting
the air for traces of the otherworldly power. It
seemed to lie just beyond the line of peaks to the
east. He lurched forward, scrabbling one-handed at
the loose scree lining the gully slope. The Usurper
scaled the steep incline with an awkward, spider-like
gait. When he was almost to the top, he turned back
to Neferem's vengeful spirit.

'*You haunt me at your peril, witch!'* he croaked. '*When
I find the dark mountain I will have the power to consume
souls and command the spirits of the dead as I once did! I'll
feast upon you, then, and silence your moaning forever!'*

But the queen did not hear him. She was gone, as
though she'd never been there.

Nagash searched for Neferem amid the shadows of
the gully for a long time, muttering bitterly to himself. Once, he called her name, but her spirit would
not be summoned so easily. Finally he turned and
scrabbled the rest of the way up the slope.

At the summit, Nagash saw only a broken sea of
foothills, stretching off to the horizon. The dark

mountain had receded from him once again. He turned his face skyward, casting about for the trail once more, and then continued his limping course eastward.

HOURS LATER, WHEN the pale moon was close to its zenith, another pack of scavengers came sniffing into the gully where the Usurper had been. They circled about the rocky overhang, hissing and chittering to each other in their own strange tongue. As with any pack, it was the largest of the creatures that decided their course, cuffing and threatening the rest into submission. They too continued eastward, moist noses bent low over the rocks as they followed Nagash's strange, unliving scent. They loped and lurched and scrabbled along, sometimes on four legs, sometimes on two.

NAGASH HAD SO far passed beyond the grasp of death, but not beyond the jaws of constant, grinding agony. Every step, every movement of arm or head, sent waves of vivid, aching pain reverberating through his wasted body. The awful wounds he'd suffered hardly troubled him at all – or at least, no more so than the agony that gripped the rest of his frame. It was a consequence of the elixir, he knew. The magical potion – wrought from blood and life energy stolen from innocent, anguished victims – allowed him to retain the vigour of youth for hundreds of years, and was the key to creating an empire unheard of since the age of Settra the Magnificent.

Normally, it would also heal nearly any injury, no matter how severe, but not since that fateful day at Mahrak, when the army of Lahmia had thrown in its lot with the rebel kings of the east and unleashed their strange weapons on him and his unliving host. He remembered the wall of fire and a crescendo of thunder from the ranks of Lahmia's black-armoured warriors, and then watching the massed ranks of his corpse-soldiers disintegrating before him. The traitors had turned on him just as he'd won his greatest triumph. Mahrak had been cast down and the sacred covenant with it. The power of the priesthood and their parasite deities had been swept aside, so that only he, Nagash the Undying, remained.

As he made his way slowly down the rubble-strewn slope of another dark ridgeline, Nagash heard a wheezing breath in his ear. It had a rasping, ragged tone, like wind blowing across the end of a broken branch.

You are no god, a man's voice sneered. *Do you remember what I said to you in your tent at Mahrak? You are a fool, Nagash. An arrogant, deluded fool who thinks himself the equal of the gods. And look at you now: a madman, clad in rags, stumbling blindly through a dead and pitiless land.*

Shouting in rage, Nagash whirled at the voice, but his footing slipped and he tumbled head over heels to the bottom of the treacherous slope. He fetched up painfully against a small boulder. His limbs were twisted awkwardly beneath him, and at first they refused to obey his will.

As he struggled to force his body into action, Nagash became aware of a ghostly figure glaring down at him from a little further upslope. Nebunefer was a frail, ancient little man, clad in the same threadbare robes he'd worn on the day he'd died. His wrinkled head lay at an unnatural angle, the stub of broken vertebrae jutting painfully against the taut skin of his bent neck. Like Neferem, the old priest's eyes glittered with pure hate.

How the mighty have fallen, Nebunefer said. *You dare to call the mighty Ptra a parasite? He created the earth, and everything that lives upon it. What little power you possess was stolen, ripped from the souls of the innocent. It's finite, and the last sands of the hourglass have almost run out.*

'Not yet, you old fool,' Nagash snarled back. 'If you were still flesh, I would wring your neck a second time! Watch.'

His limbs felt leaden, his joints frozen like corroded bronze, but Nagash would not be denied. Slowly, clumsily, he forced his good arm to work, and then his legs. Minutes later, he stood shakily on his feet again, but Nebunefer was gone.

'Jackals,' he spat into the darkness. 'We'll see who laughs last.'

IT TOOK MORE than an hour for Nagash to climb the opposite slope, snarling curses and burning with fever all the while. His limbs were growing stiffer by the moment. He drove himself onward with nothing more than the belief that the dark mountain was just ahead, right over the top of the next ridge.

It had to be.

He would not succumb. He would not fail. He was the rightful King of Khemri, heir to Settra's throne, and by extension the master of all Nehekhara.

A faint wind hissed along the ridgeline, just a few yards out of reach. A voice drifted down to him, riding on the sandy breeze.

Usurpation is not a right, brother.

Thutep stood at the crest of the ridge, his face turned towards the moon hanging low overhead. His older brother seemed damnably at peace, staring up at Neru's beaming face. Only his fingertips, worn down to stumps of splintered bone, hinted at his last, awful moments, buried alive inside his own tomb.

'The strong have the right to rule,' Nagash hissed. 'You were weak. You did not deserve the throne. Khemri's fortunes suffered under your reign.'

Thutep shrugged, never taking his eyes from the moon and the open sky. *That was the will of the gods,* he said. *You were a priest, and a prince of the realm. You wanted for nothing–*

'Nothing except an empire,' the Usurper said bitterly. 'Had I been firstborn, the people of Khemri would have served me gladly, and the city would have prospered. If you would blame anyone, blame those damned gods you so adore. It was they who made me no more than a second son. It was their will who ultimately sealed you inside that tomb.'

His brother had no answer to that. By the time Nagash reached the summit, Thutep was gone.

Beyond the ridge was a broad, rocky plain. The dark mountain, and its promise of power, might have loomed among the company of a dozen other peaks along the horizon to the east. Beyond their jagged summits, the sky was already paling with the light of false dawn.

THERE WAS NOWHERE to hide. No caves, no overhangs, no brush-covered depressions to crawl into and escape the fire of the sun. Nagash knew it would sear his skin in minutes, but that was of little concern to him. Far worse was its effects on the elixir. The older he and his immortals had become, the more that sunlight sapped the strength of their stolen vigour. When he and his armies marched to war, they moved in a perpetual darkness wrought by fearsome sorcery. Even at the peak of his powers, Nagash doubted he would have survived a full day's exposure to the sun.

As things were now, he didn't think that he'd last more than a few minutes.

Gritting his teeth, Nagash began scraping at the baked ground. Ptra could not have him. He would sooner cover himself in dirt like an animal than concede defeat to god or man.

May I be of service, great one?

The voice was soft and too sincere, the kind of tone a servant would take to mock his master to his face. It sounded right by Nagash's ear. With a monumental effort, he turned his head and glanced up at the ghostly figure kneeling by his side.

Khefru was holding out his hand to Nagash, as though to help him stand. The former priest, who had helped Nagash learn the secrets of necromancy and later conspired with him to seize the throne, smiled down at his former master through a mask of flame. As the Usurper watched, the priest's body became wreathed in sorcerous fire, just as it had centuries past when Nagash had learned of Khefru and Nekerem's betrayal.

'Traitor,' Nagash hissed. '*Snivelling coward! Enslaving your spirit was too good for you! I should have consumed you utterly when I had the chance.*'

To Nagash's surprise, the ghost's burning face turned bitter. *More is the pity,* Khefru said. *Better oblivion than an eternity wandering in the cold places of the world. You'll understand soon enough.* The former servant turned, gauging the time until dawn. *Not long now.*

But the Usurper refused to be cowed by the spirit's ominous words. '*Let it come!*' he said. '*What do I care if I'm freed from this broken husk of a body? You were never a match for me in life, Khefru – not you, nor Thutep, nor even Nebunefer or Neferem. You shall be my slave again, you cur. Watch and see.*'

Khefru's smile broadened as the flames bit deep into the flesh of his face. *Do you imagine that it's just the four of us? Oh, no, great one. We're just the ones who could reach you the easiest. There are others out there in the shadows, waiting for your demise. All the people of Mahrak, slaughtered in their thousands and cast adrift, without Usirian to judge them or Djaf to conduct them to the afterlife. All the soldiers of both sides who fell in the final battle, and all the skirmishes who came after, and all the common folk who perished in the famines and plagues that wracked the land afterwards. You cannot imagine so many,* the former servant said. *But you will have all eternity to entertain them.*

This time, Nagash watched the spirit go. Khefru simply stood up and walked away, without so much as a backwards glance. He headed westwards, into the fleeing shadows, and dissipated like smoke.

THE SCAVENGERS HEARD him raving long before they actually saw him. He was lying face down in the middle of a rocky plain, spitting curses in a tongue they didn't understand and directed at nothing they could see. The wasteland had obviously driven the hairless one mad, not that it made any difference to them. His meat would taste the same regardless.

The four of them were starving. There had been six of them once upon a time, when they'd been sent from the tunnels of the Great City to scour the World Above for the hidden gifts of the Great Horned One.

During the second year of their great hunt, they'd seen the claw of their god trace a green arc across the sky, and had followed its trail into the depths of the wasteland, where they'd found a scar gouged in the packed earth and a handful of treasures nestled together like a clutch of new-laid eggs.

Great was their fortune, or so they'd believed. Great would be their glory when they returned with their bounty to the clan master! But tracing their steps back out of the cursed waste had proved much more difficult than they'd bargained for. After the first few months the food had run out, and hunting in the rat-forsaken wasteland was slim. Mad with hunger, they'd turned on one another, and the two weakest had become food for the rest.

When the last of that meat ran out, more than a month ago, the four hunters had spent weeks waiting for one of their fellows to slip up and become the next meal, but none of them were so careless. Finally, growing more and more desperate, one of the band began gnawing at the Horned God's sky-gift, in hopes of gaining the upper paw over his companions. Out of self-preservation, the other hunters began to nibble their share of the god-stone as well. It tore like a knife through their guts and set their nerves on fire, but it lent them enough vigour to survive and keep the stalemate going.

The hunters ate of the god-stone sparingly, fearing the wrath of the clan-master when they finally did manage to return to the city. Their fur was falling out in patches, and awful, glowing lesions appeared on the raw skin beneath. Catching the scent of the hairless one was a gift from the Horned One himself, they reasoned. They hoped to find enough meat on the prey's bones to last them until they could escape the wasteland and make their way home.

When they caught sight of the prey's shrivelled, leathery body they began squabbling over the spoils at once. Knives were drawn. Threats were spat. Alliances were formed and broken in the space of minutes. Finally, the leader of the little band put an end to the bickering and declared that each hunter was entitled to one of the prey's limbs. Once those were cut off, the torso would be divided four ways, and then they'd all get turns sucking the sweetmeats out of the skull. With dawn looming close on the horizon, the band grudgingly reached an agreement. They shuffled about the hairless one, choosing which limb they wanted and scheming how to steal the rest when an opportune moment arose.

The leader of the pack hefted his knife and flipped the prey onto his back – the better to get at the entrails when the time came. To their surprise, the prey was still alive, its eyes widening at the sight of the knife in the pack leader's hand. The hunters chuckled. The meal would come with a little entertainment as well.

Hissing expectantly, the pack leader bent down and grabbed the bony wrist of the prey's one good arm. He started to stretch it out for a clean cut when the hairless one reared upward with a howl and sank its teeth into the hunter's throat!

Flesh tore. Hot blood sprayed across the rocky ground, and the pack leader let out a choking squeak. The hairless one was clumsy and slow, but the hunters were weak themselves and stunned by the sudden ferocity of the attack. They barely had time to react before their would-be prey grabbed the knife from the dying pack leader's hand and buried it in the chest of the hunter to his right. Then, with an exultant howl, the hairless one leapt upon the third hunter and the two fell to the ground, stabbing wildly at one another with their knives.

In the space of just a few seconds, the pack had been all but destroyed. The realisation proved too much for the fourth hunter's fragile courage to withstand. It abandoned its pack-mates and fled squeaking into the pre-dawn shadows.

NAGASH PULLED THE crude knife from the monster's throat. Dark blood bubbled from the wound. He bent over it at once, gulping down the hot liquid as the creature shuddered in its death throes.

The power! He could taste it in the vile thing's blood. The Usurper drank deep, marvelling at the fire that raced through his withered limbs.

When the monster was dead he leaned back, chest heaving, face bathed in gore. His emaciated body shuddered as successive waves of agony wracked it, but he welcomed the sensation for what it was. A semblance of power was coursing through his form once more, restoring to him a small amount of vitality.

One day he would thank Khefru for the incentive to try his luck with the beasts. Had he not been so persuaded to survive, the battle might not have gone half so well as it did.

The Usurper glanced about the plain, looking for where the last of the monsters had gone, but the creature had vanished from sight.

What monsters were these? For the first time, Nagash could study his attackers in detail. They looked like nothing so much as diseased men with the heads and naked tails of *rats*. They were even dressed in filthy kilts made of some sort of woven plant matter, now frayed and begrimed with the dust of the wasteland. Silver earrings glittered from their rodent-like ears, and one wore a thin, gold bracelet around its right wrist. Each of them carried bronze knives of surprising quality, as well made as anything forged in distant Ka-Sabar.

The only other possessions they carried were rough, leather bags, tightly-knotted and secured to their leather belts. Nagash reached down and tugged at the one on his last victim's belt – and felt a shock of power like a live coal burning in the palm of his hand. He dropped the bag with a start. Then after a moment's thought he carefully sliced open the side with the point of his bloody knife.

At once, a sickly green glow emanated from the slit. Working carefully with the knife, Nagash opened it further and dumped the bag's contents onto the ground.

Two small lumps of glowing green stone, each about the size of his thumb, rolled onto the hard ground. The light they cast was intense. Where it touched his bare skin it set his nerves to tingling.

Nagash reached down and carefully picked one up. Heat suffused his fingertips, radiating from the stone in a steady, buzzing stream. He inspected the stone carefully, and was shocked to find what looked like teeth marks chiselled into its rough surface. The creatures were *eating* the rock? That explained the traces of power in their blood.

The Usurper's heart began to race. The creatures must have come from the dark mountain. How else could they have come by the same power he sought? No other explanation made sense.

Already, the pain was fading from his limbs, settling into a dull ache that pulsed like a hot ember in his chest. He considered the glowing rock for a moment more, and abruptly reached a decision. Setting the stone back on the ground, he took the hilt of his knife and broke it into three smaller pieces.

With only a moment's hesitation, Nagash picked up the smallest piece and swallowed it.

Fire burst along every nerve in the Usurper's body. His muscles swelled with power; his scalp tingled until it burned. Nagash's mind reeled under the onslaught. It was far wilder and harder to channel than any power he'd known before, but the intensity was still nothing like the enormous energies he'd wielded in the past. It raged through his body, wreaking havoc on flesh and bone. He seized it with his will and directed the raging torrent where he wished it to go.

There was a crackle of bone and a creak of decayed sinew. The Usurper threw back his head and howled his suffering to the sky as his ruined left arm knit back together. Next, foul smelling smoke poured from the holes in his torso and forehead. He doubled over, still shrieking in pain, as flesh and organs were shifted aside.

Thump. Thump. Thump. One after another, three small, dark metal balls thudded to the ground, wreathed in pale greenish steam.

Seconds later, Nagash the Usurper was whole again, in body if not in mind.

The first rays of dawn were breaking over the distant peaks. With a trembling hand, Nagash gathered up the rest of the stones and tucked them back into the slit pouch. As he quickly dragged the bodies of the creatures over to him, he could sense that more stones resided in the pouches of the other creatures he'd killed.

It wasn't much, but it would be enough, the Usurper vowed. The stones would sustain him and guide him to the great mountain, where he would learn to master its fearsome power.

As Ptra's light burned overhead, Nagash curled up on the rocky ground, shielded beneath the bodies of those he'd slain, and dreamed of the doom that would befall Nehekhara.

ONE

Balance of Power

Lahmia, The City of the Dawn, in the 70th year of
Basth the Graceful
(-1650 Imperial Reckoning)

THE YELLOW SILK roof of the Hall of Rebirth rippled like a great sail in the freshening wind blowing from the coast, and its polished cedar timbers groaned like a great ship at sea. The comparison seemed particularly apt, Neferata thought bitterly, given the legion of shipwrights that had been hastily drafted to build it.

Preparations for the great Council of Kings had gone on for three solid months, beginning on the very day that the fateful news had arrived from Ka-Sabar. Even as word raced through the winding city streets that the City of Bronze had fallen at last, and the long war against the Usurper had finally come to an end, King Lamashizzar was already digging into the city treasury in anticipation of his royal peers' arrival. Commissions by the hundred flowed from the palace and descended like flocks of sea birds on the astonished city merchants and trading factors: jars of fine wine by the hundreds; casks of beer by the *thousands;* cunning gifts of gold, silver and bronze; bales of silk by the ton and a queen's ransom in fine spices and rare incense.

And that was only the beginning. Swift trading ships plied the fickle seas between Lahmia and the Eastern Empire's trading cities to bring back the finest, most exotic delicacies that the Silk Lands could produce, while the dockyards were stripped of every able hand to build a vast tent city on the Golden Plain. As spring gave way to summer it seemed as though every able-bodied man, woman and child was working feverishly to complete the king's grand design.

When the rebel leaders finally arrived, in the last month of summer, they were met at the edge of the Golden Plain by Lamashizzar himself, at the head of a richly-dressed panoply of courtesans, artists, musicians and servants. After being showered with small gifts – from rings and bracelets to fine swords and splendid chariots – the rulers were conducted across the great, fertile plain to the sprawling city of silk tents set aside for their servants and retainers. The gentle breezes that caressed the plain turned the tent city into a rippling banner of festive colour: sea green for Zandri, gold for Numas, blue for Lybaras and brilliant red for Rasetra.

The royal processions descended upon their encampments with weary delight, and allowed a few hours to rest and refresh themselves before the celebrations began in earnest. Then, at sunset, Lamashizzar and his panoply summoned his royal guests with a blare of golden trumpets and led them in a triumphant procession through the streets of his city.

The people of Lahmia commemorated the end of the war for seven ecstatic days, and from the halls of the palace to the mean streets near the dockyards, the king's royal guests were treated like saviours. They wanted for nothing, except perhaps a few hours' rest here and there between revels and enough room in their baggage to carry all of Lamashizzar's rich gifts back home with them.

It was only at the end of the week, when the king's guests were thoroughly worn out and more than a little overwhelmed by the Lahmians' wealth and generosity, that Lamashizzar convened the Council of Kings to decide the future of Nehekhara.

The great Hall of Rebirth had been built by the city's carpenters and shipwrights in the space occupied by the palace's grand royal gardens. In fact, the wooden structure encompassed the gardens themselves, creating the illusion that the council chamber was surrounded by a tamed wilderness. Brilliantly coloured songbirds, many imported at great cost from the Silk Lands, filled the space with music, while fountains burbled serenely just out of sight. Servants came and went along hidden paths, bearing refreshments to the guests, who sat around a huge, circular mahogany table in a clearing at the far end of the garden. The effect of so much vibrant, harnessed life on the desert rulers was nothing short of stunning.

The entire spectacle, from start to finish, had been calculated as carefully as any military campaign, Neferata understood. It was couched to tempt, seduce and intimidate the rulers of east and west, and muddle whatever alliances they might have forged against Lahmia's interests. It was also stupendously, ruinously *expensive*. The city's treasury was virtually empty. All of the wealth that their father Lamasheptra had so carefully built during the dark years of Nagash's reign was gone. Their last reserves had been thrown away on a single, extravagant throw of the dice. There was not enough gold in the coffers to make even a quarter of the coming year's payment to the Eastern Empire; if Lamashizzar's negotiations did not bear fruit, the City of the Dawn faced certain disaster.

While the king gambled with his city's future, Neferata was left to watch the proceedings from a broad balcony that spanned the rear of the great hall and overlooked the great council table. Her hand-maidens lounged on silk cushions and ate candied dates while they gossiped in hushed tones about the scandals from the previous week's celebrations. A delicate fog of incense curled just above their heads:

myrrh spiced with black lotus, to relieve the boredom. Servants knelt at the fringes of the chamber alert to the queen's every need. A low table, with sheets of paper and an ink brush, had been hastily set beside her as she studied the visiting rulers from behind a polished wooden screen.

As precarious as Lahmia's future might be, judging by the appearance of their guests it was evident to Neferata that the other great cities were in a far worse state. During his unnatural reign, Nagash the Usurper had recreated the Nehekharan Empire in principle if not in name, subjugating the other great cities through the power he held over Khemri's hostage queen, Neferem.

For centuries, each city had been forced to pay tribute to the Usurper in the form of gold and slaves, driving them to the brink of ruin. When the priests of Khemri – at the urging of their superiors on the Hieratic Council in Mahrak – finally attempted to unseat Nagash and end his blasphemous reign, the Usurper retaliated with a terrible curse that struck down two-thirds of Nehekhara's priesthood in the space of a single day.

It was that one act of infamy that finally caused the priest kings to rise up in revolt, but the Usurper fought back with dark magics and terrible atrocities that devastated the Blessed Land and slaughtered thousands. Yet even when the Usurper's army was finally defeated, close to a dozen of his immortal lieutenants escaped destruction and continued to bedevil the land for decades.

Rather than celebrate their hard-won triumph at Mahrak, the Priest Kings were faced with a long, gruelling campaign of terror and attrition as they hunted down every last one of the Usurper's minions. Since Nagash's body had never been found, it was secretly feared that one of them still possessed the Usurper's corpse and, if given the opportunity, might be able to restore the dreaded necromancer to life. It had taken ninety years to finish the task, slaying the last of Nagash's immortals after a lengthy siege at Ka-Sabar, the City of Bronze.

The long years of war had left an indelible mark on each of Nehekhara's rulers. They were gaunt from strain and deprivation that no amount of easy living could ever erase. Few wore jewellery, or gilt adornments on their robes of state, and the fine fabrics of their ceremonial attire seemed shabby and worn. Even now, amid the verdant luxury of the great hall, their expressions were haunted and fretful, as though they expected fresh horrors hiding in every shadow.

Neferata was vividly reminded of that night in the cellars, now decades past, when Lamashizzar and his cabal had returned from the war. *And they'd scarcely fought more than a handful of battles, while these men and women have known nothing else their entire lives,* she thought.

Yet as beleaguered and broken as these rulers might be, they were not to be underestimated, the queen knew. When the doors to the great hall were opened, Lamashizzar's guests had filed through the gardens in solemn procession, led by the Priest Kings of

Rasetra and Lybaras and the young Queen of Numas. Each of the three rulers bore a sandalwood box in their hands, and when they reached the great council table they set the boxes before the smiling Lahmian king and drew forth their contents.

The severed heads of Raamket, the Red Lord, and Atan-Heru, the Great Beast, had been treated with nitre and the sacred oils of the mortuary cult, and looked much as they had at the moment of their deaths. Their pale skin was mottled with burns from the touch of the sun, and their lips were drawn back in savage, almost bestial snarls, revealing teeth that had been filed to points and stained brown with human blood. The third head, by comparison, was round and fleshy as a suckling pig's, with small, beady eyes hidden by a thick band of kohl.

Memnet, the former Grand Hierophant of Ka-Sabar, who murdered his king and served Nagash in exchange for eternal life, had wailed like a babe as he was dragged before the headsman. An expression of craven terror was still etched on Memnet's jowly face.

The heads still sat in the centre of the table, their hideous expressions turned to face Lamashizzar. The message – to Neferata, at least – was clear. *We've done our part, while you sat in your city by the sea. Now you'll help us rebuild, or there might be one more head on this table by day's end.* At this point, it was difficult to say whether Lamashizzar's display of wealth had successfully undermined his guests, or simply strengthened their resolve.

The queen bit her lip in irritation. We should be deciding this on the battlefield, she thought. We can always make more soldiers. Gold is much harder to come by.

It was mid-afternoon. The council had been in session for almost five hours, during which time Lamashizzar enquired of the needs of each of his guests and made offers of assistance in the form of monetary loans and trade agreements. Dizzying sums of gold were haggled over, while scribes hurriedly drafted copies of proposals that would govern the flow of goods across Nehekhara for generations to come.

Trade with the Eastern Empire would rejuvenate the Blessed Land's economy, and open up a vast new realm of markets for Nehekharan goods – and all of it would pass through the City of the Dawn. Each of the rulers had been given the chance to speak, and a brief lull had settled over the table while each of the council members took stock of their current positions. Off to the east came a distant grumble of thunder as a late-summer rain shower made its way towards the coast.

Neferata heard a rustle of cushions behind her, followed by a familiar cat-like tread as her young cousin Khalida came to sit beside her.

'Great Gods, is it finally over?' the girl asked, slumping theatrically onto the queen's lap. 'We've been trapped in here *forever*. I wanted to go out riding before the rain came in.'

Neferata chuckled despite herself. Khalida hadn't the least interest in courtly gossip or affairs of state.

At fifteen she was tall and coltish, full of so much restless energy that even the sprawling Women's Palace wasn't large enough to contain her. She was much like her father, Lord Wakhashem, a wealthy nobleman and close ally of King Lamasheptra, who had secured a strategic marriage to Neferata's aunt Semunet. Both had died when Khalida was very young, and according to tradition she had been returned to the keeping of the royal family until such time as a husband could be found for her. She was passionate about horses, archery – even swordplay – and had little interest in the finer aspects of courtly behaviour. Lamashizzar dismayed of ever finding a nobleman who would take Khalida, but Neferata was secretly proud of her.

The queen reached down and stroked the girl's dark hair. She kept it in dozens of tight, oiled braids, like the Numasi horse-maidens of legend. 'The real work has scarcely begun, little hawk,' Neferata said fondly. 'Up until now, the council has merely argued matters of taxes and trade. Trivial matters, in the grander scheme of things.'

Khalida looked up at the queen. The goddess Asaph hadn't blessed her with the radiant beauty that Neferata and most of the Lahmian royal bloodline possessed. She was striking, in a fierce, angular way, with a sharp nose, a small, square chin and dark, piercing eyes. She frowned. 'Trivial compared to what?'

The queen smiled. 'Compared to power, of course. The decisions made here will determine the balance of power in Nehekhara for centuries to come. Each of the rulers seated below us has their own idea of how that balance should be struck.'

Khalida took the end of one of her braids between her fingers and twirled it thoughtfully. 'Then who decides which idea is best?'

'We do, at the moment.' *And Lamashizzar had best exploit this opportunity to the fullest.* Neferata took Khalida by the shoulders and pulled her gently upright. 'Pay attention to something other than horses for a moment and I'll try to explain.'

Khalida sighed heavily. 'If it will make the time go faster.'

The queen nodded approvingly. 'It begins with Khemri,' she said. 'Since the time of Settra the Magnificent, the living city was the centre of power in Nehekhara. Even after Settra's empire fell, the Living City and its mortuary cult exerted tremendous political and economic influence from one end of the Blessed Land to the other. Their interests were guaranteed before all others, and that translated to power, comfort and security. Next in line came Mahrak, the City of the Gods, then Ka-Sabar, Numas, Lybaras, Zandri, Lahmia and Quatar.'

'Numas was more powerful than Lybaras?' Khalida exclaimed. 'They're farmers, mostly. Lybaras had airships!'

'The Numasi provided the grain for most of Nehekhara,' the queen said patiently. 'You can't eat an airship, little hawk.'

'I suppose,' the girl said. 'But what about us? Why were we so low on the list?'

Neferata sighed. 'Because we were so distant from Khemri, for starters. Zandri was closer, and was somewhat richer due to the slave trade. And unlike other cities, we preferred to keep to ourselves.'

'But Nagash changed all that.'

'That's right. Khemri is nothing but ruins now, as well as Mahrak, and most of the other cities suffered greatly thanks to the Usurper. Now that the war is over, everything lies in flux.'

It was then that King Lamashizzar's voice rose above the muted murmur of the hall. 'My honoured friend, Priest King Khepra; do you wish to address the council?'

A heavy wooden chair creaked as Khepra, Priest King of Lybaras, rose slowly to his feet. The son of the late King Hekhmenukep looked much like his illustrious father: he was tall and lean, with narrow shoulders and a square-jawed, hangdog face. Unlike his father, though, Khepra's arms and shoulders were thick with muscle, and his hands and face bore the scars of dozens of battlefields.

Like the kings of Lybaras before him, Khepra wore a fine gold chain about his neck, hung with a bewildering assortment of glass lenses bound in gold, silver or copper wire. It was a relic from a more prosperous, peaceful age, when the engineer-priests of Lybaras crafted wondrous inventions for the greater glory of Tahoth, patron god of scholars.

The king nodded to Lamashizzar. 'Great king, on behalf of your esteemed guests, I wish to thank you for this splendid display of generosity on our behalf.

I'm also grateful to see that all of us have come together today to ensure the continued prosperity of our great cities, and the land of Nehekhara as a whole. It is a welcome beginning, but there are still very serious matters that require our attention.'

Neferata's eyes narrowed. 'Now it begins, little hawk. Watch the faces of the rulers around the table. How are they reacting to the Lybaran king?'

The young girl frowned, but did as she was told. 'Well… they're looking curious, I suppose. Politely interested.' She paused, her head tilting slightly to one side. 'Except for the King of Rasetra.'

'Oh?' the queen asked, smiling faintly.

'He's not even looking at Khepra. He's pretending to sip his wine, but really he's watching everyone else.'

Neferata nodded approvingly. 'Now you know who is truly asking the question. King Khepra is speaking on Rasetra's behest, while King Shepret can devote his full attention to gauging the reactions of his rivals.'

Rasetra and Lybaras had been close allies during the war, and had borne the brunt of the fighting from beginning to end. Whatever it was that Rasetra was now after, King Shepret could almost certainly count on Khepra's support in the council. She'd tried to warn Lamashizzar to find a way to drive a wedge between the two kings; if he didn't one of the other kings wouldn't hesitate to try.

Neferata turned to the table at her side and picked up the waiting ink brush. She wrote hurriedly in the sharp-edged pictographs of the Eastern Empire's trading cant: *Divide Rasetra and Lybaras, or they will outmanoeuvre you!*

She paused, tapping the end of the brush against her lower lip as a thought occurred to her. *King Khepra's son is in need of a wife. Perhaps Khalida?*

She plucked a pinch of fine-grained sand from a tiny box by the ink-pot and scattered it across the pictographs to help set the ink, then held out the page for a servant to carry downstairs to the king.

'While we now have plans in place to ensure the stability of our own homes, there are still three cities that are desolate and devoid of leadership,' the King of Lybaras said. 'We cannot sit idly by and watch them fall to ruin.'

'Generous words from a man who just spent the last four years desolating one of the very cities in question,' Lamashizzar replied good-naturedly. The other rulers laughed at the gentle jibe, but for a moment King Khepra was put on the back foot. He faltered for a moment, unable to come up with a proper response.

'The city of Ka-Sabar is the least of our concerns at the moment,' King Shepret said in a flat voice. He was lean and muscular, with his late father's broad shoulders, but where the legendary king Rakh-amn-hotep was stout and pugnacious, Shepret had the aquiline features of an up-country patrician.

Though he was just over a hundred years old, well into middle age, his thick black hair only showed a few streaks of grey, and his green eyes were as vivid and sharp as cut emeralds. 'The Living City has lain in ruins for almost a century.' He set down his wine cup and turned his piercing gaze on Lamashizzar. 'Now that the war is over, we must reclaim the city and restore the rightful order of things.'

Agitated murmurs rose around the council table. Khalida grinned. 'Lamashizzar made Shepret state his own case,' she said proudly. She glanced sidelong at Neferata. 'That is what happened, right?'

Neferata sighed. 'With Lamashizzar it's difficult to tell, sometimes. But possibly, yes.'

'But why does King Shepret care about restoring the Living City? Doesn't he have enough worries with the lizard folk?'

The queen gave her young cousin an appraising stare. Apparently Khalida wasn't as oblivious to matters of state as she appeared to be. Rasetra was the smallest of the great cities, but because of its proximity to the deadly southern jungles and its tribes of Lizard Folk, their army was second to none. But the war had bled Rasetra white, and now the city was fighting for its survival against growing attacks by lizard war parties.

Neferata considered the question carefully. 'It's not entirely unexpected,' she said. 'Rasetra was originally settled by Khemri, just a few hundred years ago. When King Shepret talks of putting another king on Khemri's throne, he means one of his own sons. They're directly related to the old royal family, and have an unassailable claim. It would give Rasetra a powerful ally on the western side of the Bitter Peaks, and allow it to exert its influence across all of Nehekhara.'

At the council table, Lamashizzar cleared his throat, and the murmurs fell silent. 'That's a very noble goal, honoured friend,' the king said, 'but also a daunting one. Khemri lies empty now. Only jackals and restless ghosts prowl the city streets.'

King Shepret nodded. As a young man, he'd been with his father's army when they'd reached Khemri, just a few months after the battle at Mahrak. He'd seen the city's sand-choked streets firsthand. 'According to my sources, many of Khemri's citizens fled to Bel Aliad, hoping to begin a new life there.' He shrugged. 'They could be resettled again, with the proper incentive.'

Khalida let out a snort. 'At the end of a spear, he means.'

The girl was absolutely right, Neferata realised. She turned quickly and took up the ink brush again. *Give Shepret what he wants,* she wrote. *Give him Khemri.* A servant scurried forwards and plucked the message from the queen's outstretched hand.

Khalida watched the servant go. 'Does the king actually follow your advice?'

'It's been known to happen,' Neferata replied.

'Is it true you actually ruled the city when he was fighting against Nagash, all those years ago?'

The question took Neferata aback. 'Who told you that?'

'Oh,' Khalida said, suddenly uncomfortable. 'No one in particular. Everybody knows it – inside the Women's Palace, at least.'

'Well, it's nothing that needs to be repeated elsewhere,' the queen warned. 'Other cities may treat their queens differently, but here in Lahmia, such things are not done.' She paused, uncertain of how much she should reveal. 'Let's just say that it was a difficult time, and we were at a delicate stage of negotiations with the Eastern Empire. I... consulted with Grand Vizier Ubaid on a number of important matters while the king was away. Nothing more.'

Khalida nodded thoughtfully, and turned to regard the council once more. 'Shepret would have been right about my age back then,' she mused. 'He looks so *old* now. Yet you and Lamashizzar still look as young as thirty-year-olds.'

Neferata stiffened. You see much more than I give you credit for, little hawk.

For the last nine decades, Lamashizzar and his cabal had been hard at work deciphering Nagash's tomes and trying to replicate his elixir of immortality. For the first few years the king had consulted her regularly, and despite her misgivings, she'd helped explain the necromancer's basic methods in crafting potions and performing incantations. Relinquishing control of the city to Lamashizzar had been much harder to bear than she'd imagined; experimenting with Nagash's books had at least given her something to *do*. Returning to a quiet, cloistered life in the Women's Palace seemed like a fate worse than death.

It had taken them four years of trial and error before they managed to create a very weak version of the elixir. After that, Lamashizzar no longer summoned her from the Women's Palace. She received a small bottle of the potion every month, which managed to slow the process of ageing, but nothing more. As far as she knew, Lamashizzar and his noblemen still experimented with the process, in an unused wing of the palace. She had no idea what had eventually become of Arkhan, the king's immortal prisoner.

'My brother and I have been very fortunate,' Neferata replied, as casually as she could manage. 'The blessings of Asaph run strong in the royal bloodline. They always have.'

Khalida chuckled. 'I hope I'm half so lucky when I'm a hundred years old,' she said.

'Time will tell,' the queen replied, eager to change the subject. 'What's was King Teremun saying just now?'

The young girl blinked. 'Ah... I think he asked Shepret what he meant by restoring the rightful order. Something to that effect.'

As Neferata considered the question, Shepret turned to the King of Zandri and replied. 'The will of the people has been worn thin by a century of warfare. We need to send a clear sign that the age of Nagash is no more. There needs to be a new king on Settra's throne, and a Daughter of the Sun at his side.'

Neferata drew in a sharp breath. That was clever, Shepret, the queen thought. Very clever indeed.

It was a proposal almost guaranteed to win Lahmia's support. From the time of Settra the Magnificent, the Priest Kings of Khemri were married to the eldest daughter of the Lahmian royal line. The Lahmian king's firstborn daughter was called the Daughter of the Sun, because she was the living embodiment of the covenant between the gods and the people of the Blessed Land. The marriage was meant to create a union between the spiritual and temporal power of Settra's throne, and it had been one of the cornerstones of Khemri's power ever since.

Clearly, the King of Rasetra was proposing an alliance with Lahmia, one that, in theory, would benefit both cities. It was also something that none of the other great cities would stand for.

As if on cue, Queen Amunet of Numas turned in her chair to face Shepret. She was the daughter of Seheb, one of the twin kings of the city, and the only survivor after the vicious cycle of fratricide that occurred in the wake of the twins' sudden deaths. She had eyes as black as onyx and a smile like a hungry jackal.

'You're putting the chariot before the horse, King Shepret,' the Queen of Numas said dryly. 'Lamashizzar and his queen have to actually produce children before your dream can become a reality.'

The rest of the council responded with nervous laughter – all except for the sickly King Naeem of Quatar, who planted trembling hands onto the tabletop and pushed himself to his feet. Naeem was of an age with his peers, but as a young acolyte he'd been among those trapped at Mahrak during Nagash's ten-year siege, and he'd never truly recovered from the suffering he'd endured there. His body was painfully gaunt, his head bald and his cheeks sunken. When he spoke, his voice was little more than a whisper, but his rheumy eyes burned with conviction.

'King Shepret speaks of restoring the proper order of things, but his priorities are misplaced,' Naeem declared. 'The greatest of the Usurper's crimes was that he broke the sacred covenant between the people and their gods. The blessings that have sustained us for millennia are slipping away. The sands press a little closer to our cities each year, and our harvests are dwindling. Our people suffer a little more each year from sickness, and do not live the same span of years as our ancestors. Unless we find a way to redeem ourselves in the eyes of the gods, within a few hundred years Nehekhara will be a kingdom of the dead.'

Khalida's eyes widened. 'Is this true?'

Neferata's lips pressed together in irritation. 'I haven't had the opportunity to measure the size of our fields lately,' she answered. 'It certainly sounds ominous enough, but remember that Naeem was a priest long before he became a king, so his convictions are more than a little suspect.'

The young girl frowned. 'What does that mean?'

'Wait and listen.'

Down at the council table, Lamashizzar spoke. 'What, then, would you have us do?' he said to Naeem.

From the look on Naeem's face, the answer seemed obvious to him. 'Why, the people must first be reminded of their duty to the gods!' he replied. 'We must spare no effort to rebuild Mahrak, and restore the Hieratic Council to its proper place in Nehekharan society.'

'Now we get to the heart of the matter,' the queen said to Khalida. 'Naeem has been listening to those bitter old buzzards that have roosted in his court.'

Throughout the history of Nehekhara, the Hieratic Council had presumed to speak on behalf of the gods themselves, issuing edicts and meddling in the affairs of kings from their seat of power at Mahrak. With temples in every one of the great cities and religious advisors in all of the royal courts, their wealth and influence had been tremendous. Their grip on Nehekharan society had finally been broken by the Usurper, and since the fall of Mahrak the remnants of the council had taken refuge at Quatar, where they continued to issue dire warnings about the passing of the old ways. As far as Nefereta was aware, none of Nehekhara's rulers seemed willing to listen to their harangues any more. Their divine powers had faded, and the glories of the Ushabti, their holy champions, were nothing more than a fading memory. Their day was done.

Lamashizzar raised a placating hand. 'Your piety does you great credit, King Naeem,' he said smoothly, 'and I'm sure that all of our friends here would agree that we would like to see the council restored to Mahrak one day. Of course, I don't need to tell you, of all people, how our cities have suffered during this long war—'

'If it wasn't for the Hieratic Council, none of us would be sitting here today!' Naeem shot back. His watery eyes widened in righteous indignation. 'It was they who forged the great alliance between Rasetra and Lybaras! They who financed the building of the armies and the engines of war! We owe them–'

'No one here has claimed otherwise,' Lamashizzar replied, his voice taking on a steely edge. 'Just as no one here has claimed to possess the resources to rebuild Khemri, either.'

Neferata straightened. Don't be a fool, brother, she thought. You have a golden opportunity here. Don't squander it!

'For a century, everyone here has given much in the service of the common good,' Lamashizzar continued, conveniently overlooking the fact that half of the cities represented at the table sided with Nagash up until the very last moment outside Mahrak. 'I think the gods would forgive us if we now focussed on regaining our strength, if only for a short while. Vast restoration projects are, in my opinion, a bit premature at this point. Does anyone disagree?'

The King of Quatar glared archly at the assembled rulers, but even Shepret sat back in his chair and stared silently into his wine cup. Neferata clenched her fists in frustration.

'Then we are all in agreement,' Lamashizzar said. 'But I thank both King Naeem and King Shepret for making their concerns known to us. I'm confident that when the time is right, we will no doubt revisit these proposals and give them due consideration.' Smiling, the Lahmian king rose to his feet. 'For now, though, may I suggest we adjourn and refresh ourselves before the evening's feast?'

King Naeema looked as though he would protest Lamashizzar's suggestion, but he was pre-empted by Queen Amunet and Fadil, the young King of Zandri, who rose to their feet without a word and took their leave of the council. Servants and scribes rose to their feet, swarming around the table, and the King of Quatar had no choice but to gather up his retainers and leave with what little dignity remained to him.

'Thank Asaph,' Khalida said with a sigh. 'King Naeem looked like he was ready to argue all night long.' She turned to Neferata, her expression hopeful. 'Shall we return to the Women's Palace now?'

'Go on,' Neferata told her. 'Take the maids with you. I'll be along presently.'

Khalida's eyes widened. 'I– I mean, I don't think that's very wise–'

'I must speak to Lamashizzar,' the queen said, anger seeping into her voice. 'In private. Do as I say, little hawk.'

The young girl shot to her feet as though stung, and within moments she was herding the bemused handmaidens from the balcony. As soon as they were gone, Neferata snatched her mask from a nervous-looking servant and stormed down the stairs to the lower floor.

She found Lamashizzar along one of the twisting garden pathways that led from the council space. The king was surrounded by a number of senior scribes, who were presenting drafts of various trade agreements for his approval. He looked up as she approached, and the self-satisfied smile on his face vanished.

'I must speak to you,' Neferata said icily. 'Now.'

The king's eyes narrowed angrily, but Neferata met his stare without flinching. After a long moment he dismissed the scribes, who wasted no time withdrawing down the garden path.

'I'm starting to think W'soran was right, all those years ago,' he growled at her. 'You seem to have a problem with understanding your place, sister.'

Neferata stepped close to him, turning her masked face up to his. 'Did you read a single thing I wrote, brother? I made the words as simple as I could,' she hissed. The vehemence in her voice surprised even herself, but she was too frustrated to hold it back. 'Give. Khemri. To. Shepret. Is that too complex an idea for you to grasp?'

'Why in the name of all the gods would I do such a thing?' Lamashizzar snarled. 'Hand control of Khemri to Rasetra? It's ridiculous!'

'It was the perfect opportunity to cripple our most dangerous rival!' Neferata shot back, her voice echoing within the confines of the mask. It took all of her self-control not to tear the damned thing off and fling it into her brother's smug face. 'Don't you see? Rasetra hasn't the strength to rebuild Khemri *and* keep the lizard folk at bay simultaneously! Shepret's greed would have been his undoing. All we had to do was sit back and give him our blessing!'

'And deprive ourselves of a major trading partner? Are you insane?' the king snapped. 'Has the black lotus permanently dulled your senses? These trade agreements will pay our debt to the Eastern Empire and cement Lahmia as the centre of power in Nehekhara.'

'Are you really as naïve as all that?' the queen replied. 'Our *honoured friends* won't abide by those agreements one moment more than they have to. As soon as they've restored their cities and rebuilt their armies, they'll form a coalition and force us to negotiate terms that are more to their liking. Did you learn nothing from the war with Nagash?'

The king's hand shot out, seizing Neferata's jaw and gripping it with surprising strength. 'Don't speak of things you know nothing about,' he warned. 'I should never have let you advise Ubaid in my absence. It put too many dangerous ideas in your head.' He shoved her roughly backwards. 'If you know what's good for you, you'll concern yourself with more proper matters, like providing me with an heir. Or would you rather I stopped sending you bottles of elixir every month? I can always marry Khalida once you're dead and gone.'

Lamashizzar's words cut through Neferata like a knife. And it was no empty threat, she could see the truth of it in his eyes. She was trapped. He could withhold Nagash's elixir any time he liked and simply wait for her to die.

Rapid footfalls sounded down the garden path. Neferata turned to see a pair of royal guardsmen appear, obviously drawn by the heated exchange. Lamashizzar acknowledged them with a curt nod.

'The queen has grown overexcited from the events of the day,' he told them. 'Conduct her to the Women's Palace at once, and inform her maids that she's to be given a draught to help her rest.'

Lamashizzar took the queen by the arm and handed her to the guards as though she were a child. Neferata felt herself moving, as though in the grip of a dream, as the warriors took her back to her gilded prison.

—◀ TWO ▶—

The Burning Stone

The Bitter Sea, in the 76th year of Asaph the Beautiful
(-1600 Imperial Reckoning)

As IT HAPPENED, using the glowing stone never did lead Nagash to the slopes of the dark mountain. If anything, it confused his course further, leading him ever deeper into the heart of the wasteland. It was a mystery that took him more than a hundred years to solve, during which time he was forced to re-learn the sorcerous arts that had made him master of Nehekhara.

The properties of the glowing rock – over time Nagash simply called it *abn-i-khat*, or 'the burning stone' – were similar in principle to the winds of magic he'd learned from his druchii tutors centuries ago, but not as easily manipulated using the rituals he'd mastered in Khemri. As near as he could tell, it wasn't truly a stone at all, but a physical manifestation of pure magic. If he used a fragment of stone as the locus of a simple ritual, the mineral consumed itself, converting to a dry, ashy substance that flaked away from its outer surface. The conversion was proportional to the amount of energy used, so far as he could determine; more than once he bitterly regretted the lack of paper and ink to document his observations. He'd learned over time how to ration the stone perfectly: a single thumbnail-sized chip provided him with enough strength and mental acuity to fulfil his needs for as much as a month, provided he didn't need to draw unduly upon its power. The flecks sustained him far better than his elixir ever did, but its chaotic energies sometimes caused his thoughts to become unmoored, or his perceptions to shift in unexpected ways.

If not kept under careful control, the stone wrought physical changes as well. His skin had retained its leathery texture, but it had taken on a green-tinged alabaster tone. As soon as he'd understood the stone's transformative properties he focussed his attention on channelling it to good use as much as possible; now he was stronger and swifter than ever before, and virtually tireless for days at a time. Lately his skin was growing mottled with faintly luminescent deposits around his shoulders and midsection, leading him to wonder how much of the stone he ate was accumulating in his bones and organs. Would there eventually come a point where its energies became too concentrated for him to control? He reluctantly conceded the possibility, even as he continued to consume the glowing stone.

Time had no meaning in the trackless expanse of the wasteland. Nagash no longer marked the passage of days, focusing all his attentions on unlocking the powers of the stone and shaping rituals to harness its power. The first rite he experimented on was creating a resonance between a fleck of stone and the source it had stemmed from.

The results were initially very disappointing. Over time, as he began to grasp the mineral's properties more closely, the experiments became merely baffling. It wasn't that the resonance failed to draw him in a distinct direction – it pointed him in a multitude of directions at the same time, including straight up and straight down. Following the many paths the ritual revealed to him caused Nagash to cross and re-cross the length and breadth of the wasteland. From time to time he would find pieces of stone, sometimes buried deep beneath the ground, but none led him towards the dark mountain. After a time, he began to think that the fickle energies of the stone were somehow *purposely* leading him astray.

Then one night, he saw a streak of green light arc across the starlit sky, and another piece of the puzzle fell into place.

Whatever the *abn-i-khat* was, it truly was not of this earth – or at least not part of the earth that Nagash knew and understood. He marked the plunging arc of green light as a soldier might trace the fall of an arrow shot, and then began a long and arduous trek to find where the stone had fallen. Eventually he came upon a shallow crater dug into the earth. Pieces of the green stone were nowhere to be found, but large, rat-like footprints were in abundance. The beasts had made it to the site mere hours before he did. Nagash tried to track them further, but soon lost their spoor across the hard, rocky terrain. After that, he resolved to kill the rat-beasts wherever he found them, for clearly they coveted the stone at least as much as he did.

Nagash mulled over everything he'd learned, and concluded firstly that if he'd been able to detect the power radiating from the mountain at such a distance, it must contain a much larger collection of *abn-i-khat* than he'd ever seen before, and its chaotic energies made magical divination difficult, if not impossible. So he abandoned his ritual and let his instincts guide him, heading ever eastward over the ridges and foothills and leaving his senses open for concentrations of magical power.

IT WAS THE hazy glow to the north-east that drew him first – a faint, greenish luminescence that limned the crooked lines of the mountain peaks, almost too faint to see against the paling of the early morning sky. He was well beyond the foothills now, crossing the first of the Brittle Peaks, and the sensations of power seemed to shift directions like the fey mountain wind.

Like everything else about the wasteland, the glow seemed just a few miles distant, but it took him nearly a fortnight to reach the last of the intervening peaks. From there, Nagash found himself staring down upon a broad, dark sea. The night was early, and the glow he'd seen on previous nights wasn't in evidence yet, allowing him to see a long way in the clear mountain air. Marshlands glittered frostily beneath the moonlight along the sea's south-eastern shore, while a broad crescent of watch fires flickered along the coastline to the north and north-west.

None of that mattered to Nagash. To the east, hard by the shores of the gloomy sea, rose the dark slopes of the mountain that had called to him for more than a hundred years. It was larger and far more imposing than the broken peaks that surrounded it; tendrils of steam leaked from fissures along its flanks, glowing faintly green in the darkness. It dominated the horizon for miles, crouching at the edge of the sea like a brooding dragon from some barbarian myth.

Looking upon the mountain, Nagash realised he had never actually seen it with his own eyes before that moment. The shadow of the power buried at its heart had somehow etched itself upon his mind's eye. Now he understood why it had always seemed to hide, just out of his grasp, no matter how hard he tried to reach it. All this time he'd been chasing a phantasm, a ghost of the true mountain. The notion both intrigued and troubled him.

Nagash reckoned that there could be dozens, perhaps even scores of stone deposits hidden within the mountain. How could they have been gathered all in one place? His gaze strayed to the constellation of watch fires lining the northern coast. Perhaps it was the rat-things. They were gathering up the stones faster than he. It all had to be going somewhere.

He would have to learn more before proceeding. The secrets of the mountain would be his, no matter what; he would need every bit of power he could muster to re-conquer Nehekhara and punish those who had defied him. If the rat-things stood in his way, then he would deal with them as well.

It took most of the night for Nagash to descend the far slope of the mountain and make his way to the outskirts of the marshland. In the early hours before dawn, when the night was coldest, a thick blanket of glowing mist rose from the marshlands and along the shores of the distant sea. The vapours curled and shifted across the surface of the water, though there was no wind to stir them; the unearthly light created the illusion of half-formed shapes capering and whirling madly within the mist.

The marsh terrain was more dense and treacherous than Nagash realised. He sloshed through foul-smelling, scummy water that rose up to mid-thigh in places. It was unnervingly warm, and where it touched his skin he felt the faintest brush of sorcerous energy. The necromancer considered the tendrils of steam writhing like serpents across the flank of the distant mountain. If there were enough burning stone buried within the mountain to taint the neighbouring sea, his vengeance upon the living world would be great indeed.

He wound between hummocks of thick, yellow marsh grass and stunted trees, listening to slithering, splashing creatures hunting through the mist. Strange howls and high-pitched cries echoed from the moss-covered branches of the trees, and once he saw a pair of faintly glowing yellow eyes regarding him intently from the shadows to the left of his path. But the creatures of the marsh shunned him, as all living beasts did. More than once he heard something huge rise up in the mist ahead of him and go thrashing off into the water at his approach. When the sun finally broke over the horizon, hours later, he crawled into a muddy hollow formed by the thick roots of a half-dead tree and waited for nightfall.

Voices and the sounds of thrashing water roused him from his meditations, many hours later. Darkness had fallen, though the moon was still low in the sky, and as he crept to the edge of the tree's sheltering roots he could see a yellow haze of lantern light playing upon the surface of the water.

The voices sounded human, guttural and strained with effort. There were at least two speakers, perhaps three, calling out to one another in a barbarian tongue unlike anything Nagash had heard before. It was difficult to tell how far away the voices were, the sounds echoing flatly from the surface of the water and the surrounding trees.

Nagash eased carefully from his hiding place, head low, and searched for the source of the noise. The thrashing continued unabated, punctuated by grunts and muffled blows. It was coming from beyond a screen of moss-covered trees just a few dozen yards away. The glow of lanterns seeped between the gnarled trunks, flickering crazily as struggling figures moved past the source of the light.

The necromancer still carried two of the large bronze daggers he'd looted from the corpses of the rat-things so many years ago. He drew one of the blades from his leather belt and crept from tree to tree until finally he caught sight of the source of the noise.

Peering through a screen of hanging moss, Nagash saw a wider patch of water just past the hummock where he stood. Perhaps ten yards away a low, flat-bottomed boat had poled up close to another small, tree-covered hummock, and within the globe of light cast by the lantern set at its bow, four men were wrestling with the thrashing body of what appeared to be a huge, whiskered fish. Two of the men stood up to their waists in the murky water, their arms thrown around the fish's scaly flanks as they tried to heave it up into the boat. A third stood in the boat and tried to grip the creature's flat, toothy head, while the fourth tried to kill it with blows from a short, thick club. From where Nagash stood, it was difficult to tell which side was winning the fight.

The men were barbarians; that much he saw at once, but they had little in common with the tall, fair-haired northerners sold on the slave block at Zandri. Their bodies were short and squat, thick with muscle but deformed in different ways. He saw hunchbacks and misshapen skulls, long, ape-like arms and bulging, knobby spines. Their heads were hairless, and their skin was a sickly, pale green. The men in the boat wore simple, belted kilts of rough leather that hung below their knees, and their chests were decorated in swirling scar patterns similar to Nehekharan tattoos.

So it wasn't the rat-creatures who inhabited the north shore after all, Nagash realised. Clearly these barbarians had lived close to the tainted waters for much, if not all their short, squalid lives. The mutations wrought by the burning stone appeared pervasive. The necromancer's eyes narrowed thoughtfully. With a little patient study, these men could teach him a great deal.

Sticking to the deep shadows, Nagash crept around the edges of the wide pool while the barbarians struggled to finish off their prey. The noise of their struggles masked his movements, until finally he reached the far side of the hummock next to their boat.

The sounds of thrashing abruptly ceased. Nagash heard the barbarians whooping and laughing, and then the sounds of feet tramping through foliage just a few yards away. Carefully, he eased through the undergrowth towards the sounds.

Within moments, lantern light was seeping between the mossy trees. Nagash heard the scrape of wood on soil, and then a meaty *thud* on the ground nearby. Peering around the bole of a gnarled old tree, he saw that the barbarians had grounded their little boat and dragged their monster catch up onto dry land to clean it and cut away the meat. The fish was huge – easily six feet long – and almost as thick as a human torso. The scales along its back were a dark grey, grimed with muck from the bottom of the pool, and its wide mouth was full of small, black, triangular teeth.

The two men who had wrestled the thing from its hiding place beneath the water had pulled on heavy, oiled leather cloaks and stood tiredly over their catch, their mud-streaked chests heaving, filthy water streaming down their legs. One of their companions was digging a leather-wrapped bundle out of the bottom of the boat, while the fourth man was busy tying the craft to the branch of a nearby tree.

Sensing his opportunity, Nagash slipped silently from the shadows beneath the tree and crept across the small clearing where the men had set down their catch. Being careful not to startle the barbarians, he walked quietly up behind one of the cloaked men. At the last moment, just as Nagash came within arm's reach, the man must have sensed his presence. The barbarian whirled about, his powerful hands poised to seize whatever was creeping up behind him. The man must have been expecting an animal of some kind, because when he saw Nagash, his beady eyes widened with surprise.

Before the barbarian could recover, Nagash darted in quickly and slashed his throat with the rat-beast's dagger. Blood splashed across the clearing and the man collapsed with a choking scream.

Nagash turned on the second cloaked man just as the barbarian leapt at him with a guttural shout. He managed to get his left hand around the man's throat as they crashed together, nearly knocking him from his feet. A stubby-fingered hand seized Nagash's knife wrist and held it in a vice-like grip, while jagged fingernails clawed for his eyes. Nagash tightened his grip on the barbarian's throat and tried to pull his knife hand free, but the man refused to let go. A knobby fist smashed into the side of the necromancer's skull; he responded by driving his knee into the barbarian's groin. The man roared in pain, but doggedly hung on.

The barbarian who had been tying off the boat snatched up a fallen branch and charged across the open ground towards Nagash, and the fourth man wasn't far behind. The tide of the battle was rapidly turning against the necromancer, and the very idea infuriated him. With a snarl, he drew upon the power of the burning stone.

Fiery strength surged through him. His hand closed about the barbarian's neck, crushing the man's spine. Nagash hurled the body like a children's doll straight into the third man's path. Both man and corpse tumbled across the ground in a tangle of limbs.

Nagash pounced on the man before he could pull himself free and drove his dagger through the barbarian's eye.

The last man stopped dead in his tracks, mouth agape in shock. Without thinking, Nagash flung out his hand and hissed a stream of arcane words – and the power of the stone responded. The man's body went suddenly rigid, as though gripped in a giant's invisible fist. The necromancer hissed in satisfaction.

'*Good,*' Nagash murmured, feeling the power crackling through his outstretched hand. '*Yes. Very good.*'

He rose slowly, careful to maintain his focus on the impromptu spell. It was more difficult than it once was; the magic was more potent, but less controlled, and fought against his will every second.

Nagash approached the man carefully. The cloth bundle was still clutched in the barbarian's hands. The necromancer reached up and carefully prised it from the man's fingers. The objects wrapped up in the greasy cloth clinked metallically.

He smiled. Kneeling down, he set the bundle on the ground and unrolled it. The tools within gleamed in the lamplight. The necromancer nodded grudgingly. Crude implements, but suitable to the task. Satisfied, Nagash turned his attention back to his prisoner.

'*I have many questions,*' he told the terrified barbarian. '*This is a strange land, and there is much I do not know about you and your people.*'

He drew a long, curved flensing knife from the pouch and inspected the bronze blade in the lantern light.

'*Fortunately, I expect you will be a font of useful information,*' the necromancer said. He rose to his feet and studied his subject carefully. He raised his left hand, and with a slight gesture, the barbarian's arms rose from his sides.

Nagash's smile widened. It had been a very long time since his last vivisection.

'*We shall begin with the muscle groups,*' he said to the man, and went to work.

❮ THREE ❯

A Silken Betrayal

Lahmia, The City of the Dawn, in the 76th year of
Asaph the Beautiful
(-1600 Imperial Reckoning)

THE EASTERN PRIESTS crouched before the queen like great, yellow bullfrogs, backs slightly arched and palms pressed to the marble floor as they filled the Hall of Reverent Contemplation with their buzzing, wordless song. Their eyes were squeezed shut in concentration, perspiration gleaming beneath the brim of their outlandish felt hats as the six elderly men emitted a basso drone that Neferata could feel against her skin. The delegation from the Silk Lands seemed to find it uplifting, judging by the beatific looks on their faces. She found the noise deeply unnerving – and it just seemed to go on and *on*. For the first time, Neferata was genuinely glad that she was required to wear a mask in public. The longer the Eastern *throat music* went, the more horrified she became.

The audience with the Imperial delegation had begun in a civilized enough fashion, with little of the outrageous fanfare that usually accompanied the arrival of a member of the Celestial Household. Normally, the first Imperial attendants would arrive well before dawn to decorate the Hall of Reverent Contemplation with silk hangings, lacquered screens and an unbroken line of royal carpet stretching all the way to the palace gate. Priests would walk from one end of the hall to the other, chanting prayers to chase away evil spirits and promote harmony, then give way to a procession of musicians and artists whose task was to tune the vibrations of the space in a manner that was pleasing to Celestial ears.

When the delegation itself finally arrived, many hours later, it would be accompanied by a small army of courtiers, bureaucrats and servants that would fill the cramped chamber to capacity. By the time that Neferata met the delegates face-to-face, it was only the relative placement of the throne-like chairs that made it clear who was actually giving an audience to whom.

By contrast, the current ambassador had arrived with very little fanfare, appearing at the palace gates promptly at midday and pausing only long enough to have a brilliant blue carpet unrolled at his feet before continuing onward to the hall. He was accompanied by a very modest retinue: five bureaucrats, a handful of courtiers, and a young woman clad in rich robes whose face was painted white as alabaster. The entire delegation could be seated in a comfortable half-circle before the royal dais, lending the proceedings an unusually intimate, almost conspiratorial air.

Of course, all the usual Imperial proprieties had to be observed. The audience had begun with a lengthy recitation of the queen's lineage, followed by an even longer recitation of the ambassador's ancestry. The ambassador, speaking through his senior bureaucrat, then offered a very appreciative and long-winded greeting, bestowing upon Neferata the acknowledgement of the Imperial Court and the hopes of continued harmony with the City of the Dawn.

Tea was served. The strange Eastern concoction, served in tiny ceramic cups, still tasted like little more than heated bathwater to Neferata, but she'd learned to nod politely and listen with feigned appreciation as the ambassador's courtiers spoke at length of the refinement of the leaves and the delicacy of its flavour.

Once the cups had been collected and a prayer offered to the Eastern gods in thanks for the tea's many blessings, it was time for the customary tokens of esteem. Neferata accepted a fine Eastern bow and a quiver of arrows on behalf of the king, as well as a half-dozen scrolls of poetry, three chests of fine silk robes and a prince's ransom in exotic spices from the far corners of the Empire. This time the ambassador even brought a gift for the queen's lovely cousin, whom the king had required to attend the audiences as part of her courtly education. A servant presented Khalida with a magnificent falcon, taken from the Emperor's personal stock. Evidently, the last ambassador had overheard Neferata's pet name for her cousin, confirming the queen's suspicion that the delegates from the Imperial court spoke perfectly good Nehekharan, and insisted on translators for their own inscrutable reasons.

After presenting the gifts, a light meal of Eastern delicacies was served, followed by more tea and polite conversation that lasted for two long hours. Then came a period of digestion and restful contemplation that normally would be accompanied by soft music or recitations of poetry. Neferata grimaced as the droning of the priests continued, and wondered if perhaps the Eastern Empire's culture was on the decline.

Meeting with the delegates from the Eastern Empire was the only official function left to Neferata. King Lamashizzar hadn't opened the palace to his citizens on the high holy days in many decades, and the temples no longer had the power to influence court affairs as they once did, so Neferata now spent the vast majority of her time locked inside the Women's Palace. The only reason she was still allowed to receive the Easterners was because Lamashizzar had never had any patience for the Silk Lords' tedious social rituals, yet couldn't risk offending his erstwhile allies by fobbing them off on one of his viziers. It was the primary reason she'd been given so much authority when the king had taken the army to Mahrak. At the time, the risk of a royal scandal paled in comparison to a diplomatic incident with the Empire.

Since the war, official visits from the east generally only happened once a year, when an Imperial delegation arrived to collect Lahmia's annual payment for the shiploads of iron and dragon-powder that Lamasheptra had purchased more than a century before. The next scheduled payment wasn't due for another three months, so the unannounced arrival of an Imperial vessel had caused considerable curiosity among the members of the Lahmian court.

Something was definitely going on, the queen knew, studying the resplendent figure of the Eastern ambassador. The Empire didn't send a prince of the blood all the way across the Crystal Sea on a mere social call.

Xia Ha Feng, August Personage of the First Celestial House and Scion of Heaven, was young and very handsome, in the coldly detached manner that all the Silk Lords affected. He was clad in layered robes of blue and yellow silk. The outer robe was embroidered with sinuous, bearded serpents whose scales were picked out in tiny garnets, and whose belly plates were fashioned from lustrous mother-of-pearl. The prince's raven-black hair was oiled and pulled back in a severe topknot, and a circlet of gold rested upon his brow. Long, artificial fingernails, also crafted of fine gold, capped all ten of the prince's fingers. Though a mark of refinement and wealth in the Silk Lands, the affectation seemed sinister, even monstrous, to the queen. She wondered idly where the young prince fell in the line of succession to the Imperial throne. Despite hundreds of years of trade and diplomatic relations with the Silk Lands, the Eastern Empire was still largely a mystery to the Lahmians. It was reputed to be vast in size, but foreigners were forbidden to travel beyond a handful of sanctioned trade cities situated along their western coast.

The Silk Lords claimed that their civilization was far older and more advanced than that of the Nehekharans, but Neferata, like most Lahmians, doubted the truth of this. If the Eastern Empire was so old and powerful, why were they afraid to let foreigners see it?

All at once, the priests' disquieting song came to an end. Rather than build to a satisfactory conclusion, like proper music did, the droning simply *stopped*. The priests bowed low to the queen and swiftly withdrew. Neferata blinked dazedly in the sudden silence, uncertain how to respond. She stole a surreptitious glance at Khalida, who sat upon a lesser throne to Neferata's right. Over the last half-century, the little hawk had blossomed into a tall, elegant young woman, though somehow she'd never outgrown her love for horses, hunting and war. She remained one of Neferata's favourites, though once the queen had given birth to her own children they had grown inexorably apart. Soon she would be leaving the City of the Dawn altogether, for Lamashizzar had arranged her betrothal to Prince Anhur, the son of King Khepra of Lybaras, during the last round of trade negotiations.

The young princess was sitting very straight in her chair. Like Neferata, her face was hidden behind a serene golden mask, but the queen could see that her chin was bobbing ever so slightly as she fought to stay awake.

As one, the Imperial delegates nodded their heads and gave a contented sigh as the priests silently left the hall. The prince turned to the bureaucrat at his right and spoke softly in his native tongue. The functionary listened intently, then bowed his head to Neferata.

'The Scion of Heaven hopes that this gift of song is pleasing to your ears, great queen,' he said in flawless Nehekharan. 'The music of the mountain priests is reserved only for the gods themselves, and those whom Heaven deems worthy.'

'I can't imagine what I might have done to deserve such an honour,' Neferata replied smoothly. She thought she heard a tiny, muffled snort of amusement from her cousin. 'The Scion of Heaven is as discerning as he is generous.'

The Eastern prince listened to the translation and inclined his head to the queen. He spoke again, very softly, and the bureaucrat smiled. 'The Scion of Heaven would be honoured to share the gifts of the gods with you whenever you desire, great queen.'

The statement sent a prickle of alarm racing up Neferata's spine. 'The Scion of Heaven's generosity is truly boundless,' she answered calmly. 'The court is always honoured to receive a visit from the Celestial Household, and we hope he travels to Lahmia often in the coming years.'

As the functionary related the queen's words, the prince smiled for the first time. The look in his dark eyes as he spoke reminded Neferata very much of the cold, predatory stare of the falcon he'd given to Khalida.

'The Scion of Heaven has no plans to travel in the foreseeable future, great queen,' the bureaucrat replied. 'And he is looking forward to sharing the fruits of our civilization with you in the coming months.'

Neferata straightened slightly on the throne. 'Do I misunderstand?' she asked. 'Are we to be graced with your august presence for a lengthy stay?'

This time the functionary didn't bother to translate. 'The Scion of Heaven will take residence in Lahmia,' he replied. 'His factors are seeking appropriate lodgings near the palace even as we speak.'

For a moment, the queen forgot all sense of Eastern decorum. 'Will he be staying long?' she asked.

The bureaucrat frowned ever so slightly at the forwardness of such a direct question, but he replied smoothly, 'The Scion of Heaven wishes to broaden his education of foreign cultures, and hopes to gain a deep understanding of your ancient and noble traditions.'

He means years, Neferata thought with alarm. She hesitated, composing herself and considered her reply. 'This is unprecedented,' she said carefully. 'And a momentous event in the history of our two peoples.'

The prince's smile widened as the bureaucrat translated. His reply was delivered with carefully modulated deprecation. 'The Celestial Household merely wishes to become closer to our Western neighbours, and hopes to offer what meagre aid we can in this time of transformation and rebirth.'

Neferata's unease deepened. 'We are naturally deeply grateful to the Emperor, and appreciate his interest in our people's wellbeing,' she replied.

The bureaucrat bowed deeply. 'The Emperor of Heaven and Earth is a dutiful son, and is responsible with the gifts that the gods bestow upon him,' he replied. 'A momentous event in Guanjian province has enriched the Empire, and he has taken it as a sign from Heaven that he must turn his attentions to our neighbours who are in need.'

'That is very comforting to know,' the queen replied, though she felt anything but. 'Might one inquire as to the nature of this blessed occurrence?'

The functionary beamed proudly. 'Imperial surveyors have discovered gold in the mountains of the province! Even the most pessimistic reports suggest that the vein is larger than any found in the Empire's history. Within two years, three at most, the Imperial treasury expects to benefit from the gods' great bounty.'

Neferata felt her blood run cold. Now she understood the reason behind the prince's sudden arrival.

'Truly, the fortunes of the Celestial Household are a wonder to the rest of the world,' she replied, as calmly as she could manage.

Prince Xian rose gracefully from his chair and clapped his hands together. His translator bowed once again. 'The Scion of Heaven thanks you for the graciousness of your welcome, and hopes that this audience is but the first of many to come.'

Neferata rose to her feet. 'The august personage of Prince Xian is always welcome,' she said, 'and we hope that he will grace us again with his presence soon.'

The queen remained standing as the prince and his entourage departed. When they were gone, Khalida leaned back in her chair and sighed. 'What an insufferable bunch of fops,' she growled. 'I think I fell asleep at some point during the meal. Did I miss anything?'

Neferata drew in a deep, silent breath. 'No, little hawk. You didn't miss anything at all.'

The prince's message had been for her and the king alone. Among the Silk Lords, even betrayal was delivered by polite implication.

RAIN HISSED AGAINST the thick glass windows, obscuring the view of the predawn city and the sea beyond. Within the bedchamber, Neferata's handmaidens lay sleeping. Every now and then, one of them would whisper or sigh, deep in the grips of a lotus-fuelled dream. The queen had pushed the bottle of dream-wine on her maids, insisting that they should all drink a cup before she partook herself. It was a rare luxury for the maids, who were expected to be ready to serve the needs of the queen on a moment's notice. Neferata appeared to sip from her own cup, but scarcely let the bitter liquid touch her lips.

Tephret was the last to succumb. The elderly hand-maiden had held on until well past midnight, until finally Neferata had been forced to feign sleep herself before Tephret would finally give in herself. The queen had lain in her bed for several hours afterwards, grim thoughts whirling through her head as she listened to the rain steal over the slumbering city. Finally, not long past the hour of the dead, she rose and slipped on a robe, then lit a small oil lamp and sat down at her writing desk.

The words had not come easily. *The Eastern devils have laid a trap for us,* she'd written in deft brush-strokes. *Within two to three years, the value of gold in the Empire will plummet.*

On the surface, the statement seemed innocent enough. She chewed the end of the ink brush. Did she need to spell it out for Lamashizzar? She sighed. *As a result, our annual payment to the Empire is certain to increase well beyond our capability to pay.*

What had possessed their late father Lamasheptra into entering such a potentially disastrous deal with the Eastern Empire would remain a mystery for the ages. He had concocted the scheme not long after Nagash seized the throne at Khemri and made the queen – Lamasheptra's daughter Neferem – his hostage. After years of secret negotiations in the

Imperial trade cities across the sea, the Imperials agreed to share with Lahmia the same arms and armour that equipped their own fearsome legions. This included enough of the Easterner's mysterious and explosive dragon-powder to equip an army of warriors, as well as weapons to employ them, which alone would be enough to make Lamasheptra's forces the dominant military power in all of Nehekhara.

In return, the Emperor demanded a staggering sum, equivalent at the time to ten tons of gold per year for the next *three hundred years*, and required nothing less than the sovereignty of the city itself as security for the trade. If Lahmia failed to make even *one* payment to the Empire, the city would become an Imperial possession from that day forward. Lamasheptra accepted the deal without qualm, despite the fact that the amount of money owed to the Empire each year was greater than the city's yearly tax revenue.

Perhaps the old king had planned to supplement his payments with plunder taken from Khemri; possibly he thought to exact tribute from the other great cities once the fearsome power of his army became known. As it turned out, the delivery of the promised arms and armour had taken more than a century. The final shipment, consisting of the dragon-powder itself, reached Lahmia some five months after Lamasheptra's death, and the young king Lamashizzar proved far too cautious with the powerful weapons he'd inherited. Meanwhile, the city treasury had dwindled steadily away. It was only through several shrewd trade deals with Lybaras, Rasetra and Mahrak during the war that Lahmia was able to survive at all.

Of course, the Empire had never intended to deal fairly with Lamasheptra. They'd done everything in their power to make it difficult for the city to fulfil its financial obligations, and now that there were only a few years left before the debt was fully paid, the Silk Lords had gone to extreme measures to ensure that Lahmia would be theirs.

Neferata was sure that the discovery of the gold mine was a lie. The Imperial household would flood the market with coin from their own treasury to convincingly drive down the value of their currency long enough to force Lahmia into default, after which point things would gradually return to normal again. It would cause a short period of suffering for the Empire's subjects, but it would be a small price to pay for a strategic foothold in Nehekhara.

The question, Neferata thought, is how do we get out of the trap before it snaps shut?

The complex web of trade deals that Lamashizzar had built after the war had produced dividends, and greatly increased Lahmia's influence across Nehekhara, but it wouldn't be enough if the Empire demanded more gold. The only way to save the city from the hands of the Easterners was to either seize more wealth from Lahmia's neighbours, or defy the Silk Lords, and Neferata was certain that Lamashizzar hadn't the nerve to do either.

To be honest, she wasn't even certain if her brother *cared* what happened to the city any more.

The confrontation in the council chamber, now a half-century past, had ended whatever feelings of affection Neferata had for her brother. There was a time once when she thought she might have loved him, when she thought he would stand up to centuries of hoary tradition and treat her as a co-ruler instead of a mere possession. Now she knew better. All he wanted from her were heirs to continue the dynasty, while he fumbled after the secrets of immortality. Nothing else mattered.

Well, Lahmia mattered to her. Neferata would be damned before she saw the City of the Dawn become a plaything for foreign lords. She could rule the city with a surer hand than her brother ever could.

The queen set aside the ink brush and listened for a while to the sound of the rain on the windowpanes as she turned the problem over in her mind. Always, she came back to the same conclusion.

Something had to be done. If Lamashizzar wouldn't take action, then she must.

Neferata took up the sheet of paper and considered it for a long moment. Her expression hardened. Slowly, carefully, she fed the paper to the flame guttering in the oil lamp on her desk.

It was no more than an hour before dawn when Neferata rose from her place by the window and dressed herself in a dark robe and slippers. She left her black hair bound up and pulled on a black wool cloak, then picked up a small gold box from her dressing table and tucked it into her girdle. Her golden mask was left on its wooden stand, its smooth curves masked in shadow.

Her maids were still sleeping soundly, though she knew that they would begin stirring as soon as it was light. There wasn't any time to waste. The queen slipped quietly from her bedchamber and hurried down the dark halls of the palace towards the Hall of Restful Contemplation.

She moved as quickly as she dared, keeping to little-used passageways as much as she could. Twice she saw the telltale glow of a lantern crossing down an adjoining corridor, but each time she found a pool of deep shadow to hide in before the sleepy servant girl passed by. Within minutes she was standing before the tall bronze doors of the audience chamber. The metal surface was cold to the touch as she pulled one of the doors open just wide enough to slip through.

Heart racing, she dashed down the length of the hall and pressed her ear to the outer doors. Would there be guards on the other side? She had no idea. After listening in vain for several long moments, she gave up and decided to take a chance. She grasped the door's heavy brass ring and opened it just a bit. The corridor beyond was dark and empty.

Neferata felt a faint thrill as she slipped across the threshold into the palace proper. Now she was officially an escapee, in violation of royal and theological law. *But only if they catch me,* she reminded herself, and grinned in spite of herself.

The going was slower once she emerged into the palace proper; she was far less familiar with its layout, and not accustomed to its routines. At least there were no guards about. Once upon a time the halls would have been patrolled by the king's Ushabti, who were as swift and deadly as Asaph's terrible serpents. She had only the vaguest memories of them now, from when she was a young girl. Neferata remembered their silent, graceful movements and their depthless, black eyes. All that remained of them now were the great statues that guarded the royal tombs outside the city.

Once again, she kept to deserted hallways and managed to avoid the few servants who were up and about at such an early hour. It took her nearly half an hour to make her way to the far side of the palace and the dusty, deserted wing where Lamashizzar hid his darkest secrets. The main doors to the wing were locked, but Neferata expected as much. Within a few minutes she located the entrance to the servants' passageways and felt her way into the oppressive darkness that lay beyond.

Cobwebs brushed ghostly fingers across the queen's face. The narrow corridor was windowless, and dark as a tomb. Neferata listened to rats scuttling across the floor up ahead and cursed herself for not thinking to bring a candle stub to light her way. Gritting her teeth, she reached out with her hand until she found the wall to her left and let that guide her onwards.

The air was cold and dank. Now and again her fingertips brushed across a slimy patch of mould. Once, something large and many-legged darted out from underneath her fingers, and it was all she could do not to let out a startled shout. For all she knew, the king or his companions could be nearby. If they caught her now, Neferata didn't care to speculate what they might decide to do with her.

After about twenty feet, her hand encountered a wooden doorframe. She continued on, counting each doorway as she went. It had been more than a century since she'd last stood inside Lamashizzar's improvised sanctum, but she knew it was in the centre of the wing, far from any windows that would reveal the telltale glow of oil lamps burning far into the night. When Neferata reached the tenth doorway she stopped and tried the latch. It moved with a faint screech of tarnished metal, the sound deafeningly loud in the oppressive darkness. She paused, hardly daring to breathe, but several seconds passed without any sounds of movement other than the scampering of rats.

The door opened with only the tiniest sound of wood scraping through the grit that had accumulated on the sandstone floor. Enough predawn light filtered through windows on the eastern face of the palace wing to provide some definition to the interior of the building. She saw that she was in a narrow corridor facing eastwards that connected to a wide central passageway that ran the entire length of the wing.

Moving as silently as she could, Neferata crept to the end of the servants' corridor. The walls of the central passageway had been stripped of their hangings, and every piece of art and furniture had been removed many years ago; they had all been surreptitiously sold in the city marketplace during lean years to help pay off the debt to the Silk Lords.

The thick dust that had settled in the central passageway had been churned by the regular passage of sandalled feet. Peering through the gloom, Neferata followed the muddled tracks down the wide hall until they stopped outside an otherwise unobtrusive door to her right.

Heart pounding, she laid her hand on the latch. This was the point of no return; once she crossed the threshold, there would be no turning back.

This is not for me, she reminded herself. This is for Lahmia.

The latch gave an oiled click as she pressed it. She pushed the door open with her fingertips, smelling the faint scent of incense and the tang of spilled blood.

There was still a faint red glow emanating from a banked brazier on the far side of the room. Neferata paused in the doorway, taking in everything she could see. There were more tables than she remembered, most of them covered in stacks of paper, collections of papyrus scrolls and jumbled piles of leather-bound books. Wooden chairs and tattered divans were scattered about the room, with wine goblets and trays of half-eaten food set nearby. The queen's lips curled in distaste. It resembled nothing so much as the cluttered library of a wealthy young dilettante.

Convinced that Lamashizzar and his cronies were nowhere about, Neferata stepped inside and shut the door behind her. She navigated carefully around the room until she reached the brazier, and within a few minutes she'd stoked it carefully back to life.

The glow of the burning coals reached into the far corners of the large room, revealing still more shelves and wide, utilitarian tables set with dusty ceramic jars and glass bottles filled with exotic liquids and powders. They were set to either side of a cleared patch of floor that had been scrupulously swept clean of dust and grime and inlaid with a complicated magical symbol the likes of which she had never seen before.

It took a moment before Neferata spied the figure sprawled in one corner on the other side of the sorcerous circle. The queen searched the tables around her for an oil lamp. Finding one, she lit the wick using a coal from the brazier, and, summoning up her courage, she crept closer to the king's prisoner.

Arkhan the Black hadn't changed one bit in the last hundred and fifty years. He was clad in filthy rags, and his bluish skin was covered in grime, but his face looked exactly as it had when she'd first set eyes on him all those years ago. A thick, iron collar enclosed the immortal's neck, connected to a heavy chain that had been bolted deep into the wall. At his side, an upended wine goblet spilled a thick trickle of dark fluid onto the floor.

The immortal's lips were stained black by lotus root. Though his chest did not rise and fall as a living mortal's would, Neferata knew that Arkhan was deep in a drugged slumber. From the very beginning, Lamashizzar kept his prisoner under control by feeding him a mixture of his weak elixir and enough lotus root to kill a half-dozen men. When he wasn't needed to translate Nagash's esoteric writings, Arkhan was kept in a stupor so he couldn't escape.

Staring at the immortal's slack features, Neferata wondered how much of his sanity still remained. She consoled herself with the thought that if Arkhan was of no further use to Lamashizzar, he would have been disposed of without a moment's hesitation.

The queen took a deep breath and drew the gold box from her girdle. Opening the filigreed lid, she withdrew the *hixa* and pressed it to Arkhan's neck. It took several attempts before the insect's abdomen arched and drove its sting into the immortal's flesh.

For a moment, nothing happened. Neferata expected Arkhan to groan as the wasp's venom burned away the effects of the lotus, but the immortal didn't so much as tremble. His eyes simply opened, as though he'd only been lightly dozing, and he fixed her with a dull, listless stare.

Neferata expected Arkhan to wonder at her presence, but the immortal said nothing. The unnerving silence stretched for several long minutes, until finally the queen could take it no more. Without thinking, she reached out and gripped his arm, and to her surprise, Arkhan the Black flinched from her touch.

The Queen of Lahmia struggled to give the ghastly creature a friendly smile. 'Greetings, Arkhan of Khemri,' she said. 'Do you remember me? I am Neferata, Queen of Lahmia, and I have a proposition for you.'

FOUR

The Barrow-Lands

Cripple Peak, in the 76th year of Asaph the Beautiful
(-1600 Imperial Reckoning)

NAGASH UNDERSTOOD NOW why the barbarians
favoured their long, oiled cloaks. It was the rain: the
steady, invasive, unrelenting rain.

North of the great sea, the coastline was a mix of
flat, marshy plains and rolling hills girdled with
stunted, grey-green thorn trees. The larger of the
barbarian villages squatted atop these bald hills,
their squalid mud-and-grass huts crouching like
clusters of toadstools beneath the never-ending
sheets of rain. Smaller villages or clan-like
communities hunched amid the yellow weeds of the
marsh plains, connected by winding, waterlogged
foot paths worn by generations of hunters and

raiding parties. The barbarians avoided travelling along those paths at night, Nagash found, for the humans were not the only hunters who favoured the paths when the moon was high in the sky. More than once, the necromancer heard the caterwauling of great cats out in the darkness, and the bellowing of a fierce creature that sounded bestial but had the timbre of a human voice. Sometimes he would hear stealthy footsteps creeping through the tall weeds as he walked the paths at night, but none came close enough to threaten him.

It had taken weeks to make his way up from the southern marshes to the sea's north coast. Since then, Nagash had moved more cautiously among the barbarian settlements, gathering information about them where he could and then moving on. They were a primitive, suspicious people, hostile to outsiders and capable of the kinds of treachery and cowardly viciousness common to the poor and the weak-willed.

The barbarians were little better than animals, subsisting on what little food they could scrape from the land or catch in the dark, bitter waters of the sea. They clad themselves in rough leather and worked with crude tools of wood and stone for the most part, although occasionally Nagash would peer from the shadows into the open doorway of a village hut and spy a tarnished bronze sword or spearhead hung from pegs close to the crude stone hearth. The style of the metal weapons was crude by Nehekharan standards but entirely functional, and obviously kept as treasures by the barbarians. He suspected they were battle-trophies, since the villagers had nothing of substance to trade with. That meant there was another, more prosperous and advanced barbarian culture somewhere nearby.

Virtually all of the barbarians he observed bore the mark of the burning stone in one fashion or another. The waters of the Sour Sea – or so Nagash called it, because it was dark and bitter with mineral salts from the *abn-i-khat* – permeated everything in the region and warped it in uncontrolled ways. Physical deformities were commonplace: most were minor, and a few even seemed beneficial. One night, as he'd crept up to peer into the doorway of a village hetman's dwelling, he was surprised to find himself staring at a young boy of eight whose eyes shone like a cat's in the reflected glow of the hearth-light. The child saw through the darkness with ease, raising such a hue and cry at Nagash's appearance that the entire village rose up in arms to try and capture him. The pursuit had lasted most of the night, and they'd come close to catching him a number of times.

At first, his interest in the barbarians had been more a matter of survival and a certain degree of scholarly curiosity, but the more Nagash learned, the more he saw the potential that lay before him. Here was a vast source of magical power, one that might even rival that of the Black Pyramid in Khemri, and a primitive people who could provide him with soldiers and slaves.

He would not necessarily have to return to Nehekhara to continue his quest for domination. His empire could begin again here, along the shores of the Sour Sea.

The barbarians were a fractious and tribal lot, not dissimilar to the desert tribes he had known in the past. They were led by whoever was strong enough and brutal enough to cow the rest into submission, supported by a strong cadre of kinsmen and allies who served as the hetman's warband. They posed little threat to Nagash; even the larger, hilltop tribes were still isolated from their neighbours, and could be brought down one at a time. No, what concerned him most were the totem-shrines of polished wood that every village boasted, and the treatment of the itinerant priests that tended them.

The totems were columns of carved wood more than fifteen feet high – no small feat in a land where the trees grew like gnarled fists and were no more than eight or nine feet tall – and were shaped to resemble tall, powerfully-built men and women. There were four to eight figures carved into each totem, always in pairs, facing outward from the trunk in poses that Nagash supposed were meant to convey strength, wisdom and prosperity.

The craftsmanship was crude by Nehekharan standards, and there was no common iconography from one totem to the next that might suggest anything like a pantheon. The only common factor he could discern was that none of the figures bore the deformities common to those who worshipped them.

Villagers made offerings of food and simple, carved tokens to the shrines, and Nagash suspected that, given the location of the totems at the centre of each village, they were the focal point of the barbarians' important ceremonies.

The priests who tended the shrines travelled from village to village, never staying in one place for more than a few days at a time. Like the priests Nagash had known in Khemri, these holy men got the best of everything. Their leather kilts were well made and often decorated with pieces of metal or polished stones, and carried polished wooden staves that they wielded both as weapons and badges of office. They were uniformly tall, well-fed and physically fit, and not one of them bore the slightest trace of disfigurement. The holy men travelled in groups of six or eight, usually with an older priest attended by a pair of functionaries and two or three young acolytes. When they stayed at a village they slept in the hetman's hut, even if it meant the hetman and his family slept outside that night.

From what Nagash could tell, the priests' duties involved anointing the totem shrines with oils and performing prayers over them, collecting tribute in the form of food, beer, clothing and tools (which the acolytes carried on their backs when the priests left) and occasionally meddling in the affairs of the villagers themselves. They decided who could marry whom, settled certain disputes involving inheritance, and in one case ordered the death of a young man

whose ravings suggested that exposure to the burning stone had rendered him mad.

The priesthood's influence and authority could be
problematic, Nagash realised. More importantly,
their lack of deformities hinted that they'd learned to
control the worst effects of the *abn-i-khat*, just as he
had done. Potentially that made them very dangerous indeed.

THE BARBARIAN VILLAGES grew larger and more elaborate as Nagash drew closer to the great mountain.
The broad hillsides had been crudely terraced, and
ranks of round-roofed huts sprawled down and
across the sodden fields, where crops of rice and
tubers were nurtured in paddies of bitter water. The
tracks were wider and better travelled, and the woodland more sparse. Only the constant rain worked in
his favour, giving him reason to conceal his face
beneath the dripping hood of his cloak and discour-
aging conversation with the barbarians he
encountered on the muddy tracks. There were times,
on moonless nights, when he would attach himself
to larger groups of travellers and follow along with
them in silence for many miles, little more than
another vague, cloaked shape in the darkness.

Now he stood beneath the dripping branches of a
small copse of trees, close to the point where the
northern coast began to curve south and east towards
the mountain, and watched a strange procession
make its way down the switchback trail of one of the
largest barbarian villages Nagash had seen yet.

Normally the crude customs of the barbarians were of no interest to him whatsoever; what caught his attention this time were the dozens of glowing green lights that accompanied the procession down the dark trail.

The necromancer clutched his sodden cloak tightly around his ever-thinning frame and edged back into the shadows of the wood as far as he could manage. As far as he could tell, the procession would make its way down the muddy trail directly past where he stood, which also meant that they were heading towards the mountain.

The procession was a long one. He reckoned that he was almost two miles from the village. The tail end of the line was still working its way down the hillside when he began to hear the low, mournful chanting of voices emanating from around a curve in the track to his left. Minutes later, a familiar glow began to seep around the muddy track, followed by a pair of young priests wearing fine robes and carrying gnarled wooden poles in their hands. The acolytes' heads were bared to the bitter rain as they led the procession down the track, their faces turned downward and their shoulders heaving as they led the rest in the funereal chant. The green light emanated from globular sacks of hide hung from the ends of the wooden poles. Each hide sack had been scraped until they were translucent and then filled with water. Glowing green shapes stirred within, occasionally darting and swimming from one end of their prison to the next.

Behind the priests and their heavy lamps came a large group of chanting, bare-headed holy men, all clad in rough vestments of cloth and hide that were decorated in glittering bits of metal and precious stones. Their faces had been painted with glowing oil that highlighted their handsome, unmarred features.

After the phalanx of chanting holy men came a column of groaning acolytes bearing a rough, wooden palanquin. Upon the palanquin rode an arrogant old man that Nagash knew had to be the barbarian high priest. He sat upon a straight-backed throne, wreathed in layers of heavy robes festooned with chains of actual gold and a kind of polished, ruddy copper. A circlet of gold rested upon his brow, inset with a glowing oval stone. The piece of *abn-i-khat* looked to be the size of a bird's egg; Nagash could feel its crackling power from a dozen yards away. His hands clenched hungrily at the sight of it. Had he more power at his command, he might have been tempted to lay waste to the holy men and take the stone for himself.

The high priest went by, heedless of the necromancer's feverish gaze. Behind him came another set of lantern-bearing priests, followed by a funereal procession uncomfortably similar to those Nagash had once presided over in Khemri.

There had been a battle, Nagash realised at once. The barbarians followed the priests in family groups, arranged by order of prominence within their village. Their fine clothes had been covered in grey ash, and many of the women had cut away their hair in a gesture of grief. They carried the dead upon their naked shoulders, resting in a woven litter made from swamp reeds. The corpses were naked, and Nagash was surprised to see that none of the litters contained trophies or grave gifts to aid their spirits in the afterlife. The tribe needed absolutely everything they could get just to survive. The dead, however honoured in life, clearly had to fend for themselves afterwards.

A pair of lantern-bearing priests marched at roughly even intervals along the length of the great procession, filling the air with their droning chant. Nagash watched the line snake its way south-eastward, apparently heading for the broken plain at the foot of the great mountain. Intrigued, Nagash waited for the end of the procession to go by, then fell into step behind him. The darkness and the steady, drizzling rain hid him effectively from view.

They passed through rocky, flat terrain, devoid of any signs of life. To Nagash's surprise, the path widened after a time and became paved with irregular, flat stones. Totem shrines appeared at intervals along the crudely-built road. Their faces had been painted some time earlier with the same glowing oil that adorned the priests, lending the carved faces an eerie semblance of life.

Hours passed. The barbarians walked for miles in the dark and the rain, growing steadily closer to the mountain. Eventually, Nagash saw a glowing, greenish nimbus in the air some distance ahead. After about half a mile he could see a line of tall, formidable-looking structures that stretched across the path ahead. More glowing orbs hung at intervals along their length, or shone from the slits of windows set into their flanks. Before long Nagash realised that he was looking at a strange kind of fort. From what he could tell, it was a series of long, high-walled buildings made of mud, brick and wood, connected end to end and stretching from a rocky spur to the north-east all the way to the shore of the Sour Sea, perhaps two miles to the south-west. A single, wide gateway provided the only access between the barbarian villages and the sea's western coast. It was also the first real attempt at fortification Nagash had seen in the entire region.

The procession led through the wide gate and into the lands beyond. There were acolytes waiting to shut the gates as the last of the mourners passed by; they had just begun to push the heavy, wooden portals closed when Nagash appeared out of the darkness and rain. They stared at the cloaked and hooded figure uneasily, but made no move to challenge him.

Nagash strode down the long, torchlit tunnel between the first and second gates as though he had every reason to be there. He studied the iconography carved into the support beams and the archways: more perfect faces, and occasionally something akin to a falling star, superimposed against a stylised mountain.

When he emerged from the second gate, Nagash strode a few more yards and then turned to stare back at the fort. There were more windows on this side, as well as long, roofed galleries that allowed the inhabitants to view the mountain and the wide plain. He could see more priests and acolytes up there, standing alone or in small groups, watching the procession continue towards the foot of the mountain. At once he realised that the huge structure was both temple and fortress combined. From here they could control the barbarians' access to the mountain and the evident power it represented.

Nagash looked up at the priests, smug and comfortable in their fortress of wood, and his lips drew back in a ghastly smile. One day he would show them the true meaning of power.

THE PROCESSION CONTINUED across the plain for another ten miles before leaving the stone road and travelling across the rocky ground between rolling mounds of earth and stone that Nagash had come to realise weren't broken hills at all.

There were hundreds of them, crowding the plain before the mountain and spreading along the eastern coast as far as the eye could see. The barrow mounds varied in size: some were not much bigger than a rude barbarian hut, while others were the size of hillocks. He supposed the priests constructed them, for no one else had access to the plain. Their foundations were shaped from fitted stones, and then were roofed over with a cunning arrangement of rocks and packed earth. The older ones were hills in truth, covered over with yellow grass and even a few small trees.

It was a necropolis of sorts, similar in some ways to the great cities of the dead in far-off Nehekhara. As he worked his way among the great barrows his mind reeled with the possibilities. Here, sealed in earth and stone, was the beginnings of an army. All that he lacked was the power and the knowledge to bring them forth.

Upon leaving the road, the procession had spread out among the barrow mounds. Each family followed a pair of lantern-bearing priests to the mound that had been built for their kin. Nagash ignored them, making for a collection of glowing orbs farther across the plain that lay almost at the feet of the mountain itself. That was where the high priest and his retinue were to be found.

There were almost a dozen families gathered around the priests; no doubt they represented the kinfolk of the hetman and his warband. The bodies they'd carried for so long had been laid side-by-side before the dark entrance to the mound. Each corpse was naked. Their hair had been shorn close to the scalp, and their physical deformities had been covered in dark ash, so that they practically vanished in the gloom. All of the men bore ghastly wounds; Nagash had seen such things often enough to know the marks of spear and axe, expertly delivered. The hetman and his chosen warriors had gone to do battle with a far superior foe, and been dealt a bitter defeat.

Nagash kept his distance, sticking to the shadow of an older mound as he watched the high priest rise from his chair and spread his arms over the dead men. In a guttural yet powerful voice, the old man began to speak. Nagash didn't understand the words, but the cadences and the inflection were all too familiar. A rite of some sort was being performed. After a few moments, the senior priests joined in, and he could feel the currents of invisible power growing between them.

The chanting went on for many long minutes. The ritual was a simple one. It made no use of magical symbols or carefully-inscribed circles, just torrents of raw power drawn from the high priest's circlet and, cleverly, the deposits glowing from the skin of the fish held in the priests' lanterns. Slowly, steadily, the rite built to a crescendo – and then he saw one of the corpses start to twitch.

A wail went up from the crowd. As if in response, another corpse began to twitch. Then another. Soon, all of them were trembling with invisible energies.

There was a crackle of dead joints as, one by one, the dead men sat upright. They moved like statues, stiff and awkward, driven by unseen hands. A number of the mourners cried out again. Some tried to crawl across the wet ground, reaching for their kin, and had to be dragged back.

The corpses paid them no heed. First the hetman clambered slowly to his feet, followed by his retainers. Then, without a backwards glance, they walked slowly through the doorway of the waiting barrow.

To Nagash's surprise, the chanting of the priests continued – and then he realised that the wailing of the barbarians was being echoed from all across the plain. The high priest wasn't just animating the bodies of the hetman and his retainers – he was interring all the dead at once. Nagash's mind raced. How many bodies had there been? A hundred? More? Enough to constitute a small army, he was certain.

The high priest and his followers weren't holy men. They were necromancers as well, drawing upon the power of the burning stone to command the bodies of the dead. And for the moment, they were far more powerful than he.

FIVE

The Word of Kings

Lahmia, The City of the Dawn, in the 76th year of Djaf the Terrible
(-1599 Imperial Reckoning)

ARKHAN THE BLACK dreamt of riding beneath an endless desert sky, with nothing but the stars and the gleaming moon to watch over him. The Bhagarite stallion seemed to float across the rolling dunes, its hooves thudding softly like the beat of a living heart. Silver bells were woven into the stallion's mane, jangling a fine counterpoint to the horse's stride, and a dry wind caressed his skin, smelling of dust and faded spice.

There was no end to the sands, no end to the emptiness of the desert night. It was a benediction, a gift that he knew he did not deserve. And yet, when rough hands seized Arkhan and shook him awake, the pain of the longing he felt was worse than any wound he'd ever known.

He found himself lying on his side, cheek pressed against the grimy floor of the king's hidden sanctum. His eyelids felt stiff and brittle, like old paper. The immortal opened them with effort and peered up at the robed figure kneeling beside him.

W'soran's bald, bony head and long neck reminded Arkhan of nothing so much as a vulture. His wrinkled face, with its deep-set eyes, hooked nose and receding chin, would not have looked out of place on a statue of the Scavenger God himself. Once upon a time, he might have even been a priest of Ualatp. Arkhan knew that the man had come to Lahmia from the ruined city of Mahrak, more than a hundred years before, and had ultimately thrown himself on the generosity of Lamashizzar's court when none of the city temples would have anything to do with him. Without doubt he possessed a wealth of arcane knowledge and sorcerous ability that none of Lamashizzar's other allies could equal, which explained how he'd found his way so quickly into the king's secret cabal.

Cold, black eyes studied Arkhan with dispassionate interest. 'It's taking more effort to wake him with each passing night,' W'soran observed. He gripped Arkhan's shoulders and upper arms, testing the rigidity of the immortal's muscles and joints. 'No obvious signs of morbidity, but his vigour is clearly waning,' he said with a sour expression.

Arkhan heard sounds of movement at the far end of the room. An oil lamp flared, filling the space with orange light and the faint reek of melting tallow. 'Perhaps we're giving him too much lotus these days,' he heard Lamashizzar say.

W'soran grunted, bending closer and peering into Arkhan's eyes as though searching for signs of deception. 'He's being given the same amount as always,' he stated flatly. 'So, therefore, his ability to recover from its effects has diminished. He's weakening.' His small, dark eyes narrowed. 'Or...'

Arkhan heard footsteps draw nearer. A wine bowl clunked down onto a nearby table, followed by the dry rustle of papers. 'What?' the king said irritably.

W'soran stared into the immortal's eyes for several long moments, as though he could reach inside Arkhan's mind and read its contents like a dusty scroll. Arkhan gave the man a flat, predatory stare. His expression was unequivocal. *Given half a chance, I'd tear your head off your scrawny neck.*

It was nothing that W'soran hadn't seen every night for decades. What he didn't know was that, for the first time in a century and a half, Arkhan was strong enough to actually do it.

W'soran straightened, his knees popping noisily. He'd been well advanced in years when he'd first come to Lahmia, and Lamashizzar's elixir could not completely halt the implacable march of time. He shrugged his knobby shoulders.

'Perhaps the elixir is less effective as the physical body ages,' W'soran muttered, turning his back on the immortal. 'His flesh and organs are four hundred years old. It's possible that we are approaching the limits of your arcane prowess.'

There was no mistaking the accusatory tone in W'soran's voice. Lamashizzar did not reply at first, but Arkhan could feel the sudden tension in the air between the two men.

'Come here, Arkhan,' the king said coldly.

The immortal's eyes narrowed in concentration as he drew his legs up underneath him and pushed himself to his feet. His limbs were stiff and clumsy – not due to the effects of the lotus root, but rather the months of *hixa* stings he'd been receiving from Neferata. The wasp's venom collected in his muscles rather than passing away as it would in a living body, making even the simplest movements difficult. He tried to turn its debilitating effects to his advantage, letting it slow his movements to something approximating the lassitude that the king and his cohorts had come to expect. If Lamashizzar had even the slightest suspicion that he no longer had complete control over his prisoner, Neferata's scheme would come to naught, and he would never be free again.

The king was standing before a long, wooden table set just a few feet to one side of the room's ritual circle, his expression preoccupied as he tried to bring some kind of order to the pile of papers and scrolls spread before him. More figures moved about in the shadows at the far end of the room, murmuring in low voices and passing jars of wine between one another. Lamashizzar was accompanied by nearly his entire cabal: beside W'soran, the immortal recognised the tall, muscular outline of Abhorash, the king's champion, as well as the reclining forms of Ankhat and Ushoran, his oldest and most powerful allies at court. The king's grand vizier, Ubaid, stood apart from the other men, politely refusing offers of drink and waiting to do the king's bidding. Opposite the doorway, young Zuhras poked at the banked coals of a brazier with the point of his dagger, stirring them back to life. Grinning slyly, he speared one of the small coals on the point of his knife and used it to light the small, clay pipe dangling from his lips. The acrid scent of Eastern pipe smoke began to spread throughout the chamber.

That left only the two libertines, Adio and Khenti. Arkhan suspected they were chasing whores or losing their money in the gambling dens of the Red Silk District. Likely they would stumble in later, reeking of sour wine and cackling like hyenas to claim their share of Lamashizzar's elixir. Why the king hadn't lost patience with them and had their throats cut remained a mystery to Arkhan. He knew all too well that Lamashizzar would turn on anyone that he considered a threat.

Iron chain links rattled dully as Arkhan shuffled across the floor to stand before the king. Arkhan studied the man warily. Outwardly, Lamashizzar had aged somewhat, with grey hair streaking his temples and a fleshiness to his face that bespoke years of self-indulgence, but he still held himself with the easy assurance of a younger, fitter man. The effects of the elixir had left its mark on the king in more ways than one, Arkhan knew. He could see it in Lamashizzar's stiff shoulders and the swift, almost furtive movements of his eyes. The immortal had seen that look many times, in the court of the Undying King. The hunger for immortality turned the strongest men into beasts, making them savage, suspicious and unpredictable. If what the queen had told him was true, Lamashizzar cared little for the fortunes of his kingdom any more. Mastering Nagash's terrible incantations was his one and only obsession, which made him very dangerous indeed.

Arkhan clasped his hands together and bowed his head. The iron rim of the collar dug into his scarred neck. 'How may I serve, great one?' he asked his captor. The words burned like molten lead on his tongue.

'Is it true?' the king asked. He never took his eyes from the occult diagrams laid out on the table. 'Does the elixir no longer sustain you as it once did?'

The immortal considered his answer carefully. He knew that the moment he was no longer useful to Lamashizzar, the king would have him killed. 'I do not deny that it is harder to shake off the effects of the lotus,' Arkhan replied. 'It is possible that the learned W'soran is right. Certainly there is much more to be learned from Nagash's tomes. You have scarcely scratched the surface of the Undying King's power.'

From the moment that he had awakened in the cellars of the royal palace, Arkhan knew that his only hope of survival was to give up Nagash's secrets grudgingly, giving Lamashizzar just enough power to whet the king's appetite while he waited for an opportunity to escape. But Lamashizzar was no fool, he saw to it that Arkhan had no personal access to Nagash's books, and the only sustenance allowed to him was the same thin gruel that the king and his cohorts drank. It left him with barely enough strength to move, much less break free from the iron collar that the king had riveted about his neck. Even the black lotus had given him little relief; he was so weak that the potion brought no dreams, only cold oblivion.

W'soran seized on Arkhan's reply. 'Listen to him, great one,' he said. 'We must go back to the source and start again.' He stepped forward and laid a hand on one of Nagash's books. 'Follow the Usurper's instructions to the letter. We *know* that the rituals work – Arkhan here is proof of that!'

'And they also led to the Usurper's downfall!' Lamashizzar snapped. 'Everyone knows the horrors that took place in Khemri before the war. How long do you think we could prey upon palace servants and criminals before people began to take notice?'

'You can buy slaves from the East!' W'soran exclaimed. 'No one would care what you did with them! Or round up the hundreds of beggars clogging the streets in the lower districts! You're the *king*, or have you forgotten?'

The words had scarcely passed W'soran's lips when there was a rasp of metal and suddenly Abhorash was standing beside the king, his iron sword held loosely at his side. There was no expression on the champion's broad, heavy-boned face: he had the look of a man about to kill a snake that had slipped inside his house.

Lamashizzar said nothing to either of the two men. He simply met the older man's stare until W'soran finally looked away.

'I apologise, great one,' W'soran growled. 'My words were intemperate and ill-considered. I meant no disrespect.'

'Of course,' the king replied, but there was an edge to his smile that belied the graciousness of the answer. He gave a sidelong glance to Abhorash, and the warrior obediently – although not without some reluctance – slid his sword back into its scabbard. It was only then that Arkhan realised how tense he had become. His hands had curled into fists, and his jagged teeth were on edge. Just like Nagash's court, so long ago, he thought. How we circled each other then, like hungry jackals, ready to sink our teeth into the weak the minute their back was exposed.

Arkhan saw the champion relax slightly. Lamashizzar returned his attention to the papers on the table, and just when it seemed that he confrontation was over, Lord Ushoran took a sip from his wine bowl and said, somewhat offhandedly, 'Our guest from Mahrak does have a point, cousin.'

The king turned, as did Abhorash, both of them with almost the same look of irritation on their faces. W'soran's eyes narrowed as he tried to divine the real purpose behind Ushoran's words. Lord Ushoran was infamous for his intrigues, both in and out of court; mostly the king tolerated it because Ushoran came from one of the oldest families in Lahmia, and because the nobleman was smart enough not to involve any members of the royal family in his schemes.

Though distantly related to the king's household, Ushoran wasn't blessed with Asaph's gifts of beauty and charm; he had the sort of face that blended easily into a crowd, with close-cropped dark hair and unremarkable brown eyes. Arkhan gathered that Ushoran had gone to some effort over the decades to keep the cabal's activities out of the public eye. Lamashizzar believed him capable of anything.

'Do you now question my claim to the throne?' the king asked with a brittle smile.

Ushoran chuckled. 'Certainly not, cousin. I merely wish to point out that our progress has been almost nonexistent these past fifty years. We continue to age, albeit very, very slowly, and possess nothing like the power that his ilk–' the nobleman gestured to Arkhan with his wine bowl– 'displayed during the war.' He shifted slightly on the divan. 'It cannot be argued that you aren't following Nagash's incantations as they were intended.'

'Blood is blood!' Lamashizzar snapped, giving in to his anger at last. 'It carries life in it, whether it's from a goat or from a man! And no one will raise a hue and cry if we decide to sacrifice an animal once a month – if anything, they'll likely laud us for our piety! This way raises less suspicion. You all know that.'

Next to Ushoran, Lord Ankhat straightened and swung his legs over the edge of the divan. He was less the dilettante than Ushoran, though his family name was just as old and respected. Though small in stature, he was still trim and physically fit, with piercing eyes and a sharp mind that has hampered only by his notorious impatience. 'I know that power is meant to be *used*, or else it is worthless.' Ankhat said, fixing the king with a steady gaze. 'If we had the full power of the Usurper at our command, we wouldn't need to fear the other cities.'

'I'm certain Nagash thought the same thing,' Lamashizzar retorted, glancing back at Arkhan as if for confirmation. When the immortal gave no obvious sign of agreement, the king continued.

'It's different now,' Ankhat persisted. 'The other great cities are but a shadow of their former glory, and the power of the priesthood is broken forever. They wouldn't dare defy us.'

'Not separately, perhaps, but together?' Lamashizzar shook his head. 'An alliance of the great cities would destroy us as surely as it doomed Nagash.'

Ankhat snorted in disgust. 'Who would lead such an alliance? All the great kings are dead. All except you, that is.'

The king ignored Ankhat's clumsy praise. 'All we need is time,' he said. 'Every passing year, the cities of Nehekhara grow ever more dependant on our trade with the East. Our influence reaches all the way to distant Zandri, and as far south as Ka-Sabar. In another hundred years, perhaps two, no one will dare to move against us. There is no need for bloody gambles and ruinous wars. All we have to do is wait, and everything we want will fall into our hands.'

For a moment, no one spoke. Even the stolid Abhorash seemed uncomfortable with the king's vision. The very idea of restraint was alien to these men, who were accustomed to getting what they wanted with a snap of their fingers. Yet they could not bring themselves to gainsay the king. At least, not for now.

But for how much longer, Arkhan wondered. How long until they start to feel the creeping approach of time, and become obsessed with their fading vitality? How long until they realise that Lamashizzar's carefully reasoned caution is a mask for something far more simple and straightforward. The man is weak. He inherited his power from Lamasheptra, and the one time he tried to gamble with it, he lost his nerve. If I hadn't arrived at his tent outside Mahrak, he might never have committed his army to battle at all, and Nagash would very likely have won.

It still galled the immortal that he'd let Lamashizzar turn the tables on him inside the Black Pyramid. Even a weak man can be dangerous in the right circumstances, he reminded himself. Greed can sometimes be a courage all its own.

W'soran took a deep breath and folded his hands at his waist, not unlike a priest lecturing a group of acolytes. 'You mention animal sacrifice and piety, great one,' he said. 'Yet you fail to mention that the greatest of holy rites specify the spilling of *human* blood instead.' He spread his hands. 'If the lifeblood of a goat is no more potent than that of a man, then why do the gods make a distinction?'

The king turned and glared at W'soran, his brow furrowing as he searched for a proper rebuttal, but here the former libertine was out of his depth. Finally he turned to Arkhan.

'Is he right?' Lamashizzar asked.

The immortal affected a shrug. 'I'm no more a priest than you are, great one,' he answered carefully. He was treading in dangerous waters now. If Lamashizzar ever bothered to read Nagash's commentaries more attentively, he would see the truth of what W'soran was getting at right away. 'It's certainly possible that W'soran has the right of it, but that isn't really the point, is it? The question is whether creating the elixir from animal blood is potent enough to grant immortality or not. And that is something we have yet to prove one way or the other.' Arkhan gave the king a black-toothed smile. 'Certainly there is still room for improvement in your performance of the incantations.'

Lamashizzar gave Arkhan a hard, penetrating stare, and for a moment the immortal thought he'd over-played his hand. Then, abruptly, the king grinned ruefully. 'There you have it,' he said, turning back to his cohorts. 'It's all my fault.'

Ushoran chuckled politely. 'Spoken like a true king,' he said, raising his wine bowl in salute. The others joined in, and Arkhan allowed himself to relax. He approached the table and pretended to study the ritual symbols. He could see places where he could suggest miniscule changes to the geometries that would suggest areas of improvement without providing any real benefit to the elixir.

The immortal bowed to the king, and smiled his ghoulish smile.

'Shall we begin, great one?' he said.

RAW, BURNING PAIN gnawed at Arkhan's nerves, banishing the thick fog of the lotus root. His muscles quivered like plucked bowstrings. Arkhan groaned, baring his ruined teeth against the pounding agony, and with an effort of will forced his stiff eyelids open.

She was standing over him, bathed in warm light from the oil lamp in her right hand. A tiny frown pulled at the corners of her perfect lips.

'Are you well?' Neferata asked. Her voice was dusky and sweet, like rich honey. Even in his wretched state, the sound of it was riveting. Large, almond-shaped eyes narrowed in concern. She raised a slender hand, and for a moment, the immortal thought she might actually reach out and lay her palm against his head, like a mother might to a sick child. The queen seemed to catch herself at the last moment, her hand pausing scant inches from his brow.

'It is nothing,' Arkhan grated. Even his jaw muscles were stiff now, despite the taste of the king's elixir he'd received little more than an hour ago.'

The immortal tore his gaze away from the queen's face and used the end of the iron chain to pull himself to his feet. For a moment he leaned against the grimy wall and tried to orient himself. It felt as though he'd only just choked down the bitter bowl of wine and lotus root that W'soran had forced on him. He blinked in the dim light, still expecting to see the king and his cohorts moving about the chamber. 'What time is it?' he mumbled.

'Scarcely an hour before dawn,' the queen replied, a note of tension creeping into her voice. 'The king was here much longer than usual. I had to hide in an adjoining room until he and W'soran left. I think they were arguing.'

Arkhan managed a nod. 'W'soran is growing impatient,' he said. 'The old vulture covets not just Nagash's elixir, but the rest of his incantations as well. The others are starting to agree with him.'

Neferata's dark eyes narrowed thoughtfully. 'All of them?' she asked. She turned and walked back to the paper-strewn worktable where her husband had stood just a couple of hours before. Every movement was sensuous and fluid, almost hypnotic. Like one of Asaph's sacred serpents, Arkhan thought. The sight of her filled him with a bewildering mix of wonderment, hunger and terrible dread.

She was so like Neferem, he thought, and yet so unlike her at the same time. The women of Lahmia were famous for their seductive beauty, but the daughters of the king bore the likeness of the goddess herself. But where Neferem's staggering beauty had been tempered by her role as the Daughter of the Sun, Neferata's allure was darker and far wilder, like

Asaph herself. A single look from her could topple kingdoms, the immortal thought. *No wonder the kings of Lahmia keep their daughters locked away and their queens hidden behind golden masks.*

'Well, Abhorash still seems loyal, but that's to be expected,' Arkhan said. 'Ushoran and Ankhat, on the other hand, are tired of Lamashizzar's half-measures. They were at Mahrak. They know how feeble the king's elixir truly is.'

Neferata stood beside the table and studied the arrangement of the papers carefully, noting their precise order carefully before picking through the pile. Lamashizzar would know if a single sheet was out of place when he returned the following night. 'What of Ubaid?'

The immortal shrugged. 'I confess I do not know. Lamashizzar only brought him into the cabal because he needed the grand vizier's help to maintain his secret. Since then he's been very circumspect with his opinions.'

'Typical,' the queen observed. 'But somewhat encouraging, nonetheless. And the others?'

Arkhan snorted. 'The young libertines? Irrelevant. Their loyalties belong to whoever supplies them with the elixir. Frankly, you would be better off without them.'

Neferata carefully peeled back several pages until she came to a yellowed sheet depicting a complex ritual circle. It was one of several versions of the Incantation of Immortality that Arkhan had tried to recreate from Nagash's books. To the immortal's unending irritation, the Undying King had not committed a definitive version of the ritual to paper, no doubt to keep its secrets firmly under his control. Lamashizzar could scarcely tell the difference between one page and the next without Arkhan's help, but Neferata's training with the priestesses of Neru gave her a degree of insight that her brother lacked.

Since she'd begun her secret tutelage under Arkhan, some eight months before, the queen's skill in the necromantic arts had grown by leaps and bounds. Sneaking into the cabal's sanctum each night, right on the heels of the king and his cohorts, she learned more in a few stolen hours than Lamashizzar had managed in more than a century.

Of course, it helped that Neferata was far less squeamish about the nature of the blood she used.

The queen studied the page intently. After a few moments, she took a piece of chalk from a clay bowl on a nearby shelf and began making precise adjustments to the circle laid out on the sanctum floor.

'Things are coming to a head quicker than I expected,' she said as she worked. 'We must be ready very soon now.'

Arkhan caught himself staring at the queen, watching the way her body moved in the lamplight. He took a deep breath and closed his eyes. 'If this ritual succeeds, then you will have all the power you need,' he told her. Together, they had already created versions of the elixir that were several times more potent than anything the king had made. The immortal licked his lips. 'Much depends on the quality of the base material, of course.'

Neferata gave Arkhan a sharp look. 'The blood of a royal handmaiden is sufficient, I should think.'

The immortal smiled. 'Younger is better than older,' he said. 'Of course, a live victim is better still.'

The queen made one last change to the circle and rose to her feet. 'And why is that?' she asked, as she inspected her work.

'The more youthful the blood, the more of life's vigour it contains, of course,' Arkhan replied.

'And using a live victim in the ritual grants even more vigour?'

Arkhan hesitated, uncertain how much he should reveal. Neferata had already gleaned far more secrets from him than he'd been willing to share. 'In a manner of speaking, yes.'

'Well, that will have to wait for another day,' the queen said. 'For now, we must be content with what we have.'

She moved past him, to a table at the far end of the room – one well out of reach of his iron chain, Arkhan could not help but note. Neferata picked up a small ceramic jar, not much larger than a nobleman's wine bowl, and carried it to the centre of the ritual circle. The immortal felt his turgid pulse quicken. Neferata never told him how she obtained the blood from her handmaidens, and, in truth, he didn't really care.

Neferata knelt beside the jar and placed a number of additional marks around its circumference, then retreated to the edge of the circle. 'The sun will rise soon,' she said, raising her arms towards the ceiling. 'Let us begin.'

Arkhan moved to the far side of the circle, taking care not to drag his iron chain across the sorcerous glyphs. He raised his own arms – stiff and yet trembling, all the same – to mirror Neferata's own. And then, together, they began to chant.

The words of power now rolled easily off Neferata's tongue, and the air began to crackle with invisible energies, harnessed to a force of will as great as any Arkhan had ever known save for Nagash himself. The immortal echoed every syllable, adding his will to her own, until the ritual circle seethed with power.

The incantation was long and complex, stretching for many long minutes, and Arkhan felt the energies of the ritual building to a furious crescendo. The jar began to tremble, its lid rattling maniacally as gusts of steam billowed from the contents within. His lips peeled back in a ghastly, feral snarl as he smelled the fragrant odour of the rapidly quickening elixir. Arkhan threw back his head and cried out the words of the incantation in an exultant voice. The centuries seemed to unwind within him, and for a single instant he was once more a mighty warrior, a master of magic and conqueror who once made all Nehekhara tremble with fear.

And then, immortal and queen cried out as one, and the ritual culminated in a shower of lambent sparks from the glyphs inscribed on the surface of the jar. Neferata staggered, momentarily stunned by the force of the power she'd commanded, but Arkhan's senses were razor-sharp. In an instant he was inside the circle, feeling the residual energies of the incantation burn across his skin as his hands closed about the curved surface of the jar.

He felt the queen's eyes upon him. They cut through his raging thirst like a knife. He clutched the jar tightly, imagining that he could feel the strength of the elixir through the glazed walls of clay. If he drank it dry, it might give him the strength enough to tear open the collar and finally escape.

Then again, it might not, and then where would he be? Neferata would not take such a betrayal lightly. And she already knew more than enough to continue studying Nagash's books without him, whether she realised it yet or not.

Arkhan sank slowly to his knees. With an effort of supreme will, he raised the jar to Neferata, as a servant might proffer wine to his master. 'Here, great one,' he said in a hollow voice. 'Drink of the fruits of your labour. Drink, and be restored.'

Neferata smiled at him, and Arkhan was secretly ashamed how it made his dead heart lurch in his chest. She came to him, graceful as a serpent, and took the jar from his unwilling hands.

The queen raised the steaming vessel to her lips and took a long draught. A delicious shudder went through her slender frame. 'Oh,' she whispered. '*Oh!*'

Arkhan watched in silence, gripped by a helpless despair. She would drink it all. He knew it. Months ago, she'd sworn to share every draught of elixir they made, just as Lamashizzar had promised him long ago. But promises meant nothing to kings and queens, except when it suited them. Nagash had taught him that lesson well.

He was surprised, therefore, when the queen lowered the jar to him once more. 'Here, favoured servant,' she said with a regal smile, her lips red with the sweet wine of stolen life. 'Take your due.'

It took all the remaining willpower he had not to snatch the jar from Neferata's hands. Still, they trembled as he brought the rim of the jar to his lips and drank.

The elixir flowed into his mouth like molten metal, setting every nerve alight. He stiffened, gulping greedily, as he felt a fraction of the old power return to his wasted limbs. It was a shadow of what he'd once felt as the Undying King's right hand, but it was still greater by far than anything Lamashizzar had wrought.

When he was done he sat back on his heels, gasping for breath. The queen was studying him, her dark eyes thoughtful. He met her gaze directly, too intoxicated for the moment to be cowed by her supernatural beauty.

'Why, great one?' he asked. 'What do you wish to gain from all this?'

Neferata's lips curved in a crooked smile. 'Besides eternal youth and power?' she asked.

'Yes.'

The queen's smile faded. 'Lahmia is in peril,' Neferata replied, 'and her king is too weak and too foolish to protect her. So I must instead.' She cocked her head and regarded him appraisingly. 'What of you? What do you wish, now that Nagash is dead and gone?'

Arkhan did not reply for a moment. He felt the power coursing through his veins and drew a heavy breath. 'What do I want? I want to ride a horse again, and cross the desert sands beneath the moonlight.'

Neferata quirked a delicate eyebrow. 'Is that all?'

The immortal gave her a tight-lipped smile and hefted a length of iron chain. 'Forty-seven links,' he said. 'That equates to exactly twenty-three and a half paces. For the past one hundred and forty years, that has been the length and breadth of my entire world. What I wish for, great one, is nothing less than paradise.'

Neferata considered this, and then, to Arkhan's utter surprise, she reached down and laid a hand upon his cheek. Her skin smelled of sandalwood, and was warm as a summer breeze.

She bent close to him, and her eyes seemed to swallow him whole. 'I know what it's like to live every day as a prisoner,' she said softly. 'Keep your oath to me, Arkhan the Black, and I swear you will see your wish fulfilled.'

Then she was gone, retreating from the circle and returning the ritual materials to the way they were as Lamashizzar had left them. Arkhan hadn't felt her pluck the jar from his hands. He hadn't even noticed it was gone until minutes after she'd departed.

It was a long time before Arkhan crawled from the circle and curled up like a dog at the base of the sanctum wall. When his mind finally quieted enough to let him sleep, he dreamt of endless, moonlit sands, and the music of silver bells. The warm desert air caressed his face, smelling of sandalwood.

◄ SIX ►

The Barrow-thief

Cripple Peak, in the 76th year of Djaf the Terrible
(-1599 Imperial Reckoning)

NOW THAT HE had reached the mountain at long last, Nagash's great work began in earnest. His first months were spent combing its slopes, crawling into each fissure like a spider and searching for ways to reach deeper into its heart. He'd hoped that the deposits of *abn-i-khat* would lie close to the surface, and that the vents were signs of ancient impacts that would point the way to the burning stone, but within the first few days he realised that his theory was only half-right. The fissures were mostly shallow crevices that narrowed quickly as they plunged even deeper into the rock. They weren't the scars of multiple impacts, but the marks of a single, giant impact some incalculable time in the past. The burning stone had been driven deep into the mountain's guts, cracking its granite flanks like a dropped wine bowl.

He searched the mountain systematically, starting at its foot and working upward in a rough spiral. By day he took refuge in one of the deeper fissures, breathing in the glowing vapour in an attempt to replenish some of the power he'd expended. Already, his exposure to the burning stone was beginning to take its toll. He found that he needed to ingest more of the *abn-i-khat* to maintain his strength, which left his skin ravaged by terrible lesions and glowing traces of the mineral in his bones. The luminescence penetrated his flesh, revealing the workings of his muscles and the shrivelled knots of organs nestled in his chest, but so long as his mind remained sharp and his limbs obeyed his will, he paid the changes little mind.

Finally, many weeks later, he found a fissure almost two-thirds up the mountain that sank crookedly into the stone for more than twenty feet, then opened into a wide, low-ceilinged cave that glowed with residue from centuries of subterranean vapours. From that moment on, the mountain was Nagash's fortress, his sanctum from the burning sun and the meddling of feeble-minded men.

Nagash spent months searching the tunnels that branched from the great cave, discovering a vast, tangled network of passageways that honeycombed the fractured mountain. He marked the passageways with hieroglyphs using the point of his bronze daggers, slowly building a map of the labyrinth as he made his way ever deeper into its depths. He scraped residue from the rock walls and collected the dust in the hood of his cloak, and conceived of different ways to strain the mineral from the steam that billowed from the deepest parts of the mountain, but he could not find a way to reach the deposits themselves. The tunnels would have to be extended; exploratory shafts would have to be sunk deeper into the earth, and structures built to haul the stone to the surface. He would need an army of slaves to conquer the mountain and plunder its treasures, and so the necromancer turned his attention back to the surface once more.

It was very late, and though well past the rainy season the mountainside was wreathed in thick layers of mist. Luminous ribbons of steam caused the cooler layers of mist to writhe and dance, teasing the eye with ghostly images in the fog. Nagash paused at the lip of the fissure and listened. It was deathly silent along the slopes of the mountain and the barrow fields below. In the distance, he could hear the lapping of waves along the rocky shore of the Sour Sea.

The necromancer clutched his tattered cloak about his chest and made his way down the slope. Power crackled along his withered veins. He'd ingested the last bits of his scavenged stone and a healthy pinch of the cave-dust as well, to ensure that he would have ample strength to complete the ritual he'd planned.

At the foot of the mountain he paused again, his senses stretched to the utmost. For the last week he'd crept among the barrows, observing the activity of the priests while he searched for the likeliest spot to attempt his experiment. He'd learned that groups of acolytes, led by one or more senior priests, would patrol the northern edge of the wide plain for several hours each night. They rarely ventured further south, where the barrows were much older, and they hastened to return to the temple fort before the hour of the dead. He suspected that the patrols were more of a punishment for lazy acolytes than a genuine attempt to guard the barrow fields from intruders. He'd crossed paths with the patrols more than once during his explorations, and they'd never even suspected he was nearby. Nagash had listened to their nervous chatter often enough that he thought that he was beginning to understand parts of their bestial language.

He'd decided that it was best to attempt the ritual after the patrols had returned to the temple, to minimise the risk of discovery, but that served to limit how far he could travel from his mountain lair and still make it back before dawn. Satisfied that there was no one about, Nagash headed north and west, among the newer barrow mounds.

The barrow where the high priest had interred the hetman and his warriors was still relatively unspoiled. Streaks of mud had drained down over the stone foundations during the rainy months, and a layer of sallow, sharp-edged grass had grown atop the mound, but the wooden cover that had been placed over the entrance was still easily accessible. The cover, round as a wagon wheel and made from layers of planed wood, had been wedged into the stone frame and the cracks filled with packed earth.

Nagash stepped into the shadow of the barrow mound's entrance and stretched forth a gaunt, faintly glowing hand. The power flared along his limbs as he focussed his will upon the wooden cover. Words of power fell like stones from his lips as he unleashed a short, concentrated spell.

Green light licked from the necromancer's fingertips and played across the surface of the wood. At once, the planks blanched, crackling from within as the energies ate through the living matter. The sound of decaying wood spread, growing in volume and intensity, until the entire cover collapsed with a hollow crash. Nagash hastened through the entrance, his bare feet kicking up dry clouds of dust with every step.

Beyond the opening was a short tunnel made of fitted stones that led into the centre of the mound. Nagash moved easily in the darkness, his eyes having long since adapted to the conditions of the deep tunnels beneath the mountain. After thirty feet or so, the tunnel gave way to the barrow proper: a dome-like chamber made of stone and packed earth that stank of mould and decay. There was nothing in the way of ornamentation on the walls, or the rotting platforms of wood and leather upon which the corpses were laid. It was a far cry from even the meanest of Nehekhara's crypts.

The hetman's body lay on a platform in the centre of the mound, surrounded by the bodies of his chosen men. The damp and the ravages of beetle and worm had worked their harm upon the corpse, causing flesh and muscle to liquefy and slough away from the bone. Much of the skin covering the hetman's skull had been chewed away, revealing part of a cheekbone and the warrior's gap-toothed jaw.

Nagash's lip curled in distaste. *Amateurs.* He'd hoped to find the corpses in better condition. It was easier to send power twitching through muscle than to animate bare bone. Looking about, he saw that none of the other bodies were in any better condition, so with an irritated grimace he drew his dagger and bent to work.

The damp earth made carving the ritual circle a simple task, though filling in the magical symbols was much harder to do with the necessary precision. He had to cut deeply into the dirt to chisel out the proper lines, taking far more time than he'd intended. By the time he was ready to begin, he reckoned that dawn wasn't more than an hour away. He hadn't even properly begun, and already the experiment had run into trouble.

Tucking away his dagger, Nagash stepped up to the edge of the circle and raised his arms. He began with a long litany of curses, focusing his anger and his desire by calling up the names of all those, living and dead, who had wronged him and cast him out into the wasteland. *Khefru. Neferem. Nebunefer. Hekhmenukep. Rakh-amn-hotep. Lamashizzar...* The litany went on and on, until finally he was hissing with rage. At some point the names gave way to words of power, and the dank air crackled with the force of the necromancer's will.

He drew deeply of the power he'd absorbed, pouring it into the circle and the hetman's body. '*Rise,*' he commanded. '*Rise. Your master commands it!*'

Slowly the chamber became suffused with a greenish glow, emanating first from Nagash, and then from the hetman's body itself. Green light pooled within the corpse's eye sockets. A tremor went through the rotting flesh: muscles constricted, stirring colonies of beetles and wriggling worms.

Nagash watched in triumph as the corpse's spine arched. One arm lolled off the side of the platform, spilling rotting flesh onto the floor. Then, slowly, as though pulled by an invisible tether, the hetman sat upright. The skull oriented on the necromancer, its bare jaw working as though trying to speak.

'*Rise!*' Nagash ordered. '*Come forth!*'

The corpse paused for a moment, as though uncertain of its strength, and Nagash redoubled his focus. The hetman's body shuddered under the lash of the necromancer's will, and haltingly swung its legs over the edge of the frame. Wood snapped beneath the shifting weight, all but tumbling the corpse to the floor. It tottered unsteadily on bare, uneven feet for a moment, but then it seemed to find its balance. Slowly, steadily, its back straightened. The corpse turned carefully on its heel to face its summoner, bale-lights flickering where its eyes had once been.

Nagash's lips peeled back in a ghastly, triumphant grin. Cruel laughter bubbled up from his chest. And then the hetman's corpse raised its bony arms and lurched forward, reaching for his throat.

He was so certain of his control over the corpse that at first he didn't recognise his peril. It was only when the hetman's grasping fingers were scant inches from his throat that Nagash backpedalled in shock. '*Back!*' he commanded with a sweep of his hand, pouring still more energy into the spell.

But the corpse did not cease. It staggered forwards, fingers grasping, bony jaws clicking hungrily together. Snarling, Nagash tried to push the monster's arms aside. It tottered unsteadily for a moment, but recovered with disturbing speed. With every passing moment it seemed to grow in strength and intelligence. Cursing the chaotic energies of the *abn-i-khat*, Nagash angrily banished the energies of the ritual.

He expected the corpse to collapse at his feet. Instead it leapt forward, seizing Nagash by the throat. Bony digits dug deep into the necromancer's own unliving flesh, clawing into the waxy muscle beneath. Stunned, Nagash struggled in the hetman's grip. He stared into the bale-fires that still burned in the corpse's eye-sockets, and suddenly realised that it was being directed by a will other than his own.

The faint sound of chanting echoed down the dark tunnel from the barrow entrance. The priests! They hadn't been so careless or so blind as he'd thought.

As he struggled with the hetman, Nagash saw that the bodies of the retainers were starting to move as well. The energies of his ritual had dissipated, but he pressed his hand against the hetman's chest and lashed out with his will. The corpse staggered slightly, but resumed the attack almost at once.

Had he been a living man, Nagash would already have been dead. As it was, he would be surrounded within moments and torn to pieces by the rest of the hetman's retinue.

Rage consumed the necromancer. He, who had mastered the energies of the Black Pyramid, and once commanded armies of warriors both living and dead, laid low by a handful of corpses and a pack of bawling savages? It was unthinkable!

With a roar, Nagash drew upon his diminished reserves of power and felt his limbs burn with unnatural strength. He seized the hetman's right wrist with his left hand and squeezed, shattering the small bones and tearing its clenching hand free, then drew one of his bronze daggers and drove it through the corpse's forehead. The monster staggered, but did not fall. Snarling, Nagash wrenched the knife left and right until the vertebrae snapped, then tore the corpse's head from its shoulders. At once the body collapsed, falling apart as the sorcery that had animated it was suddenly dispelled.

Nagash had time to draw his second knife before the hetman's retainers closed in. There were five of the shambling creatures, their eyes burning with malice as they reached for him with claw-like hands. He slashed with his heavy blades, severing fingers and shearing through hands, but still the corpses closed in. They jabbed at him with splintered bones and snapped at him with their rotting jaws. He smashed the skull of one leering corpse, obliterating it like a rotting melon, and then shattered the knee of another. It fell at his feet, wrapping its mauled arms around his legs.

Another arm slipped around Nagash's throat and tightened with frightening strength, while a fourth creature fastened its jaws on his left arm. He felt himself being dragged off his feet. Snarling, he kicked at the creature holding his legs and succeeded in crushing its neck and shoulder with one savage blow. It fell back, one arm hanging uselessly at its side. Free of its grasp, Nagash twisted at the waist and drove his dagger into the throat of the creature whose teeth were savaging his side. Rotten flesh parted like damp cloth; he twisted his wrist and the monster's head came loose with a wet, popping sound.

The last of the corpses crashed into him, hands pressing on his chest. Nagash fell backwards, slashing wildly with his blade as he fell. He landed on his back, and the creatures fell atop him, pinning him down and tearing at him with their jaws. The necromancer writhed and kicked. Teeth sank into his cheek, tearing at the waxy flesh. Nagash brought up his left-hand blade, driving it so deeply into one corpse's ribcage that it became hopelessly entangled. Enraged, he let go of the dagger's hilt and drove his hand deeper, past the shrivelled organs and leathery muscles until his fingers closed around the creature's spine. He squeezed, crushing the vertebrae, and then shoved the crippled monster aside. Moments later, the last corpse collapsed with its skull crushed beneath the pommel of his dagger.

Growling like a beast, Nagash kicked himself free of the corpses and staggered back to his feet. Grisly wounds had been gnawed into his face, chest and arm, but he felt no pain. His flesh burned and his bones shook. Smoke curled from the ragged ends of skin hanging from his cheek.

He burst from the barrow mound with a Nehekharan war cry on his lips, his eyes blazing with wrath. Half a dozen priests were waiting outside, standing in a semi-circle and chanting, their arms raised to the sky. Perhaps a dozen acolytes attended upon them, holding aloft lantern-globes that were already half-dead from the strain of the priests' incantation.

Nagash flung out his hand and spat words of power. Arcs of green fire burst from his fingertips, spearing half of the priests. They fell screaming, their skin blackening as they burned from the inside out. Lantern poles toppled as the acolytes fled in panic, the globes bursting as they hit the ground.

The rest of the priests recoiled in shock and horror. He waited for them to strike back, unleashing searing blasts of their own, but no such counter-strike came. Nagash advanced on them, dagger poised. He slashed out with the blade, and one of the savages toppled with his throat slashed open. The last two turned to flee, wailing and babbling imprecations to the heavens. Nagash leapt upon them, hacking and stabbing until both lay silent and broken at his feet.

Nagash staggered, bloody and torn, chest heaving with exertion. His power was all but spent, his flesh savaged by combat and the fire of the abn-i-khat. He could still hear the screams of the acolytes, fading in the distance off to the north-west. Nagash threw back his head and howled after them. I'm coming, he thought savagely. There's nowhere you can run in this forsaken place that's safe from me!

Muscles quivering, he turned, heading back for the safety of the mountain – and saw that he was not alone. A single acolyte stood watching him, eyes wide and jaw agape with fear. He was young, scarcely old enough to be a man, and he clutched his lantern-pole with a white-knuckled grip.

When Nagash's merciless gaze fell upon him, the acolyte sank slowly to his knees and bowed low. The necromancer studied him for several moments, debating on what to do. Finally he simply nodded silently and walked away. Truth be told, he wasn't certain he had enough strength left to kill the young man and still make it back to the foot of the mountain.

Power. It all came down to power. He'd thought he'd had enough, and nearly paid for that mistake with his life. As he lurched across the lifeless plain towards the distant mountain, with dawn less than half an hour away, Nagash vowed that he would not make the same mistake again.

⤙ SEVEN ⤚

The Right of Queens

*Lahmia, The City of the Dawn, in the 76th year of Djaf
the Terrible
(-1599 Imperial Reckoning)*

'PLEASE, GREAT ONE. Try one of these.' Tephret reached
for a golden bowl with one ancient, palsied hand
and tried to fish out a few candied dates. 'You'll waste
away if you don't eat something.'

A light supper had been laid out for the queen at
the edge of the small pond that served as the centre-
piece of the palace garden. Neferata leaned against
the bole of a small ornamental tree, surrounded by a
constellation of golden dishes laden with uneaten
sweetmeats and Eastern delicacies. It was late spring,
the rainy season, but the night was surprisingly clear.
Neru shone high in the sky, and drops of rain from
the evening's rainstorm glittered like diamonds on
the blooming garden flowers. The night air was warm

and heady with their perfume. Large fish swam in lazy circles just beneath the surface of the water, their opalescent scales glimmering ghostly white beneath the moonlight. If she listened very closely she could hear the whisper of the currents they stirred in their wake.

Neferata stilled Tephret's hand with a gentle touch and a warm smile. They were alone in the great garden, she'd sent her other handmaidens away as soon as the dinner had been laid out.

'These foreign foods have lost their savour, I'm afraid,' she said to Tephret. The woman's skin was soft and wrinkled beneath the queen's fingertips. At a hundred and sixty-five years of age, her most favoured handmaiden was nearing the end of a long and faithful life. The queen had watched her grow from a nervous slip of a girl into a grey-haired old woman, and in all that time, Tephret's devotion hadn't wavered.

Had she ever wondered why her mistress had never lost the bloom of youth? Had she ever resented Neferata's enduring beauty, even as her own faded with the passage of time? If she did, Tephret had never let it show. Other handmaidens had come and gone over the decades, but she had remained, until now the queen could not imagine life without her.

Tephret returned the queen's smile, her rheumy eyes glittering. 'Shall I catch you a fish, then?' she said, and a sudden memory made her chuckle. 'Do you remember that time when you gave little Ismaila that bowl of Rasetran liquor, and she got so drunk she waded out into the pond and tried to catch the fish with her hands?'

'And she nearly drowned half of us trying to get her out,' Neferata added. 'I had weeds in my hair, and a frog went down the front of your robe.'

'That's right!' Tephret exclaimed, her face lighting up. 'I didn't realise it until we got back to your bed-chamber, and then we spent half the night chasing the little thing around the room!' She threw back her head and laughed, transported by the memory, and Neferata joined in.

'Oh, she was such a silly one,' Tephret said, wiping tears from the corners of her eyes. 'But a good girl, bless her. What ever happened to her?'

Neferata sighed. 'Oh, her family had her married off to some petty lordling. Suheir, I think his name was. It was years and years ago, now.'

'Years and years,' Tephret echoed, shaking her head. 'It seems like that was just yesterday to me.'

'I know,' Neferata replied softly, feeling a sudden pang at the wistful look in Tephret's eyes. She gently gripped the handmaiden's arm. 'It must have been hard for you, watching all the other girls go on to raise their own families.'

'Oh, no,' Tephret replied, slowly shaking her head. 'I had no such illusions. I had no family after all, no one to search out a suitable husband.'

'I could have,' the queen said. 'I *should* have. It was my responsibility. I just couldn't bear to part with you.'

The handmaiden smiled, a little sadly. 'That's very kind of you to say, great one.'

'No,' the queen said. 'Call me Neferata. Nothing more. Tonight, let's talk as friends do. All right?'

At first, Tephret didn't quite know what to say. Finally, she nodded. 'You have been a friend to me,' she managed to say. 'Perhaps the only friend I've really known. Does that seem strange?'

'Not to me,' Neferata said, and felt tears prickle at the corners of her eyes. 'Here,' she said, picking up a wine bowl. 'Drink with me, and let's talk a little more about old times.'

The handmaiden hesitated for a moment. Tephret had never much enjoyed the taste of wine, and had always been the one to keep her head when Neferata and the rest of her handmaidens were deep in their cups. She started to speak, perhaps to voice a polite refusal, but then she met the queen's eyes and her resolve melted away. Without a word, she took the wine bowl in both hands and raised it carefully to her lips.

Neferata smiled to herself as she watched her handmaiden drink. Once upon a time, she could have ordered Tephret to partake of the wine, but now she could command others with nothing more than a gentle suggestion. Moreover, they *wanted* to obey, as though nothing might please them more. It was another gift of Nagash's elixir, she knew. It had manifested itself over time, growing in power as she and Arkhan continued to refine the necromancer's formula. Until now, the queen had been careful to use her newfound gift sparingly, but tonight, she would test it to its limits.

They sat and talked quietly for hours. Tephret drank wine while the two of them talked of times past, while Neferata kept a careful watch on the moon's stately progress overhead. As the hour drew close to midnight, she took a deep breath and said, 'How long has it been since you left the Women's Palace, Tephret?'

The handmaiden paused, her lips working silently as she tried to puzzle through the question. It was fairly late, by the queen's standards, and Tephret had consumed the better part of an entire jar of wine.

'Blessed Asaph, let me see…' the handmaiden muttered. 'It would have been the sixty-second year of Geheb, I believe. That was the year I was presented to the king, and he made me your handmaiden. I was just eight years old. That was…'

'More than a hundred and fifty years ago,' the queen observed. She considered Tephret for a moment, then reached over and plucked the empty bowl from the handmaiden's grasp. 'Walk with me,' Neferata said, taking Tephret's hand and gently pulling the old woman to her feet.

Tephret frowned in bemusement. 'Where? Is it time to return to the bedchamber, or do you wish to visit your cousin Khalida?'

The queen shook her head. 'Khalida is gone, remember?' she reminded Tephret. 'She was married to Prince Anhur, years ago. Now she rules as Queen of Lybaras.'

'Oh, of course,' Tephret said, chiding herself. 'Forgive me, great one. My memory plays tricks on me sometimes.'

The queen squeezed her hand. 'There's nothing to forgive, except that you forgot to call me by my name. Now come.'

'Where are we going, then?'

'Into the palace proper,' the queen replied. 'You've been shut up in here too long, Tephret. It's time to set you free.'

To the queen's surprise, Tephret stopped dead in her tracks, pulling against the queen's grip with surprising strength. 'We can't!' she said, her eyes widening. 'It's not allowed!'

Neferata turned, stepping close to the aged handmaiden and peering deep into her eyes.

'Do you trust me, sweet Tephret?' she asked.

The handmaiden fell silent, a reply half-formed on her trembling lips. She met the queen's eyes and relaxed at once.

'With my life,' she answered faintly. 'But... but what will the king's servants say? What about your mask?'

'They will say nothing,' Neferata said firmly. 'Tonight of all nights, we will go wherever we wish, and we will not hide who we are. Do you understand?'

'No,' Tephret said, shaking her head. 'But that's no matter. I go where you go.'

Neferata squeezed her hand and smiled. 'That's right, dear one. Just follow me.'

The queen led her most favoured handmaiden down the lamplit corridors, through rooms and galleries that they had both known all their lives. Servants made way for the pair, marvelling at how queen and handmaiden walked hand-in-hand, like close friends. They spoke to one another as they walked, sharing memories and laughing softly at one another's tales.

They passed through the Hall of Reverent Contemplation, still lost in times past. Tephret barely paused when the queen reached the end of the hall and pulled open one of the heavy outer doors. As luck would have it, a pair of palace servants were just passing the chamber as the queen emerged. One of the servants, a younger woman, took one look at the queen and fainted. The other was transfixed, his eyes wide and his jaw hanging open as Neferata approached.

'Tend to your companion,' she said, peering into the servant's eyes. 'And tell no one of what you saw.'

Trembling, speechless, the servant fell to his knees and pressed his forehead to the floor as the queen and her companion glided past.

Tephret followed the queen like an obedient child, clutching the queen's hand and staring openly at the unfamiliar surroundings. Neferata felt giddy, her pulse racing as she openly walked the halls that she'd been forced to skulk through for nearly a year. Other servants crossed her path, and each one she left prostrate on the marble tiles, stunned and quivering in shock. She relished their stunned, slack-jawed expressions, their instant subservience. This is how it shall be from this night forward, she swore to herself. I shall walk these halls whenever it pleases me. I shall see my children again. And no one will dare say otherwise.

Moving openly, Neferata covered the distance to the abandoned wing of the palace much faster than expected. For a moment, all she could do was stand at the servants' entrance. Her heart was in her throat.

Tephret was weaving on her feet. The late hour and the wine were weighing heavily on her. 'What are we doing here?' she said bemusedly.

The queen drew a deep breath. 'I have a gift for you,' she said. 'It's not much further now.'

The handmaiden peered through the doorway. 'It's so dark in there.'

'I know,' Neferata said. 'I know. Just hold my hand. Everything will be all right.'

And with that, her course was set. She could not turn back now. If nothing else, her pride wouldn't allow it.

Tephret followed her into the darkness without hesitation. She said not a word as they walked through the dust and debris, nor did she fret at the sounds of creatures scurrying just out of sight. All she did was tighten her grip on the queen's hand, and pressed on.

Neferata scarcely paused as she pushed open the door to the sanctum, as though she was entering nothing more than a room inside the Women's Palace. She took Tephret to the banked brazier, and then stirred the coals to sluggish life.

The handmaiden turned slowly in place as the orange light filled the room. Her gaze drifted past the laden bookshelves, the stained divans and the cluttered worktables. Neferata saw the look of innocent wonder on her face and realised that the old woman was looking for the gift she'd been promised. She watched as Tephret's eyes moved to the ritual circle at the far side of the room… and then she saw the huddled form of Arkhan, just at the edge of the light. Immediately, Tephret turned towards the immortal and then gripped the queen's arm.

'Someone's there!' she hissed, her voice quavering.

'I know,' the queen said. 'It's all right, Tephret. There's nothing to fear.'

Arkhan stirred, his head rising slowly at the sound of the handmaiden's voice. He leaned forward, into the firelight, and Tephret saw his face.

'Oh!' Tephret cried, her eyes widening in terror. She pressed a hand to her mouth, even as her voice built to a scream. 'Oh, merciful gods. Asaph protect us!'

Neferata batted Tephret's hand aside and seized her by the chin. 'Hush!' she commanded, turning the handmaiden's head so she could stare into her eyes. 'Do not be afraid. There is nothing to fear, do you understand?'

Tephret's voice fell to a whimper. Neferata heard a rattle of heavy, iron links, and then Arkhan spoke.

'What's going on?' he demanded. 'What's *she* doing here?'

'It's time,' the queen told him, never taking her eyes from Tephret. 'It's been a month. Lamashizzar will gather the cabal together to create his elixir. Correct?'

'Yes,' Arkhan replied. 'But what does that have to do with her?'

'Then this is the moment we've been waiting for,' Neferata replied. 'But before we confront the king, we'll need to be at the peak of our strength.'

The immortal let out an exasperated sigh. 'All right, but that doesn't explain–'

Neferata tore her gaze away from the handmaiden and fixed Arkhan with her stare. 'Months ago, you told me that the elixir can be made even more powerful using a living vessel.' A small part of her mind was surprised at how calm she sounded.

Arkhan was taken aback. 'No,' he stammered, shaking his head. 'You misunderstand. She… she's too old–'

'What's that got to do with anything?' Neferata snapped. 'She's alive, and she's here. If you are half as skilled as you claim to be, you should be able to make this work.'

A moan slipped past Tephret's trembling lips. She was weeping now, trembling from the strain of containing her fear. 'What's going on?' she asked in a fearful, almost childlike voice. 'What are you talking about? I don't understand…'

Neferata touched a finger to the handmaiden's lips. 'Hush, dear one,' she said, and forced a smile. 'You're about to receive your gift.'

She took Tephret's hand and led her across the room. She held the handmaiden's gaze the entire time.

'You've done so much for me,' Neferata said to her. 'For so many years you've served without hesitation or complaint. And now, dear one, I'm going to set you free.' The queen manoeuvred her into the centre of the circle and placed her hands on the woman's cheeks.

'Don't be afraid,' the queen said, drawing on the power of the elixir coursing in her veins. 'Everything is going to be all right. Stand here but a moment, and then no one in all Lahmia will ever command you again. Do you understand?'

Slowly, by degrees, Tephret relaxed. When she spoke again, her voice sounded small and frail. 'I understand, Neferata.'

The queen smiled, tasting tears on her lips. 'That's right, dear one.' She leaned forward, touching her forehead to Tephret's. 'You've done so very much for me, for so many years. You've earned your rest. Part of you will be with me always,' she said, and then stepped back until she stood outside the circle.

Arkhan was waiting for her. The immortal's expression was strange and troubled. 'You do not understand,' he said, so softly that only she could hear. 'If you truly love her, then you must not do this.'

The queen studied Tephret for a moment, then shook her head. 'No,' she said. 'It's too late for that. I need her, this one last time.' She turned to the immortal, and bore down on him with the full weight of her stare. 'Do what you must,' she told him. 'The king will be here in little more than an hour.'

Arkhan stiffened. 'Very well,' he said in a hollow voice. 'Prepare yourself, great one.'

Neferata nodded, wiping more tears from her eyes. 'I am ready,' she said.

The immortal bowed to her, then went to a nearby table. She watched, surprised, as he picked up a small knife and tested its edge against the ball of his thumb.

She was not prepared for what happened next. She was not prepared at all.

THE SOUND OF footfalls echoed through the darkness. Neferata focussed on the sound. Her senses were sharp as a razor; she could hear nine distinct sets of footsteps. One moved with catlike grace, which she took to be Abhorash, the king's champion. Two more were loose-limbed and clumsy. The drunkards could be virtually anyone.

The steps drew closer, then suddenly there was a hiss of surprise, and everyone stopped, just outside the sanctum door. Neferata heard Lamashizzar's voice, whispering urgently. Doubtless he'd seen the light of the brazier seeping beneath the sanctum door.

She heard a rasp of metal – it rang faintly, and she could tell it was sharp iron by the note, as distinct as a musical tone. Then came the catlike tread, and after a moment the door to the chamber swung slowly open. Abhorash entered, sword ready, with the king and the rest of the cabal close behind.

Neferata waited for them at the edge of the ritual circle, her head held high. Arkhan stood to one side, his hands clasped behind his back. Behind them, Tephret's bloody remains still lay sprawled in the centre of the circle. The queen's hands were spread at waist level, palms out, like a welcoming goddess. Her linen robe, from neck to sleeves, was stained crimson, and her chin was red with fresh blood.

Abhorash, the grim, implacable warrior, recoiled from the sight of Neferata with a cry of shock and wonder. Even Lamashizzar, who had known her all his life, was momentarily stunned by the sight of her naked, bloodstained face. The rest of the cabal looked upon her as though she was the vision of a vengeful goddess, come to wreak a terrible judgment upon them. Ubaid sank to his knees with a groan, his face filled with rapturous terror.

Given the scene spread before him, it was a wonder that the king could manage find his voice at all.

Lamashizzar took a halting step towards Neferata. 'How dare you!' he said. The words welled up from his throat in a choked whisper. 'This is an outrage. An offence against the crown!'

Neferata met his gaze without flinching, yet it was not her husband she saw. Her mind's eye could see little past the horrors of the hour before. She could still hear the echoes of Tephret's screams in her mind. She had lingered for a very long time, given the hideous things Arkhan had done to her. The queen had watched every agonising second of it. She had owed poor Tephret that much.

'This,' Neferata said in a leaden voice, 'is for the future of Lahmia. You have forgotten your duties to your people, brother, so I am taking matters into my own hands. Starting now.'

Lamashizzar's face went pale with rage. 'You stupid, arrogant bitch!' he growled. He rushed towards her, seizing both of her arms and shaking her roughly. 'When I get you back to the Women's Palace I'm going to flog you within an inch of your life! Do you hear–'

Neferata's small, slender hand moved too fast for mortal eyes to follow. She laid her palm against the king's chest and pushed, and Lamashizzar was hurled backwards as though he were nothing more substantial than a straw doll. Abhorash dodged nimbly aside, leaving the king to crash into the drunken forms of Lords Adio and Khenti. They fell to the ground in a tangle of thrashing limbs.

'I am the queen,' she said coldly. 'And from this night forward, there is no place in this palace that is barred to me. You shall remain king over Lahmia, brother, but know that I am Queen of Lahmia, and when I speak, you will take careful heed of what I say. Henceforth, we shall rule this city *together*. Do you understand me?'

Lamashizzar broke free of the paralysed libertines. His face was a mask of hatred, but Neferata could see a glimmer of fear in his eyes. Still, he managed a defiant snarl.

'Seize her!' he ordered Abhorash. 'She has gone mad! Strike her down!'

'He will do no such thing,' the queen replied calmly. She glanced at the king's champion and smiled. 'These men are mine now, brother – each and every one of them. They will serve me gladly, because I can give them something you cannot.'

That broke the spell. W'soran stirred, his eyes alight. 'The elixir!' he hissed.

Neferata nodded. 'I will offer you the power that you have so long craved,' she said. 'And in return, you will serve me as you would your king.'

Abhorash stirred. 'I want nothing of power,' he said in a deep voice.

The queen took a step towards him, well within reach of the champion's sword. 'No, you crave something far more elusive. You crave *perfection*,' she said. 'It's not enough to be the champion of the king; there are six others in Nehekhara who can rightfully claim such a title. No, you want to be the greatest of warriors, the epitome of fighting men. That's why you accepted the king's offer in the first place, didn't you? So that you could have all eternity to hone your skills beyond mortal ken.'

The mighty warrior blanched at the queen's unsparing assessment. The others looked at her as though she was an oracle, never pausing to think that, through Arkhan, she had more than a century's worth of knowledge about their every hope and desire.

She surveyed the assembled noblemen. 'Lamashizzar has failed you for the last time,' she said to them. 'Bow to me, and I will give you all that you desire. The choice is yours.'

W'soran did not hesitate. He sank to his knees and prostrated himself before the queen. Ankhat and Ushoran followed suit, and the three young libertines, Adio, Khenti and Zuhras followed suit.

Ubaid, already kneeling, simply nodded deferentially to the queen, as he had done so many times before.

That left only Abhorash. The queen turned to regard him with a raised eyebrow. He held her stare for a long, silent moment, then slid his sword back into its scabbard.

Lamashizzar, who only moments before had been the undisputed ruler of the greatest city in Nehekhara, could only look on in helpless fury.

'What is it you want, sister?' he snarled.

Neferata smiled.

'For now, fetch a hammer and an iron chisel,' the Queen of Lahmia said, savouring her triumph. She pointed a bloodstained finger at Arkhan the Black. 'You're going to set him free.'

—< EIGHT >—

The Eye of the Burning God

*Cripple Peak, in the 76th year of Djaf the Terrible
(-1599 Imperial Reckoning)*

AFTER THE AMBUSH at the barrow, the priests organised large hunting parties to comb the plains and the mountain slopes to find Nagash's lair. For weeks they searched the mountain, sending acolytes down into the fissures as far as they could manage. Almost a score of them died in the attempt, overcome by the concentration of glowing vapours, and their bodies were never recovered. Despite their best attempts, the hunters never came close to him; he'd become far too adept at navigating the labyrinth of tunnels and caves beneath the deeper fissures. Whenever they drew too close he would simply retreat deeper into the maze until the hunters lost their nerve and withdrew.

Eventually, the barbarians' hunger for vengeance faded, and they abandoned their hunt. The stormy season was about to begin, and the older priests had no desire to spend day after day out on the mountain slopes in the rain. They retreated back to their temple fort and doubled the patrols out on the barrow fields, in case the terrible grave robber should return again.

Nagash spent weeks studying the movements of the patrols out on the plain, sometimes moving among them on nights when the rains were heavy and the brassy notes of thunder rumbled across the surface of the Sour Sea. He'd come to realise that the priests were not true necromancers; their skills were limited and extremely crude compared to his. What they lacked in sophistication they made up for in numbers and raw power, though, and the priests he encountered on the plain took their duties very seriously indeed. They were sharp-eyed and vigilant, even under the worst conditions, and they knew the plain far better than he.

If it came to battle, Nagash had no doubt that he would win, but the fight would cost him resources he could ill afford to spare. Though he spent nearly every day combing through the tunnels in search of more dust, there was now little left to scavenge. He'd filled his cloak hood to almost three-quarters full; perhaps two pounds, more or less, and mingled with all manner of impurities. It was his sole source of strength, unless he managed to find a way to reach the deposits buried deeper inside the mountain.

Thus, Nagash was forced to surrender much of the barrow fields to the priests, restricting his activities to the southern edge of the plain where they rarely patrolled. The barrow mounds there were very old, many having collapsed altogether under the weight of centuries and their contents long gone to dust. Any corpses left within the mounds would be nothing more than bones, and much harder for him to control, but for the moment they would have to serve.

Nagash searched the southern barrow fields for some time, examining the barrow mounds carefully before he found one that suited his purposes. Like the rest, its stone foundation had settled into the earth over the centuries, completely burying its entrance-way, but the weeks of steady rain had softened its earthen roof enough that he could dig through it with his bare hands. Night after night, he clawed at the soft ground, tearing it away in chunks and casting it aside. Flashes of green lightning illuminated him as he worked, revealing his grotesque, almost skeletal figure. Sickly emerald light seeped from his bones, revealing the dark, rope-like muscles working beneath his tattered skin. More skin hung like torn parchment from his cheeks and forehead, revealing the leering skull beneath. The necromancer's eyes had long since rotted away, boiled from within by the heat of the burning stone. All that remained were twin, green flames, flickering coldly from the depth of sunken eye sockets. His limbs were held together not by sinew, but by sorcery and willpower alone.

Finally, late one night, Nagash's efforts bore fruit. His fingers tore through the last layers of root and soil covering the barrow, releasing a hissing cloud of noxious air that would have slain a breathing man within moments. Redoubling his efforts, Nagash widened the hole far enough to allow him to slither his way inside.

He had chosen this particular barrow because it was one of the largest ones still intact on the southern end of the plain. Nagash hoped it had belonged to a great warlord or hetman, and thus hold the remains of a large retinue that he could raise as well. What he found was far better than he'd hoped for.

Nagash slid through the muddy channel he'd carved in the barrow's roof and found himself in a moment of freefall as he plunged some twelve feet to the barrow floor. He landed hard, snapping his right collarbone like a dry twig; irritated, Nagash focussed his will on the surrounding muscles to pull the broken ends of bone back into place, and then healed the break with a small measure of his power. Frowning, he bent down and laid a hand on the barrow floor. It had been laid with crude paving stones, now cracked and slimy with age.

Lightning flickered high overhead, casting a shaft of brilliant green light through the hole in the barrow's roof. It pierced the gloom, revealing a carved stone bier at the centre of the barrow. Laid upon the bier was the skeleton of a once-powerful man, clad in a mouldy shell of thick leather armour. A belt of heavy gold links hung loosely about the warrior's shrunken waist, and a circlet of gold, tinged black with corruption, lay against the corpse's bony brow. The warrior's hands were folded over the hilt of a long, black sword that had been laid atop his chest. It was straight and double-edged, and it seemed as though it had been shaped from a single piece of obsidian. Crude glyphs had been carved into the surface of the blade and then filled with a familiar green dust. The *abn-i-khat* still glowed faintly after so many years.

Nagash turned about slowly, his burning stare taking in the rest of the chamber. There were no less than a dozen other skeletons interred with the warlord, laid on stone biers and arrayed in a circle about their lord with their feet pointing towards the walls of the mound. Ten of the skeletons were clearly warriors, clad in rotting leather armour and carrying crude stone weapons of their own. The other two appeared to be female, judging by the tattered scraps of fabric and the tarnished golden jewellery that adorned their fingers and necks. Wives perhaps? There was no way to tell, and it mattered little to him at any rate. So long as they could dig, they would be of use to him.

Taking out his dagger, Nagash began to carve a ritual circle into the barrow's stone floor. It was different in design and intent than the one he'd used months before, and similar to the arcane circles he'd placed in the Black Pyramid at Khemri. This circle would not contain magical power; it would broadcast it in very specific ways.

When the circle was complete, Nagash took a moment to inspect it and make certain that every line, every symbol was correct and properly aligned. Then he retreated to the far side of the chamber and pulled a tightly closed bag from his frayed leather belt. Very carefully, Nagash opened his makeshift bag and studied the glowing dust contained within. It was slightly less than half-full at this point.

A growl rose from his ravaged throat. Power. In the end, it all came down to power – and the willingness to use it.

Nagash raised the bag, tilted back his head, and poured a stream of glowing dust down his throat.

A whirlwind of fire burst inside his chest and went howling up into his brain. The entire world seemed to shudder under his feet. When he finally lowered the bag, he could hear the thunder of rain on the earthen roof of the barrow and feel the slightest wrinkles in the leather of the bag clutched in his hands. His gaze pierced the gloom of the barrow, until every detail of the dank chamber was sharply etched in his brain.

That's when Nagash realised that the walls of the chamber were not raw earth, as he'd supposed. The builders instead had covered it with a kind of lime mixture, creating smooth, white surfaces that they had then decorated with paint. He saw crude representations of battles between human tribes, focusing on the triumphs of a tall, dark-haired man with piercing eyes: no doubt the very warrior whose bones now resided in the tomb. Of greater interest to

Nagash was the woman depicted next to the warlord, whose eyes flashed with green fire and who flung bolts of burning energy to slay the warlord's foes. His gaze turned once again to the two female skeletons, whose corpses were arrayed by the warlord's head – and then he saw the mural that had been painted on the wall above them.

Fiery eyes blazing, Nagash approached the fading mural. At its feet he stared up at the curving wall and the image of a dark, broad-shouldered mountain, looming up over a bare, rocky plain. A long, burning line, like a spear, had been driven into the mountain's side, piercing it to its heart. At the centre of the wound there burned a green, lidless eye.

Nagash's burning heart raced. Quickly, he turned and stepped into the ritual circle. Raising his arms before the warlord's corpse, he focussed his mind by hissing out the names of those he hated. Then, with visions of dark vengeance glimmering in his brain, he began the incantation of awakening.

The necromancer infused every arcane syllable with power until his shrivelled lips were ragged and the air clashed like a cymbal with every word he spoke. Nagash turned his implacable will upon the ancient corpses. *Rise*, he commanded. *Your master summons you. Rise!*

More power washed over the skeletons, stirring flakes of decaying leather from their armour and scattering scraps of moulding cloth – then the blackened bones began to emit a faint, green glow. There was a crackle of decaying hide and the creak of bending sinew, and Nagash saw the warlord's hands tighten on the hilt of his blade.

'*Rise!*' Nagash said aloud, his voice rising to a furious howl. '*The Undying King commands you!*'

There was a rasp of metal and bone. Slowly, the warlord rose at the waist, like a man sitting up from a long slumber. Tiny points of green fire glittered from bony eye sockets as the skeleton regarded Nagash.

Around the barrow chamber, the other skeletons were doing the same. They rose from their beds of stone and studied Nagash in cold, pitiless silence. The necromancer clenched his fists in triumph.

'*Come to me!*' he ordered.

Bones clattered as the warlord and his retinue slid from their biers and walked haltingly to stand before Nagash. With every passing moment they seemed to stand a little straighter, their movements a little stronger and more assured. Their bones radiated the chill of the grave, and ancient malice gleamed in their flickering eyes.

Nagash pointed a bony finger at the painting on the far wall. '*Now, show me,*' he told his ghastly retainers. '*Take me to the burning eye.*'

THE UNDEAD TOOK no notice of the rain, or the mud, or the sprawl of barrow mounds that had risen up across the plain since their death. They led Nagash across the barrow field to the east, and then skirted the southern slope of the mountain until they reached a path that only they could somehow perceive. Nagash wondered if the warlord and his retainers saw the mountain as it had been at the time of their deaths, or if they were simply following the course of ancient memories, heedless of the reality laid before them.

They climbed steadily up the slope through the darkness, and the more that Nagash studied the surrounding terrain, the more he began to see faint remnants of a roadway, and the outlines of foundations that might have once supported wooden structures. He'd paid them no mind during his initial searches, focusing on natural caves and fissures instead. Now he began to see telltale clues of a large complex – a palace perhaps, or a temple – that had once been built into the side of the mountain, many hundreds of years ago.

His servants led him to a wide depression in the mountain's flank, its edges rounded in places by the passage of years. He spied more outlines of foundation stones, now that he knew what he was looking for. Once upon a time, a huge, wooden structure had been built here – and perhaps there had been tunnels as well, burrowing into the mountainside. Clearly this was the place where the huge piece of burning stone had impacted, then was buried by hundreds of tons of shattered rock and smouldering earth. Apparently the barbarians' ancestors had witnessed the fall of the great stone and had decided to worship it, a tradition now aped by their debased descendants.

The warlord climbed the slope without hesitation, certain of his bearings even in the darkness and rain.

At the base of the depression was a wide, rounded shelf of earth that Nagash now realised had been excavated in ages past to form yet more building foundations. The rain-slicked skull glanced left and right, as though expecting to see squat, wooden towers, or tall statues flanking the entrance to a hallowed place of worship. After a moment's hesitation, the warlord continued forward, marching stiffly for another thirty paces into the depression before coming to an abrupt halt by a steep slope of grassy earth.

Nagash smiled in satisfaction. '*Dig*,' he commanded. At once, the skeletal women stepped forward and began clawing at the slope. The warriors paused long enough to set aside their weapons before joining in as well.

By the time dawn broke through the scudding clouds overhead, the skeletons had carved a small cave out of the muddy earth. Nagash took refuge within and stood watch while his servants worked tirelessly through the day. By late afternoon, the skeletons were digging up squared-off pieces of stone that must have once belonged to a building's foundation. By late evening, they'd reached the broken pieces of a collapsed stone arch. Whatever passage the archway had once anchored had collapsed during the intervening centuries.

That night, Nagash went out into the barrow fields once more and returned with another dozen skeletons to add to his workforce. Less than a handful of dust remained in his bag. It was all or nothing now. They had to reach the burning stone. They *must*.

The skeletons worked through the night and into the following day. They shored up the walls with piles of broken stone and packed earth as the shaft descended at a steep angle into the side of the mountain. Then, during the third night, the skeletons clawed through a layer of earth and rock and broke into a narrow tunnel made of closely-fitted stones.

Nagash heard the hollow clatter of bony feet against flagstones and pushed his way to the front of the group. Sensing his thoughts, the skeletons paused and stood aside to let him pass.

The necromancer stood on a broad, stone staircase that sank still deeper into the side of the mountain. The walls of the staircase were carved with intricate reliefs, depicting men and women carrying offerings of food and grain down the stairs to set before the waiting god. Nagash descended the slimy steps as quickly as he dared, trying to gauge how much further the staircase went before they reached bottom.

After only a few minutes, the steps led to a small antechamber. Four thick stone columns supported the antechamber's low ceiling; they had been carved with reliefs depicting a pair of men and women, their hands held against their chests in a gesture of supplication. They reminded Nagash of the totem statues in the barbarian villages to the north-west, though these figures were not quite so idealised as the others. Wide, earthen bowls were scattered across the antechamber floor. The offerings that had once been heaped inside them were nothing more than dust now.

Nagash crossed the small chamber and came to a tall, rectangular doorway. The wooden doors that had once sealed the portal lay in heaps of dust across the wide threshold. He stepped through the drifts, scattering them with his bare feet, and entered a much larger rectangular chamber. This room's ceiling was supported by four pairs of squat stone columns, each one carved to represent a man or a woman kneeling in worship towards an undefined point at the far end of the chamber. There, in the darkness, Nagash sensed a steady buzz of magical power.

The necromancer walked carefully past the ancient pillars. Those on the left were male likenesses, he noticed, and the ones to the right were female, and each pillar represented the same person as the one before it, but with a critical difference. As Nagash progressed across the chamber, the carved figures grew stronger, more handsome – more perfect in shape. By the time he stood at the far end of the chamber, he was flanked by a pair of stone gods, still poised in supplication before an invisible god.

There was a pair of tall doors at the far end of the chamber, made of a grey metal that blended cunningly with the stone surrounding them. Nagash ran his hands across the surface of the doors, and was surprised to find them warm to the touch. There were four holes in each door at shoulder-height, arranged to accept a man's fingers. Without hesitation, the necromancer slid his bony fingers into the holes and pulled on the great doors.

At first, the metal panels refused to budge. Nagash let out an impatient hiss and called upon his ebbing power. His muscles burned, and he heaved upon the doors with all his might. There was a crack of corroded metal, then a squeal of hinges, and the doors began to move. They were immensely heavy, Nagash realised, far heavier than bronze, though not quite as heavy as gold. As they swung open, a fierce green glow poured out over Nagash and spilled into the ancient hall.

The necromancer felt his skin prickle at the touch of the sorcerous light. Beyond the heavy metal doors was an alcove of rough stone that had been chipped away to reveal a hemisphere of glowing, green stone as large as a wagon wheel. Aeons past, some foolhardy barbarian had braved the stone's searing touch to carve the semblance of a pupil and an iris into the surface of the stone, transforming it into an unblinking, blazing eye.

Nagash raised his hands covetously to the eye of the burning god and began to laugh. It was a sound of madness and murder, of devastation and despair. It was a ringing portent of ruin for the kingdoms of men.

Far up the tunnel, where the storm winds were rising, the warlord and his retainers heard the terrible sound and awaited their master's bidding.

⊰ NINE ⊱

Among Thieves

Lahmia, The City of the Dawn, in the 76th year of
Khsar the Faceless
(-1598 Imperial Reckoning)

IT WASN'T THE tireless white horse of his dreams, but the chestnut-coloured Numasi warhorse was as fine as any animal Arkhan had ever ridden. Long of leg, with a broad chest and powerful hindquarters, the stallion had been bred for agility, strength and stamina – qualities meant to keep it and its rider alive on the battlefield. Presented as a gift from the Horse Lords to the King of Lahmia, the animal had been stuck in a stable, surrounded by sleek-limbed palfreys meant for nothing more demanding than an occasional hunt or ceremonial parade. The immortal had taken to the sullen, snappish creature at once;

both of them had been locked away and largely ignored for far too long.

They passed through the palace gates at a trot, barely eliciting a response from the royal guard, and followed the broad processional that wound downhill amid the grand villas of the city's elite. It was just past nightfall, and the city's young lamp-lighters were still making their rounds down the narrow city streets. One boy with a long, reed taper had to leap nimbly to the side to avoid a bite from Arkhan's horse as he went by. Sounds of music and conversation flowed from the open windows of the walled villas as nobles gathered for an early evening meal before heading out into the city for a long night of debauchery. For the moment, the streets were relatively clear, and the immortal made good time. He was already impatient for the wide road and the rolling hills west of the city.

It had only been six months since Neferata had ordered the king to set him free – she'd forced him to wield the chisel personally, to Lamashizzar's utter humiliation – and already his memories of the last hundred and fifty years were fading away, like a long and tortured fever-dream. Neferata had chosen to maintain her quarters in the Women's Palace, far from her husband, and had been careful not to make too great a spectacle of her own newfound freedom. Where he'd once been confined to a single corner of a large, dingy room, Arkhan now had the run of the entire palace wing. Servants had been ordered to clean the corridors and begin refurnishing a suite of rooms, and he had been provided with a fine wardrobe of rich, dark silks and fine leather accoutrements.

Neferata had even gone so far as to provide him with a sword – not the curved, bronze khopesh that most Nehekharan warriors favoured, but a heavy, double-edged weapon made from dark Eastern iron. It was more than just a gesture of trust and esteem, Arkhan knew. The queen was also demonstrating her authority, both to him and to the rest of Lamashizzar's small cabal.

The queen gave him a weapon as a sign that she had nothing to fear from him. She opened the king's stables to him to show that she understood he had nowhere else to go.

After a short while the processional reached the bottom of the great hill and entered the city's eastern merchant quarter, where fine goods from all over Nehekhara were sold to the city's nobles and wealthier merchants. Business was still brisk, despite the hour. Trade with the west was finally on the rise again, with caravans arriving every few months from as far away as Numas and Zandri. Small crowds of citizens and servants browsed through the lamp-lit bazaars, buying bronze goods from Ka-Sabar, leather saddles from Numas or exotic spices from the jungles south of Rasetra. Merchants in the short capes and linen kilts of the desert cities haggled with silk-clad Lahmians and even a few haughty-looking Imperial traders, looking for luxury goods to carry back to their homeland. At one point, Arkhan heard a loud crash and a series of hoarse shouts across the wide square, and turned to see a pair of city guardsmen dragging a struggling, spitting young urchin away from a Rasetran spice trader's stall. If the young thief was very lucky, the city magistrates would only sentence him to a year's labour on a Lahmian merchant ship, otherwise, he'd be chained to the rocky shoreline north of the city and left for the crabs to eat.

Beyond the merchant district sprawled the cramped districts that were home to the city's many artisans and labourers. Here the streets were mostly quiet, as the tradesmen and their families retired to their rooftops or their small, walled courtyards after a long day's work. Children ran about or played games in the cool of the evening, enjoying a few precious hours of freedom. One group ran past Arkhan, led by a tall boy wearing a ghastly clay mask. They were pursued by another group of children brandishing sticks and wearing crude circlets or crowns woven from river reeds. They were intent on catching the masked boy, while his companions brandished sticks of their own whenever the pursuers drew too close.

'After them!' the young kings shouted gleefully. 'Death to the Usurper and his minions! Death to Nagash!'

The masked figure turned and made an obscene gesture at his pursuers, sparking more laughter and threats. Arkhan reined in his horse as they dashed across the street in front of him. The grotesque mask turned his way for a brief instant, and then the boy was gone, leading his young immortals into the shadows of a nearby alley.

Arkhan was still shaking his head in bemusement when the tightly packed mud-brick homes gave way to the cruder, sprawling mass of huts and wicker enclosures that crowded up against the range of rounded hills at the western edge of the city. The people here were mostly descendants of refugees from distant Mahrak, left to eke out a miserable existence among Lahmia's outcasts. Beggars, whores and would-be thieves skulked around the fringes of the trade road, eyeing the immortal's rich attire with predatory interest. Arkhan gave the boldest of them a black-toothed grin and they quickly looked away, seeking easier prey.

He spurred the warhorse to a canter, eager to be free from the stench and squalor of the dispossessed. Within minutes he was heading up into the wooded hills, leaving the noise and the lights of the city behind at last. Scraggly trees pressed close to the trade road, and the sky was just a narrow band of stars and moonlight overhead. Arkhan breathed in the cool air, fragrant with cedar and pine, and gave the horse its head. The stallion leapt eagerly into a gallop, and for a while he was able to put aside thoughts of formulae and incantations and simply feel the wind upon his face.

They had made great progress in the past few months, now that Neferata was in the position to obtain human subjects for their experiments. It was easy enough for Arkhan to snatch a beggar or a whore from the edge of the city, drug them with lotus root and slip back with them into the palace in the dead of night. Afterwards, the body could be dumped amid the condemned thieves north of the city and within a few days there would be nothing but bones, picked clean by the hungry sea. So long as they were suitably cautious, the city's refugee population would keep them safely supplied for hundreds of years. Their mastery of Nagash's complex ritual was still far from complete, but the elixir they created was more than potent enough to ensure the continued loyalty of Lamashizzar's cabal.

As usurpations went, the queen's move was as clever as it was subtle. Unbeknownst to the rest of the city, Lamashizzar had been transformed overnight from a king to a mere figurehead, issuing Neferata's edicts in his own name. He couldn't expose Neferata's scheme to the rest of the city without implicating himself in the practice of necromancy, and he couldn't move against her in secret without being opposed by the rest of the cabal.

Now that Ushoran, Abhorash and the rest had been given a taste of what the elixir could really do, they would have to be idiots to want a return to the thin gruel of goat's blood offered by the king. So far, Lamashizzar had accepted the new balance of power with what little grace he possessed, spending most of his time drinking and sulking in his quarters. It was possible that the coup had broken his nerve completely; Neferata seemed to think so, but Arkhan wasn't so sure. Losing a crown was one thing; losing control over Nagash's elixir was something else again.

He rode on, up into the hills and onto the edge of the great Golden Plain, where countless farmers reaped harvests of grain, corn and beans from the fertile soil. The vast fields now lay dormant and bare, awaiting the return of the spring. Arkhan reined in the warhorse and stared in silence, savouring the wide-open expanse. The crushed white stone of the trade road glimmered like a mirage beneath the moonlight, beckoning him ever westward, towards the Brittle Peaks and the lands beyond

The stallion slowed to a walk, its flanks heaving from the long ride, and Arkhan let the horse choose its own pace as they continued down the road. He was tempted, as he was every night, to simply keep going, past Lybaras and the desolate streets of Mahrak, through the Valley of Kings and the distant Gates of the Dawn. From there, he could slip past hated Quatar, and then to the citadel he'd built in the southern desert, or even to the deserted streets of Khemri itself.

The Black Pyramid remained at the centre of the city necropolis; the great crypt had been built to defy the ages, and would endure long after the sun had gone dark and cold. There were secret ways inside that no mortal knew of, and with the proper sacrifices, the dark winds of magic could be his to command once more.

And then... what? The memory of Nagash's terrible reign was still fresh in the mind of most

Nehekharans. If the kings of the great cities knew he still survived, they would spare no effort to destroy him. He could either cower in the shadows like a rat and hope to escape their notice, or else try to raise an army and defy their combined might for as long as he could.

Lahmia, on the other hand, held out the promise of immortality and the comforts of a wealthy and powerful kingdom. He had little doubt that, under Neferata's capable leadership, the city would become the undisputed centre of power in all of Nehekhara. Within a few centuries it might even become the seat of a new empire, something that not even Nagash had been able to achieve.

When that day finally arrived, Neferata would need a strong right hand to lead her armies in the field and expand the borders of her domain; a faithful and ruthless lieutenant – perhaps, in time, even a consort.

Listen to you, he sneered. Arkhan the Black, bald-headed and broken-toothed, consort to the Queen of the Dawn. What a fool! The damned woman has you under her spell. Can't you see that? The farther away from her you can get, the better!

Except, of course, that he had nowhere to go.

Brooding on his fate, Arkhan continued down the road for more than an hour, passing farmers' houses and dark, fallow fields. Dogs barked in the distance; owls hooted, hunting prey, and bats flitted across the face of the moon. After a while, he came to a section of the plain that was still subdivided by stretches of dense woodland. Each time he came upon a stand of trees he paused and took a deep draught of night air.

Soon enough, his preternatural senses detected a faint hint of cooking fires and sizzling grease. He turned off the road and headed south, down a game trail that led deep into the shadows beneath the trees. The horse picked its way forwards carefully: even Arkhan had a hard time seeing much farther than the stallion's drooping head. Yet it wasn't long before the immortal could feel that he was being watched.

The camp was large and cunningly concealed within the thick trees. Undergrowth had been cleared away to create a series of linked clearings, then used to make a cluster of lean-tos and overhangs surrounding a small, banked cook fire. More than a dozen gaunt, filthy men – as well as a number of women and children – all clad in a motley collection of robes and desert kilts stood and stared warily as he emerged from the woods into the firelight. The women gathered the children and retreated swiftly into the next clearing down the line, while the men drew battered swords or hefted spears at his approach.

Arkhan reined in and gave them all a long, calculating look. Lips pulled back in a predatory grin. 'Well met, friends,' he said. 'I smelled wood smoke as I was passing along the road. Is there room for one more traveller around the fire?' He drew a fat wineskin from one of his saddle hooks and showed it to the men. 'I've two skins of Lybaran red I'll be happy to share in exchange for a hot meal, and then I'll be moving on.'

From where he sat, it was difficult to tell how many people occupied the camp: it could be anywhere from a few score to as much as a few hundred. Bands such as these moved like nomads up and down the plain, never staying in one place for too long lest they draw unwanted attention from the city. Mostly they stalked along the edges of the trade road, preying on merchant caravans for food, trade goods and horses. Arkhan had been seeking out their camps for several months. Many of the bandit gangs had grown adept at hiding in the woods and hollows scattered across the plain, but he'd learned his trade hunting Bhagarite desert raiders, and there were only so many places a large group could make camp without attracting attention.

The brigands cast questioning glances at a short, stocky man standing closest to the fire. He studied Arkhan for a moment, then nodded curtly. 'You can sit by me,' he said, and the rest of the men lowered their weapons. 'We've grain mash and a little rabbit we can share. Where are you headed?'

Arkhan slid easily from the saddle and tossed the wineskin to the brigand leader. He shrugged. 'Oh, here and there. You know how it is.'

He might not have any place he could truly go, but in this, Arkhan was far from alone.

THE BRIGANDS DRANK every last drop of Arkhan's wine, and in return gave him a bowl of greasy stew and some news about the comings and goings of bandit gangs across the plain. The immortal chewed his gristle thoughtfully and listened to every word. Much of it was lies and exaggerations, he knew, coupled with a few honest facts about rival gangs, in the event he was a spy for the city guard. Later, when he'd returned to the palace, he would compare what he'd learned with the notes he'd taken from previous encounters, and look for common threads.

As the hour drew close to midnight, he took his leave of the brigands. Their leader and his lieutenants, who'd gotten the lion's share of the wine, made no protest, friendly or otherwise, as he said his farewells and led his horse back into the dark woods in the direction of the trade road. He could sense the movements of other bandits pacing him through the darkness, all the way to the edge of the wood line and beyond. They shadowed him across the bare fields, their brown capes blending with the dark earth. Most likely they were making sure he wasn't reporting back to a waiting troop of city guardsmen, but it was also possible that they meant to avail themselves of his fine horse and expensive iron sword. It had been tried a few times before.

They followed him all the way to the trade road, but pressed no closer than a few dozen yards. Once the horse was back on stable footing, the immortal swung into the saddle and waved farewell to his erstwhile shadows before setting off towards the city at a brisk trot.

He gauged that the camp contained a good hundred or so bandits, and a third as many women and children. It was one of the largest such gangs he'd encountered to date. There were enough armed men wandering the Golden Plain to amount to a small army; most were fairly organised and they were all heavily-armed. All they lacked was a strong leader to unite them under a single banner.

The more such gangs he encountered, the more Arkhan believed that his plan had merit. He could start with the largest gang, gain their loyalty through a mixture of charisma, fear and bribery, then begin forming ties with other, smaller groups. With the right mix of ruthlessness and reward, he could build an organization fairly quickly, and having an armed force at his command occupying the Golden Plain would give him an outside source of power that he currently lacked. That was a lever that he could apply to any number of inconvenient obstacles.

Before he knew it, Arkhan was at the edge of the plain and heading downward through the wooded hills. The lights of the city glimmered on the horizon, unimpeded by the barrier of high city walls. Of all the great cities of Nehekhara, only Lahmia disdained such fortifications. Siege warfare had been unheard of before the war against the Usurper, and old King Lamasheptra trusted in his dragon men to keep the city safe. He wondered if the queen would take steps to correct her father's mistake.

Suddenly the stallion tossed its head, checking its stride and snorting in surprise. It was the only warning the immortal had before the arrows struck home.

Two powerful blows struck him on the left side, one just below his ribcage and the other in the side of his thigh. Searing pain stole the wind from his lungs. He pitched forward against the horse's neck, tasting blood in his mouth and fumbling at the reins. Gritting his teeth, he tried to spur the horse forward, only to find that his left leg wouldn't move. The arrow had passed completely through his thigh and buried itself in the thick leather of his saddle, pinning it in place.

A third arrow hissed out of the darkness, missing him by a hair's-breadth, then a fourth punched deep into his left shoulder. This time he cried out, cursing at the ambushers. He'd grown careless during his long confinement, letting himself walk into such an obvious trap. With the moonlight glowing on the white stone road he might as well have hung an oil lamp around his neck. The archers could see him clearly, while he was all but blind.

The warhorse sidestepped, tossing its head and snorting at his confused commands. Even if he managed to get the animal under control the archers would put an arrow in its neck before he'd gone half a yard. As near as he could reckon, he only had one option left. Gritting his teeth, the immortal grabbed the arrow jutting from his thigh and tore it free, then simply let himself fall from the saddle.

He landed on the right side of the horse, striking the road with a bone-jarring crunch that consumed him with another wave of blinding pain. Pure reflex forced his limbs to work, rolling him off the road and into the brush. He fetched up against a tangle of briars and lay still, pretending to be dead. Were it not for the elixir coursing through his veins, he likely would have been.

The stallion bolted as he fell, galloping down the road and out of sight. For a moment, nothing moved. Arkhan bit back waves of agony and listened for the slightest signs of movement.

Before long he heard quiet footsteps edging from the tree line on the opposite side of the road. It sounded like just two men. The bandits must have left camp long before he did in order to set up such an ambush. How had they known he would be heading back towards the city?

He heard the men make their way cautiously nearer. His right hand, shielded beneath his body, edged towards the hilt of his sword.

The ambushers paused in the middle of the road, just a few yards away. 'Not so tough as we thought,' one of them said. Arkhan thought he recognised the voice.

Arkhan heard the rasp of a sword being drawn. 'He'll want proof,' said another familiar voice. 'We'll take back his head. Roll his body out of the brush.'

The two men drew nearer. A hand gripped his right shoulder and pulled. Arkhan rolled onto his back, drawing his iron blade with a bestial snarl. The two ambushers cursed, their faces exposed by the same lambent moonlight.

They weren't bandits at all. Arkhan found himself staring at Adio and Khenti, two of the king's young libertines.

Arkhan cursed. He'd been a fool. An utter and complete fool.

The two libertines stared back at the immortal with wide eyes. Khenti still clutched a powerful Numasi horse bow in his left hand, while Adio had left his on the white stone roadway so he could grip a curved, bronze khopesh in both hands. They were both clad head to foot in dark, cotton robes and short cloaks. Neither wore armour, as far as Arkhan could tell. No doubt they'd expected to kill or incapacitate him with a volley of arrows, then collect their trophy and ride back to the city. Had they been proper archers, they likely would have succeeded.

Careless, the immortal thought angrily. He'd all but planned the ambush for them. The cabal knew about his nightly rides out to the plain, and a few coins in the hand of the right stableboy would tell them exactly when he left. All they would have to do is ride the same route and pick out the best place to lie in wait.

The two fools hadn't killed him yet, but the powerful, broad-headed arrows had done their damage. His left leg felt leaden and unresponsive, and the arrow in his left shoulder made it difficult to move his arm. The third arrow had sunk deep into his vitals. It and the shaft in his shoulder had snapped when he'd rolled off his horse, leaving two bloodied and splintered stubs jutting from his robes. Agony washed over his body in cold waves, but he scarcely felt its bite. Pain held no power over him any more, not since the war. Not since Quatar.

He only had moments to act; if he was still on his back when Adio's shock wore off, even a pampered Lahmian libertine would have little trouble hacking him to pieces. Gritting his ruined teeth, he rolled onto his right side and then, using just his sword arm and his right leg, he pushed himself onto his feet. The moment he put any weight on his left leg it began to buckle. Desperate, he drew upon the power of the queen's elixir to lend him strength and speed.

For an instant, the immortal felt his veins catch fire, but the heat began to fade almost at once. Neferata's potion was powerful, but it still had its limits. Darkness crowded at the corners of his eyes, until for a moment he feared that he'd drawn too much and he was about to do Adio's work for him. The pain ebbed, held for a dizzying instant... and then swept back in again, pushing the threatening shadows aside. His leg remained weak, but at least the muscles responded to his will. It would have to be enough.

Adio was already lunging forward with a choked cry. He was a tall man, with long, lean arms, narrow shoulders and bony knees. His brown eyes were wide with fear, bulging above a long, hooked nose, and his narrow lips were stained by years of exposure to lotus root. His swing was swift enough, but lacked skill. Arkhan parried it easily with his iron blade and countered with a swipe to the nobleman's throat, but after more than a century his skill was little better than Adio's. The libertine clumsily blocked the strike and fell back towards the road, his sandals scuffing across its stone surface. The clash of bronze and iron galvanised Khenti as well. With a startled shout the paunchy nobleman turned and ran back the way he'd come.

Cursing, Arkhan charged after his would-be ambushers. He would have just as soon see Adio break and run as well, but the nobleman either didn't like his odds in a foot race, or was possessed of much more courage than the immortal had given him credit for. Adio threw another wild swing that missed the immortal by more than a foot, then abruptly shifted direction, swinging around to the immortal's left. Arkhan tried to match Adio's movements, but his wounded leg hindered him. The libertine slashed at him again, and Arkhan's sword was too far out of position to block it. The bronze blade gouged across the immortal's upper left arm, leaving a shallow cut through the muscle. Had the blade been sharper, it would have cut him to the bone.

Snarling, Arkhan planted his right foot and spun on its heel. The iron sword flickered in the moonlight, arcing around to catch Adio from an unexpected direction. The libertine reacted with surprising speed, just barely raising his curved sword in time to block the heavier blade. Still, the nobleman let out a high-pitched shriek as Arkhan's weapon sliced open Adio's sword arm just above the elbow.

Then a powerful blow hit the immortal in the back, punching into his torso just beneath his right shoulder. Arkhan staggered, shouting in surprise and anger. Khenti hadn't been running away at all; the pudgy little bastard had simply been getting enough room to start firing arrows again.

You've gotten soft in a century and a half, Arkhan thought, as Adio regained his balance and rushed at him, khopesh raised high for a skull-splitting blow. In a moment of cold clarity, Arkhan wondered if this was how he was going to finally die, struck down by a callow young gambler and left in a ditch for the vultures.

The khopesh swept down, its nicked edge whistling through the air. Arkhan's limbs moved without conscious volition, driven by instincts honed on countless battlefields. His iron sword swept up in a sweeping block, meeting the khopesh just past the height of its arc. There was a discordant clang, and the lighter bronze weapon snapped in two.

Adio reeled backwards, staring in shock at the ruined sword, and Arkhan was on him like a wolf. A backhanded blow from his heavier sword shattered the nobleman's right elbow, eliciting a scream of raw agony. The cry turned to a bubbling wail as the immortal's second stroke slashed Adio's throat all the way to the spine. The libertine fell backwards, his left hand trying to stanch the dark blood pouring from the gaping wound. He had no sooner hit the ground than the immortal was standing over him, sword raised. Arkhan ended the nobleman's thrashings with a single blow to the head.

Another arrow hissed out of the darkness, flying a handspan over Arkhan's bent back. The immortal pulled his blade free from Adio's shattered skull and turned, throwing back his head and howling like a fiend as he charged across the road.

His wounded leg hobbled him, turning his charge into a headlong stagger, but Arkhan pushed forward as quickly as he could. His bloodcurdling shout echoed from the dense trees. It was a calculated move, meant to rattle Khenti. Every second brought the immortal closer to his foe, and it took nerves of stone to calmly draw and nock an arrow in the face of a charging enemy swordsman.

Arkhan glimpsed movement across the road, then heard a muffled curse. Teeth bared, he oriented on the sound and tried to increase his pace. A moment later he could make out Khenti's head and shoulders, then the raised arm of his horse bow. The immortal was close enough to hear the *twang* of the bowstring, then Khenti's arrow smashed into his chest. It missed his heart but pierced his left lung; Arkhan staggered, but the sight of Khenti reaching for another arrow spurred him forward once more.

Crying out in fear, Khenti fumbled for another shaft from the hunting quiver at his hip. Arkhan reached him in eight long steps and smashed the bow from the nobleman's hand with a sweep of his sword. Forgetting the khopesh at his side, the libertine made to turn and run, but Arkhan's left hand seized him by the throat and held him fast. The point of his iron sword came to rest against Khenti's chest, just above his heart.

'I have some questions for you,' Arkhan grated. Flecks of dark ichor stained his pale lips. 'How long you live depends on how well you answer.' He drove the point of his sword a fraction of an inch into Khenti's chest for emphasis. The young nobleman moaned in terror.

'Who else is part of this?' the immortal demanded. He didn't know whether to be relieved or insulted that Lamashizzar had sent the two libertines to kill him. Had Abhorash been waiting for him instead, his headless body would already be cooling by the side of the road. Did that mean the king's champion might not be a part of the plot, or was he being reserved for a more important task?

Khenti squirmed in Arkhan's grasp. His puffy features were pale and mottled with fright. 'The king–'

Arkhan shook the nobleman like a dog. 'I *know* the king's involved, you idiot,' he snarled, revealing ichor-stained teeth. 'Who else?'

'I – I don't know,' Khenti stammered, his tiny eyes very wide. 'I swear! He claimed there were others, but he wouldn't name them!'

Which could mean anything, Arkhan mused angrily. It was entirely possible that Adio and Khenti were the only ones stupid enough to turn on Neferata, and the king lied to lend them some extra courage.

The immortal's grip tightened. 'Is the queen in danger?' he said. 'Was this just about killing me, or does the king have plans for Neferata as well?'

Khenti let out a groan. Tears of fright rolled down his round cheeks. 'It's too late,' he said pleadingly. 'She's already dead. You were – *ghurrrk*!'

The libertine's body spasmed. Arkhan hadn't realised he'd stabbed the man until the point of his blade burst from Khenti's back. The nobleman's body sagged in death, and the immortal let it sink to the ground. He left his blade sticking out of Khenti's chest, reached up with his right hand and grimly pulled the arrow shaft from his chest. The arrow in his back was more problematic. He groped at it for several moments, only succeeding in breaking off the shaft close to his torso. The exertion left him reeling. He turned his face to the night sky. How much stolen life did he have left, he wondered. More importantly, what should he do with it?

If Neferata was dead, there was nothing left for him in Lahmia. Lamashizzar would have him killed on sight. On the other hand, if Khenti was wrong, and the conspirators hadn't yet reached the queen...

For a long while he stood, staring up at the sky, feeling cold and weak. He tried to think about endless, rolling dunes, and the citadel he'd built in the middle of the empty desert, but Arkhan's mind kept coming back to the startling touch of a hand against his cheek, and the queen's depthless eyes staring into his own.

It was possible Khenti was wrong. In fact, it was more than possible. There could still be a chance to reach Neferata before Lamashizzar's trap could spring shut. Or so Arkhan cared to believe.

'Damn me,' he snarled up at the cold face of the moon. 'First Nagash, and now this.' He bent forward and pulled his sword from Khenti's chest. 'When will I ever learn?'

Gritting his teeth, Arkhan staggered down the trade road, towards Lahmia. With luck, his damned horse wouldn't have run too far.

TEN

The Hour of the Dead

Cripple Peak, in the 76th year of Khsar the Faceless
(-1598 Imperial Reckoning)

THE STORM WAS the worst of the season by far, and it broke upon the shores of the Sour Sea with little warning.

It had been a cloudy, windy day, with sudden gusts of rain interspersed with long periods of drizzle – nothing out of the ordinary for that time of the year. But shortly after sundown the wind picked up, howling like a chorus of hungry ghosts across the barrow fields, and flickers of lightning danced behind the roiling clouds out to sea. The barbarians along the north coast heard the ominous rumble of thunder, saw the height of the waves dashing against the shore, and rushed to their low, rounded huts.

Lowland tribes flocked to the hills, begging the hetmen for shelter from the coming storm.

The reaction was altogether different among the Keepers of the Mountain, as the barbarian priests were known. Their lookouts reported the rising winds and the ominous clouds to the High Keeper, and after a moment's thought he ordered the patrols of the barrow fields doubled until the storm had run its course. The High Keeper was an old and cunning man, or he never would have risen to claim the God's Eye in the first place. The elder Keepers were certain that the grave-robbing monster who'd killed their brethren had been driven away by their hunting parties, but the High Keeper wasn't convinced. He was certain that the creature was still close by, perhaps hiding somewhere on the mountain in spite of his order's best efforts to find it. If so, the storm would draw it out of hiding. The wind and the rain would conceal its movements, providing the perfect opportunity to resume its grisly deeds. And when it did, the Keepers would be waiting.

A few hours later, well past nightfall, the storm broke upon the coast in all its fury. The wind raged, lashing at the men out on the barrow fields with blinding sheets of rain. Visibility dropped to twenty feet, then fifteen, then ten; had the Keepers not known the plain like the backs of their hands, they would have been utterly disorientated. Even still, the patrols could do little more than huddle together against the furious gale and creep from one mound to the next, trusting that the Burning God would lead them to the monster if it were about.

Then, around midnight, with the storm still scouring the plain, the patrols spied a pillar of green fire blazing fiercely to the south, towards the older barrow mounds. The sight lifted the Keepers' hearts. At first, they believed their prayers had been answered, and, in a bitterly ironic sense, they were right.

The four patrols made their way independently southward, converging on the source of the god's own flame. They had learned their lesson after the first disastrous encounter with the monster. The ostentatious lantern-globes had been left behind, and the acolytes had been armed with bronze swords and spears from the fortress's ancient armoury. The Keepers in each patrol had been entrusted with even more precious treasures: reliquaries of tarnished bronze, each more than a thousand years old, containing polished spheres of god-stone to fuel their invocations. It was more raw power than any of the Keepers had ever seen, much less controlled. Each patrol felt confident that they could deal with the monster on their own, and pressed forward as quickly as they could in hopes of securing the glory for themselves.

NAGASH STOOD IN the eye of the raging storm, shielded on all sides by a whirling column of power. Beyond the pillar of fire, the tempest roared, clawing at the shield like a frenzied beast, while within the air was still, and silent save for the scratching of his dagger through the damp earth. Where the bronze knifepoint passed, the earth was left blackened and smouldering by its touch.

The chunk of *abn-i-khat* burned like molten lead in his shrivelled stomach. He had carved a piece of stone the size of his fist from the centre of the Burning God's eye and had forced it down his throat, and the tempest raging within his flesh made the storm above seem as gentle as an evening breeze. He could feel every nerve, every muscle fibre, every inch of flesh and bone with sharp-edged detail. He felt every blade of grass beneath his feet, and every tiny mote of power within them – he could even feel the lingering vestiges of life force in the hide cloak that lay across his shoulders. A veritable sea of sensations raged within him from one moment to the next: it might have been pain, or pleasure, or a mingling of both. Nagash could not tell any longer. He was long past the point of making distinctions between the two.

Yet his mind was absolutely, utterly clear. His thoughts were gleaming and sharp-etched as obsidian, and beggared the lightning for speed. What mighty deeds could he have accomplished in Khemri with such clarity of thought? The power of the Black Pyramid paled in comparison.

The site he'd chosen for the great ritual was a flat region surrounded by four barrow mounds near the exact centre of the plain. He'd chosen the spot not only because it would allow him to cast his invocation over the entire area, but also because the pathways around the barrows would serve to channel the barbarian patrols in predictable ways. Nagash had no doubt that they would appear, once his work began in earnest.

There were more of them than he expected, and by either luck or design they struck at more or less the same time. Thin cries rose and fell amid the howling gale as sword- and spear-wielding acolytes charged blindly across the open ground towards the beacon of flame. Behind them, tiny pinpoints of green light glowed like sullen coals as a dozen priests brandished their bronze reliquaries and made ready for battle.

The necromancer straightened, gauging the acolytes' approach. To his mind, they seemed ponderous and slow, stumbling haltingly across the wet ground towards him. When they were halfway to him, he raised his dagger skyward and reached out with his will.

Slay them!

Blinded by eagerness and lashing curtains of rain, the acolytes did not register the figures rising up from the dark ground until they'd charged in among them. The skeletons reared up with disturbing speed, rain coursing from their age-darkened bones, and closed in on the barbarians from all sides. Obsidian blades flashed, severing limbs and spilling entrails. Bony hands grabbed at the acolytes, dragging them to the ground by their robes or by their hair. Leering skulls closed in, jaws snapping, their eye sockets alight with green flame. In moments, the acolytes' bloodthirsty shouts had turned to confused and agonised screams, punctuated by the clang and clatter of blades as the survivors rallied and fought for their lives.

It took several long seconds for the priests to grasp what was happening, and when they did their response was potent but poorly coordinated. Nagash felt a ragged volley of invocations from across the field as the priests tried to seize control of his warriors. Here and there one of the skeletons stumbled beneath the onslaught, and the acolytes lashed out at them, smashing several to pieces. The barbarians took heart, sensing that the tide of battle was about to turn – and then Nagash raised his left fist skyward and hissed a dreadful invocation of his own.

An ominous rumble echoed through the clouds overhead, followed by stuttering flashes of lightning. Moments later, the priests were stunned by a single arc of burning, green light that plunged to earth and struck the barrow mound between them with a sputtering hiss. Another glowing mote fell from the bruised clouds, then another, and then there was a clap of thunder and a shower of burning hail the size of sling stones plunged down upon priests and acolytes both.

Men fell dead with their skulls dashed in or their necks broken. Others shrieked in agony as their robes burst into greenish flames that the rain could not quench. The priests scattered under the onslaught, running in every direction to escape the attack, and the sight of their panic unnerved the beleaguered acolytes, who tried to break free from the clutches of the undead and escape into the darkness. Many were cut down as they tried to flee, or were dragged to the ground by claw-like hands and torn apart. The last thing the survivors heard as they fled for their lives was the sound of soulless, mocking laughter riding the howling wind.

The skeletons made no effort to pursue the fleeing barbarians. Heedless of the sizzling hail, those undead warriors with no weapons of their own began plucking weapons from the bodies of the dead, while the warlord and his skeletal retinue went about killing the wounded that had been left behind. Perhaps a third of their number had been destroyed in the fighting, their bones scattered across the smouldering ground.

The losses mattered little to Nagash. Close to forty-five dead barbarians littered the battleground, some still burning as the magical fire consumed their flesh. They would more than make up for the numbers he had lost.

Grinning cruelly, Nagash returned his attention to the ritual circle. His army had only just begun to grow.

THE GREAT CIRCLE took another hour to complete, while the wind and the rain raged unabated over the barrow fields. As the hour of the dead approached, Nagash cast aside his bronze dagger and drew the oilskin bag from his belt. He bent over the great circle and poured the last of the stone dust into the channels he'd burned into the earth. When he was done the ritual symbols glowed with latent power.

It was time. The necromancer tossed the bag aside and stepped into the centre of the circle. He felt each tiny tremor of energy in the web he'd created – a net of sorcerous power that he merely had to speak the proper phrases and draw tight over the plain.

Nagash looked out across the open ground. Skeletal figures waited in the darkness, silent and patient as death itself; the hetman stood among them, his rune-sword glinting balefully.

Clenching his fists, Nagash threw back his head and began to chant, spitting the arcane words into the sky. The arcane symbols within the ritual circle blazed with light, and the bruised clouds recoiled overhead, receding in every direction as the power of the necromancer's invocation spread in a great wave across the barrow plain.

Power flowed in a torrent from Nagash's body, racing across the fields and sinking like claws into the hundreds of barrow mounds. The energies sought out every corpse, burrowing into rotting flesh and yellowing bones and stirring up the ghosts of old memories buried within. The spell was attuned to the worst passions of the human soul: anger, violence, jealousy and hate, and it lent those memories a semblance of life.

Bodies trembled. Limbs twitched. Dead hands clenched, scattering dust from decayed joints. Pitiless flames burned in the depths of old, dead eyes.

Nagash felt them stir, hundreds of them, caught within the strands of his sorcerous web. Ragged lips pulled back in a triumphant snarl. *'Come forth!'* he shouted into the tumult. *'Your master commands it!'*

Sealed up in their earthen barrows, the dead heard Nagash's command, and they obeyed.

Hands clawed at muddy earth, or tore at wooden boards. The earthen surfaces of the barrow mounds rippled and heaved. Flashes of lightning silhouetted the stark outlines of skeletal figures dragging themselves free from their graves.

Silent figures shambled out of the stormy night, drawn by Nagash's command. When the southern barrows had been emptied, and a horde of more than a thousand skeletons stood at his back, the Undying King stepped from the glowing circle and ordered his army to advance.

THE UNDEAD HORDE marched northwards, growing in size as it went. Keepers and acolytes who'd panicked and lost their bearings in the storm were the first to die, their terrified screams rising and then quickly vanishing amid the howling wind. The revenants let the bloodied corpses fall where they were slain and continued onwards, towards the temple fortress to the north. Within minutes the mutilated bodies began to twitch, preparing to join the implacable advance.

The lookouts had all retreated into the safety of the fortress the moment the storm had broken, so there was no one to witness the emptying of the sacred barrows. It was only when the survivors of the slaughtered patrols came stumbling out of the darkness that the rest of the order became aware of the doom that approached. Concealing his fear, the High Keeper ordered his brethren to the armoury, and them commanded that the ancient alarm-horns to be sounded, summoning aid from the villages to the north-east. The great horns had not been blown for hundreds of years, and only two out of the dozen instruments still worked. The urgent, wailing notes sounded for more than an hour, rising and falling with the wind. The hetmen nearest the fortress heard the call, but their warriors refused to leave their families and brave the fury of the storm. When dawn came, they would march, but until then the Keepers would have to fend for themselves.

Believing that reinforcements would soon arrive, the Keepers emptied the armoury and barricaded the southern gates. Lookouts were ordered out onto the walls, but there was little to see in the darkness and the rain until the walking dead were almost upon them.

The men guarding the gates heard the first shouts of terror from the acolytes atop the walls, and then, moments later came the eerie sound of fingers scratching against the wood. One of the Keepers, hoping to encourage the others, laughed at the pitiful noise.

At once, the scratching fell silent. The men held their breaths, hands tightening around the unfamiliar grips of their weapons. A young voice up on the wall was babbling in fright, begging for the Burning God to save them.

And then the Keepers felt an invisible wave of power wash over them, and the southern gates began to rot before their very eyes. Iron-hard planks cracked and splintered, filling the corridors with clouds of dust and snuffing out the torches. And then the scratching began again, louder and more insistent, followed by the sound of rending wood.

Within seconds, pairs of flickering, greenish fires shone out of the gloom. Claw-like fingers raked across the Keepers' wooden barricades. Men screamed and called out to their god for aid, while those in front who had no way to escape hefted their weapons and threw themselves at their foes. Bronze and stone blades hacked and stabbed. Ancient bones cracked and splintered, and blood spattered across the walls.

The Keepers of the Mountain were no cowards. Though unused to battle, they stood their ground and defended the fortress with strength and determination. The gateways limited the number of enemies that could be brought to bear against them at any one time, and for a while they managed to hold the invaders at bay. Some of the senior Keepers arrived with reliquaries of god-stone, and tried to hold back the undead by force of will. At some of the gates they were successful, holding the corpses fast so that their brethren could strike them down.

Yet the enemy was implacable. They knew no fear, nor pain, nor fatigue. When their legs were smashed, they dragged themselves across the floor and grabbed at the Keepers' legs. When their arms were torn off they snapped at the Keepers' flesh with their broken teeth.

Worst of all, every brother who fell rose up and joined their ranks. Before long, the Keepers found themselves fighting against the savaged corpses of men whom they'd known for years or even decades. It was too much for any sane mind to take.

At one gate after another, exhausted Keepers were overwhelmed, and resistance began to collapse. Acolytes fled, shrieking in terror, to the deepest parts of the fortress. They hid themselves in wooden chests, in dry cisterns and bins of dusty grain, trembling and weeping and whispering prayers for their deliverance right up to the moment that bony hands seized them and dragged them to their doom.

THE MAIN GATE on the temple's south face was the last to fall. Most of the order's senior priests were marshalled there, aiding in its defence, and they had already thrown back three successive assaults. They had learned enough from the last few attacks to try a different strategy: instead of hurling their energies at the army en masse and trying to halt it in its tracks, the priests were focusing their will on isolated elements, attempting to seize control and turn them against the rest of the undead horde. Though Nagash's force of will far eclipsed any of the individual priests, he found it difficult to control his army and resist a score of individual attacks simultaneously, and the cursed priests were starting to inflict significant damage.

A cheer went up from the priests as the third assault foundered. Piles of shattered corpses clogged the gateway, and the stink of blood and spilled entrails hung heavy in the air. The defenders had paid dearly since the gate had fallen, but they'd learned hard lessons since the first assault began. More barricades had been erected to break up the undead advance, and the priests had organised themselves to operate in three groups. One group fought while the second performed the grim task of destroying the corpses of their brothers who fell in battle, so that they could not be turned against them. The third group rested and tended the wounded, or formed a new set of barricades for the defenders to withdraw behind. It was a potent and effective defence; so long as they kept their heads, they could hold the gate almost indefinitely.

Nagash struck them just as the defenders were rotating groups. All at once, the piles of old bones glowed a furious green and then exploded, filling the tunnel with jagged splinters. Men fell screaming, their bodies raked by the needle-like fragments, and the rest reeled back in shock. Before they could recover, Nagash himself burst through the gate, his hideous body wreathed in sorcerous flame. He spat words of terrible power, and darts of fire shot from his fingertips – where they struck, men collapsed in agony, their bodies consumed from within. Behind the necromancer came his retinue of ancient warriors. The undead warlord stepped past Nagash and began slaughtering the stunned priests with his rune-sword.

The surviving defenders recovered quickly, retreating back to another set of barricades and forming another, smaller defensive line. Nagash caught a glimpse of the High Priest and his senior servants clustered behind the barricade, along with perhaps a few score acolytes and holy men. They had been driven back almost the length of the tunnel; the north gate stood only ten yards behind them.

Nagash's hands clenched in anticipation. Teeth bared in a feral snarl, he advanced on the defenders.

The acolytes and the younger priests gaped in terror at his approach, their pale faces lit by the greenish flames wreathing the necromancer's body. Skeletons poured into the tunnel behind Nagash, filling it with the dry clatter of bones.

The High Priest saw his opportunity. Here was the chance to stop the attack in its tracks, if the glowing abomination could be destroyed! His old voice rang with authority as he shouted exhortations to the elders, and at once they linked their voices in a sacred chant. The rest of the defenders took heart from this, standing shoulder to shoulder and raising their weapons once more as the enemy approached.

Nagash flung out his hand and spat an angry invocation. A blast of green fire sped down the tunnel – and the priests responded, focusing their energies in a crude counter-spell. The bolt disintegrated a few feet from the terrified defenders, leaving them unharmed.

Smiling, Nagash hurled another bolt. Then another. Cold, mocking laughter echoed down the tunnel.

The priests deflected the second blow, and the third, but each one seemed to get a bit closer before breaking apart. A fourth bolt came close enough to singe the robes of the defenders. Lines of strain appeared on the faces of the holy men as they tried to withstand the onslaught.

A fifth blast was deflected. Then a sixth. Thunder reverberated in the confined space, deafening human ears. The seventh blast broke up with a blinding flash, close enough to cause the defenders' robes to smoulder. One of the senior priests slumped silently to the ground, blood streaming from his nose, eyes and ears.

The eighth blast slew five acolytes before the rest of its energy was dissipated. Another senior priest collapsed with a groan, clutching at his chest. The defenders' lines wavered, and then an acolyte, his mind overwhelmed by horror, hurled himself at the oncoming skeletons with a wordless shriek of terror and rage. Another acolyte succumbed, then another, and then the defenders' lines broke as they launched a last, desperate charge into the face of certain death.

Nagash blasted a charging acolyte point-blank, scattering burning body parts back down the tunnel towards the High Priest. The elders of the order began to waver, their minds strained to the breaking point by the contest of power. His laughter took on a harsher, wilder edge as he hurled a final bolt, straight at the High Priest's face.

The holy men summoned the last of their strength, and the bolt dissipated with a thunderous crash less than a foot from where they stood. The concussion hurled men's bodies against the tunnel walls, breaking old bones and crushing skulls. Others were slain instantly by the sudden flash of heat, their bodies charred beyond recognition.

Only the High Priest survived, his body largely shielded from the blast by the men in front of him. His robes smouldering, the old man tried to crawl backwards, away from the necromancer.

Nagash loomed over the barbarian, bending low and seizing him by his wrinkled neck. He pulled the old man up until their faces were scant inches apart. The High Priest stared into the necromancer's burning eyes and saw in them the death of all living things. Nagash's fist clenched; old bone snapped, and the High Priest's head lolled to one side. The barbarian's feet thrashed spasmodically for several seconds more, then went still.

Slowly, Nagash lowered the old man's body until his feet touched the stone floor. He released his grip, and the High Priest remained upright. Green flames flickered in the depths of his glazed eyes. Gripped by the necromancer's will, the old man sank to his knees, then reached up with wrinkled hands and gripped the golden circlet set upon his head. Haltingly, as though some part of the old priest's soul still struggled within the broken frame, the corpse removed the circlet and offered it to Nagash.

The necromancer took the symbol of the order in his bony hands, and, grinning cruelly, he twisted the soft gold until the setting holding the *abn-i-khat* burst apart. Nagash plucked the burning stone from the circlet, and tossed the mangled gold band aside.

THE STORM RAGED through the night and into the dawn of the next day, finally spending the last of its strength well past daybreak. As soon as the winds had dropped off, the hetmen of the nearby villages summoned their warriors and set off as quickly as they could down the muddy tracks towards the temple fortress.

When they arrived, the great fortress was silent and still. The gates along the north face were shut and locked, and no amount of shouting would bring one of the Keepers out onto the wall. Finally, one of the hetmen ordered runners to fetch a tall ladder from his village, and they sent a young lad scampering up to the top of the wall to see what he could find.

The warriors waited in silence as the boy disappeared from sight. The minutes stretched, one after another, and the hetmen exchanged nervous glances. After half an hour, they knew something had gone terribly wrong.

Finally, the main gate swung open. The boy appeared, trembling and pale. No amount of questions, cajoling or threats could make him relate what he'd seen inside, and nothing on earth could get him to go back in again.

Weapons ready, the hetmen led their troops into the fortress. At once, they saw that a terrible battle had raged inside the walls. Blood was splashed on the walls and the floors, and the stench of death hung heavy in the air. A mere ten yards from the north gate, one of the hetmen let out a cry of dismay and picked up a mangled band of gold. The other village leaders recognised it at once. If the God's Eye had been taken, it meant that the High Keeper and the order had been destroyed.

And yet, no matter how hard they looked, the villagers found no bodies inside the temple fortress. None at all.

—◄ ELEVEN ►—

Necessary Sacrifices

*Lahmia, The City of the Dawn, in the 76th year of
Khsar the Faceless
(-1598 Imperial Reckoning)*

UBAID BOWED HIS tattooed head at the queen's
approach. 'All is in readiness, great one,' he said, as
though he were speaking of nothing more untoward
than a palace feast.

Neferata acknowledged the vizier with a nod. It
was fast approaching midnight; the audience with
Xia Ha Feng had lasted much longer than she'd
expected, but it had been important not to appear
rude and hasten away too early. She needed the
august personage to be receptive to her overtures, to
believe that he could win her confidence and thus
gain a lever to use against the king. So long as he

believed that he had power over her, she was free to lay the trap that would ultimately ensnare him – and possibly the whole Eastern Empire as well.

A thin line of warm light shone beneath the door to the sanctum. Ubaid had been busy for hours, preparing for the ritual. The grand vizier was the only member of the cabal that she permitted into the chamber; the rest were now required to pay their respects and receive their draught of elixir in the funereal confines of the Hall of Regretful Sorrows. She'd chosen the location for the express reason that it was the least used of the queen's three audience chambers – and also because she wanted Lamashizzar and his former allies to never forget that she alone now stood between them and the realm of the dead.

Lamashizzar, of course, was furious at the thought. She knew that it was dangerous to provoke him in such petty ways; he lacked ambition, but he could be ruthless when his pride was offended. Perhaps, in time, she would release him from the obligation, but right now he needed to kneel before her and acknowledge her authority. He needed to be humbled. He needed to know what it was like to live at the whim of another. It was the one concession to her feelings that she allowed herself to make.

For the most part, she had been careful not to abuse her power. For all their reputation for decadence, in some ways the people of Lahmia were just as hidebound as other Nehekharans. None outside the palace knew that she no longer confined herself to the Women's Palace, and none other than the members of the cabal knew that the city was ruled by anyone other than its king.

Neferata intended it to remain that way. Nagash might have believed that he could rule as an Undying King in Khemri without tempting the wrath of the other great cities, but she knew better. Now that she had access to her children once more, she had plans to ensure that, to all outward purposes, the ruling dynasty would continue as before. When her son Lamasu reached marriageable age, she would find him a proper wife, and then it would be time for Lamashizzar to join his ancestors in the afterlife. Naturally she, as the dutiful wife, would appear to drink from the poisoned cup and join him in his journey to the underworld, and to all intents and purposes she would be dead and gone.

The trick would be to convince the other members of the cabal to engineer their own deaths as well. Already their long lives – and miraculous vitality – were giving rise to unwelcome rumours both at court and even as far away as neighbouring Lybaras. According to Lamashizzar's spies, Queen Khalida had hinted at suspicions of her own on more than one occasion, though she'd never come out and publicly accused her royal cousins of any unnatural dealings.

Neferata had tried to reach out to Khalida on more than one occasion, hoping to use their past friendship to build strong ties between the two cities, but so far the Lybaran queen had found compelling reasons not to accept any of her cousin's invitations to court.

At some point she would also have to decide what to do about Arkhan. For now, his knowledge of Nagash's sorcery still outweighed the risk of keeping him alive, but that balance was shifting fast. She was starting to grasp the finer nuances of the Usurper's incantations. Soon she would allow W'soran to begin studying the more esoteric aspects of Nagash's necromantic lore, using it to both control him and expand her own base of knowledge through his studies. Once that was underway, Arkhan would only be useful for his sword arm and his ability to procure victims for the cabal, two functions that she was certain Abhorash and Ushoran could perform just as well. It had been pathetically easy to win over the monster's loyalty, though it had required her to open herself to Arkhan far more than she would have liked. Neferata was already looking forward to the day that she could order Abhorash to put an end to the whole tiresome business.

The queen pushed open the sanctum door and hastened within, mindful of the sands hissing through the hourglass. Ubaid had laid out the ritual implements and lit the incense in preparation for the incantation. The sacrifice had likewise been prepared and awaited her in the centre of the circle. His wounds had been cleaned and he'd been given a potion that would banish his fatigue and leave him awake and alert for the ceremony to come.

He was part of an experiment that Neferata was conducting in an attempt to better refine the outcome of Nagash's ritual. Arkhan had found him amid the squalid refugee districts west of the city: a young man, relatively fit and healthy enough to survive a full week of suffering. The subject was chained to an iron ring that had been set in the ceiling at the centre of the ritual circle, and the dark stone around his toes was layered with thick spatters of blood. The incisions that covered his body in precise, intricate patterns had been inflicted according to the diagrams provided in Nagash's tomes, and represented the culmination of the torturer's art. The wounds left every nerve in the victim's body throbbing and raw, but the injuries themselves were not serious enough to kill.

According to the necromancer's experiments, no victim had survived the nightmare of constant pain for more than eight days. By Neferata's estimation, at seven days the victim's energies would be at their peak; past that point they would start to ebb as the body began to fail.

Now would come the true test. Neferata crossed to the worktable at the edge of the circle. The razor-edged torture knives had been scrupulously cleaned and set aside on a clean linen cloth. In their place, Ubaid had set out the curved sacrificial blade, the golden bowl and the jewel-encrusted goblet that she used to drink the first draught of the elixir. The heavy tome containing the great ritual lay open to the proper page at the table's edge, but she hardly spared it a glance. She'd learned the necessary phrases and gestures by heart a long time ago.

Neferata breathed deeply, drinking in the delicate incense that permeated the room. She reached down and touched the blade of the sacrificial knife; the sharpened bronze was cold to the touch. The queen smiled, tracing a fingertip along the narrow, wooden hilt, then picked it up. It felt light and comfortable in her hand.

She entered the circle with care, and sought the young man's eyes. His gaze was fixed upon her, both terrified and hopeful all at once. A faint groan escaped his lacerated lips.

The queen held him with her gaze. Arkhan had taught her to draw upon the power inherent in the elixir. She used it now, and watched a spark of longing catch fire in his eyes. He drew in a deep, shuddering breath, and from the expression that crossed his tortured face, she knew that the agony wracking his body had been transformed into something far sharper, far sweeter and much more agonising than anything he'd felt before. How she had made him suffer in the last few days of his life. And yet he *loved* her, with all his heart and soul. He ached for her, through and through.

Smiling, Neferata placed the knife in her belt, and drew so close to him that she could feel his laboured breathing against her cheek. She stretched, almost languidly, reaching up to undo the chains that held his wrists. He staggered as the bonds were released, yet he did not fall. Her gaze held him upright.

Her smile broadened. 'You have pleased me,' she told him, and the words sent shudders through his frame. 'Now there is one last thing you must do, and then, my sweet, you will be with me forever.' She drew out the knife. 'Will you do this for me?

His mouth worked. Broken sounds issued forth, until tears of frustration gleamed at the corners of his eyes. Finally, he managed a shaky nod.

'I knew you wouldn't fail me,' she said softly. 'Take this,' she said, and held out the knife.

The young man reached out a trembling hand and grasped the gleaming blade. 'Good,' Neferata whispered. 'Wait here.'

She retreated to the edge of the circle. The hour had come. Ubaid appeared at her side, silent and ready.

Neferata raised her hands. Her eyes had never left her victim's. 'Now,' she told him, 'Repeat after me.'

And so she began to chant, slowly and purposefully, and the man in the centre of the circle joined in. She drew him into the ritual, weaving his pain and passion into the incantation, and he surrendered himself to it willingly, eagerly. At that moment, he wanted to give her everything her heart desired.

The incantation built slowly and steadily. Minutes passed into hours, until time lost all meaning. The climax, when it came, took both of them by surprise.

'Now!' she gasped. 'The knife!' Neferata raised a trembling finger to her throat, right over the pulsing artery. 'Give me your heart's blood!'

A beatific smile crossed the young man's scarred face. He brought the knife to his throat and sliced it open with a single, graceful motion. Ubaid was beside him at once, the golden bowl held in his upraised hands.

The man stood there, bleeding his life away, his face transported in ecstasy. She held him with her gaze until his heart ceased to beat, and his lifeless body collapsed to the stone floor.

Neferata let out a long, shuddering breath. Her nerves were afire. She reached for the golden goblet as Ubaid rose from the victim's corpse and brought her the brimming, steaming bowl.

Slowly, carefully, the grand vizier poured a measure of blood into the gleaming cup. Neferata inhaled the heady scent. It was sweeter than any fragrance she'd ever smelled before.

Suddenly, there came a sound in the corridor outside the sanctum. It sounded to Neferata like the scuff of sandal leather across stone. Ubaid frowned, and carefully set the sacrificial bowl upon the floor. The dagger he drew from his belt was anything but light and utilitarian. He circled around the bowl and moved quietly towards the closed door.

Neferata turned to watch him go. Something was wrong. She thought of Lamashizzar, and felt a sudden sense of foreboding.

The goblet was warm in her hands. She stared down at the still surface of the elixir, sensing the power seething in its depths. Neferata raised the cup to her lips and drank deep. The taste was painfully bitter, yet it filled her with a power the likes of which she had never known before.

Ubaid was struggling with someone at the door. Was it Lamashizzar? She could not tell, and at that moment, she did not care. Neferata let out a throaty chuckle. 'Stand aside,' she said to Ubaid. 'Let him pass.' Whoever it was, he would bow at her feet and beg her forgiveness for the unwelcome intrusion.

The grand vizier retreated from the doorway, and a lone figure staggered into the room. It took her a moment to recognise who it was.

'Arkhan?' she asked. She could smell the stink of blood on his robes. 'What is the meaning of this?'

The immortal lurched towards her. As he stepped further into the light, she could see the bloody stubs of arrow shafts jutting from his shoulder and side. His ghastly face was paler than usual, and the iron sword she'd given him was held in his hand. Its edge was dark with dried blood.

'The king is moving against you,' Arkhan croaked. He sounded as though he was at the very limits of his strength. 'Lamashizzar sent Adio and Khenti to murder me on the trade road. He means to kill you as well.'

Neferata shook her head. Arkhan wasn't making sense. She laughed softly, drunk with sudden power – and then a cold spike of pain lanced through her heart.

The queen had time for a single, startled gasp before the poison took hold and dragged her down into darkness.

* * *

ARKHAN WATCHED IN horror as Neferata collapsed. The golden goblet tumbled from her hand, spilling the last, thick dregs of elixir at her feet. He lurched towards her, his body stiff and clumsy from his wounds. 'Help me!' he snarled at the grand vizier as he collapsed to his knees beside the queen.

'There is nothing to be done,' Ubaid replied in a dead voice.

Neferata lay upon her side, head resting on one out-flung arm. Her skin was cold to the touch. Arkhan rested his fingertips against her slender throat, but could not feel the pulse of her heart. He brought his cheek close to her lips. There was barely a whisper of breath.

The immortal's gaze went to the dented goblet. There were scarlet drops of elixir beading its rim. As he watched, they turned dull red, then black. Realisation sank into him like a knife. It was one thing to murder a man on the trade road and leave his body in the ditch; killing a queen was something altogether more risky. Her body would be handled by the priests of the mortuary cult, and viewed by thousands of grieving citizens. Her death would have to appear natural.

'This cannot be,' Arkhan snarled. 'No poison in all Nehekhara could overcome Nagash's elixir.'

'It is the venom of the sphinx, a poison both natural and supernatural,' Ubaid said. 'Even before the fall of Mahrak it was vanishingly rare. The gods alone know how Lamashizzar obtained it.' The grand vizier approached the queen. His expression was inscrutable as he studied Neferata's still form. 'According to the old texts, the venom attacks the blood, rendering it lifeless. Death is instantaneous.' He shook his head. 'It's a wonder that the queen is alive at all.'

Something in Ubaid's dispassionate voice kindled a black rage in Arkhan's heart. He surged to his feet, seizing the grand vizier by the throat. The immortal could feel the last vestiges of elixir boiling in his veins. Dimly, he was aware that Ubaid still held a knife in his hand, but the immortal scarcely cared. The point of his own sword was scant inches from Ubaid's belly.

'Why?' Arkhan growled.

The grand vizier glowered at the immortal, but his expression was bleak. 'Because, like Abhorash, I serve the throne,' he replied. 'Lamashizzar is weak and feckless, but Lahmia has survived such rulers before.' Ubaid squirmed a little in Arkhan's grasp. His voice rose in frustration. 'The queen did not keep her word. Instead of advising the king, she usurped his power entirely. It's not right–'

Arkhan's hand tightened around Ubaid's throat. 'She thinks only of this city! Lahmia will prosper under her rule! And for this, you *betray* her?'

Ubaid's eyes widened in anger. 'Who are you to judge me?' he hissed. 'Arkhan the Black, who betrayed his own king in favour of the Usurper, then even turned upon Nagash when it suited your purposes. What do you know of loyalty, or devotion?' He spread his arms. 'Kill me, if you wish, but you may not presume to pass judgement on me.'

Arkhan's grip tightened on the hilt of his sword. His mind whirled. Snarling in disgust, he turned and shoved the grand vizier towards the door. Ubaid staggered a dozen paces, an uncomprehending look on his face.

'I will leave it up to the queen to decide your fate,' Arkhan said coldly. 'Now go.'

Ubaid shook his head. The snake tattoo on his neck seemed to slither in the shifting light. 'Don't you understand? The queen will never wake. The elixir's power may slow the venom for a time, but it's just a matter of hours now. Days at the most.'

'*I said get out!*' Arkhan roared, and took a step towards Ubaid. The grand vizier saw the murderous look in the immortal's eyes, and his nerve finally deserted him. Tucking his knife back into his belt, he fled the room with as much dignity as he could muster.

Arkhan listened to the grand vizier's footsteps retreat down the corridor. He swayed on his feet. I must be out of my mind, he thought. How did I let Neferata do this to me?

He spun on his heel, surveying the chamber. Ubaid would go back to the king and report what had happened, and the king would swoop in like a hawk to seize the queen's body and reclaim Nagash's tomes. There was no time to waste.

With a trembling hand, Arkhan slid his iron blade back into its scabbard, and limped over to the golden bowl. The immortal knelt, placed his hands against the bowl's curved surface, and raised it to his lips. The liquid inside was still warm and fragrant.

He drank it all; it was far more than he needed, filling his innards to bursting, but he was careful not to waste a single drop. Stolen vigour seethed through his veins. The power of the elixir staggered him; it was nearly as powerful as Nagash's own, and far sweeter. Grinning mirthlessly, he plucked the remaining arrow stubs from his torso and cast them aside.

The immortal searched through the room until he found a large, linen sack, then filled it with a half-dozen carefully selected tomes. If the elixir was potent enough to resist the effects of the sphinx's poison, then perhaps there was a chance to defeat it entirely. First, however, he needed a place where he could work in relative safety. At the moment, only one option seemed open to him.

Arkhan knelt carefully and took the queen in his arms. Her body was already stiffening, as though in death, and felt as light and brittle as old paper. Once again, the immortal was struck by the sheer folly of what he was doing. He ought to be fleeing the city with as many of Nagash's books as he could carry. Once on the Golden Plain he could escape Lamashizzar's wrath with ease.

The immortal looked down at the queen's unconscious form and was reminded once again of Neferem, another daughter of Lahmia who was a pawn of kings and suffered for centuries while he stood by and watched.

Neferata didn't have to set you free, he reminded himself.

Cursing under his breath, Arkhan carried the queen from the room. With luck, he could make it to the Women's Palace before the king realised that she still lived.

It APPEARED THAT King Lamashizzar hadn't entertained the possibility that his wife might survive the poisoned cup. There were no palace guards roaming the corridors as Arkhan hastened to the southern edge of the palace. Just to be safe, he crossed into the Women's Palace via the rarely used Hall of Regretful Sorrows. The immortal fought down a sense of grim foreboding as he bore the queen's body past the great marble bier where the queens of Lahmia had been laid in state for millennia.

The Women's Palace was echoing and empty. For more than a century, the sprawling sanctuary housed only Neferata herself, along with the bare minimum of servants and handmaidens that protocol demanded the king provide. And yet his presence in the dusty halls was detected almost at once. Within minutes, the immortal found himself surrounded on all sides by pale, outraged women, some of whom were armed with small, wicked-looking knives. Had he been alone, he had no doubt that they would have set upon him like a pride of angry lionesses. Only the sight of the queen's motionless corpse held them at bay. They paced alongside him in mute shock for close to an hour while he wandered aimlessly through the sprawling palace.

Finally, his patience stretched to the breaking point, he turned to the women and asked where the queen's bedchamber lay. They stared at him as though he were mad – all but one young woman, dressed in fine robes, who stepped forward and silently beckoned for him to follow.

Her name was Aiyah. Much later, Arkhan learned she had served Princess Khalida as one of her hand-maidens during the last year she'd lived at the palace. Despite her youth, she was calm and controlled in the face of catastrophe. She led Arkhan to the queen's chambers, then banished the crowd of servants to the outer corridor while the immortal laid out Neferata's body on the bed. The handmaiden returned as the immortal was unpacking Nagash's tomes, and waited quietly by the door. No protests, no tedious questions or hysterics. She simply waited, patient and composed, ready to serve the queen in whatever capacity she could. Arkhan's first instinct was to dismiss her, but the more he considered the difficulties of trying to work inside the confines of the sanctuary, the more he had to admit that he was going to need her help.

He knew that it wouldn't be very long before Lamashizzar learned where he'd taken the queen: hours, perhaps a day at most. So Arkhan told the handmaiden a partial truth – that the king had conspired to poison Neferata because he resented her claims to equality. Aiyah accepted the story without comment while the immortal took ink and brushes and began to inscribe out a ritual circle on the bed-chamber floor. At some point during the process, the handmaiden slipped quietly from the room again, and he knew that his tale was winging its way through the Women's Palace. Arkhan reckoned that once the story was known, the palace servants would block any attempt by Lamashizzar to enter the sanctuary in search of the queen. As it was, the palace guard would baulk at any command to enter the forbidden halls of the palace; even though the palace was technically open now, hundreds of years of tradition carried a weight that was very difficult to overcome. That left only the king's fellow conspirators, and Arkhan was certain he could deal with any of them save for Abhorash – if the king's champion was even involved. He still had no idea how deep the conspiracy went.

The rest of that first night was spent sitting vigil at the queen's side and poring through the Usurper's tomes in search of an incantation or ritual that might banish the poison from the queen's blood. Hours passed, and Neferata began to turn pale. Her breath was still very faint, and only Arkhan's preternatural senses allowed him to hear a heartbeat. So far, the elixir was holding the poison at bay, but she was clearly weakening. As dawn began to break, far out to sea, Arkhan was no closer to finding a solution. He had Aiyah draw the curtains tight across the tall windows and continued his search. By the time night fell once more, he still had nothing to show for his efforts, and the queen's condition was becoming steadily worse.

Growing desperate, Arkhan set the books aside and placed the queen's body inside the ritual circle. Aiyah watched the immortal spread open three magical tomes on the floor by the circle, then gather up the inkpot and horsehair brush once more.

'Undress her,' he said to the handmaiden, and then began riffling through the pages of the three books.

The young woman hesitated. 'What do you intend to do?' she asked coolly.

Arkhan shot the handmaiden a hard stare. 'She will need help to overcome the poison in her veins,' he said. 'So far, her… blood is strong enough to at least slow the venom's progress.' He paused, studying a detailed drawing of a human figure on one yellowed page. After a moment he shook his head and continued his search. 'So I must find a way to increase her vigour enough to overcome it.'

The handmaiden took a step towards the circle and frowned. Her dark eyes lingered on the strange markings painted on the floor. 'I could send for an apothecary,' she offered. 'The priestesses of Neru have tended to the health of the royal line for centuries. They have experience with poisons–'

'If I thought there was an herb or potion that could save her, I would have carried her to the temple myself,' Arkhan snapped.

Aiyah took a deep breath. 'But this,' she began. 'What you're doing–'

'What I am doing is trying to save your queen,' the immortal said. He paused in his search, studied another image, and nodded to himself. Arkhan removed the inkpot's ceramic stopper. 'The longer we wait, the weaker she becomes,' he told her.

The handmaiden hesitated a moment more, brows knitted in consternation, before making her decision. She knelt carefully within the circle and began to deftly pull away Neferata's robes.

Arkhan laid out the runes with care. The work took hours, winding in intricate ribbons from Neferata's scalp to her toes. The immortal was conscious of each minute slipping away; it seemed to him that her skin was growing steadily cooler beneath his touch.

It was well past the hour of the dead by the time the preparations were complete. Arkhan stood and pressed the book into Aiyah's, hands. 'Go and stand at the edge of the circle, by her feet,' he said. 'When I begin, repeat the words as I say them. They are marked on the page there.'

Aiyah looked dubious, but accepted the tome nonetheless. 'Is that all?'

'Do you wish the queen to live?' he asked.

'Of course!'

'Then make that uppermost in your mind,' Arkhan told her. 'Think of nothing else. With luck, it will be enough.'

Arkhan took his place on the opposite side of the circle. Standing at the head of the queen, he spread his arms and began to chant.

The ritual was little different from the incantation of reaping that was used to create Nagash's elixir. He had made several modifications to the arrangement of the runes to account for the elixir already present in her body. He wasn't interested in transmutation so much as enhancing what was already there. In theory, the problem seemed simple enough.

Drawing on the surfeit of elixir filling his body, Arkhan poured a steady stream of power into the incantation. At once the air grew heavy above the circle, and he saw the queen's body begin to tremble. Tiny wisps of steam curled from the sigils painted on her skin.

The immortal felt the elixir boil inside him and directed the released energy into the arcane words rolling from his lips. And, within the circle, Neferata's body suddenly spasmed. Her back arched painfully, arms splayed and chest thrust skyward. Arkhan could see the tendons in her neck and along the backs of her hands grow taut as bowstrings; her mouth gaped, emitting a billowing gout of black vapour.

Arkhan watched as the queen's skin began to change. Her rich, brown skin, already pale, began to lose all trace of colour, taking on the cold tone of bleached linen or alabaster. He stopped the incantation abruptly, fearing that he might already be too late. The backlash of forces tore through him; he staggered, his hand going to his chest as invisible knives tore through his vitals. A thin trickle of ichor ran down his chin.

The immortal sank slowly to his knees. Neferata's body had gone limp again, shrouded in tendrils of steam. The runes painted on her skin had already begun to fade, running together in dark blue threads that formed pools on the stone floor. Aiyah sank to her knees, her eyes wide with shock. She crawled gingerly into the circle and laid a trembling hand against Neferata's flank. The handmaiden jerked her fingers away as though stung.

'She's cold,' Aiyah said. 'Colder than the desert night. What happened? What have you done?'

Arkhan stared at the queen's near-lifeless form. The runes had all but melted away in the heat that had radiated from her skin. Beneath the bluish tinge of the ink, he could see that her veins had turned black at her temples and throat.

The immortal rubbed the back of a hand across his lips. It came away slick with a film of ichor. Anger and revulsion roiled in his chest. What horror had Lamashizzar unleashed?

'I don't know,' Arkhan said in a hollow voice.

FIVE MORE DAYS went by. Arkhan never relented, searching through Nagash's books again and again for something he could use to defeat the sphinx's venom. The queen scarcely breathed now; her flesh was cold and stiff as marble. Her heart still beat, stubbornly driving the elixir through her veins, but it had grown inexorably weaker with each passing night. Every ritual he attempted, no matter how great or small, only seemed to worsen her condition. It seemed that the sphinx's deadly venom had somehow bonded with Neferata's ensorcelled blood, transforming it from within. Any attempt to increase the elixir's vigour empowered the poison as well.

Now, as the seventh night fell upon the city, Arkhan believed he knew the answer. He sat at Neferata's writing desk and studied the words and symbols of the incantation one last time, checking carefully to ensure he'd made no errors. Satisfied, he took the large sheet of paper and set it on the floor at the edge of the circle. Next, he laid out the tools for the ritual with care, and then went to kneel at the queen's side. The immortal took her limp body in his arms and carried Neferata to her bed. He laid her body gently upon the silken sheets, and then returned to the freshly-drawn ritual he'd made. Arkhan took off his sword belt, and then let his robes fall to the floor. He turned to Aiyah and spread his arms.

'Follow the diagrams exactly,' he said to her. 'The symbols and their positions are crucial, or the energies will not conduct properly.'

The handmaiden nodded, but Arkhan could see the weariness and apprehension in her eyes. She had laboured every bit as hard as he had, yet without the benefits of the elixir to sustain her. When she wasn't participating in Arkhan's rituals she was trying to glean information about Lamashizzar and the other members of the cabal. Despite her best efforts, however, there was no way to find out who had chosen to side with the king in the wake of Neferata's disappearance. All that could be learned was that the king was incommunicado, conferring with his advisors. Arkhan knew he was simply waiting for news that the queen had succumbed at last. With luck, the king's strategy could be used against him. He had ceded the initiative to Neferata, if only she could make use of it.

This was their last chance. If this ritual failed, Arkhan was certain that the queen would not last until the dawn.

Aiyah stepped forward, brush and inkpot in hand. She studied the paper carefully for a moment, then dipped the brush in the inkpot and went to work. Her brushstrokes were tentative at first, but her confidence increased steadily as the hours went by and the ribbons of arcane symbols wove their way along Arkhan's skin. Still, it was close to dawn by the time the last symbols were inscribed upon the immortal's flesh.

'Well done,' Arkhan said, and hoped it was true. There was no way he could tell for certain. 'Now, quickly, take your place at the circle. There is very little time left.'

The immortal went and stood in the centre of the circle. 'No matter what happens to me, do not falter,' he told the handmaiden. 'Complete the incantation, no matter what. Do you understand?'

Aiyah nodded. Her eyes were now wide with fear.

'Then let us begin,' he said gravely. 'We are almost out of time.'

As before, they chanted the incantation together. At once, the immortal felt his veins begin to burn as the ritual tapped into his remaining reserves of elixir. But rather than draw out the stolen power, this ritual was meant to shape it instead, transforming it into a tool designed for a very specific purpose. Arkhan gritted his teeth as stabbing pains shot through his torso and limbs. His vision began to dissolve into a reddish fog, and a hollow roaring filled his ears. His skin drew painfully tight, until he thought it would split apart, but through it all, his chant never faltered. He'd suffered far worse in the past.

Time lost all meaning for the immortal. The incantation went on forever, and the agony only grew worse, until it was as boundless as the desert itself. Arkhan's voice was little more than a ragged howl of pain, but he still spat out the words that kept the incantation going. His entire body was afire; a small part of his mind was certain that his flesh and bones were melting in the heat.

An eternity passed. He did not feel the culmination of the ritual when it finally arrived; for him, there was only a shift in the roaring whirlwind that filled his ears, signifying that Aiyah had finished her chant. It took several long moments before she could make him understand anything else.

'Now?' her voice echoed in his skull. It sounded small and far away.

Arkhan tried to see beyond the red mist that filled his vision. He nodded, or at least he thought that he did. 'The... knife...' he gasped. The words sounded impossibly loud.

Aiyah let the page fall from her fingers. Her gaze fell to the small, curved knife at her feet. The edge, honed to a razor's sharpness, gleamed bright in the lamplight. When she tried to speak again, her voice caught in her throat. 'Are – are you certain?'

The immortal responded with a tortured groan that made the handmaiden flinch. 'Do it!' he moaned. His eyes were orbs of dark red, the pupils completely obscured, and yet she could feel the weight of his stare. 'This is… her only hope,' Arkhan continued. 'She is certain… to die… otherwise.'

Aiyah took a deep breath. Swiftly, she bent and took up the knife. It felt terribly heavy in her hand.

She crossed to the bed. But for her unnaturally white skin, the queen might have been sleeping, lost in a deep lotus-dream. Aiyah laid a trembling hand upon the queen's forehead, grimacing at how cold she felt.

'Asaph forgive me,' the handmaiden said faintly. Then she took the knife and sliced open the side of Neferata's throat.

Black liquid, hot and foul-smelling, poured from the wound and spread across the silken sheets. Neferata shuddered faintly, then went deathly still.

'It's done,' the handmaiden said, stepping back from the bed to avoid the rain of droplets pattering on the floor.

'Good,' the immortal replied. He climbed unsteadily to his feet. He beckoned to her. 'Help me. Quickly.'

Aiyah hurried to Arkhan and took his outstretched hand. She led him, stumbling, to the queen's side.

The immortal knelt beside her, leaning in until his face was inches from hers. He nodded. 'Not long now,' he rasped. 'Hand me the blade.'

Aiyah handed over the knife and stepped back, wringing her hands. 'I never imagined there would be so much,' she said, staring in horror at the spreading pool of ichor. 'I've killed her. She's going to die!'

'It must be done,' Arkhan insisted. 'Her blood has been corrupted. Can't you see? We have to remove it, or she is doomed.'

The immortal watched in silence for another minute, watching the flood of ichor slowly ebb away. When it had become no more than a trickle, he took the knife in his left hand and pressed the point into the skin of his right forearm, just behind the wrist. He cut deep, slicing open one of the major veins. There was no pain. All he could feel now was fear.

The knife clanged to the floor. Left hand trembling, he cupped the back of Neferata's head and raised it from the sodden pillow. 'Live, oh queen,' he said, his voice shaking as he pressed the pulsing wound to her pale lips. 'Drink of me, and live.'

Arkhan felt her body tremble as the ichor touched her lips. His skin tingled as her lips brushed the inside of his forearm; they moved against his skin, almost like a kiss, and then she began to drink.

'Yes… yes!' Arkhan breathed. The red mist began to recede. *Drink!*

And she did. Hungrily, greedily, with gathering strength, she drew the liquid from the wound. Her mouth opened, teeth pressing into his flesh. Arkhan clenched his fist. As he watched, the cut in her neck closed up with startling speed.

'It's working!' he gasped. 'Aiyah, do you see? It's working!'

The roaring in his ears was receding. Within seconds he could see clearly again, and the pain had begun to fade. Arkhan's muscles felt loose and weak, and a chill settled into his bones. Neferata still drank from him, her eyes clamped tightly shut.

And then, without warning, her body began to convulse. Arkhan felt the muscles in her neck writhe like serpents. She tore herself from his grasp, her mouth agape and her chin stained dark with fluids. The queen thrashed upon the bed, arms and legs flailing. A cloud of steam boiled up from her throat, followed by a long, terrible howl.

Arkhan watched in horror as the queen's body began to change. Her flesh shrivelled, stretching the skin across her bones, and her lustrous, black hair grew faded and brittle. Neferata's eyes sank into their sockets, and her cheeks turned gaunt, transforming her face into a ghoulish, bestial mask.

Shrieking in agony, Neferata reached for him with one flailing hand. It clawed at the sheets, just inches away, but Arkhan could not bring himself to touch her.

Neferata's screams turned to a choking rattle. She collapsed back upon the bed. Her head turned towards Arkhan, and the immortal saw that her eyes were wide and staring. They were still vivid green, but the pupils were slitted, like those of a cat.

She stared at him for barely a moment, her expression filled with pain, and then all the air went out of her lungs and her body went limp. Arkhan heard Aiyah let out a long, heart-wrenching moan.

Neferata, Daughter of the Moon and Queen of Lahmia, was dead.

⟨ TWELVE ⟩

Apotheosis

*Cripple Peak, in the 76th year of Khsar the Faceless
(-1598 Imperial Reckoning)*

THE SLAUGHTER OF the barbarian priests had been
more than just an act of vengeance on Nagash's part;
it had served a pragmatic purpose as well. The mountain would become the seat of his power, just as the
Black Pyramid had been in Khemri. From here he
would raise the armies that would cast down the
kings of Nehekhara. He envisioned sprawling mines,
foundries, armouries and great laboratories from
which he would continue to master the arts of necromancy. The construction alone would last centuries,
and occupy his undead army both day and night.
Eliminating the priests was necessary to keep them
from interfering in his designs, and to swell the ranks
of his workforce.

Construction began the night after the battle at the fortress temple. The undead rose from their beds across the barrow plain and converged on the south face of the mountain. Guided by Nagash's will, they began constructing the first stage of fortifications around what would be the first of many mine complexes. Within the first month the southern barrows had been dismantled, and the foundation stones hauled up to the mountain to help form the first buildings. Earth and stone excavated from the mountain were used as well, but Nagash knew he would need much more before he could say the great work was well and truly begun. The fortress would take many centuries before it was complete, and much of it would be underground, sheltered from the burning light of the sun.

At the same time, Nagash kept a close watch on the temple fortress. He knew that he hadn't managed to kill every member of the order. At any given time close to a hundred junior priests and acolytes were travelling between the barbarian villages, tending to each of the totem statues and performing the ceremonial duties of the order. Sure enough, almost two months later, a few score of the holy men returned to the fortress and began making it fit for habitation again. That night, he sent a large force to slay them and add their numbers to his own. Nagash especially savoured the irony of using the undead members of the order to slay their younger brethren and deliver them into his hands. After that, no one else attempted to take residence in the great fortress.

Nagash suspected that the superstitious barbarians thought it to be haunted and, in a very real sense, they were right.

Surprisingly, the burials on the barrow plain continued. The families of the deceased would cross the Sour Sea in boats, making landfall just after sunset and bearing their dead kin to a spot on the northern end of the plain. They would bring tools with them, and under the moonlight they would dig a deep hole in the ground and lay the body inside. Then, to Nagash's amusement, they would turn their attention to the mountain and utter some kind of absurd prayer before filling up the hole again. Once the family had gone, Nagash would summon up the corpse and find a place for it on one of his work parties.

A year passed. Work on the mountain continued, and then the rainy season returned. Not long after, burials on the plain increased sharply. Scores of bodies were brought across the sea and laid to rest, usually in large groups. Nagash noted that the corpses were men of fighting age, and all of them had been slain by sword, spear or arrow. The barbarian tribes were at war again, though against whom Nagash did not know. One night, Nagash saw an orange glow on the horizon to the north-west, and realised that one of the larger hilltop villages was on fire.

Another wave of burials occurred, twice as large as the ones before. The war continued unabated, Nagash reckoned – and the barbarians were losing badly. Their loss was his gain, he reasoned. And then something unexpected happened.

One night, in the midst of another spate of burials, a small group of men made their way across the barrow plain in the direction of the mountain. They were dragging a large sledge behind them, bearing a large, cylindrical object wrapped in ragged sheets of muslin.

The men hauled the sledge over the muddy ground, until they reached the eastern edge of the plain. There, virtually in the shadow of the mountain, they took up tools from the sledge and went to work digging a deep hole. When one of the men judged the hole deep enough, he gestured for his companions to proceed, then he knelt before the hole and bowed his head, spreading his arms as though in supplication, or in prayer.

The rest of the men returned to the sledge and pulled away the muslin sheets. Then they took their places to either side of the cylinder and lifted it from its cradle. Struggling under the weight of the object, they inched towards the hole. Finally, after long minutes of effort, they let the end of the cylinder drop into the cavity and pushed the object upright. The kneeling man rose to his feet, his hands turning upwards in a gesture of triumph, as the men shovelled loose earth into the hole and stabilised the object. Once they were satisfied that the object was secure, the men gathered their tools and began the long trek back to the shore.

Nagash had observed this through the eyes of several of his servants, who stood watch over the plain to mark the arrivals of the burial parties. The object left at the foot of the mountain intrigued him. When the men had disappeared to the west, he sent one of the undead sentinels to inspect it.

What the sentinel found was a totem-statue, similar to those found in the barbarian villages. But where the other statues were four-sided and depicted two pairs of men and women, this statue was carved to represent one figure only.

The workmanship was crude. Nagash, looking through his servants' eyes, stared at the statue for some time, until he saw the suggestion of a cloak about the figure's shoulders and realised that the skeletal monster carved into the wood was meant to be him!

Nagash didn't know what to make of the statue. Was it some pathetic attempt at an abjuration, meant to forbid him from trespassing upon the plain, or was it simply a crude attempt at defiance on the part of the barbarians? At length, he decided to wait and see if the men visited the statue again.

And visit they did, just a few nights later, when the next wave of burials landed upon the shore. Nagash watched the men approach the statue, and this time he noted that the men were young and clad in robes – and, most importantly, bore none of the physical deformities that marked the rest of the villagers. They were members of the old order that Nagash had thought extinct!

To his amazement, the men surrounded the statue and laid plates heaped with offerings at its feet. They knelt in supplication and offered up prayers, then anointed the statue with oils. The whole ritual took almost an hour, and then the men hurriedly withdrew.

Nagash continued to study the statue throughout the night, trying to puzzle out the meaning of the ritual offerings and prayers. Were they actually offering up adulation and worship, or were the offerings more of a bribe to keep him from interfering in their business? The fact that the ritual coincided with another round of mass burials wasn't lost on him, but the timing didn't argue one way or the other.

He continued to watch and wait, though now he made sure that a small group of warriors were always kept close by the statue each night. The men returned each night that a burial took place, laying out more offerings and taking care of the great statue. On the fifth visitation, Nagash's patience was rewarded.

As the men gathered about the statue and laid out their offerings, another group of men and women approached from the north, where the latest round of burials were taking place. They accosted the supplicants, brandishing cudgels and shouting threats. The leader of the supplicants – a young man whose mannerisms seemed strangely familiar to Nagash – seemed to try reasoning with the second group, but his arguments fell on deaf ears. There were more shouted threats, and finally the supplicants chose to depart. The second group pursued them for a while, waving their clubs in the air, then, satisfied, they returned to the sombre ceremonies to the north.

The confrontation suggested a great many things to Nagash. The supplicants considered Nagash a god, and sought to worship him, but their newfound devotion wasn't popular with the rest of their kind. What was it they hoped to accomplish? Had the confrontation convinced them to abandon their heresy? The questions only served to pique his interest further.

ANOTHER WEEK PASSED before the next spate of burials occurred. Again, the supplicants journeyed across the plain to kneel before the statue. This time, Nagash was ready for them.

The supplicants had no sooner begun their rite when a much larger group of villagers came charging out of the darkness, brandishing cudgels and knives and shouting threats at the kneeling men. The young leader of the supplicants rose to his feet and approached the villagers, but it was clear to Nagash that the mob wouldn't be interested in talking this time. They were out for blood.

Nagash issued a series of commands to the warriors that lay in wait just a short distance from the totem statue. They rose silently from their places of concealment and crept towards the unsuspecting barbarians.

The leader of the supplicants started to speak, but a burly villager stepped from the crowd and lashed out with his cudgel, striking the young man in the head and knocking him to the ground. The attack galvanised the rest of the mob; they rushed forward, shouting furiously, and fell upon the other worshippers. The holy men fell to the ground, covering their heads with their arms to ward off the avalanche of blows.

No one saw the undead warriors until it was too late. Half a dozen skeletons appeared out of the darkness, stabbing at the villagers with spears or slashing with tarnished bronze blades. Shouts of anger turned to screams of fear and pain as the mob was cut apart by the remorseless skeletons. The survivors reeled away from the attackers and fled into the darkness, abandoning their wounded compatriots to their fate.

The leader of the mob lingered a moment too long, pausing to deliver a final, vicious kick to the leader of the supplicants before trying to make good his escape. As he turned and prepared to run, he found himself face-to-face with a leering skeleton; the flat of the undead warrior's blade crashed into the side of his head, knocking him senseless.

The fight was over in seconds. Nagash's warriors surveyed the scene of carnage for a moment, and then a pair of the skeletons seized the leader of the mob by the shoulders and dragged him away. Two more of the warriors went to the leader of the supplicants, who was trying to force his battered body to stand upright. They seized him by the arms and dragged him away as well.

The remaining two skeletons hefted their weapons and slew the wounded villagers one by one. As the supplicants watched in horrified wonder, their oppressors died screaming – then, with the last of their lifeblood still flowing from their wounds, the corpses rose to their feet and followed their killers into the night.

A SINGLE TOWER reared up from the ugly sprawl of buildings, mine works and fortifications that now girdled the mountain's southern flank. Five storeys tall, square and built from stone, it would have been thought crude and artless in the civilized cities of Nehekhara, but it dominated the surrounding countryside and provided good fields of view over the southern barrow fields and the mountains to the south-east. It was no palace, but it allowed Nagash to oversee the labours on the mountainside and continue his necromantic studies in solitude until such time as a proper sanctum could be built.

The top storey of the tower was a single, windowless chamber, lit only by the pulsing green glow of a huge chunk of burning stone that rested on a crude metal tripod at the left of Nagash's new throne. The high-backed chair had been wrought of wood and bronze, shaped to resemble the Throne of Settra that had once rested in Khemri. The necromancer sat back in the tall chair, his hands steepled thoughtfully, as his warriors dragged the two barbarians into his presence.

The former leader of the village mob struggled in the skeletons' grip, spitting curses and roaring oaths in his bestial tongue. Blood flowed freely from a cut at his temple, but otherwise he appeared none the worse for his experience. The young supplicant, on the other hand, had been beaten within an inch of his life. He hung almost limply from the bony arms of the warriors. It took all of his strength to hold his head upright and look about in dull wonder at the shadowy interior of the tower.

With a mental command Nagash directed his warriors to drag the mob leader into the centre of a ritual circle he'd prepared some time before. They forced the man to his knees. When he tried to rise, one of the skeletons dashed him to the floor with another blow to the head.

The supplicant was deposited on the floor a short distance from the circle, at the very edge of the light shed by the chunk of burning stone. His wide-eyed stare fell upon Nagash, and immediately the young man bent forward, prostrating himself before the throne. The gesture triggered a memory: this was the young acolyte he'd seen outside the barrow during the ambush. Nagash smiled thinly. His instincts had been correct. This one could prove useful.

Nagash rose slowly from the throne. He was clad in robes that had been looted from the temple fortress, which concealed much of the changes that time and the *abn-i-khat* had wrought upon his body. It was only his hands and his face that hinted at the horrors concealed beneath the rough-spun cloth. His flesh, once paper-thin, had begun to liquefy under the heat emanating from his bones, giving it a sickly, gelid appearance. Muscles and tendons glistened in the open air where the flesh and skin had been worn away, and only the barest shreds of flesh remained at cheek and brow to lend the hint of life to Nagash's skeletal face.

He approached the leader of the villagers, whose eyes widened in pure terror. The barbarian screamed curses at the necromancer, his voice rising in pitch as his sanity neared breaking point. When Nagash entered the ritual circle, the barbarian surged to his feet, but before he could take a single step, the necromancer seized him by the throat.

Wide-eyed, gasping, the barbarian began to thrash and kick. Nagash spoke a single word, and the villager's muscles contracted savagely, putting so much stress on his limbs that the long bones of his arms and legs broke like dry twigs. His curses became shrieks of agony, growing ever more shrill and frenzied as the necromancer reached up with his left hand and began methodically pulling away handfuls of the barbarian's black hair. When the man's scalp was bald and bleeding, Nagash pulled a knife from his belt and began carving runes into the barbarian's skin.

The preparations took almost half an hour. When it was complete, Nagash dropped the villager in a heap at the centre of the circle and then withdrew. Once outside the circle, the necromancer raised his arms and began to chant. At once, the sigils etched into the circle flared into life, and the spell began to unravel the barbarian's mind and soul.

It was a variation on the ritual of reaping that he'd perfected in Khemri, and then reconstructed from memory in the years he'd spent wandering the wasteland. The difference between this version and the original was the way it separated the constituent elements of a victim's spirit. As he tore the villager's soul from his body, Nagash picked the elements he wished and discarded the rest, like a lord picking at a resplendent feast.

The barbarian's memories meant nothing to him; he cast those aside with a contemptuous flick of his wrist. Nagash learned that the man was an apprentice woodworker by tasting the flavour of his skill with chisel and saw. Those, too, he cast aside.

There! Nagash tasted the rough flavour of language in the stew of the man's thoughts. He drew that out and consumed it. Crude, guttural words came and went in his mind, etched one by one into his memory.

Finally, the necromancer consumed the barbarian's life essence. He tasted its potency and compared it to the power of the burning stone. Nagash's lip curled in distaste.

'*Disappointing,*' he sneered, as the shrivelled corpse collapsed onto the floor. With a wave of his hand, he sent a flow of power back into the sack of bones and sent it shambling off to the mines.

Nagash turned to the supplicant, who had watched the entire ritual in terrified silence. The necromancer searched his memory for the right words.

'*Who are you?*'

The supplicant pressed his forehead to the floor. 'Ha… Hathurk, mighty one,' he stammered.

'*Hathurk,*' Nagash echoed. '*Who are you to worship me? You served the temple once.*'

The necromancer expected the former acolyte to equivocate, but instead, Hathurk nodded matter-of-factly. 'I served the Keepers of the Mountain,' he admitted readily. 'In time, I would have become a Keeper myself. But their time is finished. The words of the Ancients have been fulfilled.'

'*How so?*'

Hathurk dared to glance up from the floor. 'The Ancients told us that one day the mountain would wake,' he explained. 'The god would come forth. And now you are here.'

Interesting, Nagash thought. '*Where are the words of the Ancients…*' he paused, realising that the barbarians had no words for the act of writing. '*How were the words of the Ancients preserved?*'

'They were passed down, generation to generation, from Keeper to acolyte.'

Nagash nodded thoughtfully. 'And do the village hetmen know these tales?'

Hathurk shook his head. 'They were not worthy, mighty one. They are ignorant, superstitious folk.'

'*Indeed,*' Nagash said.

Sarcasm was lost on the likes of Hathurk. The supplicant nodded quickly. 'They know of you, though,' he continued. 'We have travelled between the villages, spreading the word of your coming. We told the hetmen that it was you who came for the Keepers, because the High Keeper refused to accept that the words of the Ancients had been fulfilled.'

'*Do they believe?*' Nagash asked.

The supplicant shook his head. 'Not yet, mighty one. They are stubborn and set in their ways. But,' he added quickly, 'the war season has begun, and the tribes of the Forsaken have come down from the northlands with fire and sword. Without the Keepers to aid them, the village warbands have suffered many defeats. Already, two villages have been destroyed, their women and children slaughtered in their homes. The other hetmen are talking openly of an alliance against the Forsaken, but even that will not be enough. They will need the power of the mountain if they are to prevail.'

Nagash considered this. More vassals were needed to labour in the mines and seek out sources of stone and timber for constructing the fortress. Empires grew on a steady diet of conquest.

The Undying King crossed the sanctum and settled once more upon his throne. His eyes guttered thoughtfully.

'*Tell me more,*' he said.

━━◄ THIRTEEN ►━━

Blood for Blood

Lahmia, the City of the Dawn, in the 76th year of Khsar the Faceless
(-1598 Imperial Reckoning)

'THE QUEEN! THE *queen!*' Aiyah wailed in horror. 'Blessed gods, what have we done?'

Arkhan reeled backwards, away from the bed and Neferata's withered corpse. The sight of her left him speechless. He shook his head, stunned at the enormity of what had happened.

'I don't understand,' he finally managed to say. 'There were no mistakes. The ritual should have worked. *It should have worked!*'

The immortal rubbed his face with a bloodstained hand. Belatedly, he realised that his arm was still bleeding. With an effort, he focussed his will and sealed the wound shut. He felt weak and stiff. His limbs were cold. He'd given her almost every ounce of vigour he possessed. *All for nothing*, he thought bitterly. *She looks no better than Neferem now.*

Arkhan forced himself to close his eyes. He took a deep breath and forced the image of the dead queen from his mind. Almost at once, his sense of regret dissipated, like the heat of the desert at sunset, leaving his mind sharper and clearer than it had been in years. Neferata was gone, and the glamour she'd cast on him had faded along with her. Arkhan was both surprised and ashamed at how keenly he felt the loss. Bitterness and hatred welled up to fill the void it had left behind.

He was himself again. And the way ahead was clear.

The immortal rose slowly to his feet and went to collect his robes. Aiyah was curled into a ball at the foot of the queen's bed, sobbing despondently.

'That's enough,' he said as he dressed. 'She's gone. All the wailing in the world won't bring her back.'

By the time he had tied on his sword belt, the handmaiden had mastered herself. She sat up, rubbing at the tracks of kohl that stained her damp cheeks. 'What would you have me do?' she asked.

Arkhan grabbed a carry-bag from the floor beside Neferata's writing desk and began stuffing Nagash's books inside. 'That's your concern now,' he said. 'If I were you, I'd gather up some changes of clothing and as many of the queen's trinkets as I could carry, and then steal a fast horse from the royal stable. Any number of merchant caravans would be happy to let you ride along with them, for the proper fee. I wouldn't advise riding the trade road alone.'

The handmaiden stared bemusedly at him. 'Leave the city?' she said dully. 'Where would I go?'

'Anywhere but here, you little fool,' he snarled, slinging the bulging bag over his shoulder. 'Unless you're keen to drink from a poisoned cup and follow your queen into darkness.'

Aiyah watched him as he headed for the chamber door, her expression full of dread. 'Where are you going?' she asked.

'To see the king,' Arkhan growled. 'There's something I've been wanting to give him for a very long time.'

THE HALLS OF the palace were quiet in the small hours before dawn. Arkhan slipped from one shadow to the next, his pale face hidden by a desert scarf and his hands concealed by dark leather gloves. He disliked the notion of creeping through the palace like a rat, but he suspected that if Lamashizzar knew he was coming, the feckless king would go into hiding, and the immortal did not have time to waste hunting for him across the sprawling royal compound. He meant to settle accounts with the king and be well away from the city before daybreak. There were secluded spots on the Golden Plain where he could lie up until nightfall and contemplate his next move.

Arkhan didn't plan on going far. He'd already come to that conclusion. With the queen dead and the king soon to follow, there would be chaos and confusion among the noble houses as the most prominent lords vied to rule the city as crown regent until Lamashizzar's young son reached adulthood. The process could last for weeks, even months – more than enough time for him to knit the plains outlaws together into something resembling an army. With a little luck, the city nobles would still be scheming against one another on the night his cutthroats came scrambling over the city walls.

The streets of Lahmia would run with rivers of blood. Her villas would go up in flame, as would the ships filling her harbour. The sack of the city would take days, and when he was done, not one stone would be left standing atop another. Then Arkhan would lead his howling mob eastward, and woe betide anyone or anything caught in their path. The petty cares of mortal men filled him with contempt; he wanted nothing more than to scourge mankind for its callowness and stupidity, to bury all of Nehekhara under a pall of suffering and despair. By the time he was done, the survivors would look back on the reign of Nagash with *envy*.

The immortal moved as swiftly as he dared, encountering few servants and even fewer palace guards as the crossed the royal compound towards the king's quarters. The royal apartments were a collection of luxurious chambers for the ruler, his children and his favoured concubines, connected by a sprawling network of common rooms, libraries, small shrines and meditative gardens. It occupied the entire north-west corner of the palace compound, with views looking out across the city proper and the wide, blue sea. What little he knew of it came from Neferata, and she'd only lived there during her early childhood. He had no idea where the king's bed-chamber lay, but he'd spent enough time in the royal palace at Khemri to know how such places operated. *When in doubt, follow the servants*, he thought.

Once past the great central palace garden and the royal audience chamber, Arkhan passed through the palace's smaller privy chambers, where the king met with his councillors to conduct the day-to-day busi-ness of the city. From there he came upon a series of increasingly well-appointed passageways. He began to encounter more and more sleepy-eyed servants, hurrying about on one errand or another in antici-pation of the coming day. Before long, Arkhan came to a tall, wide doorway, flanked by basalt statues of Asaph and Ptra. Hieroglyphs carved into the stone lintel proclaimed, *Here dwell the most favoured of the gods, the mortal seed of Asaph the Beautiful and great Ptra in His Glory*. With a wolfish smile, the immortal drew his iron sword and crept across the threshold.

Beyond the great doorway was a small, silent antechamber, with passageways leading off in three directions. Arkhan continued through the doorway on the opposite side of the room, and soon found himself in a small, shadow-filled garden. Narrow paths wound among the ornamental trees and clus-ters of ferns. Somewhere a fountain chuckled to itself, and captive songbirds chirped sleepily in the branches. Was this the central garden for the royal apartments, or just one of several? Arkhan's confidence began to ebb. He couldn't afford the time to search every path and passageway until he found the king. The first hints of false dawn were already paling the sky overhead.

Suddenly, he caught the sound of soft voices approaching him from behind. Arkhan slipped off the path as quietly as he could and hid behind the bole of a palm tree. Moments later, a pair of bare-chested slaves walked past, murmuring to each other in quiet tones. One carried a polished bronze bowl filled with steaming water, while another bore clean cotton cloths and a small, bronze shaving knife.

The immortal was surprised. He had no idea that Lamashizzar had become such an early riser. Arkhan waited until the men had disappeared from sight before easing himself back onto the path and following along in their wake.

It took several minutes to reach the far side of the garden. The paths wound a meandering course through the lush foliage, creating the illusion that the garden was much larger and more secluded than it actually was, and effectively concealed the routes into and out of the open-air space. It had been so cunningly designed that Arkhan hadn't realised he'd reached the opposite edge until he rounded another sharp turn in the path and came upon another tall, imposing doorway, flanked by a pair of royal guards.

Arkhan froze, his sword held low at his side. The two men were clad in lacquered iron armour and polished skullcaps, and were armed with heavy, straight swords like the one he carried. Neither man saw him at first; his dark clothing blended well with the shadows, and it was clear that their senses were dulled from a long, quiet watch.

They were less than fifteen paces away. Arkhan gauged the distance carefully, and drew upon what little remained of the queen's elixir. Strength swelled in his limbs, and he dashed forward, almost too quickly for the eye to follow. His blade whickered through the air. The first man barely had time to register the movement before his head toppled from his shoulders. Blood sprayed across the second man; Arkhan saw his eyes widen in shock, stunned by the speed and ferocity of the attack. The hesitation was fatal.

Arkhan paused just long enough to drag the two bodies beneath a nearby stand of drooping ferns, then crept carefully through the doorway into the king's personal apartments. Beyond was another dark antechamber, thick with a fog of cloying incense. He glimpsed low divans and wooden tables arranged together in tight clusters around the room. Empty wine jars and bronze trays littered with scraps of food covered most of the tables.

On the opposite side of the antechamber was another open doorway, filled with the shifting orange glow of lit braziers. Arkhan paused at the threshold and glimpsed what appeared to be another long rectangular chamber. There was a set of tall blue-painted doors on the far side of the room, and the doorway was carved with intricate hieroglyphs of protection, wealth and good fortune. The king's bed-chamber had to lie on the other side of those doors, he reckoned. Arkhan steeled himself, acutely aware of how little vigour remained to him. He would have to make this quick. The thought galled him, but better swift vengeance than none at all. Tightening his grip on his bloodstained sword, he raced for the doors.

The guards rushed him the moment he stepped across the threshold.

There were six of them, waiting with swords drawn, three to either side of the doorway. Doubtless one of them had heard something as he'd despatched the guards at the edge of the garden, and they'd lain in wait for him. Now they leapt at him with triumphant shouts, moving quickly to cut him off from the king's bedchamber.

Arkhan had little time to curse his own careless-ness, and no choice but to draw upon the elixir once more. The guardsmen were swift and skilled, but lacked experience; in their haste they got in one another's way, fouling the sweep of their own swords. The immortal gave them a bestial snarl and struck first, ducking low and spinning on his heel to strike at the man just behind and to his right. The heavy iron blade slashed across the guard's thigh, through the narrow gap between the edge of his armoured skirt and the top of his iron greaves. The sword sliced through flesh and muscle and left him thrashing on the floor in a spreading pool of blood.

The guardsman to Arkhan's immediate left chopped downwards with his sword. He parried the blow swiftly and drove the man back with a feint to his throat. The warriors shouted curses at him and at one another. A blade scored across his back, and another jabbed into his side, just above his hip. Arkhan scarcely felt the blows. He whirled left and slashed upwards, catching another guardsman's sword wrist and severing his hand. The man reeled backwards with a scream and slipped in the dark blood pouring from the other guard's leg.

Two down, but now the other guards had more room to manoeuvre. Arkhan sidestepped a fearsome downward slash, and then had to whirl out of the way of a thrust angling in from his far left. Then a powerful blow on his back cut deep into his shoulder blade and nearly sent him sprawling. This time he felt the sharp pain of broken bone, but he sealed the wound with a thought and kept fighting, lunging upwards and catching a guard in the throat with the point of his sword.

The remaining guards circled around him, harrying him with a flurry of strikes that were meant to test his defences and keep him off-balance. He kept moving, turning in place and batting the attacks aside, waiting for his moment. A warrior lunged at him from the right, thrusting at his sword arm. He turned on his heel, sweeping the point aside with his own blade and causing the man to stumble slightly forwards. The guard saw his peril and moved swiftly to regain his balance, but it was already too late. Arkhan's blade flashed, and the guard's head bounced across the floor.

The two surviving guards struck at once, hitting him from behind. One sword bit deeply into his right hip, its edge grating against bone, while the other stabbed into his back, just below his left shoulder blade. Arkhan staggered, tasting blood in his mouth. He turned, almost tearing the sword from the grip of the man who'd stabbed him, and slashed his blade across the man's face. The guard fell with a scream, clutching at his ruined eyes. His sword was still trapped in Arkhan's back, lodged between his ribs.

With a savage jerk, the last guard tore his blade free from Arkhan's hip. Seeing his foe gravely wounded, the guard rained a storm of ringing blows down upon the immortal's guard. Sparks flew as the iron blades clashed, and the immortal's counter-blows began to slacken. The guard cut him three times in swift succession, once above the right elbow, once in the left thigh, and once across the chest. Sensing triumph, the warrior redoubled his attacks, aiming a lightning-fast blow at Arkhan's neck that the immortal barely turned aside. The block left his torso unprotected, and the guard leapt forward with a shout, thrusting his sword straight at Arkhan's heart.

But the blow never struck home. Arkhan had given him the opening to draw him in, then spun on his heel and let the guard's sword go past him. His own blade smashed into the side of the man's head, shattering his iron skullcap and driving shards of bone into his brain. The warrior was dead before his body hit the floor.

Arkhan staggered, nearly toppling as well. The battle had lasted only a few seconds, but no doubt it had woken everyone in earshot. The alarm would be spreading through the palace even now. He groped at his back, fumbling for the sword that jutted from his ribs. It took several more agonising seconds to pull it free, and then a moment more to focus his will and use just enough power to seal the wound. He had very little remaining now. If he used much more he might not have enough strength left to escape.

It would be enough, he thought, gritting his ruined teeth. *It would have to be enough.*

Arkhan lurched forward, gathering speed, and shoved open the doors to the king's bedchamber.

The room was large, much more so than the queen's, and dominated by a wide bed piled with silken pillows. Two braziers along the walls to the left and right had been recently stoked to life, revealing rich, painted carvings etched into the sandstone that depicted the great journey of the Nehekharan people from the southern jungles millennia ago. Tall, basalt statues of Ptra and Asaph stood watch over the royal bed, their stone faces uncharacteristically smiling and beneficent. More padded divans and low tables were clustered around the edges of the room, along with a little-used writing table near the tall windows on the room's opposite side. Gauzy window hangings shifted lazily in the breeze blowing in from the sea.

The two body servants cowered at the foot of the bed, their eyes wide with terror. The upended bowl and the bronze knife gleamed at their feet. Arkhan ignored them, searching the room for the king. Just then, the wind shifted, drawing back the window hangings, and he caught sight of a silhouette between two of the windows. The figure moved suddenly, raising his right arm.

Arkhan was faster. His left hand shot up, fingers outstretched, and he spoke a single word. The last vestiges of his power flowed through his fingertips, and the silhouette stiffened.

A slow, cruel smile crossed the immortal's face. 'Did you imagine I'd forgotten?' he told the king. 'Oh, no. That little trick won't work a second time.'

He forced his stiff limbs to move, making his way haltingly across the chamber. When he passed the great bed, the two servants bolted from the room. He could hear their hysterical shouts receding in the direction of the garden. As he drew nearer to the windows he could see the king clearly now. Lamashizzar was clad in a silken sleeping robe, stained here and there with splashes of wine. The strain of the last week had taken a toll upon him: his face was gaunt and sallow, and his eyes were sunken deeply in their sockets. Arkhan saw that the king's lips were stained from the steady use of lotus root. How long had Lamashizzar kept himself here, surrounded by guards, waiting for word that Neferata had died?

The short dragon-stave was gripped in the king's outstretched hand. A faint wisp of smoke rose from the wick held in his left hand. The little red coal had burned very close to his fingers, but the king could not let it go. He stared at Arkhan, his expression transfixed, as a bird watches the dreadful approach of the cobra.

Arkhan stared deep into the king's eyes, savouring the terror he saw there. 'As you can see, I've learned a few tricks of my own,' he said. 'It took some time to perfect the technique, but I knew I'd need it when this day finally came. Thanks to you, I had plenty of time to practice.'

Never taking his eyes from the king, Arkhan set his sword carefully upon the floor. He straightened, his ghastly smile widening. 'There's something I've been wanting to share with you for a very long time,' he said. 'You know, it was very clever of you, shooting me in the heart with that damned stave of yours. When the bullet pierced, I honestly thought you'd killed me. Everything went black, but then I realised that I could still hear and feel everything around me. How I screamed then. How I raged. After a while, I even begged. I called upon gods I'd forsaken centuries ago, praying for the mercy of death. Naturally, it never came. It was the worst torture I'd ever felt, and if you knew anything about my past, you'd know just exactly how profound that statement is.'

Arkhan reached up and carefully took hold of the dragon-stave. One by one, he plucked the king's stiff fingers from the haft of the weapon. 'Do you know what sustained me in that darkness? The only thing that allowed me to keep what little sanity I had left was the slim hope that one day, I'd visit the same awful fate upon you.'

He took the weapon carefully from the king's hand. 'It was worth it, teaching you the secrets of the Undying King's elixir. Without it, my vengeance would not have been possible. Now, when the bullet strikes your heart, you'll know the same smothering darkness, the same helplessness. The same despair.'

The immortal pressed the gaping muzzle of the dragon to Lamashizzar's chest. A faint tremor shook the king's body. His eyes widened a tiny, terrified fraction. It would have taken a prodigious, desperate exertion of will to manage even so small a movement.

Arkhan plucked the wick from the king's left hand, and blew softly upon the end. The tiny coal blazed to life.

'When your servants find you, they'll think you've been slain, of course,' the immortal continued. 'Doubtless, they'll summon the mortuary priests, who will bear your body to the House of Everlasting Life and prepare you for the ages to come. If you're lucky, you'll die when they remove your heart and seal it in a canopic jar. If not… you'll have a very long time to regret you ever dreamt of crossing me.'

Arkhan touched the wick to the stave's touch-hole. 'The queen is dead,' he said to Lamashizzar, 'but at least she's free. I hope you rot in darkness until the end of time.'

The weapon discharged with a flash and a muffled *thump*. The impact knocked the king from his feet.

He hit the wall and slid to the floor, his body going limp. Arkhan knelt, staring into the king's wide eyes, and then reached up with his fingertips to slowly push them shut.

Arkhan studied his handiwork a moment more, then rose and tossed the smoking weapon aside. The sky beyond the windows was paling. He was nearly out of time.

Snatching up his sword, he made his way across the bedchamber. His mind was already racing ahead, planning his route to the royal stables, when he heard a loud commotion in the chamber beyond.

Arkhan reached the doorway and saw a score of royal guardsmen dashing into the chamber from the direction of the garden, led by the king's champion. Abhorash's face was pale with fury. Two long iron swords gleamed in his scarred hands.

There would be no escape. Arkhan knew that at once. He was spent, and Abhorash was too skilled an opponent to be taken in by his tricks. For a moment, the immortal thought wistfully of the warhorse waiting in the stables, and the feel of the desert wind on his face.

He had his revenge upon the king. That would have to be enough.

Raising his sword, Arkhan went to meet his fate.

THE SCOPE OF the tragedy was immense, the carnage terrible to behold. The royal apartments looked like a battlefield, heaped with the mangled remains of Lamashizzar's valiant guard. Though Abhorash, the king's champion, had slain the assassin in the end, it was a bitter victory for the people of Lahmia. Lamashizzar, the great king, was dead.

It was a crushing blow for the royal household to bear. Functionaries and servants alike were overwhelmed by the news, not realising that it was only a fraction of the greater catastrophe. Only Ubaid, the grand vizier, and the few remaining servants of the Women's Palace knew that Neferata was dead as well.

For a handful of hours, just after dawn, Ubaid held the fate of the city – and by extension, all of Nehekhara – in his hands. His first act was to order the king's champion to seal off the palace, allowing none to enter or leave upon pain of death. One of the queen's handmaidens was already missing, probably having fled in the small hours of the morning, but the rest of the household was kept from spreading the word to the city at large. Orders were given not to inform the king's children of his death, at least not yet. That bought the palace precious hours to organise a proper response.

After careful consideration, the king's privy council was summoned. Lords Ankhat and Ushoran answered the call at once, as well as the old scholar W'soran. Lord Zuhras, the king's young cousin, could not be found for hours, having gone drinking with his friends in the Red Silk District the night before. It was mid-morning by the time his servants brought him, pale and trembling, to the palace gates.

While the council met in secret to discuss the shocking turn of events, the priests of the mortuary cult were quietly summoned to begin their ministrations to the dead. Rituals began at once for the great king, preparing his body for transfer to the House of Everlasting Life. The protocols for the queen were different. By tradition, her body was to be washed and clothed by her handmaidens, and at dusk they would bear her upon their shoulders to the Hall of Regretful Sorrows. There she would be given into the keeping of the priests, who would tend her while her body lay in state for the proscribed three days and three nights. Only then, after the citizens had been given time to pay their last respects, would Neferata join her husband in the House of Everlasting Life.

SHORTLY BEFORE THE appointed hour, just as the sun was setting far out to sea, Ubaid, the grand vizier, appeared at the door to the queen's bedchamber.

The last of the queen's handmaidens – half a dozen women ranging in age from youthful to elderly – were crouched on their knees around the perimeter of the queen's bed. The traditional preparation of the body had lasted for almost the entire day, and most of the handmaidens were slumped and silent with exhaustion. The rest rocked slowly on their heels, keening softly in mourning.

Ubaid stood in the doorway and carefully surveyed the room. He'd been told what the handmaidens had found when they'd entered the room that morning, but all traces of Arkhan's desperate rituals had been scrupulously removed. The ritual circle had been scrubbed away, along with the pools of dried blood that had stained the floor around the bed. The bed-clothes themselves had been stripped away, and now lay in a tightly wrapped bundle in one corner of the room. The grand vizier made a mental note to have them burned before the night was out.

Neferata lay on a bare white mattress, her body wrapped in a fine cotton robe that had been marked with hieroglyphs of protection and anointed with sacred oils. Her arms were folded across her chest, and her golden mask had been laid across her face. Only the bare skin of her hands, marked with intricate bands of henna tattoos, showed how cruelly wasted her body had been at the time of her death. The sight of it sent a pang of guilt through the grand vizier, but he stifled it with an effort of will. What was done was done. His responsibility now was to look to the future, and ensure the continuation of the dynasty.

One of the older handmaidens caught sight of Ubaid and straightened. 'You shouldn't be here!' she said. 'It's not proper!'

'These are not proper times,' Ubaid replied. He approached the bed. As one, the handmaidens scrambled to their feet, forming an implacable barrier between him and their charge.

The grand vizier addressed the old handmaiden. 'Forgive the intrusion,' he said, inclining his head respectfully. 'I meant no disrespect. This has been a hard day for us all, and I wanted to make certain that the queen and her quarters had been seen to properly.'

'We know our duty,' the handmaiden said, folding her arms indignantly. 'Do you imagine we would allow any slight to her honour?'

'No, naturally not,' Ubaid replied. 'It must have been hard, preparing the queen and... restoring her chamber to its proper appearance. Did you manage all of it alone?'

'Just the six of us,' she replied grimly, though her head was held high. 'We couldn't trust such an important task to anyone else.'

'Yes, of course,' the grand vizier said, inwardly breathing a sigh of relief. He studied each of the handmaidens in turn, committing their faces to memory. All of them would have to die. Hopefully they would all choose to follow the queen into the afterlife, but if not, he would take matters into his own hands. Once they were gone, there would be no one left who knew the real circumstances of Nefer-ata's death.

The cabal – what was left of it – could continue its work in secret. Ubaid had little doubt that W'soran would be able to take up where the queen left off. Lord Ankhat or Lord Ushoran would be named regent, and life in the city would go on much as before. In fact, the grand vizier thought, the oppor-tunities for power and influence for the surviving cabal members would be even greater.

Ubaid took a step back and composed himself, then bowed solemnly to the handmaidens. 'It is time,' he said. 'The priests and the privy council await in the Hall of Regretful Sorrows. Let the people of

Lahmia look upon Neferata one final time, and weep.'

The handmaidens grew subdued at the grand vizier's solemn words. The old one sighed and gestured to her companions, and they turned their attention once more to their beloved queen. Three of the women circled around to the far side of the bed, then they all hung their heads and intoned a ceremonial prayer to Usirian, god of the underworld. Ubaid listened to the low, mournful chant, as the sun sank low on the horizon and the light fled from the room. The prayer came to an end, and the chamber was plunged into a funereal gloom. As one, the handmaidens began their keening wail again, and bent over the queen's recumbent form.

Suddenly, there came a dreadful sound from the bed. It was a faint, wet, rippling crackle, like the popping of joints grown stiff from disuse. Then the keening of the handmaidens spiralled into a threnody of horrified screams.

Bone crunched and flesh parted with a sound like a knife through wet cloth. The two handmaidens closest to the head of the bed were hurled backwards in a welter of blood, their throats reduced to ragged pulp. Ubaid's stunned mind barely had time to register the horrifying sight before there was a blur of motion above the bed and the sickening sound of crunching bone. Two more handmaidens collapsed, their skulls crushed by swift and terrible blows.

There was scarcely time to breathe, much less react. The last of the queen's devoted servants seemed to reel away from the bed in slow motion, their hands rising to their faces as a lithe, bloodstained figure reached for them with gaunt, grasping hands.

The grand vizier stared in shock as Neferata lashed out at one of the handmaidens with an open hand. The blow crushed the woman's skull like a melon and flung her corpse against the far wall. The last of the handmaidens, younger and swifter than the rest, turned and fled towards Ubaid, her hands outstretched and her face twisted into a mask of absolute terror.

She managed less than a half-dozen steps before Neferata leapt upon her back like a desert lioness. Fingers tipped with long, curving claws sank into the handmaiden's throat. The impact jarred the golden death mask from the queen's face, its cold, smooth perfection falling away to reveal the snarling face of a monster.

The queen's face was horribly gaunt, her cheeks sunken and the flesh stretched like parchment across the planes of her face. Her eyes were twin points of cold, pitiless light, shining with animal hunger as she fell upon her prey. Neferata's shrivelled lips were drawn back in a feral snarl, her delicate jaw agape to reveal prominent, leonine fangs. The handmaiden scarcely had time to scream before the queen's head plunged downward and those terrible fangs sank into the young woman's throat. Flesh tore and vertebrae popped, and the girl's screams dwindled into a choking rattle.

Ubaid pressed a trembling fist to his mouth, biting back a scream of his own. His legs trembled, threatening to betray him completely as he backed towards the bedchamber door. No matter how hard he tried, he could not take his eyes from the handmaiden's body. He dared not turn and run.

Each step lasted an eternity. The handmaiden's body twitched as the queen worried at her throat, gorging on the young woman's blood. He had to be close to the doorway now, Ubaid thought. Another few feet at most, and then–

Suddenly the grand vizier realised that the sounds of feasting had stopped. Neferata's head was raised, her mouth and chin soaked in bright, red blood. His own veins turned to ice as she turned her unearthly gaze upon him.

'Ubaid,' she said, her voice liquid and menacing. The power of her stare left him transfixed. His heart laboured painfully in his chest. '*Loyal servant.* Fall to your knees before your queen.'

The grand vizier's body obeyed. His knees cracked painfully on the stone as he all but prostrated himself before Neferata's terrifying visage.

The queen smiled, her teeth slick with gore. Her eyes glinted cruelly.

'Now tell me all that has transpired.'

THE GATHERING IN the Hall of Regretful Sorrows was silent and subdued. The only sounds in the vault-like space were the soft sounds of the mortuary priests' robes as they went about their preparations to receive the body of the queen. Votive incense had been lit, and the proper sigils of preservation had been laid across the marble bier. Lord Abhorash stood at the foot of the cold slab of stone, his head bowed and his hands resting upon the hilt of an ancient ceremonial sword. Lord Ushoran and Lord Ankhat stood apart from one another, each lost in their own thoughts as they contemplated the difficult days ahead.

When news of the king's death became widely known it would send ripples throughout the entire land. It would require adroit manoeuvring to keep the other priest kings in check. Behind the powerful nobles, W'soran stood with his hands folded at his waist and his head bowed, as though in prayer. The old sholar had an impatient expression on his face. He now had unfettered access to Nagash's works, and he was eager to begin his studies. Behind W'soran stood young Lord Zuhras, who lingered close to the door as though he might bolt from the hall at any second. The king's cousin looked pale and stricken, though from grief or guilt, none could truly say.

They had been waiting for more than an hour already, having gathered long before sunset to view the body of the queen. It had already been decided that once Neferata's body had been laid in state, the word of her and Lamashizzar's death would be announced to the city. When the doors at the far end of the chamber swung silently opened, a stir went through the small assembly as they braced for the beginning of a new era.

None expected to see the queen emerge from the shadows of the Women's Palace, pale and terrible in her glory. Her beauty, once the gift of the goddess, now took on a divine power all its own. They did not see the dark blood that stained her white robes and painted her hands and face. Her eyes, dark and depthless as the sea, banished thought and replaced it with a yearning that was deeper and more all consuming than any they had known before.

Beside the queen came Ubaid, the grand vizier. He stepped past Neferata, head bowed and shoulders hunched. He descended the shallow steps that led to the waiting bier, and regarded the assembly with haunted, hollow eyes.

'Rejoice,' he said in a bleak voice. 'Rejoice at the coming of the queen.'

—◄ FOURTEEN ►—

The Dark Feast

*The Plain of Skulls, in the 76th year of Phakth the Just
(-1597 Imperial Reckoning)*

THE WARRIORS OF the Forsaken had pitched their tents upon the Plain of Skulls, a broad, roughly triangular plain some three leagues north-east of the Sour Sea. As the only navigable terrain between the coastline and the village-forts of the northlanders, the plain was where the barbarians – or the Yaghur, as Hathurk knew them – and the Forsaken had met to do battle for centuries. By ancient custom, the warbands of both sides normally encamped along the northern and southern edges of the plain, but after a series of recent victories of the Yaghur, the northlanders were no longer abiding by the old rules. They had taken note of the absence of the Keepers, and believed that the strength of the tribes had been broken. The destruction of the Yaghur was finally at hand.

For the last month, Forsaken raiding parties had struck southward from the plain at will, destroying a number of lowland settlements and storming a pair of hilltop villages. They left behind heaps of charred skulls as offerings to their four-faced god, Malakh, and sent scouts further westward to test the defences of the remaining Yaghur villages. Unless they were driven off the plain, the Forsaken would decimate the Yaghur to the point that the survivors would have little chance of surviving the winter.

According to Hathurk, the war between the Forsaken and the Yaghur had nothing to do with resources or territory; there was nothing the Yaghur possessed that the Forsaken could possibly desire. Indeed, according to Hathurk, the Forsaken once ruled the entire coast, down past the great mountain where a narrow strait led to the great Crystal Sea. It was they who had witnessed the fall of the star-stone that had pierced the side of the mountain, and who had built a great temple-city to venerate their new-found god. They had used the power of the burning stone to dominate the surrounding tribes and carve out a kingdom of their own. In those days, *they* were known as the Yaghur, which in Hathurk's tongue translated as 'the faithful'.

But the kingdom's glory days were short-lived. The noble houses, which ruled from the temple-city on the southern flank of the mountain, turned paranoid and cruel. Madness infected the ruling clans, and soon the kingdom was torn by civil war. Clans fought over the god-stone buried beneath the mountain, and thousands died. Finally, the noble houses of the Yaghur were overthrown when an exiled prince returned from the northlands with the teachings of a new god: Malakh, the Dark One, Master of the Four-fold Path. Malakh's power gained the prince many followers, and in time they conquered the temple city and slaughtered the maddened Yaghur nobles in a grand sacrifice to their god.

Afterwards, the prince sealed up the tunnels beneath the temple city and led his people northwards, where they settled far from the mountain and its corrupting god. But the insatiable desires of Malakh turned out to be just as bad – if not worse – than the lunatic rule of the old Yaghur kings, and once again the people were torn by civil war. Eventually, a schism occurred. Those who rejected Malakh broke away and returned to the shores of the Sour Sea in a vain bid to reclaim the glories of the kingdom they had lost.

The war had raged ever since. The Forsaken would not rest until the last Yaghur had been offered up to their four-faced god. Malakh would be satisfied with nothing less.

Watch-fires flickered across the Plain of Bones, picking out the curved flanks of hide tents and tall, wooden trophy poles festooned with rotting human skulls. Here and there, warriors dozed drunkenly around the fires. As far as they knew, there were no Yaghur warbands for miles; had there been any, their scouts would have warned them long before.

Those selfsame scouts now crept silently towards the Forsaken camp, their eyes burning with necromantic fire. Nagash's warriors had hunted down every one, tracking them by their life energies across the dark, lifeless plain. Now the small, skeletal army was less than fifty yards from the Forsaken camp, crawling inexorably across the rocky ground with the tireless patience of the dead.

A hundred yards further south, Nagash and Hathurk waited with the Yaghur hetmen. The barbarians had taken too long to unite against the northlanders. After months of fighting, the hetmen could barely muster two hundred warriors against an enemy force almost ten times that size. Most were armed with nothing more than crude spears and clubs, and none wore anything resembling proper armour. Nagash wasn't surprised that the Yaghur had hardly ever won a pitched battle against the Forsaken; indeed, it surprised him that they'd survived as long as they had. The Keepers must have been hard-pressed indeed just to maintain an uneasy stalemate against their foes.

The hetmen themselves were armed and armoured with bronze wargear that had been brought from the northlands during the time of the schism. They nervously fingered tarnished bronze swords or clutched at the hafts of bronze-tipped spears and cast fearful glances at Nagash and his undead bodyguard. Hathurk had suggested to the necromancer that bribery would be the best way to win over the hetmen, but Nagash had opted for a more direct approach. When the village leaders had gathered to formally seal their alliance, he had arrived unannounced during the evening feast, riding upon a palanquin borne by the corpses of the High Keeper and his senior subordinates. That served to get the village leaders' attention with a minimum of expense and effort. The rest would hinge on the outcome of the battle that was about to unfold.

As before, Nagash sat upon the palanquin that had once belonged to the High Keeper, which in turn rested upon the motionless shoulders of his servants. It gave him a slightly better view of the battlefield. He could see his warriors crawling forward steadily under the fading light of the moon; another few minutes and they would be at the edge of the watch fires. The necromancer stirred, turning his burning gaze upon the hetmen.

'The time has come,' he said. 'The hour of your victory is at hand. We will slaughter the northmen and drive them from the plain, as I have promised.'

The hetmen shared sidelong glances. Finally, one of them stepped forward. He was a large man for the Yaghur, with dark hair and a shelf-like brow. A third eye, covered with a cataract-like green film, tracked lazily from his forehead. His name was Aighul, and among the barbarians he was reckoned a mighty warrior. The hetman threw out his chest and clutched at the haft of his bronze axe, but he could not quite bring himself to meet Nagash's burning eyes.

'What about the rest of your promise?' Aighul replied. 'You said–'

'I said I would give you the secret of the northmen's prowess,' Nagash almost sneered, 'and so I shall. After the battle is won.'

'And after you bow before great Nagash and accept him as the new god of the mountain!' Hathurk added, in the steely tones of a true believer.

Nagash fought the urge to slay each and every one of them. Men such as they weren't even fit for the slave dock at Zandri. They were little better than animals, unworthy of the attentions of a king. Even Hathurk's credulous worship disgusted him. And yet, for the moment, they were all he had.

'Go now,' he told the Yaghur. 'My warriors are nearly ready.'

Aighul looked as though he was about to say something more, but at the end his nerve deserted him. He and the other hetmen nodded curtly and fanned out into the darkness to meet their warbands. Before long the Yaghur were on the move, loping across the stony plain with admirable stealth. Nagash watched their progress carefully. The barbarians moved much faster than his undead warriors, hence the need to hold them back until his own forces were almost on top of the camp.

Hathurk and his disciples crowded around the palanquin, their expressions earnest. 'How may we be of help, master?' the young supplicant asked.

'By doing nothing and saying less,' the necromancer hissed. 'I must concentrate.'

The Yaghur had almost overtaken his warriors. Nagash willed forth his commands. As one, a mix of two hundred and fifty skeletons and rotting, shambling zombies reared up against the moonlit sky and closed in on the northmen sleeping around the watch fires.

Quick. Quiet. Nagash impressed his will upon his warriors. He'd learned long ago that the undead did not need to be guided through each and every movement of a given order; there were memories and reflexes that lingered in their rotting bodies, though he could not say precisely how. All he needed to do was provide the impetus, and the corpses would do the rest. Those that performed poorly made good sword-fodder so that the rest could fulfil his wishes.

Long, angular shadows crept towards the northmen. Nagash watched swords rise and fall; powerful hands clamped over mouths and tightened about throats. A few northmen thrashed in the grip of the zombies, but never for more than a few moments. Nagash smiled to himself, whispering an incantation into the night air. Most of the slain northmen rose slowly to their feet.

Now the fire, Nagash ordered.

Several of the skeletons turned towards the watch fires. They reached their hands into the dying flames and drew out pieces of burning wood. One by one, they raised their torches skyward, signalling the Yaghur.

Out on the plain, the barbarians saw the signal fires and broke into a ground-eating charge. Then one of the Yaghur, overcome with bloodlust, threw back his head a howled a savage war cry.

'*Idiots!*' Nagash snarled. More and more howls rent the night as the other Yaghur gave into their rage and bayed for the blood of their foes. Already, shouts of alarm were answering the cries from deeper within the camp. *Attack!* The necromancer commanded. *Kill! Burn!* His lips moved, hissing out another incantation.

The undead warriors surged forwards, moving with a sudden burst of speed and agility. Northmen staggered from their tents, sluggish from sleep and the lingering grip of wine. Most barely had time to gape in shock at their attackers before they were slain. Torches were pressed against the oily hides, and within seconds half a dozen tents were ablaze.

Howling like fiends, the Yaghur came charging into the camp. They swung their clubs at anything that moved, adding to the pandemonium. At Nagash's command, the undead pressed further into the camp. Speed was critical, the necromancer knew. The attackers had to stay ahead of the enemy's ability to organise a proper defence, or the defenders' greater numbers would quickly tip the scales against them.

And yet, many of the Yaghur were milling about the edge of the camp, tearing down tents and looting bodies! Nagash's fingers clawed furrows down the arms of his chair. *Forward*, he commanded the corpses carrying his palanquin. If the barbarians were still there when he reached the edge of the camp he would slay them where they stood!

More fires were spreading through the camp, but now came the sound of fighting as well.

Nagash gazed through the eyes of his warriors, and saw that the Forsaken were reacting quickly to the surprise attack. The northmen were huge, powerfully-built warriors, far larger than their deformed southern kin and almost as large as the giant, bronze-skinned fighting men of faraway Ka-Sabar. They wore leather kilts like the Yaghur, studded with wide disks of bronze, and broad belts hung with polished skulls and long chains of finger bones. Some of the warriors were bare-chested, their skin marked with elaborate scar patterns that wound from their thick necks all the way to their waists, while others wore heavy leather vests covered in layers of small, bronze squares.

They showed no fear at the sight of Nagash's warriors. Instead, they charged headlong into their midst, swinging huge axes or long-bladed swords and screaming the name of their strange god. Bones shattered; rotting bodies burst apart. The Forsaken waded through their foes, heedless of peril. They fought on despite terrible wounds, intent only on slaying as many enemies as they could before they were brought down.

In the darkness and the confusion the northmen even attacked one another, further adding to the chaos. Nagash knew that if the enemy's confusion could be fanned like the flames already consuming the camp, the Forsaken would ultimately defeat themselves.

Then the air over the centre of the enemy camp flickered with orange and red light, and series of small thunderclaps shook the air. Nagash felt the aether tremble with invisible energies, and knew that dozens of his warriors had been obliterated. Hathurk had warned him that the Forsaken warlords were often accompanied by a trio of witches, a custom that dated back to the earliest days of the Yaghur kingdom. Their power, he saw, was considerable.

On the heels of the detonations came the baying of horns. Nagash spat out a curse. The warlords were trying to rally their warriors and organise a counterattack. The necromancer knew that he had to deal with the enemy leaders, and quickly, or his meagre forces would be quickly overwhelmed.

The palanquin had nearly reached the perimeter of the camp. Snarling impatiently, Nagash rose from his seat and leap to the ground. Around him, Forsaken warriors were charging out of the darkness, their blades glinting hungrily in the firelight. The Yaghur attacked them with guttural shouts, but the northmen hacked the unarmoured warriors to pieces.

Snarling, Nagash swept his hand in a wide arc, and unleashed a fan of sizzling green bolts that cut down three northmen who sought to bar his path. He charged towards the centre of the camp, forcing his limbs to move at preternatural speed. The tents weren't laid out in neat lines, like a proper Nehekharan army camp, which forced him to weave his way left and right past one shelter after another. Bodies were strewn across the open ground between the tents, half-glimpsed in the firelight.

Another series of flashes lit the air above the camp, followed by a rumble of thunder. His warriors were being decimated. Nagash called back the survivors, drawing them in towards him in hopes that it would force the warlord and his witches to follow. He found a tent blocking his path and raced around it, coming upon a small, cleared area where eight or ten Yaghur were trading blows with six northmen. Nagash let fly with a volley of glowing missiles, spearing friend and foe alike. The survivors scattered in every direction, clearing the necromancer's path.

Moments later, Nagash found himself at the edge of a much larger, open square. Tall trophy poles marked the corners of the square, festooned with dozens of fresh skulls. Within the square stood perhaps a score of Nagash's warriors, engaged in a fighting withdrawal with a large force of northmen. At the forefront of the enemy warriors was a tall, powerfully muscled warrior, clad in bronze scale armour and swinging a huge, bronze sword. Runes had been engraved along the length of the heavy blade, and the air around the sword seemed to shimmer, like the haze over a desert dune.

At Nagash's arrival, the undead warriors halted their retreat and the Forsaken crashed against them in a howling wave. Over the heads of the warriors, Nagash and the enemy warlord locked eyes, and both recognised the other for who and what they were. But the necromancer spared the warlord only a moment's thought. He wasn't the greatest danger inside the enemy camp. Nagash reached out with his arcane senses, seeking the source of the magical energies that had destroyed so many of his warriors.

There! He sensed swirling vortices of power on the far side of the square, well behind the line of savage northmen. Here was the heart of the Forsaken host. He had to seize it quickly and tear it apart.

Nagash reached out across the camp, summoning every one of his surviving warriors. Then he uttered a powerful incantation, increasing the vigour of the warriors in front of him threefold. They surged forwards, into the Forsaken line, their weapons moving almost in a blur. The sudden push caught the northmen by surprise. Several of them fell, slain outright or bleeding to death from mortal wounds. The rest, including their warlord, found themselves on the defensive. It wouldn't last for long, Nagash knew, but it would give him the time he needed to deal with the witches.

Or so he thought. Almost at once he sensed tendrils of magical energy pulling at the forces contained within his invocation, seeking to dispel it. Angered, Nagash threw out his hands and hissed out another spell. A trio of burning green globes flashed from the space between his hands, arcing like arrows over the enemy line and hurtling towards the witches. But before they could plunge onto their targets, the spheres burst apart in thunderous detonations that buffeted the warriors struggling in the square. The witches' counter-magic was potent indeed.

Within moments, Nagash discovered that their offensive sorceries were deadly as well. Tendrils of dark mist coalesced out of the night air around his warriors and wrapped like ropes around their arms and legs. In seconds, they were thoroughly enmeshed, limiting their movements and the strength of their blows. The Forsaken warriors struck back with bloodthirsty shouts, breaking apart many skeletons in the front rank.

Nagash ignored his warriors' plight. He could not afford to become distracted in a contest of spell and counter-spell with the Forsaken witches. So long as the mists clung to his warriors, it meant one or more witches were occupied with maintaining the spell. That was one or more witches who weren't able to act directly against him. He hurled another volley of magical bolts over the warriors' heads. Again, the bolts were dissipated before they could reach their mark, but only barely so.

By this time, more undead warriors were converging on both sides of the square. Nagash launched another storm of sorcerous missiles, then unleashed his reinforcements on the northmen's flanks. The Forsaken found themselves beset on three sides. More of the northmen fell, and despite the exhortations of their warlord, the courage of the Forsaken began to waver.

Sensing his opportunity, Nagash hurled another volley of bolts – this time aimed right at the faces of the Forsaken warriors. Several of his own warriors were caught in the volley, but that mattered little to him. Men fell to either side of the warlord, their bodies consumed in burst of green fire; the warlord himself was driven back, but some kind of magical protection deflected the force of Nagash's bolts away from his body.

Through the gap created by the dead men, Nagash caught sight of the witches at last. They stood in a loose semicircle, clutching tall, wooden staffs topped with skulls and strings of ritual ornamentation. Nagash sent another stream of bolts hissing their way, and the witches quickly brandished their staffs and chanted counter-spells. The fierce energies burst about them, but once again failed to inflict any damage.

But magic was not the only danger threatening the witches. No sooner had they turned aside Nagash's latest attack than a flight of spears plunged into their midst from the northmen's right flank. One of the weapons struck the right-most witch in the chest. She collapsed, blood pouring from her mouth, and her sisters recoiled in surprise and fear.

The cries of horror from the Forsaken witches was the last straw for the northmen. The Forsaken warriors fell back in confusion, believing that they were on the verge of being surrounded and destroyed. The warlord retreated with them, roaring curses at his men, but no amount of shouting or threats was enough to get them to stand their ground.

With a snarl, Nagash drove his warriors forward, pushing them in a rough semicircle towards the warlord and the surviving witches. He let fly another volley of bolts, and watched as one of the witches was wreathed in green flame. The energies set her robes on fire and wracked her with terrible burns, but somehow she survived the necromancer's spell.

The Forsaken were in full retreat now, fleeing north through the square and into the maze of burning tents beyond. The witches held their ground, and the warlord retreated to stand among them. He turned, his eyes blazing with hatred, and Nagash prepared to crush them beneath an avalanche of sorcerous might. Yet no sooner had be begun the incantation than the last of the witches spat a savage string of syllables and smote the ground with her staff. The shadows around the two witches seemed to enfold them and their master like a cloak. It swallowed them up, and then simply vanished, right before Nagash's eyes.

What manner of sorcery was this? Nagash had never seen the like. Not even his druchii tutors in Khemri had ever hinted at such a thing. What else did these barbarians know that he didn't?

Nagash ordered his warriors to pursue the retreating northmen. Without their leaders, the rest would flee the destruction of their camp, possibly even going so far as to return to their homelands beyond the north edge of the plain. It had been a close-run thing, Nagash realised, much closer than he'd expected. His small force of warriors had been almost destroyed, and there was no telling how many of the Yaghur still survived. Had the battle in the square lasted another few minutes, the outcome might have been very different.

The necromancer made his way across the square, stepping over crushed skeletons and bleeding bodies. He made his way to the witch and stood over her, studying the woman's corpse carefully. She was dressed in fine, dark robes, and wore a curved dagger at her hip. A necklace of bronze plates, engraved with strange runes, rested against her collarbones.

Nagash knelt beside her and picked up her staff. The skull that capped the length of wood wasn't human. He studied it for a few moments in the flickering light before he realised that it was the skull of a huge rat.

Shouts split the air behind him. Nagash turned to see Aighul and the rest of the Yaghur hetmen come charging into the square. Most of them bore battle-wounds, and their weapons dripped with blood. Hathurk accompanied them, his eyes blazing with triumph.

'They're fleeing!' the supplicant cried. 'The northmen are running for home! It all happened as you said it would, master!'

Hardly, Nagash thought. He had underestimated the Forsaken. They were far more powerful than he'd expected. They'd won because the enemy had been overconfident and unprepared. Next time, things would be different.

And there would have to be a next time. The fighting would continue until the Forsaken had been conquered. There was no choice now. The campaign could take years, or even decades, but it would only end when one side or the other was broken. And

Nagash intended to make them subjects of his growing empire. They would prove far more useful than the Yaghur.

Aighul approached the necromancer slowly, his expression a mix of fear and wonder. He stopped a few yards from Nagash and sank to his knees.

'All hail the god of the mountain,' he said in a hollow voice. The hetman bent at the waist, pressing his forehead to the blood-soaked ground. One by one, the other hetmen followed suit.

Nagash rose to his feet. Their obeisance meant nothing to him. He recalled how the barbarians had very nearly ruined the attack at the outset, and felt nothing but contempt for them.

Hathurk approached the necromancer, an ecstatic look on his crude features. He came right up to Nagash and bowed deeply. 'The hetmen are ready to receive their reward, master,' he said proudly.

Nagash suppressed an angry sneer. When he'd promised to give them the secret of the northmen's strength, he'd meant skills like metalworking and simple tactics. But such things were lost on these animals. No doubt they expected some kind of magical gift – or worse, a damned miracle!

A cruel idea came to him then. He looked at Hathurk and smiled, as a man might smile at an obedient dog.

They want to make the strength of the Forsaken their own? Very well. Tell them this: the power of a man lies in his flesh and his bones. His heart is the fount of his strength. The liver is the seat of his courage. If you would become like them, you must consume them, down to the very bones.'

Hathurk's eyes widened in shock. 'You... you mean–'

'Tell them!' Nagash commanded. *'I command it! Tell them that they must feast upon the dead. It is the only way.'*

The supplicant stared at Nagash. A look of dread crept across his face. After a moment, the necromancer thought that Hathurk would refuse, but then the fool bowed to him once again and turned to give the hetmen the first commandment of their new god.

⊰ FIFTEEN ⊱

The Shadow of the Hawk

*Lahmia, the City of the Dawn, in the 76th year of
Phakth the Just
(-1597 Imperial Reckoning)*

THE NEWS OF King Lamashizzar's death took flight within hours of the announcement by the palace. Swift messengers raced across the Golden Plain, carrying word to Lybaras and Rasetra, and then past ruined Mahrak to the Valley of the Kings and the cities of the west. Within months, royal processions from each of the seven cities were underway, heading east to pay their respects to the dead king and to gauge the new state of affairs in the City of the Dawn. It was rare for a queen to assume the throne in the great cities of Nehekhara, and unheard of in Lahmia itself. Speculation was rampant on how this would affect the complex web-work of trade deals that the city had woven during Lamashizzar's reign. The priest kings hastened to Lahmia as quickly as they could manage, suspecting that those who reached the queen first would stand the best chance of profiting under the new regime.

Queen Amunet of distant Numas was first to arrive, having journeyed by barge up the River Vitae and deep into the mountains, where the great trade stations had been built around the shores of the wide Vitae Tarn. From there the Numasi had off-loaded two score of their fine steeds and rode swiftly through the twisting mountain passages until they reached the northern edge of the Golden Plain.

King Teremun of Zandri followed the same path and arrived less than a month later, leading a procession of northern slaves laden with gifts for the new queen. The delegation from Zandri had been bedevilled by bandit raiders as they crossed the plain, losing several of their number along the way before finding refuge within the city.

Next to arrive was dour, white-haired King Naeem of Quatar, accompanied by a solemn retinue of ash-daubed priests. Beset on all sides by the dispossessed hierophants of Mahrak, the Quatari ruler had spent his entire life trying to restore both his city and theirs, with minimal success. Had it not been for a quick-witted captain at the city gates, the delegation might have been taken for beggars and turned away.

Two weeks after the Quatari delegation came a much larger procession, led by King Ahmun-hotep of

Ka-Sabar and a score of nobles clad in the old armour of the once-mighty Legion of Bronze. Though the city still lay mostly in ruin following the dreadful siege a half-century before, Ahmun-hotep intended to show his peers that he and his city remained a force to be reckoned with. His servants bore rich gifts for the queen that likely had been stripped from the royal palace itself, and the blood staining the tips of his warriors' spears told of the bandits who'd come to grief trying to wrest those treasures from Ahmun-hotep's grasp.

Curiously, the cities closest to Lahmia were the last to send delegations to honour the queen. First came King Shepret of Rasetra, hard-faced and armed for war, at the head of a procession of royal guardsmen armoured in glossy lizard-scale. Unlike the other delegations, who bore treasures of gold and precious stones, the Rasetrans brought with them the riches of the deep jungle: raw amber, polished thunder lizard horn and jars of exotic herbs found nowhere else in all of the land.

As lavish as the gifts were, they were also a message for the queen: Rasetra had regained much of its strength since the dark days after the war, driving back the lizard tribes and reclaiming much of their lost territory. In short, the Rasetrans meant to show the queen that Lahmia would be far better off treating them as friends and allies rather than rivals.

Last of all, more than three months after the arrival of the Numasi delegation, came the Priest King of Lybaras and his fierce warrior-queen. They arrived

with even less pomp than the dour Rasetrans,
attended by a retinue of nobles and spearmen clad in
glossy plates of dark iron.

The sight was a shock to the Lahmian nobility. For
years there had been rumours that the Lybarans had
been hard at work searching for local sources of iron
in the Brittle Peaks. Not only had they evidently succeeded, they had also divined the art of working the
dense metal, something that even the Lahmian royal
artisans hadn't been able to achieve. It was also clear
that the rumours of cooperation with Rasetra was
borne out in the martial skill of the warriors under
the Lybaran king's command. Unlike Lahmia, the
City of Scholars had dealt aggressively with the rov-
ing bands of raiders that had plagued the trade road
within their sphere of control, and it was said that on
more than one occasion the Lybaran queen herself
had led expeditions to run down the largest and
most stubborn raiders. She rode in full armour
alongside the marching warriors, her hair bound
back in tight braids and her expression as unsparing
and fierce as her namesake.

Rather than keep the royal delegations at a lavish
remove by housing them in tent cities, as Lamashizzar had once done, Neferata instead welcomed each
procession into the royal palace. They were assigned
luxurious quarters, as befitted their stations, and
treated with generous, if sombre, hospitality. The
opportunity provided by the queen wasn't lost on
her guests, each of whom made use of the proximity
to the throne to press for their individual agendas.

For weeks, Neferata met each ruler in private, discussing matters of state deep into the night – all but the kings of Rasetra and Lybaras, who treated the queen's representatives with careful courtesy but chose to keep their own counsels nonetheless.

By the time all the kings and queens were assembled, Lamashizzar had been more than six months in the tomb. Rather than take part in a funeral procession the visiting rulers took part in a solemn ritual of remembrance in the great necropolis to the north of the city, then spent another six days attending lengthy afternoon councils and sumptuous feasts held in the great palace garden.

The guests used the council meetings to test the success of their private dealings with the queen and determine where they stood in relation to their peers. Each and every one soon discovered that, no matter how ruthlessly they'd pursued their agendas, not one of them had emerged in a better position than their peers. If anything, their strengths and weaknesses had been carefully exploited to neutralise their counterparts, creating a status quo that left each city prosperous and stable only so long as they fulfilled their obligations to Lahmia.

The net of trade and debt, first envisioned by Lamasheptra, then laid down by Lamashizzar his son, had finally been drawn tight by Neferata, trapping the great cities at last. And not one of Nehekhara's rulers could say just exactly how it had happened. They had understood the danger when they'd begun the journey to Lahmia, had plotted and schemed diverse ways to counter it, and yet their cunning had all come to naught when matched against the wiles of Lahmia's canny and seductive queen.

By the end of the sixth day it was clear to the visiting rulers that they had journeyed to Lahmia not just to bear witness to the passing of a king, but to also formalise the city's ascension as the centre of wealth and power in all Nehekhara.

In private councils, sometimes well into their cups, the royal guests confessed their dismay to one another in rueful whispers. They wondered how all their plans could have gone so wrong, pitted against a cloistered and untried queen. The rulers of Rasetra and Lybaras listened closely, but kept their suspicions to themselves.

THE HALL OF Kings glittered like a treasure vault in the slanting rays of the afternoon sun. The gifts of five great kings and queens had been heaped upon the gleaming marble floor, at the feet of towering basalt statues that flanked the long processional leading to the Lahmian throne. No less than eight of Nehekhara's lost gods looked down upon the supplicants of the court. The first two, closest to the chamber's great double doors, were grim, jackal-headed Djaf, the death-bringer, and faceless, hooded Usirian, who judges the worth of the souls of the dead. Sixty paces onward stood lion-headed Geheb, god of the earth and giver of strength, standing opposite Phakth, the hawk-faced bringer of justice. Yet another sixty paces further, at the feet of the wide steps leading to the great throne, rose sensuous, cat-faced Basth, giver of love and beauty; her feline eyes seemed to stare mischievously across the great hall at slender Tahoth, giver of knowledge and keeper of lore. Finally, towering to either side of the throne, stood Lahmia's patron goddess Asaph, giver of magic and architect of the sacred covenant, and mighty Ptra, god of the sun and father of all Creation.

The guardians of the throne faced westward, towards the sea. Sunlight streamed through high, rectangular openings set above the chamber's entrance, bathing the statues in golden light. Only the great throne room in Khemri had rivalled the chamber in splendour and regal glory; now it was without equal in all the land.

So, too, the great throne of Lahmia had been wrought from the same fine-grained, dark wood as the one that had once sat in the palace of Khemri. There was nothing like it in all of Nehekhara, and legends said it had been brought out of the deep parts of the southern jungles during the Great Migration of mankind. The throne was high-backed and deep, shaped in sinuous curves that suggested it had been grown rather than carved by the hand of man; its thick, rolled arms were glossy and smooth, polished by generations of royal hands. They felt warm beneath Neferata's touch as she leaned back in the ancient chair and studied the approaching figures of the Imperial delegation. Even at a hundred paces she could read their discomfort in the curt *swish-swish* of their slippered feet and the thin whistle of breath through their tightly-pressed lips.

The queen was clad in her richest robes of state: layers of rich saffron embroidered with gold and thousands of tiny pearls. A girdle of gold thread and lapis circled her narrow waist, and a thick necklace of gold plate circled her alabaster throat. Her lustrous hair had been bound up with golden pins and more strands of pearl, and thick bracelets of gold circled her slender wrists. Nestled in the crook of her left arm was the sceptre of Asaph, a heavy rod of solid gold wrought in the shape of a pair of twining asps and inset with tiny scales of onyx. Upon her face rested the cold, lifeless contours of her golden mask. It was the first time she had worn it since rising from her deathbed. She had resolved that the scheming barbarians of the far east deserved nothing more.

Sunlight shone from the mask's polished surface, almost too bright to look upon. Neferata felt its rays upon her bare hands and felt little more than a faint discomfort, like the fading ache of a *hixa* sting. Even Nagash and his immortals had grown to shun Ptra's searing rays, but the queen found that she could move about in the morning and afternoon with little trouble. She was nothing like the necromancer or his minions; somehow she had been reborn in a crucible of poison, sorcery and death. The interactions of the sphinx's venom with the powers of the elixir and the workings of Arkhan's rituals had transformed her into a being of flesh that existed beyond the reach of death.

She was no mere immortal. Neferata had become like unto Asaph herself, and the secrets of the world were laid bare at her feet. She could sense the passage of the sun through the sky and feel the rhythm of the tides through the stones beneath her feet. She sensed the presence of each and every living thing in the echoing audience chamber, from the members of her privy council who stood at the feet of her throne to the Celestial Prince and his retainers and even the stolid-faced royal guards who stood just outside the chamber door. She could hear their every movement, smell the scents upon their skin and taste the rich, sweet blood hissing through their veins.

It was blood, always blood, that was uppermost in her mind. If there was one weakness to her new existence, it was the endless thirst for human blood. It was the wellspring of her power, a thousand times purer and more potent than Nagash's petty brew, but almost as soon as she had drunk her fill of it, she found herself craving more. Neferata found that she had to drink each and every night to sustain her strength. Fortunately, with a city of souls at her beck and call she knew that she would never go without.

The queen smiled languidly behind the implacable curves of her mask and studied Prince Xian's young, handsome face with the cold intensity of a hungry lioness. His expression was set in a mask of calculated disdain as he and his retinue approached to within a dozen paces of the queen's privy council and came to an abrupt halt, as though noticing the Lahmian nobles for the first time. As before, the

Scion of Heaven was accompanied by a fawning translator, a handful of imperious-looking bureaucrats and a silent, demure young woman whose face and hands were painted as white as Neferata's own. The queen could not be certain if she was the prince's wife or merely a favoured concubine. Her hands were clasped at her waist, and her eyes were focussed on a point just behind Xian's heels.

Xian gestured almost imperceptibly with one long, golden fingernail, and his translator immediately took one small step towards the throne. 'The Scion of Heaven offers his condolences on the death of your husband, the king,' he said stiffly. 'He cannot help but observe your sorrow, so deep that even the simplest ceremonies are too terrible a burden to bear.'

Neferata's smile sharpened. 'The Scion of Heaven is mistaken,' she said simply, careful to keep her tone neutral and unaffected. 'I am conscious of my obligations as ruler and host. Has he not been treated with all due courtesy and respect?'

The translator paused, pressing his lips together tightly as he struggled for a proper response. 'It is to my eternal shame that I must inform you that your guards have refused to admit the Scion of Heaven's servants to prepare the hall for his arrival.' He spread his hands. 'Where is my lord and master to take his ease, while he indulges you with fine tea and civilized conversation?'

'There is but one chair in the Hall of Kings,' Neferata replied coldly, and watched with satisfaction as the translator shivered in response. 'And it is a place for conducting affairs of state, not indulging in idle chatter.' The queen waved her hand dismissively. 'Though the Scion of Heaven can be forgiven his misapprehension, since this is the first time he has been invited to attend upon the throne.'

One of the prince's bureaucrats let out a strangled gasp; the rest kept their composure, but Neferata could hear their hearts beating angrily in their chests. She couldn't have insulted the prince any worse if she'd walked up to him and slapped him across the face.

The translator was completely taken aback. Uncertain how to proceed, he turned and stared at Xian, whose own expression might have been carved from stone. Once more, the Son of Heaven gestured to the functionary with a tiny flick of one curved nail. The man bowed deeply to the prince, then drew a deep breath and turned back to the queen.

'The Scion of Heaven has the honour of bearing tidings from his divine father, the Emperor of Heaven and Earth,' the translator said with as much affronted dignity as he could muster. 'He wishes you to know of the great fortune bestowed upon the Empire in the form of the gold mines of Guanjian province. So great is their bounty that the value of gold is not as it was when your father incurred his debt to the Empire.' A tiny glint of satisfaction shone in the functionary's eyes as he bowed before the throne. 'A single payment remains to settle the matter between Lahmia and the Celestial Household, but it must be no less than triple the agreed upon amount in order to satisfy the terms of the debt.'

Silence fell across the great hall. The prince and his retainers watched and waited, expecting cries of outrage and growing ever so slightly concerned when none was forthcoming. Finally, after a long moment, the queen shook her head.

'No.'

Now the cries of outrage began in earnest, but it was the prince's retainers who shouted their anger at the insult to the Scion of Heaven's honour. One of the functionaries even went so far as to take a step forward and raise his fist to the queen. Before he could take a second step Abhorash was blocking the man's path. The tip of the champion's iron sword rested in the hollow of the bureaucrat's throat.

'Enough,' Neferata said, her voice carrying clearly over the tumult. 'Prince Xian, the insolence of your retainers offends me. They will remove themselves at once.'

The translator puffed up his narrow chest. 'It is not for you to dictate–'

'Go,' Neferata commanded, exerting her will. The Imperial functionaries fled, all but stumbling over the hems of their robes in their haste to obey the queen's command. Within moments, the prince and his woman were alone.

Neferata rose slowly from the throne. Her movements were fluid and graceful, as mesmerising as the movements of a cobra. She descended the stairs and approached the Scion of Heaven, who held his ground out of sheer, stubborn pride. The queen drew close enough to touch him, staring deeply into his dark eyes.

'What your father asks is impossible,' Neferata said softly. She exerted her will and listened with satisfaction as the prince's heart quickened in response. 'You know that as well as I.' The golden mask cocked slightly to one side as she studied him. 'You're a clever man, Prince Xian. Pragmatic too, else you'd have never agreed to come here in the first place. So perhaps there is a way to settle Lahmia's debt with a currency other than gold.'

Prince Xian frowned slightly. He hesitated but an instant before answering the queen. 'What have you to offer?' he said in fluent Nehekharan.

The queen took a step closer and laid a hand on his chest, right at the juncture of neck and collarbone. She could feel the pulse of blood vessels throbbing sweetly beneath the prince's skin. Her lips parted, brushing against the tips of razor-sharp fangs.

'For you, oh prince,' she whispered. 'I offer the gift of life eternal.'

Xian's eyes widened. She could sense the struggle within him, as reason warred with the seductive force of her will. He wanted to disbelieve her, to heed his father's wishes and close the trap around Lahmia, but his heart refused to obey.

A tiny frown creased the prince's smooth forehead. 'How?' he asked faintly.

Neferata held up a tiny, ceramic vial. Within lay a single dram of her blood. 'Take this,' she said. 'Return to your home in the city, and when the sun has set, drink it down. Then you will understand.'

Moving as though in a dream, the prince reached out and took the vial from her hand. The vigour stored within faded much quicker than Nagash's elixir, but its potency was a hundred times greater. She had tried it already on the members of the cabal, and was well pleased with the results. 'Return to me tomorrow,' she continued, 'and we will discuss our arrangement in more detail.'

Xian gripped the vial tightly. His heart bade him obey, but still his mind tried to resist. 'I… I cannot defy the will of the Emperor,' he protested.

'Might the Emperor's will not change when he hears of this?' Neferata said, tapping the vial lightly with a lacquered nail. 'Or with this power at his command, might a son not rise up to supplant the father, and become Emperor himself?'

'I…' the prince began. His expression grew troubled, but then slowly he nodded. 'I will think on this.'

Neferata smiled. 'Then go,' she said, 'but tell no one of what we have discussed.' Her gaze drifted to the woman standing in the prince's shadow. On a whim, the queen said, 'She will remain here in the meantime, to vouchsafe your discretion.'

Xian turned and looked at the woman, as though suddenly remembering that she was there. 'Her?' he asked, clearly surprised by the queen's request. 'She is nothing to me.'

Neferata saw the woman stiffen slightly. 'Then she will remain here at my pleasure,' the queen said coldly. 'I thank you for the gift. Now go. Your servants await you.'

Xian turned back to her, as though to protest further, but with one last look in Neferata's eyes, the last of the prince's resolve was swept away. He sketched an awkward, uncertain bow, and then retreated dazedly from the hall.

The queen contemplated the woman. Her thin shoulders trembled faintly, but she continued to stare resolutely at the floor. Neferata frowned slightly. She reached out and touched a finger to the woman's chin and gently raised her head. For a moment they regarded one another, their expressions concealed by carefully constructed masks.

'What is your name?' Neferata asked.

The woman frowned slightly. The queen sighed. Naturally the woman wouldn't speak Nehekharan. 'Ubaid,' Neferata snapped. 'Show her to the Women's Palace and see that she's made comfortable.'

Ubaid hurried to the woman's side. The queen's displeasure had crumpled the once-proud grand vizier; he had bent beneath her will to the point that he was hunched over like a whipped dog. His eyes were wide and furtive, and his hands trembled as though with palsy. Silently he took the young woman's arm and led her into the shadows at the rear of the hall.

As they left the queen returned to the great throne and stared down at her privy council. Not for the first time, she found herself wondering who had sided with Lamashizzar. Lord Zurhas, the king's young cousin, had most likely been one of the king's supporters. Abhorash, perhaps? Certainly not W'soran; the king would never have given him the freedom to explore Nagash's works as she had. Or would he? Such an offer would have made for a powerful bargaining tool.

None of them knew how to react to her now. She could sense their unease, now matter how hard they worked to conceal it. On one level they were repelled by her transformation, while on another level they craved the power she possessed. Only Abhorash, the stoic master warrior, seemed unaffected by the allure of her newfound power. In the end, all of them would have to accept the poisoned cup, Neferata reckoned, whether they wanted it or not. She needed their support in order to rule the city; the only way she could guarantee that was if they shared the same degree of risk that she did. She now had Arkhan's notes in her possession, and Ubaid had led her to the vial of sphinx venom hidden in Lamashizzar's quarters. In time, Neferata was certain that she could reproduce the process.

Lord Ankhat waited until Prince Xian had left the hall before he spoke. 'It might work,' he mused. 'Much depends on the amount of influence he wields at home. The Emperor might simply send another, more powerful envoy to demand payment.'

Whatever his loyalties might have been, Ankhat had proven invaluable to her since Lamashizzar's death. It was he who concocted the story that a priest of Sokth, patron god of assassins, had crept into the palace to murder the king in reprisal for his treatment of refugees from Mahrak. As the story went, the assassin-priest had attacked the queen first, slaughtering her handmaidens and striking her with a poisoned needle, then fighting his way to the king's chambers and slaying him before being slain in turn by Abhorash and the royal guard. It was a cunning move, one that focussed the need for revenge on a group of outsiders that were already held in contempt by much of the populace. More importantly, Neferata's recovery had been touted as nothing less than a miracle, reminding Lahmia and the rest of the land of her divine lineage. Support for her rule had been absolute.

It was also Ankhat who arranged for the disappearance of Arkhan's decapitated corpse. W'soran and even Abhorash had been adamant that the immortal's body should be incinerated, but at the last moment, Neferata found that she could not bring herself to permit it. Instead, Ankhat discreetly purchased a pauper's tomb in the great city necropolis and had the immortal interred there at the same time King Lamashizzar was being placed inside his own, far greater tomb farther north. Neferata felt she owed the ghastly creature at least that much.

The queen considered Ankhat's counsel and nodded thoughtfully. 'Perhaps, but it would take many months, possibly even years, for another delegation to arrive. That gives us time to build up the treasury and consolidate our power.' She shrugged. 'If the Emperor is a pragmatic ruler, he'll take our final payment and accept the fact that his gambit failed. If not… well, we will be in a far better position to defend our interests.'

Abhorash turned and looked up at her. He did that very rarely now, which hinted at his surprise. 'You mean war with the Silk Lands? That would be ruinous!'

'That is certainly not my intent,' Neferata said smoothly. 'But I will defend this city with every power at my command. You may be assured of that.'

'Then you should worry more about enemies closer to home,' Ushoran said quietly.

Neferata straightened. The Lord of Masks was infamous for his intrigues within the city, and she knew that he spent lavishly to maintain a vast network of spies within Lahmia and elsewhere. 'Enemies within the city?'

'At present, yes,' Ushoran replied. 'My sources tell me that the King of Lybaras is… uneasy about your ascension to the throne. And he's been sharing his concerns with others.'

The queen frowned. Ushoran liked to savour his revelations, but she wasn't in a patient mood. 'Such as?'

'The King of Rasetra, for a start. Since he's been here, he's also held late-night meetings with the King of Quatar and the Queen of Numas.'

'And what exactly are his concerns?'

Ushoran shook his head. 'That I do not know, great one. But it is safe to assume that Rasetra will be sympathetic, if for no other reason than the age-old friendship between the two cities. Quatar and Numas might not be receptive yet, but...'

Neferata sighed irritably. 'What lies at the heart of this? What are the Lybarans' concerns, exactly?'

The Lord of Masks shrugged. 'That I cannot say, great one. King Anhur has been very careful to avoid details.'

Lord Zurhas shifted uncomfortably, clearly torn between the desire to appear useful and the fear of gaining the queen's attention. 'Perhaps you could ask Queen Khalida? Surely she would tell you.'

Neferata sighed under her breath. How long had it been since she'd spoken to Khalida? Years, certainly. After a moment, she shook her head.

'There is no need,' she said, rising from the throne. 'As it happens, I had already planned on a pair of announcements at tonight's feast that will put an end to these intrigues. No doubt the Lybarans covet Lahmia's newfound power, but we've laid our plans with care. The treaties have been signed and sealed. Nothing short of war can break them, and no city in Nehekhara would contemplate such a thing.'

Neferata reached up and pulled away her mask. As one, the assembled nobles lowered their heads – in respect, to be sure, but not without a certain amount of fear as well. That was well, as far as she was concerned.

The queen smiled down at the men. 'Lahmia's time of glory is at hand. Savour this, and thank the forgotten gods that you were alive to see it.'

* * *

NEFERATA'S GUESTS WERE feted in the great palace garden that night, seated at the same wide, circular table that had served them during the long council sessions with Lamashizzar more than a half-century before. The feasting had begun an hour after sunset and had lasted well into the evening. Rich courses of fish and fowl, prepared with fiery spices imported from the Silk Lands, were served with jars of fine wine and bowls of thick, yeasty beer. Musicians and silk-clad dancers beguiled and entertained the royal guests between courses, allowing time for the food to settle and the potent drink to mellow their moods. Small braziers had been discretely situated around the wide clearing, filling the air with sweet-smelling, slightly narcotic vapours.

The queen sat in the tall chair that had once belonged to her husband and studied her guests from beneath heavy-lidded eyes. She pretended to eat a little when each course was served, and the servants were instructed to clear her dishes away first. Since her transformation, food and wine had lost their savour; in fact, even the smallest taste caused her throat to tighten and her stomach to knot in pain. No amount of lotus root or drugged incense could dull her senses, either. Fortunately, the small goblets of hot, red liquid Ubaid served her between courses more than made up for the absence of solid sustenance.

She watched the gathered rulers closely for signs of suspicion or discontent. King Fadil of Zandri was raucously drunk, laughing loudly and hissing salacious whispers into the ear of a pale-skinned barbarian concubine. To his left, Queen Amunet of Numas made no effort to conceal her disdain as she picked at a bowl of spiced eels with a long-tyned copper fork. King Naeem, grey-haired and gloomy beyond his years, sat amid a flock of querulous old priests who stolidly refused to share in the queen's entertainments.

That left the kings of Rasetra and Lybaras. King Shepret sat to Neferata's left, sipping from a jar of beer like a common soldier. The elderly Rasetran king, still hale despite the passage of years, had eaten well from all the fine offerings at the feast table, and had taken great pleasure in the procession of silk-clad dancers that had whirled past him during the course of the evening. Yet Neferata could not mistake the tension in the warrior king's shoulders, and the wary glances he cast about the table when he thought no one was watching. She also couldn't help but notice that the dagger hanging from the king's belt was anything but ceremonial.

The King of Lybaras sat to Shepret's left, almost close enough to touch, and yet they had spoken scarcely two words to one another since the feast began. Instead, Anhur had spent nearly the entire time in quiet, sometimes heated, conversation with his queen. Neferata hardly recognised her beloved cousin; her years in Lybaras had transformed her, not into a quiet, submissive queen, but into the fierce, radiant warrior she'd always longed to be. She had shed the soft flesh of a cloistered princess and become lean, tanned and muscular, with sword-scars on her hands and a Rasetran warrior's tattoo marked in red ink along the right side of her slender neck. Her black hair was done up in a score of tight braids and bound with a gold pin at the base of her neck, accentuating the sharp lines of her face. She was a scandal in royal society; not even the queens of war-like Rasetra were permitted to learn the ways of sword and spear, much less march with the common soldiery. But Khalida did as she pleased, riding, fight-ing and hunting like any man, and public opinion be damned. Supposedly the Lybaran people loved her for it, which filled Neferata with equal measures of pride and bitter envy. They hadn't spoken at all since Khalida had returned to the city. Even at the feast table she avoided Neferata's gaze. When she wasn't speaking to the king she was trading whispers with a young, nervous-looking woman that the queen was certain she'd seen somewhere before.

Had she offended Khalida somehow? Neferata couldn't imagine how such a thing was possible, unless her cousin somehow resented her arranged marriage to Anhur. She found herself studying the young Lybaran king and wondering if perhaps her relationship with her cousin might improve if Anhur were to have an unfortunate accident. The idea had its merits, she thought.

It was late in the evening now. Servants were emerging from hidden paths to carry away the last courses of the feast. Ubaid appeared at Neferata's side with another brimming goblet to slake her thirst. She sipped at the hot liquid as the servants finished their work, savouring the rush of strength and vitality that flooded her limbs and took the chill of the evening away.

When the servants had finished their work and withdrawn, Neferata returned the goblet to Ubaid's trembling hands and rose smoothly from her chair. The nobles of her privy council, who were seated either side of the queen, immediately set aside their drinks and gazed at her expectantly. Within moments her royal guests took note and paid heed as well. King Shepret studied her over the rim of his beer, his expression neutral. Anhur folded his arms tightly across his chest, his gaze darting uneasily between Khalida and Neferata. Only Khalida failed to meet her gaze; her cousin stared stubbornly at the tabletop, tracing patterns across the polished surface with a close-bitten thumbnail.

For a fleeting instant, she was tempted to use her power to bend these kings and queens to her will. It was so tempting, so easy… and yet, Ushoran's warnings about Rasetra and Lybaras gave her pause. If she tried, and somehow failed, the backlash might be catastrophic. And there was no sense taking such a risk when she had other sources of power to draw upon.

'Beloved friends,' she said, lifting her arms and smiling warmly, as though she meant to take them all into a wide embrace. 'Words cannot express how truly honoured I am that you made such a long and arduous journey to pay your respects to my husband, whom we pray has reached the company of his ancestors in the Lands of the Dead. His loss is a terrible blow to all of Nehekhara, but after speaking to most of you over the course of the last few months, I'm hopeful that his legacy of prosperity and renewal will continue to live on.'

Neferata allowed her smile to fade, transforming her luminous expression into one of wistful regret. 'If there is one thing I have learned from this awful experience, it's that there are still a great many Nehekharans who are still suffering from the horrors wrought by the Usurper. The breaking of the sacred covenant and the passing of the old gods have left a terrible wound on our collective soul. We no longer think of this as a blessed land, nor we a blessed people.'

That got the attention of King Amunet and his gaggle of priests. Their sullen expressions vanished, replaced with looks of genuine surprise and faint, dawning hope. That sent a ripple of interest through the other rulers as well. Anhur's bemused expression turned increasingly wary.

'Beloved friends, honoured kings and queens, I say that the gods are with us yet. The bloodline of Lahmia remains strong. The blessings of Asaph have not deserted us, even in these dark times! It was she, great goddess of beauty and magic, who persuaded great Ptra to take pity on our people and make this land a paradise.'

Neferata's gaze went around the table, meeting the eyes of each ruler in turn. 'Hear me, friends. The goddess lives on through me, as she has lived in each of my ancestors since the dawn of civilization. We are not forsaken. If we come together and restore what Nagash cast down, perhaps we can forge a *new* covenant – one that will lead us into a golden age of rebirth.'

'Praise the gods!' cried an elderly hierophant. The old man rose to his feet, his age-spotted hands rising skyward. 'Praise be! We are delivered at last!'

The queen smiled fondly at the old man. Go on believing that, she thought. It will help convince the others.

'In the past, my husband believed it was wiser and more compassionate to focus on the needs of the living rather than the memories of the dead,' the queen continued. 'And it is not for me to question the wisdom of his policies at this late date. But now that our cities are well on their way to recovery, and we have a plan to ensure our continued trade and prosperity, I believe that now is the time we moved to erase the last traces of Nagash's infamy. Mahrak, the City of Hope, must be rebuilt. Khemri, the Living City, must be restored to her former glory once more.'

Everyone, even drunken King Teremun, stared in shock. Several of the priests began to whisper prayers of thanks to their gods, silent tears trickling down their lined cheeks. Neferata paused, letting the moment build, until finally King Shepret took the bait.

The old warrior-king of Rasetra put aside his beer and leaned forward, resting his elbows on the table.

'And how do you plan to oversee such a restoration?' he asked.

Neferata acknowledged the question with a respectful nod. 'In truth, I wouldn't presume to do such a thing at all,' she said, 'not when there are better people, like yourself, who have already demonstrated a desire to undertake the effort. Rasetra was born from distant Khemri; the bloodline of her royal house runs in your veins. By rights, it should be for you and your children to determine the city's future. I merely wish to share some of Lahmia's riches to make the task possible.'

Shepret didn't know how to respond at first. That wasn't nearly the response he'd expected. 'How... how much do you propose?' he asked.

'Ten thousand talents of gold each year, until such time as we agree that the city's reconstruction is complete,' the queen replied.

King Telemun gasped in shock. Queen Amunet's eyes went as wide as dinner-plates.

King Naeem drew in a long breath and pressed his palms against the tabletop. The look on his face hinted that he was afraid he might be dreaming. 'What of Mahrak, great queen?' he said. 'Surely you can do no less for the City of Hope.'

Again, Neferata nodded. 'Nor shall I. You shall have ten thousand talents of gold each year for you and Mahrak's surviving hierophants to use for the city's reconstruction.'

Pandemonium ensued. Mahrak's priests erupted in loud cries of joy, praising King Naeem and Queen

Neferata with equal fervour. Queen Amunet rose from her seat and went around to speak intently to King Shepret, whose eyes were half-glazed with shock. King Telemun threw back his head and roared for more wine.

They were fabulous sums of money, far richer than either ruler could have reasonably hoped for, but in truth they were little more than half of what Lahmia had been paying annually to the Empire. Lahmia would still profit, and while Rasetra and Quatar would spend decades, even centuries, focusing their efforts on rebuilding two cities that would never again enjoy the wealth and power that they'd once possessed. By the time they realised they'd been duped, Lahmia's pre-eminence would be unassailable. It was the crowning triumph to decades of carefully laid schemes.

'LIES!'

The shout cut through the din like the peal of a war horn. Khalida was on her feet, hands clenched into fists and trembling with rage. Her face was pale and her expression anguished.

'Queen Neferata lies,' Khalida declared. 'It's not the blessings of Asaph that lend her beauty and unnatural youth, but vile necromancy! She consorts with monsters, and practises the damned sorcery of Nagash himself!'

Neferata stared at her cousin in stunned silence. 'Khalida?' she finally managed to say. 'How... how can you say such things?'

'I have a witness!' Khalida snarled. She pointed to the woman seated beside her. 'Aiyah was there when the pale-skinned creature appeared at the Women's Palace with your body in his arms! She witnessed the rituals, and the obscene bloodletting! It was a miracle she managed to escape the palace and reach Lybaras with the truth!'

Now Neferata knew where she'd seen the girl before. Aiyah the handmaiden would not meet the queen's eyes, as though she feared that her very soul would be forfeit if she did so. Betrayed, by a mere handmaiden? The very idea galled her.

'I don't know what the little fool is talking about,' Neferata shot back. 'You'd take the word of a handmaiden over that of the rightful Queen of Lahmia?'

Khalida continued, as though she hadn't heard. 'How long?' she demanded. 'How long had you been worshipping at the feet of the Usurper? I always wondered why you never aged, cousin. Did Lamashizzar know? Is that why he poisoned you?'

Neferata's hand came down on the table like a thunderclap. '*You go too far!*' she snapped, transmuting shock and sudden fear into burning anger. 'How *dare* you sit at my table, share my bread and salt, and then accuse me of such terrible things, when I alone in all of Nehekhara still bear the mark of the gods' favour!'

'Beware, cousin! If the gods still hear us, they will not suffer such blasphemy lightly!' Khalida shot back.

'It is you who blaspheme, Khalida!' Neferata cried. 'The innocent have nothing to fear from the gods!'

'Then challenge me,' Khalida said. 'Prove your innocence beyond a shadow of a doubt.' A glint of triumph shone in the warrior queen's eye. 'Let us cross blades, and see who the gods truly favour.'

Too late, Neferata realised she'd gone too far. Khalida had laid the trap, and she'd charged headlong into it. She did not dare refuse, especially not in front of a gaggle of priests and hierophants. It would undermine everything she had worked so hard to achieve.

'So be it,' she said numbly. 'Abhorash, bring me a blade.'

The preparations were made largely in silence. Lord Ankhat led Neferata away from the table to the far side of the garden clearing. For a wonder, there were no clouds overhead, and the queen marvelled at the vault of stars glittering coldly over the palace. Khalida followed several minutes later; King Anhur dogged her heels, whispering urgently, but she paid him no mind. She had bound back her voluminous sleeves with a pair of leather cords, and the hem of her feast robe had been pinned back so that it wouldn't tangle her feet. Neferata saw that Khalida was wearing sturdy leather sandals instead of slippers, the kind that soldiers wore on the battlefield. On any other day it might have amused her, but now the sight left her cold. *She was planning this all along*, the queen realised. *One way or another, this evening was going to end in blood.*

Abhorash appeared before her, gripping a bronze blade in his hands. The champion's expression was stricken. He held out the hilt to her; it took Neferata a moment to realise he meant her to take it. The leather wrapping felt cold against her palm. The weapon was short and straight, like an oversized dagger about two feet long, but it seemed to fit her hand well. She stared morbidly at the tip of the blade. 'Not iron?' she asked.

The champion shook his head. 'You'll notice that Khalida isn't using iron either,' he said, nodding slightly in her direction. 'Bronze is lighter and quicker. She was hoping you'd take iron and give her one more advantage.' He paused, pressing his lips together as if uncertain what to say next. 'Have you any training, great one? Any at all?'

'Don't be stupid,' Neferata snapped.

Abhorash grimaced. 'Then you're going to have to make this quick,' he said to her. 'You're faster and stronger than she is. She doesn't know it yet. Use that to your advantage.' He reached forward and gripped her wrists tightly, his gaze burning into hers. 'And when you strike, don't hold back. She's not your cousin any longer. Khalida will kill you if she can.'

Neferata pulled her hands away. 'Let's be done with this,' she said, and stepped into the circle formed by the assembled crowd.

Khalida gently pushed her husband aside and went to stand before Neferata. She carried a bronze sword nearly identical to the queen's, though Khalida held hers easily, as though it were an extension of her hand. Her face was emotionless now, her eyes cold and remote, like an executioner.

Neferata surveyed the crowd, seeking out the priests. There were formalities that had to be observed. 'Is there a priest or priestess of Asaph in attendance?'

The priests and hierophants shifted uncomfortably. The eldest shrugged his narrow shoulders. 'That honour falls to you, great one,' he said.

Neferata growled under her breath. She closed her eyes and raised her hands to the heavens, struggling to remember the proper words.

'Great Asaph, goddess of beauty and the mysteries of the world, we beseech you to preside over this contest of arms and judge it fairly, lending your strength to the righteous and casting down the false claims of the wicked. Let justice prevail in your name.'

'Let justice prevail,' Khalida echoed faintly, and rushed forward, her sandals gliding on the grass, as though hurrying to her cousin's embrace. Neferata saw the glinting tip of her blade at nearly the last moment and tried to leap aside. She swung her own weapon in a wide, clumsy block, and connected with a discordant clang of metal.

Khalida's blade flickered again, and the point tugged at the billowing sleeve of Neferata's left arm. The queen circled right, trying to get away from the slashing sword, her own weapon hanging forgotten in her hand. She felt a burning pain in her left hand and jerked it back with a cry. Khalida's blade had slashed cleanly across her palm. Neferata stared at the wound in horror, watching beads of dark blood well up from the cut.

But Khalida never paused. She leapt forward, grabbing Neferata's sword wrist and stabbing at the queen's chest. Neferata felt the point of Khalida's sword pierce her robe and sink into the skin beneath her left breast. Without thinking, she seized her cousin's sword wrist with her wounded left hand before Khalida could drive her weapon home.

They grappled for an agonising moment, nose-to-nose, feeling each other's gasping breaths against their skin. Khalida dug in her heels and pushed for all she was worth. Neferata could feel the muscles working in her cousin's arms as she tried to drive the sword deeper. Khalida's lips were drawn back in a rictus of fury, her dark eyes burning with battle-lust.

Cold terror clenched Neferata's throat. Without thinking, she drew upon her power and shoved Khalida backwards. Her cousin was hurled off her feet, flying back for nearly five feet before landing hard on her back. Khalida turned the impact into a backward shoulder roll and sprang swiftly back onto her feet. Blood glistened on the tip of her sword.

Now she knows how strong I am, Neferata thought. *She won't make that mistake again.*

They circled one another for a moment, contemplating their next moves. Neferata's left hand ached dully, and the wound in her chest felt like it was on fire. Abhorash's words echoed dully in her mind. *You're going to have to make this quick.*

She stared at Khalida, her eyes pleading. 'Don't do this,' she whispered.

But Khalida was beyond hearing. With a snarl she rushed forward again, sword held low. She was on the queen in moments. Neferata tried to twist aside again, but felt the point of Khalida's blade dig into her hip. She cried out, groping instinctively for Khalida's wrist again, but the attack was only a feint. Swift as a snake, Khalida jerked the blade away and brought it around in a swift, looping motion, straight for the side of Neferata's throat.

She saw the blade arcing towards her out of the corner of her eye. With a scream, Neferata called upon her power once more and surged forwards, deeper into Khalida's embrace. Her cousin's sword missed its mark by inches, carving a furrow across the back of Neferata's neck.

The queen held her cousin for just a moment, and she could feel Khalida's heart hammering wildly through the thin fabric of her robe. Then they parted. Khalida took one step back, her expression slack. Her gaze fell to the hilt of Neferata's blade, jutting at a downward angle from her side. Slowly, wonderingly, she grasped the hilt with her left hand and with a strangled gasp, pulled the weapon free. Dark blood poured down Khalida's side.

Neferata watched in horror as her cousin sank to the ground. An agonised cry split the stunned silence. It was Anhur, his face a mask of anguish.

The queen fell to her knees beside Khalida. Her terror was gone, replaced with a bottomless well of sorrow. Without thinking, she pressed her hand to the wound in her cousin's side, but the bleeding would not stop. The warm fluid ran over her fingers and stained the sleeve of her robe. Khalida made a choked sound and tried to move, but she was already growing weak. Her eyes were open, searching wildly about for something or someone.

'Oh, gods,' Neferata whispered. 'Oh, great gods.' Her eyes burned, but no tears would come. She laid a trembling hand against Khalida's cheek, staining it with blood. 'Forgive me, little hawk. Please, please forgive me...'

She could still be saved, Neferata realised. She took her lower lip in her teeth and bit down hard, tasting blood. She bit until her lip was bitter with the taste.

Neferata took Khalida's head in her hands and turned it until their eyes met. She lowered her face, until all they could see was one another's eyes.

'Kiss me,' she said to Khalida. 'Kiss me, little hawk, and you'll live forever.'

Khalida stiffened. Tears welled in her eyes. Her head trembled, and her hands pressed weakly at Neferata's shoulders. When she spoke, her voice was almost too faint to hear.

'No,' she said.

'*Please*,' Neferata said. She pressed closer, and felt Khalida push back with the last of her strength. 'I never wanted this. I never wanted *any* of it, but Lahmia needs me. Please, let's kiss and be friends again, like before.'

Khalida resisted a moment more, and then Neferata felt her body relax. With a gasp of relief, the queen pressed her bloody lips to Khalida's.

Her cousin did not return the kiss. Khalida's body was utterly still.

After a long, painful moment, Neferata raised her head again and stared into Khalida's vacant eyes. Slowly, she became aware of people shouting, and a man's voice wailing in misery. Hands grasped Neferata's shoulders and pulled her away from Khalida's body. Her robe was heavy with blood.

Ankhat stepped close, whispering in her ear. 'Say something,' he urged. 'Everyone is waiting to hear the goddess's verdict.'

Neferata's gaze fell to her cousin's body, and felt her heart break.

'Justice is served,' she said in a hollow voice.

— SIXTEEN —

The Glory of Nagash

North of the Plain of Bones, in the 96th year of Ptra the Glorious
(-1350 Imperial Reckoning)

COLD, DEAD HANDS seized the priests and dragged them towards the towering wooden statue of Malakh that stood in the hill fort's ceremonial square. Pieces of splintered wood, scavenged from the fort's shattered gates, had already been piled around the statue's base and soaked with pitch from the temple's own storehouses.

The Forsaken priests screamed and kicked, crying out to their god to bring down bloody vengeance on the invaders, but the skeletal executioners paid them no heed. The four old men were all that remained of the god's temple at Maghur'kan, the chief hill fort of the northmen's petty empire. Those members of the cult that hadn't died in the bitter defence of the main gate were dragged from the temple cellars and their bodies left to bleed out in the muddy street.

Every man, woman and child still living after the month-long siege of Maghur'kan had been herded to the edges of the square to bear witness to the death of their god. The night air trembled with their muffled wails. Most were so weak from hunger that they could manage little else.

Nagash sat upon a palanquin of polished oak at the southern end of the square, surrounded by the skeletal warriors of his bodyguard and a score of northmen vassals drawn from hill forts conquered during the long war. The struggle against the Forsaken hadn't lasted years, or decades, but *centuries* – nearly two hundred and fifty years since that first, confused night battle upon the Plain of Bones.

The northmen had proven to be mighty warriors, and their witches possessed of great skill and cunning. Nagash had lost count of the number of battles that had been fought down the years, but in most cases the Forsaken had given as good as they'd got. Ultimately, the path to victory had rested on the simple fact that the Forsaken had to eat, and his army did not. By keeping up constant pressure on one hill fort at a time, he prevented the northmen from adequately tending their fields and setting back enough food for the winters to come, until finally they had been so weakened by hunger and sickness that they couldn't resist Nagash's constant attacks. And so the northmen had been enslaved, one hill fort at a time, until only Maghur'kan remained.

The necromancer watched as the priests were lashed to the great totem of their god. Off to the east, near the circular wall of the hill fort, one of the Yaghur let out a bone-chilling howl. Children squealed in terror, burying themselves in their mothers' skirts. No doubt the barbarians were feasting well tonight.

When the ropes had been drawn tight, Nagash rose from his seat and stepped onto the stinking mud of the square. Heavy, leather robes, faced with polished bronze medallions inscribed with runes of protection, flapped about his lean limbs. A deep hood, its hem ornamented with tiny disks of gold, concealed all but the flickering flames of his eyes. There was a dry clatter of bone as his bodyguard made to follow him, but he held them back with a wave of his hand and a curt mental command.

His legion of undead servants had grown so vast that he could no longer keep them all under control at the same time. Most functioned more or less autonomously, operating on a strict set of commands according to their function. It was an arrangement he'd perfected out of necessity during the long campaigns in the northland. Unfortunately he'd yet to find a way to impose the same degree of control on his human minions without ultimately killing them. He was instead forced to rely upon intangibles such as loyalty and devotion, which, as far as he was concerned, was a kind of sorcery all its own.

Thus, the death of the priests was a ritual in more ways than one, Nagash mused, as he approached the condemned men.

Malakh's high priest had been lashed to the statue facing Nagash. He and the two senior priests to his left and right glared at the necromancer with pure, fanatical hatred.

'You have not won!' the high priest spat. The Forsaken spoke a purer, somewhat more cultured form of the tongue once spoken by the Yaghur. 'You will not defeat great Malakh by ending our lives! He is eternal! He will triumph after–' the holy man's curse faltered.

'After my works are dust, and I am nothing but bones?' Nagash chuckled cruelly. *'Your curses mean nothing to me, old man. I am eternal. What can your petty god do to one who has passed beyond life and death?'*

The high priest thrashed against his bonds. 'May pestilence find your house! May it burrow in the walls and consume your treasures!'

Nagash shook his head in disgust. The Forsaken had been worthy foes. He'd hoped for better from their high priest. He raised his right hand. The energies of the burning stone had permeated the flesh that remained, until it was swollen and foul with cancerous tumours. Black veins, thick and pulsing with unnatural life, penetrated muscle and tendon and sank their roots into bone, where they drew sustenance from the deposits of burning stone. He reached out and seized the priest's jaw, cutting off his tirade. Nagash's fingers left streaks of slime on the northman's cheeks.

'There is nothing your god can do to me that I have not willingly inflicted upon myself,' Nagash said. 'Malakh's days are done. Go and tell him, when your soul is wandering the wastelands beyond death's door.'

Nagash released the high priest and withdrew a few steps. On cue, Thestus, the leader of his Forsaken vassals, came forward with a blazing torch in his hand. The northman, once the chieftain of a hill fort nearly as large as Maghur'kan, wore leather and bronze armour in the Nehekharan style, and his scalp had been shaved bare. His hard, craggy features showed no emotion at all as he approached the bound priests and held his brand aloft. It was important that the people of Maghur'kan saw one of their own feeding their god to the flames.

'Witness!' Thestus cried. 'Malakh rules here no longer! From this moment forward, Maghur'kan serves only Nagash, the Undying King!'

The high priest spat upon Thestus. The Forsaken warrior's only reaction was to bend low and thrust the torch into the wood directly beneath the holy man's feet.

Flames *whooshed* through the pitch-soaked wood, until the totem and the men tied to it were wreathed in hungry blue flames. The priests began screaming at once, their cries of agony piercing the night. From the narrow mud lanes of the hill fort, the Yaghur began to howl in reply. Nagash listened to the gruesome chorus for a moment, savouring the sound, then left Thestus and his warriors and headed to the opposite side of the square, where the warlord's great hall could be found.

The Forsaken built their halls the same way they built their barrows. It was large and dome-shaped, with a roof of wood and thatch, and the only building in the entire fort with a thick, stone foundation. As he approached the hall, dark, humanoid shapes glided from the shadows and paced along behind the necromancer. They wove back and forth in Nagash's wake like a pack of two-legged hounds, panting and sniffing at the sweet smell of roasting flesh.

There were no guards stationed outside the hall's large, round door; only a pair of lit braziers, vainly trying to hold back the shadows of the night. The Yaghur raised clawed hands to shield their faces from the hateful light; their eyes shone a pale yellow in the firelight, like a jackal's.

Nagash passed through the open door, noting the sorcerous wards that had been incised into its wooden foundation. Protection against misfortune, against pestilence and evil spirits... he felt not the slightest murmur of power from the old symbols. Perhaps they had died along with the men burning in the square outside.

Beyond the door was a wide passageway leading to the centre of the hall, flanked by branching corridors that ran left and right around the building's circumference. Tapestries hung along the walls, depicting glorious victories against the northmen's many enemies. Nagash saw human tribes defeated and enslaved, and fierce battles against hulking, green-skinned monsters that walked upright like men. He also saw one old, threadbare tapestry that depicted the Forsaken triumphing over a horde of rat-things like the ones he'd encountered in the wasteland.

Interestingly, there were no tapestries showing mighty victories over their old foes, the Yaghur. Nagash wondered what his long-time vassals thought of such an omission – if they thought of it at all.

At the far end of the passageway, Nagash entered a large, circular great room, dominated by a crackling fire pit in the centre of the space. A crowd of silent, grim-faced warriors stood around the dying flames, their scarred faces fixed in masks of anger and despair. They turned as the necromancer appeared, and retreated slowly to the perimeter of the room.

These were the Forsaken warlord's few remaining allies, as well as the survivors of his own personal warband, gathered together at Nagash's command to bear witness to Braghad Maghur'kan's submission.

Over the tips of the crackling flames, he could see Bragadh, the last of the Forsaken warlords. Even in defeat, the young leader of the northmen was proud and defiant, flanked on his right hand by Diarid, his scarred, grey-haired champion, and on his left hand by Akatha, the last of his witches. Akatha's two sisters had died horrible deaths during the battle at the fort's main gate. She had survived Nagash's sorcerous bolts only because of the heroism of another of Bragadh's champions, who had stepped in front of the blast and had died in her place. Like Bragadh, she was very young, perhaps twenty-five or twenty-six. In Nagash's day, as a priest in Khemri, they would have been considered little more than children. It was a sign of how badly the northmen had suffered during the last, bitter years of the war.

Nagash paused just inside the great chamber, pointedly ignoring the hateful stares of the Forsaken as he studied the many war trophies hung along the walls. Eventually his gaze came around to where Bragadh stood. The necromancer smiled coldly.

'*I had expected a throne, at the very least,*' he said.

The warlord nodded at the timber crackling in the fire. 'You're looking at it,' he growled. He was a huge, broad-shouldered giant, with a forked, red beard and a heavy, brooding brow.

Nagash inclined his head to the warlord. That kind of bitter spite was something he could understand. '*It is time,*' he said.

Bragadh raised his chin stubbornly. 'Let's hear your terms.'

'*Have I not already given them?*' Nagash countered.

'I want my people to hear you say them as well.'

Nagash considered the request. Bragadh had been a fearsome war leader in his time: bold, cunning and ruthless to a fault. The necromancer did not take him for a petty man; that suggested his allies did not necessarily support his decision to surrender.

'Very well,' Nagash said. '*You will receive the same terms as every other fort which has surrendered to me. To begin with you will reject the worship of Malakh from this night forward. In addition, two-thirds of your fighting men will return with me to my fortress, where they will serve in my army until death and beyond. The rest will*

remain here, along with the women and children, to tend
the fields and grow the population. Two-thirds of each
male generation will be called to serve, while the village
will supply them with shipments of meat and grain twice
each year. These are the only tithes that you will owe to
me as your master.'

The Forsaken glanced sidelong at one another. The
terms were very generous, as far as Nagash was concerned.

Diarid folded his muscular arms. Like Bragadh, his
long face was framed by a dark, forked beard, and
polished finger bones were plaited into his hair.
'How will our people defend themselves against our
other enemies?' he asked. 'You would leave us with
too few warriors to survive.'

Nagash chuckled. '*I have walked your lands from one
end to the other,*' he said. '*There are a great many graves
here. Enough for a very large army indeed. They can be
called to war at any time.*'

Diarid's dark eyes narrowed thoughtfully. The
implication hadn't escaped the young champion. If
any village were foolish enough to rebel, their own
ancestors would rise up to punish them.

Bragadh nodded. 'All this you will swear to, if our
villages submit?'

'*I would not have said so otherwise,*' the necromancer
replied.

'No!' cried one of the Forsaken to Nagash's right.
He was an older man, with streaks of grey in his
beard, and a barrel-like body clad in bronze and
leather armour. He stepped forward, shaking his fist

at Bragadh first, then at Nagash. 'We are true men, not slaves!' he said. He turned to face Nagash, his expression savage. 'I would sooner choose death than to betray my god and serve the likes of you!'

Nagash regarded the old village leader for a moment. *'As you wish,'* he said.

At once, the Yaghur were upon him. Sleek, mis-shapen figures burst from the passageway, racing past their master and leaping on the man. Their bodies were hunched, naked and hairless, covered in layers of dried blood and filth, and they propelled them-selves across the packed earth floor using all four limbs, like mad, bloodthirsty apes.

A baying chorus of terrible, ululating howls filled the great hall as they seized the old man in their clawed hands and dragged him off his feet. Jagged, rotting teeth sank into the barbarian's face and neck. He tried to struggle, screaming in terror and pain, but the creatures held him fast. Flesh tore like rotting cloth; hot blood sprayed through the air, and the man's screams became a choking death-rattle. The Yaghur tore at the man's body with their claws, rip-ping apart his armour to get to the warm meat beneath. Their howls transformed into slobbering, chewing sounds as the monsters began to feast.

'Before the sun rises, every man, woman and child in his hill fort will be dead,' Nagash said into the stunned silence that followed. *'The fields and buildings will remain, and will be given to someone with better sense than he.'* His gaze swept across the crowd. *'Your choice here is simple. Serve me, and your people will survive.*

They will even prosper, as well-tended vassals should. Otherwise, they will die, and their bones will serve me in the mines for centuries to come. Do you understand?'

No one spoke. Finally, the witch – a tall, dark-haired woman with large eyes and a narrow, pointed face – folded her arms and glared at the men. 'Don't be fools,' Akatha snarled. 'The time for defiance has passed. We must be pragmatic. The True People must survive.'

One of the Yaghur raised his head as the witch spoke, blood drooling from his jaws. His flat nostrils flared, and he growled hungrily. After a quarter millennia of feasting on human flesh, the Yaghur had developed an especial love for the soft meat of women and children.

Bragadh glared hatefully at the ghoul, and the Yaghur quickly turned back to its meal. The warlord sighed. 'The witch speaks true,' he said wearily. 'We must all take the long view now, and look to our people's survival.'

Groans went up from a dozen throats as Bragadh walked around the fire pit towards Nagash. When he stood before the necromancer he drew the great, bronze rune sword from its sheath and sank to his knees.

'I am Bragadh Maghur'kan,' he intoned. 'Warlord of the True People.' He carefully set his blade at Nagash's feet. 'And I submit.'

For a moment, no one moved. Then, one by one, the village leaders came forward to lay their weapons at the necromancer's feet.

Nagash accepted the submissions in silence, his expression of triumph lost within the depths of his hood. Across the chamber, Diarid and Bragadh's chosen men watched with stricken expressions as they watched their honour and traditions laid at the feet of their long-time foe.

Only Akatha met the necromancer's eyes. Her expression was hard as stone. Pragmatic, but no less hateful for that, Nagash noted. *Well enough*, he thought. *So long as she serves.*

The Yaghur watched the ceremony with feral disinterest, chewing noisily.

THE LONG PROCESSION marched from Maghur'kan just after sunset on the following day. First came Nagash, borne upon his oaken palanquin and attended by his skeletal bodyguard. Behind them came his vassal lieutenants, Bragadh, Thestus and Diarid, and the witch Akatha. They marched from their ancestral home with their heads high, but their expressions were bleak.

In their wake marched the columns of Nagash's infantry – human and undead, more than four thousand strong, their ranks replenished by the corpses of those they'd slain. Then, shoulders hunched and heads hung low, came the remnants of the once-mighty Forsaken host: four hundred barbarian warriors, stumbling from exhaustion and the pain of their wounds. Not all of them would survive the three-week march to the mountain. The Yaghur loped along the army's flanks, sniffing the air and waiting for the first of the barbarians to stumble.

South the column wound, through conquered territories that had lain under Nagash's hand for many decades. The hill forts were well maintained, the fields tended and the muddy lanes kept clean of filth. Silence and despair, heavy as a funeral shroud, hung over the entire region. Food and water were brought out for the human soldiers by hollow-eyed men and women, none of whom seemed to understand the simplest of questions posed by Bragadh or his kinsmen.

After the second week the army was close to the northern end of the Plain of Bones, and on bright, moonlit nights they could see a pall of dark grey clouds hanging low on the southern horizon. At first, the enslaved barbarians thought they were seeing storm clouds hanging over the Sour Sea, but night after night, the sight was still the same.

Three nights later the army had reached the Plain of Bones. The old battlefield had changed a great deal in the last two-and-a-half centuries, as Nagash had pursued his campaign against the northmen. A wall of stone had been built across the narrow, northern approach to the plain, anchored on each end by a citadel garrisoned by human and undead soldiers. A wide gate in the centre of the wall creaked open as the army approached, and the warriors marched through a tunnel of stone some ten yards long before emerging onto a wide expanse of tortured earth. Every square foot of the plain had been churned by pick and shovel over the centuries, digging up the bones of those who had fallen there over the millennia and adding them to Nagash's undead army.

A pall of stinking, ashen cloud hung low over the plain, plunging it into perpetual darkness, and a heavy, almost tangible silence clung to the broken land. Even the baying of the Yaghur was muted beneath the churning shadow cast from the south.

From that point on, the army marched day and night through the perpetual gloom. Hard-bitten warriors who had endured the bitter siege and the torturous march south became unmanned as they stumbled through the nightmarish landscape. Some broke ranks and tried to flee, raving and screaming in terror before the Yaghur pulled them down. Others simply fell by the wayside, their hearts gone dead between one step and the next as the burden of fear and despair simply grew too heavy to bear.

Two days later, as they crossed the southern edge of the plain and began the long descent to the coast, the vassals got their first sight of the great mountain. *Nagashizzar*, it was now called, which in Nehekharan meant 'the glory of Nagash', and a quarter millennium of constant labour had transformed it into a vast and impenetrable fortress. High walls girdled the wide slopes in seven concentric rings, each one higher and more forbidding than the next. Hundreds of towers clawed at the ashen sky, interspersed between barracks buildings, storehouses, foundries and mine works.

Wavering tongues of ghostly green fire flickered from scores of bronze forges, and twisting plumes of noxious vapours poured from countless mineshafts carved deep into the mountainside. The great barrow plain that once stretched westward towards the coast was now covered in vast piles of crushed stone and poisonous tailings from the mines, spilling down into the dark waters of the sea. To the north, where the Yaghur still dwelled, the marshland had turned into a poisonous waste, devoid of all life save for the flesh-eaters and their squalid lairs.

As the army descended onto the coastal plain the barbarians' fears mounted. Howls rose from the wasteland as the Yaghur sensed the return of their master, and shrill, wailing horns echoed them from the phantasmal towers. Down they went, across the lifeless slope and through the ruins of the old temple fortress, and then along a wide road of crushed stone that led to the first of the fortress gates.

Men began to wail in horror as they approached that dark portal. It yawned wide like the mouth of a hungry beast, eager for their souls. And, in a sense, they were correct.

Slowly, inexorably, the fortress gate swallowed them whole. The screams of the Forsaken echoed for a long time afterwards, until the huge gates crashed shut behind them.

As vast and ominous as Nagashizzar was upon the surface, the fearsome array of walls, towers and industry only represented a fraction of the fortress's true size. Much of the enormous stronghold had been burrowed into the mountain itself, with miles upon miles of tunnels, mineshafts, laboratories, vaults and storehouses. Night and day, Nagash's undead servants toiled in the darkness, extending tunnels and hollowing out still more chambers to support Nagashizzar's ever-growing population. No one knew for certain how deep the tunnels went any more, or even where many of them led. There were exploratory tunnels and deep shafts that had not been trod in a hundred years or more.

Deep, deep within the earth, in the very lowest levels of the mighty fortress, bare hands clawed relentlessly at dirt and stone. When at last they broke through into a vast, half-finished gallery, the exhausted tunnellers all but fell onto their snouts in the open, echoing space. They lay there on the smooth stone for several seconds, wringing their taloned hands and panting shallowly. Their smooth, pink noses tasted the dank air. Oil and metal, old bone and the teasing scent of man-flesh. Could this be the place the Grey Seer had sent them to find?

Yes! The Seekers caught the scent at almost the same moment. Quivering, they scrambled to their feet, wringing paw-like hands in excitement. They licked their noses, tasting the bitter dust. Sky-stone! Gifts from the Great Horned One, in numbers uncounted!

The Seekers froze, still as statues but for the wrinkling of their noses and the twitching of their ears as they searched for signs they'd been discovered.

Always, always there was the risk that something vigilant waited in the darkness; some horror with teeth or blades to rend rat-flesh. Such was the way of life in the tunnels. Every one of the Seekers had secretly picked out which of their companions they could safely throw in the path of danger so they could make good their escape.

Nothing stirred in the abandoned gallery save for the Seekers themselves. Such luck! Such glory to the first one who carried the news back to the Council! Minds buzzing with dreams of power and schemes of treachery, the Seekers turned about and fled back the way they'd come, their long, pink tails twitching behind them.

SEVENTEEN

The Deathless Court

Lahmia, the City of the Dawn, in the 96th year of Ptra
the Glorious
(-1350 Imperial Reckoning)

By DAY, NEFERATA slept, yet she did not dream. Instead, the sounds of the great city washed over her, filling her mind with fragments of mortal life that existed beyond the cold palace walls.

Sailors shouted bawdy boasts to whores walking the city docks, or sang songs of foreign shores while they made their ships ready for another long journey at sea. Servants gossiped in the market squares, or haggled over the price of melons or grain. Beggars called out to passers-by, pleading for a copper or a crust of bread. A tavern-keeper opened his doors with a muttered prayer for a good day's custom.

Lovers argued over an imagined slight. A thief jeered at the city guard as he made good his escape. A young mother sang a lullaby for her baby. An old man wept softly, mourning the wife he'd lost the year before.

She awoke at sunset, in the utter darkness of her bedchamber, her legs tangled in silken sheets. Her limbs were stiff and cold. Thirst tightened her throat. No matter how much she drank the night before, the thirst was always with her when she woke.

The faintest sounds of movement came from beyond her bedchamber door. Neferata swiftly wiped the tears from her cheeks as her attendants swept into the room to prepare her for the long night ahead.

Lamplight filled the room as the women went about their tasks with swift and silent precision. They were all priestesses of the highest order in the secretive Lahmian Cult: orphans raised within the precincts of the former Women's Palace and trained to serve the sacred bloodline of Asaph, as manifested in the person of the queen. Only the cult's inner circle knew the true nature of the living goddess whom they served, but by that point their hearts and minds belonged to Neferata alone. The initiates of the cult wore robes of purest samite and masks of fine, beaten gold, wrought in the image of Asaph herself.

She waited as the priestesses laid out her robes and drew open the heavy, bronze shutters that covered the windows and shielded her from the sun. A sea breeze stirred the curtains, caressing her icy skin, and she heard the distant murmur of waves. The riot of voices in the city below faded to a dull roar, not unlike the sound of the restless surf.

A priestess knelt by the side of her bed, her masked face carefully downcast. The mask she wore had been modelled on Neferata's own face, and wrought with exacting detail. With both hands she offered a golden goblet brimming with blood.

'For you, holy one,' she intoned in a hollow voice. 'An offer of love, and life eternal.'

Neferata took the goblet from the priestess and held it to her breast, savouring its warmth. The thirst grew suddenly, painfully sharp; her hand tightened on the metal rim, and she became horribly aware of the curved fangs pressing against her lower gums. As she did each night, she forced herself to remain still and calm until the feral impulse subsided. Slowly, deliberately, she raised the goblet to her lips and drained it in a single draught. Not one precious drop escaped her lips.

When she was done, she handed the vessel back to the priestess. The ritual would be repeated again at midnight, and once more just before dawn. Bloodletting in small amounts was a central tenet of the Lahmian Cult; from the lowliest acolyte to the most senior priestesses, each initiate surrendered a small portion each night as part of rituals intended to bring them closer to the goddess.

The cult had been a clever scheme on the part of W'soran, who envisioned it as both a cover for their predations and a safe haven from which to continue their rule over the city. Under Neferata's leadership it had also become a useful political tool as well, lending the Lahmian throne a degree of divine authority that the other Nehekharan cities lacked. The cult boasted a single, grand temple, converted from the Women's Palace during the latter days of Neferata's official reign. The temple's inner sanctum, a small complex of buildings in its own right, encompassed her private apartments and the palace's old central garden and still retained the opulence of its former existence. Nagash's tomes were kept in an arcane laboratory inside the sanctum, its doors sealed by physical and magical locks that only Neferata and W'soran together could open.

Fresh strength flowed through Neferata's limbs and lent her a small measure of warmth. She rose from the bed and spread her arms, allowing the priestesses to dress her. They garbed her in the raiment of an empress: robes of the finest Eastern silk, in layers of saffron, crimson and sapphire, embroidered with gold and silver thread and hundreds of tiny pearls. A girdle of fine, hammered gold was draped about her hips, its plates inset with dark, polished rubies. Deft hands slid precious bracelets onto her wrists, and a necklace made of heavy, gold links was fastened about her neck.

When the priestesses had completed the elaborate costume, they led her to the dressing table and bade her sit. Jewelled slippers were placed on her feet, and her eyes were darkened with kohl. All the while, Neferata stared out the open windows, listening to the sea. The steady whisper of the deeps soothed her mind as almost nothing else could.

As the priestesses worked, another pale figure slipped silently into the room and sat gracefully upon the edge of Neferata's bed. She was slim and delicate of feature, like the porcelain dolls from the land of her birth, and favoured elegant silk robes cut in the Eastern style. Her raven-black hair was swept up behind her head, held there with golden pins and a comb of polished jade. It drew attention to her slender neck, and emphasised her artful, elegant sense of poise.

Everything about her was carefully crafted, from the precise angles her hands made as they rested in her lap, to the patient, composed tilt of her pointed chin. She had been a courtesan once, expensively educated and trained from early childhood to be a companion to princes and emperors. Her purpose had been to moderate the baser appetites of noble men and elevate their public appearance with her refined manner. She had been an ornament, like a jewelled songbird that hovered about the shoulders of the wealthy and powerful. In those days, she hadn't even had a proper name. To her master, Prince Xian, she had simply been known as White Orchid. Neferata called her Naaima, and in her court she wanted for nothing.

The priestesses finished their work and withdrew as silently as they'd come. As they left, Naaima rose from the bed and went to her mistress. She ran slender fingers through Neferata's long hair, deftly teasing out the tangles, and then chose a silver-backed brush from the table.

'You called out in your sleep,' Naaima said softly, in the oddly lilting tongue of the Silk Lands. She drew the brush through Neferata's hair in long, smooth strokes.

Naaima slept in a luxurious bedchamber just across the corridor from Neferata's own. Centuries ago, when Neferata had persuaded her to take the poisoned cup, she had kept Naaima as close to her as she could, often taking comfort in the former courtesan's embrace while she slept. It did not last, however. As time wore on, Neferata felt only the coldness of Naaima's embrace, the deathly stillness of her body as she slept. There was no comfort to be found in the embrace of the dead.

The question irritated her. 'Perhaps I was dreaming,' Neferata said coldly. Even after two hundred years, the language of the easterners felt strange on her tongue. 'Do you always listen to me while I sleep?'

'Sometimes,' Naaima replied, ignoring the brittle edge in Neferata's voice. She was silent for a time as she finished her brushing, then gathered up a handful of golden pins. As she drew back Neferata's long hair she said, 'It sounded as though you were calling to a hawk.'

Neferata's body betrayed nothing. The pain was still sharp, even now, like a needle in her heart. The passage of years wore away the softer emotions first, she'd learned, while the harder, crueller ones endured.

'You must be mistaken,' she managed to say. 'I know nothing of hawks. Falconry never held any interest for me.'

'Of course,' Naaima replied smoothly. She did not pursue the matter any further. When she was finished with Neferata's hair, she went to the wooden box that sat on a pedestal in one corner of the room. Opening it, she drew out Neferata's golden mask. The delicate metal of the mask bore the weight of centuries upon its cold face. She studied it for a moment, frowning slightly. 'You should have a crown,' she said. 'You deserve better than this.'

'The crown is for the Queen of Lahmia,' Neferata replied. 'I am merely its ruler.' She beckoned to Naaima. 'Bring it here. I have work to do.'

She forced herself to hold still as Naaima slipped the mask onto her face. Every time she felt the touch of metal against her cheeks she was reminded of her own funeral. It reminded her now of nothing but death and loss. When it was in place she rose without a word and made her way from the chamber. Naaima fell into step a precise six paces behind her; the habits of a lifetime and were nearly impossible to overcome, and only became more so in the unlife that followed.

The corridors of the inner sanctum were funereal in their stillness. There were never more than three hundred acolytes and initiates of the cult at any one time, and they were swallowed up whole by the vast size of the temple complex. Neferata walked in silence down the dimly lit passageways, then across the broad expanse of the former palace garden. The trees and tall ferns grew wild and untended now, and many of the rare flowers had died without the care of the gardeners. Bats circled overhead, darting and dancing in the moonlight. She listened to their strange, almost plaintive cries, as she did every night, and wondered who or what it was they were calling for.

They crossed the wild garden, and then entered another set of silent, echoing chambers on the far side. Moments later they arrived at a pair of bronze doors, attended by silent, masked priestesses. Ubaid waited beside them. Though he still looked as young as the day he'd tasted Lamashizzar's elixir, his back was hunched and his hands trembled like that of an old man. His eyes were round and bright like polished glass. As Neferata approached, he managed a clumsy bow.

'The court awaits, holy one,' he said in a ragged voice. The former grand vizier sounded as though his inner workings had been crushed to pieces, then carelessly reassembled.

Neferata ignored him. With a curt nod, the priestesses pulled open the doors. Warm, yellow light poured over her as she crossed the threshold into the audience chamber. The blocks of polished sandstone and the lacquered wooden screens of the Hall of Reverent Contemplation had been dismantled and rebuilt within the inner sanctum when the Women's Palace had been renovated. She knew she would no longer have any need for the vast, echoing court chamber that she'd presided from in the palace proper, and she'd thought the familiar surroundings would be a comfort in the ages to come. How little she had known.

She climbed the back of the dais and stepped around the tall, wooden throne. It was the one concession to her ego that she'd allowed when she surrendered her crown. A vast fortune had been spent to hire a small expedition to scour the southern jungles for a match to the wood that had been used for the original throne, and a still greater sum paid to find and commission an artisan skilled enough to shape it into an exact copy of the original. The whole process had taken almost as long as the construction of the temple itself. Neferata had never gotten around to asking Lord Ushoran what had become of the artisan afterward. Certainly no one ever found the body.

Neferata settled gracefully into the ancient chair and surveyed the audience chamber. Lord Ankhat stood closest to the dais, attended by a pair of enthralled retainers burdened with stacks of ledgers and bundles of scrolls. Lord Ushoran waited at a careful remove from Ankhat, his expression distant as he meditated on his intrigues. This evening W'soran was present as well, accompanied by an enthralled young scribe who was busily copying down his master's muttered dictation. As always, Lord Zurhas lingered furthest from the throne, his arms folded tightly across his chest and a look on his face that said he would rather be gambling away his fortune in some squalid dice house.

Each one bore the marks of unlife in their own, unique way. Lord Ankhat, was, if anything, more lordly in mien than before, possessing a dominating presence that nearly rivalled her own. Ushoran, on the other hand, was just the opposite. He seemed more changeable, more chimerical than before. There were times that Neferata was certain his features looked subtly different from one moment to the next. Unfortunately for Lord Zurhas, his features were entirely fixed. Neferata couldn't help but think he turned more craven and rodent-like with each passing year.

Then there was W'soran. The old scholar had been the first to ask Neferata to drink from the poisoned cup, and since rising from his deathbed he had grown even more gaunt and skeletal than before. Now, centuries later, he was a hideous creature, more resembling a walking corpse than a man. The very sight of him filled her with dread. For the longest time, she was afraid that some error in the ritual had caused his transformation, and that he secretly hated her for it. But Lord Ushoran insisted that W'soran was actually *pleased* with what he'd become.

When she was seated, Naaima glided soundlessly around the dais and took her place at Neferata's right, head bowed and hands clasped at her waist. Moments later, Ubaid shuffled around to Neferata's left and cleared his gravelly throat.

'Pay heed to the throne of Lahmia,' the grand vizier intoned, his voice echoing in the nearly empty chamber. 'The court of Neferata the Eternal is convened. Let all bear witness to her glory.'

* * *

'THE LAST OF the annual tribute has arrived,' Ankhat said, scanning the contents of the ledger in his hands. 'Zandri has come up short again.'

Neferata sighed. 'What is the excuse this time?'

Ankhat shrugged. 'Pirates, of course. Cut down profits on the slave trade by nearly a third, according to them.'

Her eyes narrowed. 'Are they telling the truth, Ushoran?'

The Lord of Masks shook his head. His network of spies now reached from one end of Nehekhara to the other. Lahmia was the centre of the civilized world, richer by far than any of the other great cities combined. The yearly tribute to pay off the interest on their debts saw to that. There were a great many powerful people who resented that fact. 'Zandri's navy is as strong as ever,' he said. 'There hasn't been a pirate spotted in her waters for more than a century.'

'And does Numas support Zandri's reckless behaviour?' Neferata asked.

Ankhat snorted. 'Given how much we're paying them for grain? I should hope not.' The city of Numas, situated on the wide Plains of Plenty, had long been the chief food producer in Nehekhara. Now, with reports that the fertile banks of the River Vitae were shrinking, and the desert encroaching on the other cities more and more each year, their power and influence had grown tenfold. Even Lahmia found itself increasingly beholden to the distant city, as increasing numbers of bandit gangs drove farmers off the Golden Plain.

'Numas has given no sign of support for Zandri,' Ushoran agreed. 'The west has changed a great deal in the last two hundred years, and the only real common ground the two cities ever had was their brief allegiance to Nagash. If anything, I suspect that Zandri is growing bold in response to Numas's growing stature.'

'And does Numas pose a threat to us?' Neferata asked. Naaima chided her often that she saw potential threats everywhere these days. When one ruled a de facto empire, it was the only way to survive.

Ushoran gave another of his shrugs. 'Now? No. A hundred years from now? Perhaps.'

Neferata sighed. 'How quickly they seem to forget,' she growled. 'Three hundred years of peace and prosperity has evidently spoiled them. Perhaps a punitive expedition to Zandri is in order.'

Ushoran glanced at Ankhat, who shifted uncomfortably.

'For that, we'll need an army, I suspect,' Ankhat said.

Neferata straightened. 'What happened to the army we *had*?' she demanded.

'Three hundred years of peace and prosperity,' Ankhat replied. 'Lamashizzar began reducing the army right after the war, and it was allowed to wither ever since. There didn't seem to be a point to maintaining an expensive army when the trade policies were working so well, and besides, it's highly unlikely the dragon power has retained its potency after so long in storage.'

Neferata glowered behind her mask. There likely wouldn't be any more opportunities to buy the exotic powder, either. The Eastern Empire was still as secretive and isolationist as it ever had been, but Ushoran's spies in the trade cities hinted that there had been great upheavals inside its borders. Prince Xian Ha Feng, scion of the Celestial Household, had defied the edicts of the Emperor for two years after his first taste of Neferata's blood, effectively resolving the matter of Lahmia's debt to the Empire.

When he was finally recalled by his august father, the prince left for the Silk Lands with two more vials of the queen's blood, and promises of much more in the future. But shortly after Xian's return, all contact with the Empire abruptly ceased, and all foreigners were barred from its trade cities on pain of death. It would be more than a century before contact was restored, whereupon it was learned that the old emperor had met with sudden misfortune, and issues of succession had turned violent. Prince Xian disappeared into the chaos of the civil wars that followed, and none knew his fate. The current emperor's view on Nehekhara was one of benign disinterest.

'What have we been doing with all the money that was supposed to be going to the army?' she inquired.

'Some of it went to the navy,' Ankhat said. 'Most of it went to expanding the City Guard and adding patrols to the trade routes across the Golden Plain.'

'And much good that did us,' Neferata replied sourly. 'No wonder Zandri feels free to withhold tribute.' She pointed at Ankhat. 'That policy changes now. How long will it take to raise a new army and train it?'

Ankhat blinked. 'I don't know for certain,' he replied. 'I seem to recall that it took your father decades–'

'That was because he was negotiating with the damned Easterners,' Neferata said, and then cast a guilty look at Naaima.

'Abhorash could tell us,' Ankhat replied. 'If he was here, of course.'

Neferata glanced at Ushoran. 'What of Abhorash?' she asked. 'Any word?'

The Lord of Masks shrugged once again. 'There are rumours he was sighted in Rasetra last year,' he said, 'The last I knew for certain, he was heading into the jungles, but it's been twenty years now. He could very well be dead.'

Abhorash had been the last member of the cabal to accept the poisoned cup; later even than Naaima by more than a decade. Having witnessed the voluntary transformation of the rest of Neferata's cabal, he wanted no part of an existence that would prevent him from fighting on the battlefield. He believed that more than a hundred and fifty years of loyal service to the throne was enough to ensure that he would never betray the cabal, but Neferata was not convinced. Finally, she lost patience. When he came to the palace to receive his elixir from the queen, she gave him the poisoned cup instead.

He had been furious upon awakening as an immortal, and refused to accept what he had become. Incredibly, he'd denied his thirst for many nights, as though it were a sickness that could be overcome, until Neferata had begun to think the mighty warrior might actually waste away. But then, one moonless night, Abhorash succumbed. By the time the sun had risen once more, twelve people – men, women, even a small child – had been slain across the length of the city. Ankhat and Ushoran had scoured the city in search of Abhorash on the following night, but the champion was nowhere to be found. He'd fled the city, and no one in Lahmia had seen him since.

'Abhorash isn't dead,' Neferata declared. 'There's nothing in the southern jungles – or anywhere else – capable of killing him. When he discovers that for himself, I expect we will see him again.' She glanced at Ankhat. 'In the meantime, my lord, we need an army.'

Ankhat bowed. 'I will inform the queen of the new policy at once.'

A group of priestesses slipped into the chamber, bearing goblets to quench the court's thirst. Midnight already. They'd been discussing matters of state for six hours. The notion surprised and dismayed her.

Neferata accepted the first goblet and drank it down, then watched the others drink. The transformation affected each of them differently, she knew. They all dealt with the thirst in their own ways, and it was reflected in the way that they fed. Ankhat took the proffered cup, studied its depths, and then drank it slowly, like wine. Lord Ushoran took his cup in an almost absent fashion, his brooding mind distracted by one intrigue or another. He drank the blood in swift gulps; for him it was fuel, and nothing more. Zurhas eyed his goblet with dread, yet he accepted the cup with a grimace and drank it down in a single swallow. Naaima accepted hers with studied calm, as with everything else she did, and drank it without evident interest or emotion.

W'soran shook his head curtly, refusing the cup as he always did. Neferata wondered at his appetites, and how he managed to indulge them.

Once the priestesses had withdrawn, Neferata sighed. 'Is there anything else to discuss?'

Ankhat and Ushoran consulted their notes. 'More reports in Numas of strange clouds seen over the mountains to the east,' Ushoran said. 'King Ahmose is thinking about sending an expedition to find its source.'

'Much good may it do him,' Neferata said. 'Anything else?'

To her surprise, W'soran spoke up. 'I have a request,' he said.

'Go on.'

The old scholar raised his chin, almost in challenge. 'I would like access to Nagash's books for a time,' he said. 'I want to begin a new field of research.'

'And what would that be?' Neferata asked, though she had suspicions of what it might be.

'An aspect of necromancy,' W'soran began.

'We've discussed this before,' Neferata growled. 'Many, many times–'

'Not raising the dead,' W'soran interjected. 'Not that. My interest lies in raising spirits and communicating with them. If I recall, Nagash made some notes regarding summoning circles in one of his books.'

Neferata thought it over. 'And what do you hope to gain from this?' she asked.

W'soran shrugged. 'Knowledge, of course. What else?'

Her first instinct was to refuse, but she knew that W'soran would ask for her reasons, and she had none. 'Very well,' she said. 'But I expect to be kept apprised of your efforts.'

'Of course,' W'soran said, and gave a small bow of gratitude.

'There is also the matter of Khemri,' added Lord Ankhat. 'The rebuilding of the city is nearly complete, and the inhabitants are clamouring for a king. Will you approve of such a thing?'

The news surprised Neferata, though she chided herself that it had been centuries since she'd made her pledge to help the late King Shepret restore the ruined city.

'I see no reason why not,' she said at length. 'It's been almost four hundred years. Nagash is nothing more than an evil memory now. And the sooner that Khemri has a king, the sooner we can stop subsidising the city's construction.'

'Perhaps it's best to wait and see if the would-be king lives to claim the throne,' Ushoran said wryly.

Neferata turned to the spymaster. 'What does that mean?' she asked.

'The Queen of Rasetra is with child, but she has never been a woman of robust health,' Ushoran said. 'The pregnancy has been very difficult. From what I gather, there is little chance that the baby will survive.'

Ankhat nodded. 'She is here right now, in fact, praying at the temple.'

'What?' Neferata said, sitting straight upon the throne.

'She's holding vigil in the presence of the goddess, praying for her child's life,' Ushoran explained. 'A pity it will do her little good.'

Neferata did not reply at first. The silence stretched, until Ushoran began to look uncomfortable.

'Is there something wrong, great one?' he asked.

Again, Neferata did not immediately reply. When she did finally speak, it caught them all by surprise.

'Nagash is just an evil memory now,' she repeated. 'A legend. One that grows more nebulous each year.'

Ankhat frowned. 'So we hope,' he said warily.

Neferata nodded – thoughtfully at first, then more decisively. 'The baby will live,' she declared.

Ushoran gave her a bemused look. 'How can you be so certain?'

'Because I am going to save him,' Neferata replied. As she spoke, the idea took shape in her mind. 'The queen will remain here in Lahmia as our guest, for the duration of the pregnancy, and I will give her an elixir mixed with my blood.'

The news stunned the cabal. Ankhat and W'soran looked visibly shaken. 'What makes you think she would agree to such a thing?' Ankhat said.

'She travelled, heavily pregnant, for weeks, just for the chance to pray for her son's life,' Neferata snapped. 'That woman is prepared to do anything to save her child.'

Ushoran frowned. 'But to what end?'

'When the child is born, he will remain here until his majority,' Neferata declared. 'It's past time that the heirs apparent to the great cities came to Lahmia for their education.'

The spymaster gaped at her. 'Hostages. You're talking about hostages.'

'Not at all,' Neferata replied. 'I am talking about shaping the future of all Nehekhara. Think of it: what if, in a hundred years, we ruled an empire from here to Zandri, and we did so *openly*?'

'The other cities would never stand for it!' Ankhat exclaimed.

'They would if the kings supported us, and soon they will,' she countered. 'We've existed under the shadow of Nagash for too long. I'm *tired* of hiding. After everything I've done, everything I've *sacrificed*, all I've done is trade one prison for another.' Her fists clenched. 'No more. Do you hear? No more.'

She rose from the throne. 'Instruct the queen to draft the summons to the other cities,' she said. 'I will speak to the Queen of Rasetra personally. I want the first children here within the next year. Offer to lower their yearly tribute if you must.'

'And if they refuse?' Ushoran countered.

'They won't, once we hear how the temple saved the future King of Khemri,' Neferata said. 'We will show them that we are not the children of Nagash. We are something altogether different. In time, they may even worship us as gods.'

She left them in shocked silence, her mind whirling with possibilities. Naaima followed behind her, for once surrendering her composure and dashing after her mistress.

'You've frightened them,' she whispered in Neferata's ear as they rushed through the dark halls of the inner sanctum.

'We've all been afraid for too long,' Neferata replied. 'I meant what I said. I'm tired of skulking here, while the world turns without me. Perhaps Abhorash had the right of it all along, fleeing Lahmia and seeking his destiny elsewhere.'

'This has nothing to do with destiny, or with compassion,' Naaima replied, her voice taut. 'This is about Khalida–'

Neferata's hand blurred through the air, seizing Naaima by the throat. One moment they were racing through the inner sanctum, then the next Naaima was dangling from Neferata's iron grip in the middle of the passageway.

'Never speak that name again,' Neferata hissed. Her fangs glinted in the faint light. '*Never*. Do you understand me?'

It took all her strength to gasp out her reply. 'I...
I understand,' Naaima said.

Neferata held her there for several agonising seconds, her face a mask of madness and rage. Slowly,
one heartbeat at a time, the anger ebbed from her
face, until she realised what she was doing. With a
start, she released the former concubine. Naaima hit
the floor hard and collapsed, clutching her throat.

'Forgive me,' Neferata said softly. 'I didn't mean to
hurt you.'

Naaima shook her head. The pain she felt in her
heart left her breathless.

'You can't bring her back,' Naaima gasped. 'Nothing you do will bring Khalida back. Why can't you
see that?'

But there was no answer. Neferata was gone.

━◄ EPILOGUE ►━

Portents of Destruction

*Lahmia, The City of the Dawn, in the 98th year of
Asaph the Beautiful
(-1325 Imperial Reckoning)*

'HERE THEY COME!' the tutor roared in his leathery,
field-of-battle voice. 'Get on your feet, boy! Get up!'

Four men in bronze scale armour hefted their
weapons and charged across the training ground,
their sandaled feet kicking up plumes of sand as they
converged on their prey. The early morning sun
slanted across the square, leaving much of the
ground still in deep shadow except for where young
Alcadizzar lay. Haptshur's pupil lay in his back in the
rocky sand, half-covered by an overturned chariot.
His bare legs were wrapped in the chariot's traces,
and a heavy sack of grain – representing the body of

389

his dead driver – lay across his chest. The young man's shield was strapped to his left arm, but his sword was ten paces away, back along the chariot's imagined trail. As a final touch. Haptshur had smeared pig's blood over his pupil's face, taking care to dab it liberally in the young man's eyes. The older warrior believed in making his lessons as realistic and messy as he possibly could – much like the brutal reality of the battlefield.

Haptshur's assistants likewise dispensed with any fanciful notions of honour or fair play – they had no intention of giving Alcadizzar the slightest chance of extricating himself and getting to his sword. They came at him all in a rush, intent on chopping him to pieces as quickly and savagely as they could.

Swathed in deep shadow behind a lacquered wooden screen, Neferata watched the oncoming collision with mounting concern. Accidents happened in training. Even wooden weapons were more than capable of breaking bones or fracturing skulls, and if an infection set it, the results were often fatal. It had never happened to any of Haptshur's royal pupils, but… She pressed the fingertips of her right hand against the screen's fragile wooden vine work, as though willing speed and strength into the young man's body.

Not that Alcadizzar needed it; despite his age, the Rasetran prince was already more than six feet tall, and more powerfully built than the burly Haptshur and his men. His mother had done everything Neferata had asked of her, remaining at the temple and drinking a vial of elixir each and every week until the baby was born, and its effects on the unborn child had been profound.

The young man's attackers covered the sandy ground in seconds, but Alcadizzar was already on the move. Cool and calm despite the angry shouts and the blood stinging his eyes, the young man paused for scarcely a moment to formulate his plan, and then sprang swiftly into action. Neferata watched as he got his hands underneath the heavy bag laid across his chest, then with a heave of his shoulders and arms he flung it backwards, over his head and into the path of the oncoming men. The projectile caught the attackers momentarily by surprise, but they recovered almost at once, dodging left and right out of its path, but the diversion bought Alcadizzar a few more precious seconds.

To Neferata's surprise, the prince didn't bother untangling his legs from the leather traces; instead, he drew back his muscular legs, propped his feet against the chariot's wicker rim, and heaved with all his strength. With a creak of wood and leather, the chariot rolled over onto its side, and Alcadizzar scrambled after it, disappearing into the open bed.

Now the prince's attackers pulled up short, suddenly without an easy target to reach. Alcadizzar had backed into the chariot like a cornered viper, and his foes could only come at him from one direction. Furthermore, the upper side of the chariot provided a roof of sorts over Alcadizzar's head, preventing the men from raining blows down on him from overhead. They would have to come right at him, thrusting with their curved khopeshes, which made their task that much more difficult.

The three men spread out, communicating with one another using glances and hand gestures. One of the attackers nodded, rushing towards the prince, while the other two circled around the opposite side of the chariot. Neferata frowned. What were they up to? Then she understood. While one man kept Alcadizzar occupied, the others were going to grab the chariot and pull it back upright, disorientating the prince and leaving him open for a blow from his attacker.

But Alcadizzar had plans of his own. As the first man rushed in, stabbing awkwardly with his curved blade, his feet came down amid tangled loops of leather traces that the prince had trailed behind him. At once, Alcadizzar jerked back on the traces, and the man flew backwards with a yell. The prince leapt onto him like a desert lion, landing on his chest and pummelling him with one powerful blow after another. Snarling, the swordsman tried to counter-attack, but Alcadizzar caught his sword-hand by the wrist and cracked his fist across the other man's chin, knocking him senseless.

Just then, the chariot lurched, rolling back onto its wheels with a loud crash. The traces jerked tight, yanking Alcadizzar away from his foe, but not before he plucked the khopesh from the unconscious man's hand. He twisted onto his back as the traces dragged him across the sand, and began trying to kick his way free of the tangled leather straps.

It took the remaining attackers scarcely a moment to realise what had happened. They came racing around the back of the chariot, eager to avenge their fallen friend. Alcadizzar, his legs still trapped, did the only thing he could: he rolled across the sand towards the charging men, closing the distance more quickly than they'd expected. The men recovered swiftly, trying to circle around the oncoming prince, but the young man moved with preternatural speed. His wooden khopesh slashed through the air, feinting low at one man's calf, then cutting suddenly upwards and striking the man in the groin. The attacker fell to the sand with a muffled groan.

There was a *whack* of wood on flesh. Neferata missed the blow, but saw the angry red weal rising on Alcadizzar's right thigh. The prince didn't utter a sound at the painful hit; his sword blurred, reaching for the last attacker's left arm. The man pulled his arm out of the way just in time – and was caught by surprise when the prince's left leg swept into his right foot and knocked him from his feet. The man hit the sand with a whoosh of tortured breath as the wind was knocked from his lungs, and before he could recover, Alcadizzar had scrambled atop him and laid the khopesh's blade against his throat.

'Enough!' Haptshur cried. At once, Alcadizzar sat back with a grin and tossed the practice weapon aside. Within moments, the three men who'd been so intent on giving the prince a thrashing were slapping him on the back and laughing ruefully as they helped to unwind him from the dust-stained traces.

Haptshur walked over, his leathery face beaming with pride, and tossed the prince a cloth to wipe the blood from his face.

'He has grown into quite the young man,' Lord Ankhat observed quietly. 'I'm certain his father would be proud if he could see him now.'

Neferata nearly jumped at the sound of the lord's voice. Ankhat was standing at the far end of the observation gallery, near the door that led to the secret corridor back to the temple's inner sanctum. He was careful to remain completely in shadow. Even so, the mere proximity of sunlight clearly made him uncomfortable.

'My lord Ankhat,' Neferata said smoothly. 'I didn't hear your approach.' Once upon a time, Naaima would have warned her, but she saw little of the former concubine these days. She kept to herself, spending her evenings in the wild garden or poring through the tomes in the temple libraries. Neferata had been offended at first, but then she had become preoccupied with Alcadizzar's birth, and after a while she hadn't missed Naaima's presence at all.

'Forgive me if I startled you,' Ankhat said with a mirthless smile. 'No doubt your attention was devoted entirely to the young prince.'

Despite herself, Neferata glanced proudly at the prince. He now stood next to Haptshur, towering head and shoulders over his tutor, his expression intent as he listened to the burly warrior's assessment of the fight. Even coated with dust and smeared with traces of blood, his face was handsome and refined, with a square chin, strong cheekbones and a sharp nose. Alcadizzar had black hair and dark, intense eyes that he offset with a brilliant, disarming smile.

'He is a wonder,' Neferata admitted. 'A true prince. One day, he will have the world at his fingertips.' Certainly he had been given the finest education in the land. Alcadizzar and the other royal children who now lived at the Lahmian court were lavished with the best of everything. The kings of the other great cities might resent sending their children to be raised in a foreign court, but they couldn't say that their sons and daughters weren't being treated as well – or in most cases, better – than they would have at home.

Ankhat studied Neferata intently. 'That day is close at hand,' he said. 'There have been letters from Rasetra. The king says that it's time for Alcadizzar to assume his duties as King of Khemri.'

'Now? Nonsense!' Neferata exclaimed. 'He's only twenty-five years old!'

'His father became King of Rasetra at his age,' Ankhat pointed out. 'People do not have the span of years that our fathers once did.'

'*He* will,' Neferata said. 'Look at him. See what the elixir has wrought! He'll live to be a hundred and twenty, perhaps more!'

Ankhat shrugged. 'Perhaps so, great one. Nevertheless, he has reached the age when he should be king in his own right.'

Neferata turned back to the practice field. Alcadizzar was walking away, still talking with his tutors and rubbing the thick dust from his bare shoulders. His smile was dazzling against his dark skin. Ubaid waited at the edge of the field with fresh clothes for the prince; at Neferata's command, the former grand vizier had been Alcadizzar's personal servant since childhood, allowing her to keep a constant watch over the boy. Even Ubaid seemed to have been charmed by the young prince's magnetism; in Alcadizzar's presence he seemed to recover a bit of his former poise and presence of mind.

'No,' she said, shaking her head. 'He's not ready yet. Tell the Rasetrans they cannot have him.'

Ankhat blinked. 'He belongs to them–'

'He belongs to *me*,' Neferata hissed. 'Were it not for me, he would have died in the womb! *I* made him what he is today, and I say I'm not finished with him yet!'

The full force of her will hit Ankhat like a gale. He visibly wavered underneath her stare.

'This is dangerous, great one,' Ankhat managed to say. 'The other kings already resent sending their children to live here as hostages. Refusing to return Alcadizzar will lead to repercussions.'

Neferata's eyes narrowed at Ankhat. Her lips drew back slightly, revealing her fangs. 'Are you threatening me?'

Ankhat bristled. 'I'm merely pointing out the risks of your... attachment to the young prince,' he replied. 'It is a danger to us all.'

'No,' Neferata said. 'That's where you're wrong. Alcadizzar is the future. Through him, we'll remake all of Nehekhara in our image, and rule over it until the end of time.'

The practice field was empty now. Neferata hurried down the length of the gallery, brushing past the stunned Ankhat.

'Tell the Rasetrans whatever you must,' she said to him as she went by. 'Khemri will have a king when I say it is time, and not before.'

ACRID SMOKE HUNG in a dense, blue cloud over the ritual circle in the temple's arcane sanctum. The incense braziers still burned after the long night's work, mingling with the candle smoke and the arcane vapours that W'soran had learned were efficacious in the summoning of spirits. Over the last twenty-five years he had summoned countless spirits from the bleak wasteland beyond death's door, until now he reckoned himself a master of the art. And yet his ultimate goal remained stubbornly out of reach.

The very thought of it galled him. W'soran had never been a strong man, but he reckoned that only one man in all of Nehekhara had ever rivalled him in matters of intellect. He was not accustomed to the notion of failure where his studies were concerned.

A glassy-eyed scribe shuffled up to him, holding out the transcript of the evening's ritual. W'soran snatched the papyrus from the thrall's hand and compared it to the invocations that Nagash had written in the yellowing tome open on the table before him. His lips pulled back in a snarl at the scribe's atrocious handiwork. The thralls made terrible assistants unless the lightest amount of pressure was brought to bear on their minds, but W'soran had little patience for such foolishness. He would have preferred the steady, tireless hand of a skeletal servant, and once again cursed Neferata's edict forbidding such creations. She was little better than her dead husband: ambitious, but too timid to make use of the tremendous power that lay in their hands. The specific tomes that governed the creation of the undead were locked away in another vault, along with Arkhan's notes on the transformation ritual he had used on Neferata. There they would remain until the end of time, if she were allowed to have her way.

'Stupid, moon-eyed bitch!' he muttered, smoothing out the papyrus next to the ancient page and reaching for an ink brush.

'The evening's work didn't go well, I take it?'

W'soran whirled, hands clenching into claws. Fleshless lips drew back, revealing long, needle-like fangs. He didn't recognise the bland features of the man standing just inside the doorway of the sanctum, but he knew the voice all too well. 'Ushoran!' he exclaimed. 'How did you get in here?'

Lord Ushoran gave the skeletal W'soran a ghostly smile. 'The door was unlocked long ago,' he said. 'You requested it, in fact.'

'Don't be impertinent!' W'soran snapped. 'You're not allowed here! If Neferata knew–'

Ushoran's smile turned cold. 'If she knew I was here, she'd no doubt be angry. I'll give you that. But that would be nothing compared to how furious she'd be if she knew what you were really up to.'

W'soran's anger vanished in an instant. 'What are you talking about?' he said, suddenly wary.

Ushoran sighed. 'You've been summoning and binding spirits for a quarter of a century. Do you mean to tell me that you haven't figured out how to do it yet?'

'Certainly not!' W'soran snapped. 'I mastered the art of summoning years ago!'

'Then I have to assume you're in here, night after night, not because you're still learning how to call up spirits – but because you're trying to call up a very specific spirit instead.'

W'soran cursed himself for a fool. Ushoran had led him right into the trap, and he'd never seen it coming. He affected a sneer, hoping it would hide his unease.

'What of it? Do you think Neferata would care if I was summoning one particular spirit over another?'

'Oh, yes,' Ushoran said. 'She most definitely would – if the spirit in question was Nagash.'

W'soran froze. How had he been found out? For a wild instant, he wondered if he were capable of killing Ushoran and disposing of the body. The Lord of Masks would often disappear for weeks, even months at a time. No one would notice his absence for a long while.

He slowly turned back to the table and began casually searching through the pile for another one of Nagash's books. There were offensive spells inside that would turn Ushoran to a blackened husk in seconds.

'How did you find out?' W'soran said, hoping to keep Ushoran distracted.

The nobleman gave a snort. 'It's my business to know things,' he replied casually. 'What I don't understand is why.'

'Why else?' W'soran exclaimed. 'Because we should have crushed the other cities long ago and built a new empire on their bones! The whole world is ours for the taking, and yet Neferata is content to hide behind her descendants and rule over a city of merchants! She might have had potential once, but killing that fool Khalida broke her nerve.' He waved his hand dismissively. 'Look at this foolishness with the Rasetran boy. Pure idiocy.'

'And how will summoning Nagash's spirit help us?'

The spell-book forgotten, W'soran whirled on Ushoran. 'Think of the knowledge he possessed! He was the only man in the world I would have called my equal. To this day I curse the fates that I was born too late to have journeyed to Khemri and served him!' He spread his hands, taking in the entirety of the room and its shelves of arcane tomes. 'With the knowledge at my command I could bind even a spirit as powerful as his to serve me.' He smiled a death's head smile. 'And then the world would truly change, Lord Ushoran. You may be assured of that!'

Ushoran was silent for a moment, his bland eyes regarding W'soran inscrutably. 'You've been at this a quarter of a century,' he said at last. 'Why haven't you been able to summon him yet?'

The answer stuck in W'soran's throat. It took an effort of will to get it out.

'I don't know,' he said.

'How is that possible?' Ushoran asked.

W'soran turned back to the tome. 'It's not difficult to summon a spirit in general,' he said, searching through the pages once more. 'The breaking of the covenant with the gods resulted in countless numbers of dead souls trapped between the world of the living and the lands of the dead; they wander in a kind of wasteland between the two, desperate for rest.' Suddenly he found the page he'd been seeking. He narrowed his eyes and quickly read over the incantation.

'Summoning a specific spirit is more challenging,' he continued, absently. His fingers traced the necromantic writing on the fragile page. 'One must possess a means of focusing the spell on that one spirit in particular.'

'Can't you just call the spirit by name?' Ushoran asked.

W'soran paused. He'd always taken the Lord of Masks for a dilettante. Perhaps there was more to him than met the eye. 'I suspected the same thing at first,' he continued. 'But either the name doesn't provide a strong enough connection, or the rituals I have to work with aren't as effective as they need to be.'

'All right,' Ushoran said. 'For the sake of argument, what would provide a stronger connection to the spirit?'

W'soran gave a bitter bark of laughter. 'A piece of his body would suffice. Failing that, perhaps a piece of a close family member, like his father.'

'Or his brother?'

W'soran paused. Slowly he turned to regard the Lord of Masks.

'Nagash's brother is entombed in a crypt outside Khemri,' W'soran said.

The Lord of Masks smiled and gave an offhanded shrug. 'That's not so great an obstacle as you might think.'

Now he had W'soran's undivided attention. 'You could do this?'

'If I put the right amount of gold into the right hands… yes, it's possible.'

Was this a trap? W'soran could not be sure. Temptation warred with his sense of preservation. Finally, he concluded that Ushoran already had more than enough to involve Neferata already. He didn't especially need anything more.

'Why would you do this?' W'soran asked.

The Lord of Masks gave another shrug. His expression was unreadable.

'As it stands right now, we're all hostages to fate,' he said. 'Neferata has seen to it that our fortunes are inextricably tied to her own. That can't be allowed to continue. We need to find a way to level the field against her before this affair with young Alcadizzar drags us all to our doom.' He regarded W'soran intently. 'Just be certain you have the means to control what you call up, sorcerer, or Neferata may well turn out to be the least of our problems.'

Nagashizzar, in the 98th year of Ptra the Glorious
(-1325 Imperial Reckoning)

AT FIRST, THE Children of the Horned God responded swiftly to the reports of god-stone buried beneath the great mountain. Within a year, packs of black-garbed scouts were pouring from the first, exploratory tunnel and scuttling silently through the lower tunnels of the fortress. Slowly, warily, they followed the bitter scent of the Horned God's spoor until finally they came upon the first of the active mine shafts. What they discovered in those dimly-lit tunnels sent the first scouts scampering back into the deeps in terror.

Glowing skeletons, they swore to their pack leaders. Skeletons that swung picks and hauled away stone, their bones glowing with god-stone dust. The first scouts who reported this were slain out of hand, for the pack leaders were foul-tempered, suspicious creatures that reacted poorly when they thought they were being mocked. The rest were sent back, and warned to return with proof if they valued their mangy hides.

And so the black-cloaks crept about the mine tunnels, whispering and watching and waiting for their opportunity. In short order, a trio of tunnel-creepers caught sight of a skeleton with a smashed foot that could not keep pace with its companions. As soon as the rest of the work party had disappeared around a bend in the tunnel the ratmen swarmed over the crippled thing. Knives flashed and teeth snapped; within seconds the skeleton had been expertly dismantled. The scouts smashed the thing's skull with a rock for good measure, then stuffed the glowing long bones into their packs and scuttled back into the darkness.

By the end of the day the bones had been snatched from the paws of the lowly scouts and were personally rushed back to the Great City by the pack leaders themselves. The sight of the bones stunned the Grey

Seers, who by virtue of their own self-interest were knowledgeable themselves in the mining of god-stone. The bones were ground to powder and mixed with various potions to determine their potency. The results surpassed their wildest expectations. Even assuming that the scouts were wildly exaggerating their reports, the amount of dust found upon the bones hinted at deposits of god-stone beyond anything the Children of the Horned God had ever seen before. At once, the seers knew that the news had to be kept secret from the Council of Thirteen at all costs until they could determine the best way to exploit it. The pack leaders who had brought the bones to the Great City were rewarded with goblets of poisoned wine, and all records of their testimony were destroyed, but by that point it was already too late. A dozen spies had already drafted coded messages detailing the discovery to their masters on the council.

The Council of Thirteen was the ruling body of the skaven, as the ratmen called themselves, and was comprised of the twelve mightiest lords of their subterranean empire. The thirteenth seat was a symbolic one, reserved for the Horned God himself. The coded messages sped by magical means to the far corners of the empire, and within days there were tangled intrigues afoot as the council members schemed to seize the mountain's riches for their own. Alliances were forged and subsequently betrayed; bribes and counter-bribes changed hands, and acts of assassination and sabotage abounded.

The great lords assembled expeditionary forces and hastily rushed them to the mountain, only to have them collide en route and decimate one another in an escalating series of ambushes and ruthless hit-and-run raids before ever reaching their destination. This went on for twenty-five years before the members of the council surrendered to reason and called for a gathering in the Great City to determine who had the best claim to the mountain's riches.

Of course, *every* lord had the best, most compelling claim. Many even had elaborately forged documents to prove it. Finally, the Seerlord, who was chief among the skaven's grey seers and a member of the council himself, came forward and explained in no uncertain terms how they had received signs from the Horned God that had led them to the mountain, and that the riches buried there belonged to the skaven as a whole rather than any one clan. He concluded his tirade with the very persuasive notion that every day they argued gave the skeletons more time to seize the stone for themselves.

That served to focus the council's attention. Within three more months, after another furious round of politicking, intriguing, bribing and assassinating, the skaven lords had agreed to an elaborate and complicated alliance of clans. Another expeditionary force was assembled, this time comprising warriors from all the great clans and their vassals, and a warlord appointed who would ultimately answer to the council as a whole. According to the terms of the alliance, every last piece of god-stone recovered from the mountain would become the property of the council, and would be shared evenly among the clans.

It was all a bunch of high-handed nonsense of course. Not one of the council members had the slightest intention of sharing such a huge treasure trove, but they were pragmatic enough to wait until they had the plunder in hand before the backstabbing began.

The mighty expeditionary force left the Great City with much fanfare, and Lord Eekrit, the warlord in command of the force, was urged by the council to return with his treasures as quickly as possible. The size of the skaven force was huge: equal contingents from each of the major clans made it the largest army of its kind in their race's history. With so powerful a force under Lord Eekrit's command, the council members felt certain that the looting of the great mountain would scarcely take more than a month to complete.

When Lord Eekrit finally arrived in the deeps of Nagash's mighty fortress, he was greeted by a small colony of scouts who had mapped out much of the mountain's lower tunnels and the routes to each and every mineshaft.

The number of shafts and the estimates of god-stone being pulled from them each day staggered Lord Eekrit. The wealth buried within the mountain was beyond his most avaricious dreams. It would take months to haul it all back to the Great City –

perhaps even *years*. The treasure trove tempted him with feverish ambitions. He had visions of conquering the great mountain and claiming it for himself, ruling from the deeps like one of the great lords who sat upon the council; there was ample precedent for such things in his race's past. But the composition of the army made such an ambition nearly impossible. He could count on the rats of his own clan (and only then so far as he could make it worth their while), but the others would turn on him in an instant. The council had put a great deal of cunning into the creation of the expeditionary force, ensuring that they wouldn't be cheated of the treasure. Eekrit roundly cursed their conniving, black hearts!

At least victory would be swift and certain. His scouts assured him that there were only a few thousand skeletons working in the mines, and there wasn't a single one of them that stood a chance against a pack of stalwart clanrats. Lord Eekrit's force was almost fifty thousand strong, not counting the hordes of expendable slaves he could use to soften up any serious resistance. They would overrun the skeletons, clear out the lower tunnels, then push into the lower levels and see where all that precious stone was being taken. Nothing would stand in their way.

The gifts of the Horned God belonged to the skaven, and to them alone.

THE NEHEKHARAN
PANTHEON

THE PEOPLE OF the Blessed Land worship a number of gods and goddesses, both major and minor, as part of an ancient pact known as the Great Covenant. According to legend, the Nehekharans first encountered the gods at the site of what is now Mahrak, the City of Hope; the timeless spirits were moved by the suffering of the tribes, and gave them succour amid the wasteland of the desert. In return for the Nehekharans' eternal worship and devotion, the gods pledged to make them a great people, and would bless their lands until the end of time.

Each of the great cities of Nehekhara worships one of the great deities as its patron, though devotion to Ptra, the Great Father, is pre-eminent. The high priest of a Nehekharan temple is referred to as the *Hierophant*. In every city but Khemri, the high priest of Ptra is referred to as the *Grand Hierophant*.

In addition to the priesthood, each Nehekharan temple trains an order of holy warriors known as the *Ushabti*. Each Ushabti devotes his life to the service of his patron deity, and is granted superhuman abilities in return. These gifts make the Ushabti among the mightiest warriors in all the Blessed Land. Since the time of Settra, the first and only Nehekharan emperor, the Ushabti of each city have served as bodyguards to the priest king and his household.

The fourteen most prominent gods and goddesses of Nehekhara are:

Ptra: Also called the Great Father, Ptra is the first among the gods and the creator of mankind. Though worshipped all across Nehekhara, the cities of Khemri and Rasetra claim him as their patron.

Neru: Minor goddess of the moon and wife of Ptra. She protects all Nehekharans from the evils of the night.

Sakhmet: Minor goddess of the green moon, also called the Green Witch. Ptra's scheming and vindictive concubine, who is jealous of the Great Father's love of mankind.

Asaph: Goddess of beauty, magic and vengeance. Asaph is the patron goddess of Lahmia.

Djaf: The jackal-headed god of death. Djaf is the patron god of Quatar.

Khsar: The fierce and malign god of the desert. A cruel and hungry god worshipped by the tribes of the great desert.

Phakth: The hawk-faced god of the sky and the bringer of swift justice.

Qu'aph: The god of serpents and subtlety. Qu'aph is the patron god of Zandri.

Ualatp: The vulture-headed god of scavengers.

Sokth: The treacherous god of assassins and thieves.

Basth: The goddess of grace and love.

Geheb: The god of the earth and the giver of strength. Geheb is the patron god of Ka-Sabar.

Tahoth: The god of knowledge and the keeper of sacred lore. Tahoth is the patron god of Lybaras.

Usirian: The faceless god of the underworld. Usirian judges the souls of the dead and determines if they are fit to enter into the afterlife.